T0108734

BEST TO LAUGH

Mayor of the Universe

BEST to LAUGH

— A NOVEL —

Lorna Landvik

UNIVERSITY OF MINNESOTA PRESS
MINNEAPOLIS · LONDON

Published by the University of Minnesota Press
111 Third Avenue South, Suite 290
Minneapolis, MN 55401–2520
http://www.upress.umn.edu

Library of Congress Cataloging-in-Publication Data
Landvik, Lorna.
Best to laugh : a novel / Lorna Landvik.
ISBN 978-0-8166-9453-2 (hc : alk. paper) I. Title.
PS3562.A4835B47 2014
813'.54—dc23   2014013927

Printed in the United States of America on acid-free paper

The University of Minnesota is an equal-opportunity educator and employer.

27 26 25 24 23 22 21   10 9 8 7 6 5 4

In memory of Betty Lou Hensen,
one of the funniest,
and for Lori Naslund,
my first comedy partner

PROLOGUE

A BLACK COCKTAIL DRESS, decorated with a smattering of sequins across the neckline, hangs like an art piece on my bedroom wall. Although the integrity of the seams might be compromised, I could probably still squeeze into it, but for me the greater pleasure is looking at it every day and remembering its lessons.

For that same reason, I have two pictures of Hollywood Boulevard in my bathroom, right above the towel rack. One is black and white, circa the 1940s, and in it bulbous limousines are lined up in front of the Roosevelt Hotel. A party has spilled onto the sidewalk and its celebrants are women draped in fur and men in top hats and tails. Some raise champagne flutes and one man holds a lighter, its flame a dot of fuzz. A swirl-haired woman leans into him, her cigarette held in a gloved hand.

The other photograph is in color and shows a blurred wrecking ball about to smash into the side of a white stuccoed building, much of which has already been knocked down. A jagged plaster and wood border frames all that remains of the second floor apartment: a wall decorated with deftly drawn caricatures, hulking silhouettes, and the odd coffee stain.

I keep the pictures and the dress on display because they remind me of the vagaries of life: what's up can take a tumble, what's down can bob up, and sometimes what glitters *is* gold.

When I lived on Hollywood Boulevard, its heyday had long passed and a tired seediness had settled in—the tuxedos threadbare, the fur stoles gone to mange, and the champagne bubbles long since popped. Buses belched smoke where limousines once idled, and a tourist was more likely to have a personal encounter with a pickpocket than a movie star.

Still, the lure was the Boulevard's reputation and not its reality, and people came from all over the world to study the cement prints in front of Grauman's Chinese Theatre, comparing the delicacy of their fingers to Marilyn Monroe's or their shoe size to Gary Cooper's; to photograph the names on the pink, black, and gold stars on the Walk of Fame; to rifle through the revolving rack of postcards at Highland Drug and sit at the counter, sipping cherry sodas as they wrote their "Wish you were here's" in dozens of languages.

And there I was, watching movies and eating popcorn at Grauman's, roller-skating down the Walk of Fame on my way to work, and buying my toothpaste and tampons at Highland Drug. Wonder of wonders, this international Mecca was my neighborhood.

MY ALL-TIME FAVORITE TEACHER, Mr. Meyers, thought it important for his sixth graders to know that English didn't just spring up on its own but contained the seeds, the pollination, the crossbreeding of the ancient languages.

"*Calendar,* for example, comes from the Latin word *calendaeium,* which means *account book.* So think of your calendar as a ledger," he said, presenting us with mimeographed and stapled datebooks. "Only it's not money you'll keep track of spending, but your days. *Make them count.*"

"Are these like diaries?" asked Dale Ferguson, roughly fanning the pages of his booklet. "What am I supposed to write in a diary?"

"Pretend you're writing to a friend," said Mr. Meyers. "A friend who's really curious about who you are."

Dear Cal, I wrote, already feeling chummy.

My name is Candy and I can't wait to tell you everything. If you asked a bunch of people to describe me in one word, they'd probably say FUNNY. Or maybe GORGEOUS, ha ha. I love to read, write, cook, and swim, although not at the same time.

Too bad Dale Ferguson is so dumb, because he sort of looks like Illya Kuryakin in The Man from U.N.C.L.E. *Only a lot younger.*

That first entry began a habit that continues to this day. I am a dedicated accountant and keep an active ledger.

On the day I moved into the apartment that would be my home for three and a half years, I wrote *Yahoo! Yippee! Yeehaw!,* a big contrast to the dark and scary scribbles I'd written just weeks earlier.

No one steps up to life's banquet, holds out her tray, and orders, "Grief, please!" but as a child I was served a heaping helping of it and burped up for years its bitter aftertaste of sadness. Just weeks after I had reached my lowest point, my nadir, my rocky bottom, I came to live on Hollywood Boulevard, a place that could have easily confirmed life's cruelty, misery, and general crappiness. Instead, it's where I found everything that matters.

So whatever the slop being ladled out, learn what I've learned: most buffet lines have a dessert section, and if you just keep going you might get to the good stuff, the happiness cupcakes, the parfaits of joy. And if you can't find them, demand to see the manager.

PART I

1

1978

OF THE UNTOLD MYSTERIES in this great wide world, the one confounding me at the moment was why none of my neighbors stocked what I considered a kitchen staple. In fact, from Maeve Mullman's reaction, you'd have thought I was asking to borrow a kilo of heroin.

"Are you aware that sugar is *poison*?" she said, hogging the doorway, as a six-foot female bodybuilder is wont to do. "Are you aware that sugar's responsible for everything from cancer to sexual dysfunction? Never forget, your body is your temple!"

As she slammed the door in my face, I murmured my thanks and apologies, all the while doubting the purity of worship going on in *her* temple. I mean, it was fairly obvious from her East-German-world-champion-swim-team physique that steroids were a part of her daily bread.

Melvin Slyke, the geriatric animator, told me he ate most of his meals at the Denny's on Sunset, but he might be able to scrounge up a packet or two of Sweet 'N Low.

"My daughter takes it with her coffee," he explained. "Every weekend she comes over to make sure I haven't keeled over, and we have a cup of Sanka—she thinks I can't handle caffeine—and while I take mine black, she'll sweeten hers up to high heaven. She's got concerns about her figure, see, so she's always got a purseful of fake sugar and—"

"Well, thanks again," I said, backing away from the conversational sinkhole I sensed opening up.

"You could always try pepper."

This stopped me in my tracks. "Uh, I'm baking a cake."

Melvin's gray dentures made a clicking sound as he smiled.

"*Madame* Pepper. That's what the lady calls herself." He widened his eyes, which were already Mr. Magoo-magnified behind the smudged lenses of his glasses. "She's the type of person who's always got whatever you need. She's over in the end building. Upstairs."

Satisfied that all business had been taken care of, he shut his door. A second later, it creaked open.

"Tell her Melvin Slyke from *Maxie the Minx* sent you," he said. "And when you bake that cake, bring me a piece, will ya? My daughter never brings dessert."

OUTSIDE IN THE SMOGGY CARBONS choking the late summer air, I regarded the sign perched on the scorched grass of the front lawn.

It read, in fancy green neon script, Peyton Hall, and it was into this complex I had just moved. The upstairs apartment that was now my swinging (one can dream) bachelorette pad was rented out by my cousin Charlotte, who had been cast in *Vegas on the Adriatic!* and whose home for the next three months was a 1,400-passenger cruise ship.

Only five days earlier she had called me.

"Okay, what's the favor?" I asked, knowing that on the rare occasion my cousin telephoned, it wasn't to chat.

"I was only going to ask how you'd like a chance to trade in your boring life for the excitement of Hollywood."

Both insulted and intrigued, I said nothing.

"All right, I do need a favor—but it's as big a favor to you as it is to me. Bigger even!"

She explained that her need to get a subletter just might coalesce with my need to get a life.

"Because, come on, Candy—how long are you going to live with Grandma anyway? Geez—you're twenty-two years old!"

When I told her I needed time to think about it, Charlotte conceded, "Fair enough. Call me back in half an hour."

My grandmother was having coffee with Mrs. Clark next door, but I didn't need to consult her to know what she'd advise. Despite a long string of losses by Team Candy, Grandma had never stepped down from her position as head cheerleader, and this news would have her shaking her pompoms, urging me to, "Go, Candy, Go!" It was the same cheer that blared inside my head, but as an expert in the art of self-sabotage, I wasn't used to flinging open the door when opportunity knocked. Most often, I pretended I wasn't home.

But as the saying goes, timing is everything, and my cousin's offer came at exactly the right time, which is why I was here in Hollywood, looking for sugar. I wanted—no, needed—to bake a cake. It had been a long time since the needle on my personal Thrill-O-Meter had cause to tremble, but stuffing a backpack with summer clothes and boarding a plane to California had made it sweep across the dial, and that was something deserving celebration.

THE HOT AIR FELT HEAVY, as if the zillions of smog particles had weight, and I stood on the brick sidewalk that led to the back apartment buildings, debating which direction to go. Melvin Slyke had said the end building, but the big complex, comprising two-storied four-plexes, had several ends. I headed east, toward the building manager's office.

Jaz Delwyn had given me a little history of the place yesterday, when I picked up the key and introduced myself as Charlotte's subletter.

His eyes were arresting because of their color and condition—crystal blue and extremely bloodshot—and they scanned the length of my body, undressing me as he addressed me.

"Peyton Hall," he said in a British accent, "was rife with stars in the '40s. Not like the Garden of Allah, certainly, but at least this place is still standing. Clark Gable, Cary Grant, Shelley Winters; they all had pied-à-terres here, and Douglas Fairbanks designed our Olympic-size pool, which Johnny Weismuller—certainly cinema's greatest Tarzan—was always splashing about in." The building manager took a deep drag of his unfiltered cigarette and allowed me to bathe in his exhale. "By the way, did I tell you I'll be playing Errol Flynn in a movie about his life?"

His smile was one I'm sure he practiced in front of his mirror—jaunty, attractive, but not infused with any particular sincerity.

"Wow, that's great."

"You do know who Errol Flynn is, don't you?"

"Sure."

Watching old movies with my grandmother had given me a basic knowledge of Hollywood legends, and holding one hand high, with the other I mimed a sword thrust, in homage to the swashbuckling star of *Robin Hood* and *Captain Blood*.

"En garde!" said Jaz, blocking my imaginary sword with his own and for a few strange moments we indulged in a pretend duel on his front steps.

Now he didn't answer the doorbell I nudged with my thumb, and when I saw a woman heading down the center brick walkway, I loped down the steps.

She was tugging at the pink leather leash of one of those tiny white dogs whose breed I can never remember.

"Excuse me," I said, catching up to her. "Do you know where a Madame Pepper lives?"

Wearing a floral sundress whose daisies had long since faded, the woman lifted the unraveling brim of her straw hat and peered at me through sunglasses whose frames were missing several of their rhinestones.

"Yes, and I could also direct you to one Mr. Salt in El Cerrito. I won a cha-cha contest with him at the Ambassador Hotel in the winter of '51."

My semi-smile reflected my uncertainty as to how to respond.

"It surprised the hell out of me, considering the length of Mr. Salt's feet," said the wizened woman. "But turns out those size-thirteen boats really knew their way around the harbor."

The furry white dog with goopy brown tears matted under its eyes yawned a squeaky bark, as if reminding its owner they were on a walk.

"Yes, my little Binky-Bink," she said, smooching her lips, but her baby talk stiffened into sarcasm when she addressed me.

"As for you," she pointed west with a grand flourish, "you can find the great Madame Pepper on the Fuller Avenue side, last building, second floor. There's a little troll on her landing."

"Thank you, uh—"

"June. Like the month. Although disposition-wise, I'm more a February."

"Oh. Well, nice to meet you, June. I'm Candy—"

Turning her back to me, she reverted to baby talk, promising the yappy little furball a stop at Rin Tin Tin's star if he behaved himself, and as she lurched away in a funny tiptoed walk I shut my unhinged jaw and headed toward the apartment whose occupant I hoped might provide me with a simple cup of sugar.

On the landing, next to a gargoyle planter from whose head a bonsai jade tree sprouted, I stood on a mat whose printed Welcome message was editorialized with a question mark. I dropped the heavy brass door knocker twice.

"Not available!" a sharp voice announced from behind the door, and I made a hasty retreat down the stairs, before any snarling dogs were unleashed or warning shots fired.

Your loss, I thought, not about to be daunted by some crank too lazy to open the door. I had places to go, people to meet, and if nobody would assist me in my cake-making venture . . . then I'd go check out the pool. It was a brand-new me; I was that flexible.

I WAS A HAPPY CHILD and there are photographs that corroborate this; in a black-and-white one whose serrated margin reads, "Candy—1 week old," I'm wrapped in swaddling clothes and lying in my mother's embrace. I look toothlessly blissful, as if my smile were an expression of joy and not a reflex of something more prosaic, like passing gas.

There's a snapshot of me at my third birthday party, merriment and frosting smeared in equal measure all over my face. One of me dressed as a cat for Halloween, my painted-on whiskers crinkled by my wide smile. Another of me as a four-year-old with a quartet of cousins at a family picnic, caught in the middle of a laugh, my head tipped back. I'm the only one of the foursome who looks thrilled, but my delight is not the only contrast between me and the shining examples of Nordic youth that are my kin.

It was at that same picnic I first met my cousin Charlotte, who informed me that I had funny eyes. Turning to her mother fixing her plate, she asked, "Mommy, why does Candy have such funny eyes?"

Even though her comment stung me, I assumed curiosity and not malice inspired it. Thinking, *All you have to do is look at my mom, dummy,* I nevertheless waited patiently for my aunt's reply.

"Uh, Candy's mother is from Korea," she said, dumping a spoonful of Sloppy Joes on the bottom circle of a hamburger bun. "Koreans have . . . uh, different-shaped eyes than us."

My Aunt Lorraine's visit was the reason for the picnic; this was her first trip back to Minneapolis after living in Wyoming for years. She had brought her two children, Todd and Charlotte, but not her husband, who was a whispered topic of conversation between her and my Aunt Pauline.

It was the first time my dad's middle sister had met me and my mother, and her reaction to us was the subject of another whispered conversation, this one between my parents and held post-picnic in the car, where they had made the erroneous assumption that I was asleep in the backseat.

"I tell you, she no like me. She no like me a bit," said my mother.

"Jo, everyone likes you. You just have to give her time. Lorraine's got a lot on her plate right now."

"What that mean?"

My dad paused for a moment, understanding that in speaking with my mother, a time-out for translation was often needed.

"That means she's got an awful lot to worry about right now."

"Not with those yum yums! She no have to worry about nothing!"

My dad's low rich laugh filled the car.

"Shh!" said my mother, laughing too. "Don't wake up Baby!"

I kept my eyes shut; even as I wanted to join in my parents' high spirits, it was one of those times when the bigger satisfaction came from reveling quietly in their enjoyment of one another. It made me feel safe, like when my mother called me "Baby."

The happy child photographs—if I wasn't grinning in them, I was laughing—ended when I was five and a half and my mother died.

There is a snapshot I came across last winter that someone (probably my Aunt Lorraine) had the lack of grace to take. In it, I'm sitting at a table in a church basement, so hunched with sadness that my chin's nearly touching the tabletop. Because of the way I'm seated and because the photograph is black and white, you can't tell that I was wearing a red-dotted Swiss dress with a sash and flouncy petticoat, a dress that caused me great shame, making me look as if I were going to a birthday party instead of my mother's funeral.

"That was such a terrible day," said my Grandma Pekkala, anchoring me with her arm as I stood at the kitchen counter. I had promised to make the North Stars' number-one hockey fan a fancy dinner in celebration of the Stars' win over the Islanders and when opening her rarely used *Better Homes and Garden* cookbook, I had found the photograph tucked between two pages featuring Beef Wellington and Beef Stroganoff recipes.

I stared at the picture, reliving the awful memories it conjured: the surreal fear and confusion of waking up to my father's howls and seeing men lift my mother onto a stretcher and race her out of our apartment; the wallop of pain and shock that had struck me hours later, when my dad staggered into my grandmother's kitchen to tell me that my mother had died. By the time of her funeral service, those feelings had frozen into a numb coldness, only to be disturbed by the itchiness of my petticoat and the fits of rage that made me want to kick or punch someone—specifically my cousin Charlotte who, after enjoying the luncheon the church ladies had put on, said, "Good Jell-O."

My life had caved in like a rotted shack and all she could say was "Good Jell-O?"

"I have no idea how that picture got there," said my grandma, but as she reached for the photograph, I pressed my thumb on it, so hard that a crescent of white appeared high on its nail.

"I want it."

There was neither Beef Stroganoff nor Beef Wellington that night; instead I took the picture and a bowl of cereal downstairs to my basement bedroom, the rattle of pipes and the clunk of the furnace accompaniment to my muffled sobs.

2

My dad met my mother, Jong Oh, during his tour of duty in Seoul, Korea, several months after the Armistice had been signed. PFC Arne Pekkala had been enjoying a weekend liberty with his friend, the similarly ranked Kermit Carlson, and exiting the PuPu Club on Itaewon Street had grabbed two bikes from a pile near the door. Having toasted several times to peace and prosperity, as well as their plans of becoming partners in the expanding Carlson family hardware empire in Hoboken, New Jersey, the soldiers weren't in any condition to ride bicycles, but it was being in that condition that convinced them otherwise. Laughter and inebriation caused them to swerve through the crowded streets and, a block later, into my mother, who'd just finished her shift at a metal-stamping plant.

Upon seeing the young woman sprawled on the street, the young private experienced a sudden sobering, helping to her feet the Korean who was bleeding from under the bangs of her shiny black hair. More dazed than hurt, the victim didn't yell at the man responsible for her injury but instead made him laugh, by miming a drunken bicycle rider and then wagging her finger at him.

This accidental (literally) meeting led to a whirlwind courtship, which, after months of unsnarling red tape, led to a marriage ceremony conducted by an army chaplain, which led, four months later, to me.

These events were reported in sporadic letters home, and with such paucity of detail that I seek meaning reading between the lines and in between those lines.

There is one letter my father wrote that doesn't need my added color commentary. It's the one announcing my birth, and although it only comprises one page, it's his most emotionally open.

May 1, 1956

Dear Mother,

I telephoned to give you the news but no one answered.
Candy Lee Pekkala was born just an hour ago, at 2:42 pm.
Weight: 7# 8oz., height: 19". Black-haired and black-eyed.
Glad we got stateside for her birth—don't US presidents have
to be born on American soil? (Ha ha.)
Her mother is doing fine, and me, well, I'm as puffed up as a
pigeon.
Things are going okay at the store. New Jersey's okay, but I miss
the Midwest.

Your son and new dad,
Arne

Of course I memorized it.

How I long to know more of my parents' lives, but my mom died before my curiosity in her background was ignited, and my dad, well, technically he lived nearly a dozen years longer, but a big part of him checked out when my mother did.

My grandmother has tried to fill in the gaps of their stories, but that's like asking someone with a trowel and a bucket of plaster to tuck-point the Great Wall of China. Desperate for the whole unabridged autobiography, I've had to make do with her anecdotes and observations.

"Imagine how hard it must have been for Jo. Brand new to the country. Hardly knows English and yet she figures out how to be funny in it."

My grandmother's memories reinforce my own: my mother was hilarious, and in cracking me up she inspired me to return the favor. I loved the sound of her laughter, so riddled with snorts that she'd cover her nose and mouth with a curled hand.

"Best to laugh!" was her frequent advice. The concept of comparatives and superlatives in the English language was something she didn't have a firm grasp of and yet I was in total agreement: it was best to laugh.

Because I was so young when the poison from her burst appendix killed her, there aren't a ton of charms on my memory bracelet, but the ones I have are golden. They have played over and over in my mind until I wonder: how much of these are real? How can I remember whole snatches of dialogue?

"You've always been sharp as a tack," my grandmother said when I once confessed that I didn't trust the truth of my memories. "What you remember is what you remember."

Her words gave me permission to believe in them, however my own imagination and wishfulness have polished and made them lustrous.

One charm: my mother and I snuggled in my bed, *Goodnight Moon* propped open between us. Having spent countless hours on her lap as she sounded out words in her English books, I had taught myself to read, and we often took turns reading my bedtime story aloud. On this particular night my mother had decided to riff on the narrative.

"Good night crazy lady in grocery store who say, 'Go back to Japan!'" she said, running her index finger under words that said no such thing. "Good night dog next door who only know how to yap yap yap!"

I didn't need an invitation to jump in.

"Good night icky Janie Larson, who won't let me play with her dumb Chatty Cathy doll!"

"Good night, Chatty Cathy doll who talk too much anyway!"

We had laughed ourselves silly, saying good night to all manner of things not listed in the book.

"Good night," my mother said finally, kissing me on the cheeks, on the forehead, on my lips. "Good night, little girl I love!"

Another charm: my mother bringing cookies to my class on Treat Day.

"You talk funny!" announced Timmy Esperson, the kid who, if kindergarten were a monarchy, would reign as king.

"I look more funny!" said my mother, crossing her eyes. "And how I dance—even more funny! She did the Twist, a dance that was all the rage, only she turned it into a series of poses that cracked up the whole class, our teacher included. When she left, King Timmy deemed my mother "nice."

Her desire to become fluent in English and "Be American!" was so strong that she seldom spoke Korean, although she did sing to me in her native tongue. I've forgotten most of the words and melodies, but every now and then a wisp of her lullabies wafts through my head, my most precious charm.

THE ONLY GOOD THING about losing your mother at a young age is young age. Wounds heel faster, even the deep gash of your mom's death. You don't know at the time that the scar never goes away and that throughout your life it will get hot and inflamed; all you know is that you're five and a half and you can be howling with sadness one minute and concentrating on a game of Jacks with your grandmother the next. I couldn't articulate it then, but I felt that my mother's love was so full and strong that, even in death, it somehow blanketed me.

My dad kicked off any such blanket. Lacking the grace of a glad heart, or courage, or resilience—whatever—he was done in by my mother's death. JoJo had been able to cajole kisses, caresses, and laughs out of the reticent Arne Pekkala, but after she was gone, he was an emotional Scrooge, locking away gestures of affection in a strongbox along with the key.

"It wasn't you," my grandma has assured me. "It was him. He thought to protect himself he had to . . . hold it all in."

Coward. Not a word a kid likes to have on her list of Adjectives to Describe My Father, but, come on, he was the adult. How could he be so selfish as to let his sorrow trump everything—including a relationship with his own daughter? He could have helped me so much, and I would have returned the favor a thousand times over, if he had only let me in.

3

"YOU'RE CHARLOTTE FIELDS'S COUSIN?"

This was asked by a guy greasy with suntan lotion, whose abdominal muscles popped out in two rows as he sat up in one of the chaise longues that ringed the swimming pool.

His surprise was a reaction I was used to; what wasn't familiar was the name Fields. My cousin's last name was Fjeldsman. I was about to correct the error, but I didn't have to channel Sherlock Holmes to deduce that my actress/dancer/singer cousin had given herself a stage name.

"Are you from Minneapolis, too?" asked Oily Man's pal, a rangy guy who didn't share his friend's sculpted stomach, slick bronzed skin, or bad manners.

Nodding, I said, "I'm subletting her apartment for three months while she's in a show."

"She got the *show?*" asked Oily Man. "She got the *Caribbean Vegas!* show?"

"*Vegas on the Adriatic!*" I said, enjoying correcting him.

"And she already left?"

When I nodded, he said to his friend, "I auditioned for that show too and nailed my song—'Where Is the Life That Late I Led'—from *Kiss Me Kate.* Nailed it. Wow. I guess they thought a really strong singer might take away from the ensemble." He turned to me. "I cannot believe Charlotte got it and she didn't even tell me!"

"They phoned her at the last minute. Someone had dropped out, and they said if she could be ready to leave in twenty-four hours, the part was hers."

Not liking the eagerness in my voice—I sounded like I was my cousin's press agent or something—I undid the towel I had wrapped around me like a sarong.

Strolling to the deep end of the pool, I bounced twice on the diving board and executed a simple but pretty swan dive, my splash as light as a librarian's cough. I swam one length, did a slick somersault turn, and swam back. For nearly an hour, I stayed in the pool, emerging every now and then to show off my repertoire of dives, and when I got out for good, Oily Man's chaise longe was empty, a vague impression of his oily body visible in the oily sags of the plastic webbing.

His nonoily friend closed his book.

"Don't tell me—college swim team MVP?"

"High school, junior year," I said, adjusting my towel like a matador's cape.

"I'm Ed, by the way. Ed Stickley."

"Candy." I shook his outstretched hand. "Candy Ohi."

The lie—my last name was Pekkala—sprang out of my mouth like a verbal jack-in-the-box.

"Like the county?"

I stared at the man with the pink peeling nose and shoulders. There *was* a county in Minnesota called Kandiyohi, a discovery I'd made long ago while heading to my Aunt Pauline's house. On these road trips to visit relatives, my dad was less chatty than a hearse driver, forcing me to entertain myself with books, crossword puzzles, or the view the passenger window offered. I remember the kick I felt seeing the roadside Kandiyohi County sign.

"Hey, Dad," I said, too excited to honor our tacit vow of silence. "Did you see that sign? There's a county named after me and mom: Kandy-Ohi!"

"Your mother's maiden name was 'Oh,' not 'Ohi,' he said sharply, "and you spell your name with a 'C.'"

Duh! I screamed silently, my cheeks burning from the shame of committing the sin of trying to have a playful moment with my father.

I asked Ed Stickley how he knew Kandiyohi was a county in Minnesota.

Scratching his thinning strawberry-blond hair, he smiled. "The same way I know Citrus is a county in Florida, Churchill's one in Nevada, and Catawba's a county in North Carolina. I like studying maps."

"For fun?"

"What can I say?" said Ed, holding up his palms. "I'm a teacher."

"Of geography?"

"Sometimes, but usually history or English. Whatever's needed. I'm a substitute." He reached into the little Styrofoam cooler beside him and held up in offering what looked like a pop bottle of chocolate milk. "Want one?"

I shook my head and instead picked up the book he'd been reading.

"So is this something you'll be teaching?" I asked, examining the cover that promised in bold print to reveal *The Truth behind the National Security Act of* 1947!

"I wish, but the school board likes our students' reading lists to be a little less . . . controversial." Opening the bottle with a church key, he took a sip. "But let's not talk about school—this is my last weekend of summer vacation. That is, if I decide to take an assignment right away."

His grin begged me to ask him why he wouldn't, and so I did.

"Because in June I won fifty-one thousand dollars on a game show."

"Whoa," I said, rearing back in my chair as if I'd been splashed. "You must know a lot of trivia."

"I prefer to think of it as 'general knowledge.'"

Metal squealed against concrete as two women on the opposite side of the pool dragged lounge chairs from out of the shade. Once in the sun, they greeted Ed.

"Hey, girls," he said, doffing an imaginary hat, and a moment later he whispered, "Sherri Durban. She works for the Hollywood Bowl. Definitely worth checking out while you're here."

"I'm not really much of a bowler."

Ed's laugh was a series of heh-heh-hehs. "The Hollywood Bowl is an amphitheater."

"Oh. I thought because of the name—"

"—which is perfectly logical. But no, this bowl's the biggest natural amphitheater in the United States. It can seat up to eighteen thousand people. They say it . . ."

We both laughed and he shrugged.

"Sorry. The teacher in me."

The smell of coconuts wafted over as the two women across the pool made a production of slathering suntan lotion up the slopes of their calves and thighs.

"What about her friend?"

Ed squinted at the minimally bikinied woman kicking off her high-heeled mules.

"Joanie Welles. She's a singing waitress at this Italian joint on Hill-hurst, but her dream—and this is a direct quote—'is to be bigger than Streisand.'"

"That's pretty big."

"And pretty delusional. I've heard her sing."

Pointing out my new neighbors, Ed was a veritable directory.

The man wearing a maroon velour robe and a copy of the show-business daily *Variety* tented over his face was Robert X. Roberts.

"He was on his way to being a big leading man and then talkies came in and his career went phhhhht. Couldn't get rid of his Bronx accent—still has a little bit of it, in fact. So he got into directing instead. He did a lot of B movies and then had a career revival in live television."

Bastien Laurent was a French photographer who accessorized his black Speedo with a black Stetson and several gold chains.

"Once he had a photo shoot with a bunch of swimsuit models down here at the pool," said Ed with a sigh. "That was a good day."

The two intensely tan men, wearing little plastic eye protectors and triangles of zinc oxide on their noses, were Bruce, a talent agent, and his boyfriend Robb, a salesman at Giorgio's in Beverly Hills.

"And that guy leaving?" said Ed of the silver-haired man who'd anchored his towel under a belly that looked like a fully inflated pink beach ball. "That's Vince Perrogio. He wrote a couple of noir films back in the '40s. Now he says he can't get a movie made because 'the fairies have taken over Hollywood.' That's why he never hangs around the pool when Bruce and Robb are here."

"Sounds like a real charmer."

"Plus he's got a policy that he'll only date women under thirty, and he's always on the lookout."

"Ick. Thanks for the warning."

I ran my fingers through my hair, surprised that it was nearly dried. Even buried in its shroud of smog, the sun shone fierce.

"So other than your name," said Ed, "what else should I know about you?"

My mouth turned down in a little grimace. "Actually, you don't even know that. My last name's Pekkala."

"Finnish, right?"

"You're good," I said, impressed.

"So why'd you say it was Ohi?"

"I don't really know," I said, feeling the flush of being caught in a dumb lie spread across my face. "It just popped out of my mouth. Maybe because when that oily guy—"

"—Win Baker. He lives in the apartment below me."

"Well, when he asked me if I was Charlotte Fields's cousin—see, her real last name is Fjeldsman—it kind of took me by surprise, and I guess I thought, 'Hey, I'm going to make up a stage name, too.' So I said Ohi."

"Are you an actress?"

"No, but I—"

There was an explosion of water and those in its wake voiced their complaints to its creator.

"Maeve Mullman," said Ed, as the woman's white-blonde head emerged from the water. "Our neighborhood weightlifter."

"She lives in my building," I said. "She told me the cup of sugar I was trying to borrow was poison."

"I didn't know people borrowed sugar anymore."

"I wanted to bake a cake, plus I thought it'd be a good way to introduce myself to my neighbors."

"What kind of cake?"

"Yellow, with my famous fudge frosting."

A sudden shadow loomed over us.

"Stickley," said a raspy, accusative voice. "You busy for dinner tonight? I've got two steaks thawing out in my fridge, and you could definitely use the protein."

Holding his hand to form an awning over his eyes, Ed looked up at the imposing body that was the bodybuilder's.

"Sorry, Maeve, I've got a date. But I appreciate the invitation."

"Like hell you do!" said Maeve, her eyebrows, nearly plucked into nonexistence, furrowing.

She took a step backwards, turned around, and dove into the pool.

"You're a popular guy," I said, watching the water churn under Maeve's Australian crawl.

"I'm straight," said Ed, "plus I'm not in showbiz, which believe it or not, acts as an aphrodisiac—or at least a relief—to a lot of women. I think they like to be reminded of what it is to be normal."

A single apartment, built above the garages and the laundry room, looked over the pool, and the sound of an alarm clock jangled through its open windows.

"Billy Gray Green," said Ed. "Greeting the late afternoon. He's a bartender down at the Toy Tiger." Looking at his watch, he stifled a big, jaw-cracking yawn.

"Was it something I said?"

Ed laughed. "I really do have a date." Collecting his book and his cooler, he stood up and said, "Pleasure to have made your acquaintance, Candy, and I hope soon to make the acquaintance of your yellow cake with the famous fudge frosting."

4

TECHNICALLY, I lived in the upper half of the duplex with my dad, but because he worked nights at the Ford Plant, I was most often downstairs at my grandma's, taking over her guest room as my own.

Tired of repeating "Lights out!" to someone who was a natural night owl, Grandma became lax in policing a bedtime she knew I wasn't tired enough to obey, and by the time I was nine all attempts at enforcement had been thrown out the window and the two of us had a regular date on the couch with Johnny Carson.

We both loved *The Tonight Show* and its host—loved watching Johnny play Carnac the Magnificent or Aunt Blabby; loved his looks of understated alarm as marsupials from the San Diego Zoo inspected his hair for nits or snakes slithered up his arm; loved the polite conversations he'd have with the old lady who collected mushrooms that looked like presidential profiles or with the condescending ten-year-old genius who had sold a patent to NASA, all the while winking at the camera to let us know he couldn't see Millard Fillmore in that particular piece of fungi either, and that this kid (the little twerp) was way over his head, too.

We liked the opera singers, the drum soloists, the authors and artists he'd have on, but boy oh boy, we loved the comedians.

During the commercials, I'd jump up and re-create their acts, the throw rug by the fireplace serving as my stage.

"I tell ya, when I was a kid, all I knew was rejection," I'd say, adjusting an imaginary tie à la Rodney Dangerfield. "My yo-yo, it never came back."

Doing Joan Rivers, I'd grouse, "I hate to do housework. You make the beds, you wash the dishes, and six months later you have to start all over again."

My grandmother's laughter was like gold to King Midas and greed pushed me to want more, more, more.

When she explained that the comics were professionals and that they, like Johnny, were *paid* to make people laugh, a light—a spotlight—clicked on.

"I want a job like that," I said.

"Oh, kid," she said, using her all-purpose expression. "You'd be so good at it."

ONE EVENING MY DAD WAS HOME—it must have been a holiday—and decided to indulge in a rarity around our household: a little family time.

The three of us were on the couch, our hands dipping into the stainless steel bowls of popcorn on our laps. I was an emotional tuning fork, thrumming with happiness, excitement, and an uncommon sense of security.

Don Rickles was calling Johnny Carson a hockey puck and any number of insults, and Johnny was both laughing and getting laughs of his own.

"Can't you just see Candy there?" said my grandmother. "Up there sitting with Johnny Carson?"

"Candy?" said my father, surprised. "Why could you see Candy sitting with Johnny Carson?"

His words cut me, and his confused expression sent the knife in deeper.

"Oh, for Pete's sake," said my grandmother. "Because she's such a performer. Because she's so funny."

"Candy?"

"Of course! Candy, do Phyllis Diller for your dad. Or be Johnny doing Art Fern!"

The look on my dad's face showed me he didn't know a thing about me, that he didn't recognize what I thought was most essential about me.

Didn't he remember my very first foray into show business when at a recital I had willingly turned the Patty Cake Party dance routine into a slapstick free-for-all? And what about the huge laugh I got playing the turkey in my fourth grade Thanksgiving play, when instead of delivering my "Gobble-gobble" line, I ad-libbed, "How's about we all go out for burgers?" And had he forgotten the recent schoolwide speech competition when Mr. Meyers had cast me to deliver a Huck Finn monologue because none of the boys could do his lines justice, and I had taken home the Best Comedic Performance certificate?

True, he had witnessed few of my triumphs on school stages because they occurred during his work hours (or the hours during which he slept), but that was little solace, reinforcing my belief that he had deliberately chosen the swing shift to avoid interaction with me.

"I'd like to see one of those impressions,'" my dad said now.

Fighting back a swell of hurt and rage, I pointed to the TV and trying to keep my voice light, I said, "Oh, man, look at that crazy hat Doc Severinsen's wearing."

As I GREW, so did my father's basic obliviousness toward me. Was he leading the standing ovation when I took my bows as one of the Pigeon sisters in our high school production of *The Odd Couple*? Nope. Or as the social worker in *A Thousand Clowns*? Nada.

Okay, so maybe he wasn't the theater type—maybe he felt more comfortable cheering me on in a gym, or better yet, a pool, considering I had broken two school records and was nominated swim team co-captain as a junior? Uh-uh.

GRANDMA EXPENDED A LOT OF ENERGY figuring out ways to help the merry laughing little girl outrun the shadow of her mother's death, and when I was in second grade she had brought me to the YWCA for swimming lessons.

"It's something your mom would have wanted for you," she told me as we rode the bus downtown. "Do you remember how she'd take you down to the kiddie pool practically every sunny day of summer?"

"Sort of," I said, trying desperately to add details to the vague picture of her in a skirted swimsuit, sitting on the concrete ledge of the pool.

"Well, she always said you took to the water like a fish. She said you were a born swimmer."

Swimming was good for me; I could beat the water with my arms, kick it with my legs, and rather than being punished my aggression was rewarded with breaking records and earning titles. I took up diving, too, practicing over and over reverse and inward pikes, finding, in that space between the final bounce and the entry into the water, flight.

IN MY JUNIOR YEAR, while I was at swim practice, Arne Pekkala's atrophied heart finally gave out. Having done what my coach called the prettiest one-and-a-half somersault tuck she had ever seen and clocking my best time ever in the two-hundred-meter butterfly, I had no idea that it would be the last time I'd climb out of the pool and peel off my swim cap, feeling that odd exhilarating exhaustion; the last time I'd goof around with my teammates as we headed toward the locker room, accusing one another of being responsible for the warm spots in the pool or the extra bubbles.

THE NIGHT AFTER MY DAD WAS BURIED, Karen Schaeffer, a girl in my art class, came clumping down the basement steps.

"Nice pad," she said of the former storage area my grandmother had allowed me to appropriate as my bedroom, letting me paint it black and red and helping me rig up a clothesline around the bed and hang gauzy curtain panels from it.

"Thanks," I said, and, exhausted from the events of the past few days, my voice expressed none of the surprise I felt over Karen's presence. She traveled in circles that didn't overlap mine, and the only social exchanges I had with her were in the art room.

"I'm sorry about your dad," she said, and her hand darted into her jeans jacket pocket. A second later she lit a thinly rolled joint with a yellow Bic lighter and held it out to me. "This might help."

It did.

As much as my father was physically and emotionally absent in much of my life, his death knocked me down, hard. Like a trapped moth, one question frantically batted around in my feelings of shock and grief: What did I do so wrong to deserve this? and that question, after a few tokes, was muted. That weekend I huddled on a matted square of carpet on the floor of a Dodge van, sharing a pipe and a bottle of Boone's Farm apple wine with Karen and two guys she worked with at the Red Barn. That helped, too.

On Monday I quit the swim team. I had already been cast as the dentist's receptionist in *Cactus Flower* ("You'll be hilarious," the drama club advisor had told me), but before the first rehearsal I told Mrs. Freeburg that I was no longer interested. No extracurricular activities were going to get in the way of my newfound priority, which was to get high.

Swimming and theater had given me a distinction, a special identity, but after I quit both, I was back to being the only "Oriental" (or at least "Oriental-looking") kid in a school whose student body looked like a reunion of the Von Trapp Family Singers. And having both a mother *and* father die—whoa!—that shoved me into a whole new category of weird-ness. I was someone people felt both apart from and sorry for, and if that wouldn't compel you to buy a nickel bag or guzzle wine that tasted like fruit-flavored petrol, I salute your strength.

5

ALTHOUGH SHE HELD A NIGHTLY COCKTAIL PARTY for herself, my grandmother didn't set an example of medication by alcohol. She strictly enforced a one-drink-only rule, and while she was prudent with portions, she was lavish with ingenuity and ingredients. Monday she might shake up a martini, Tuesday stir a Manhattan, but what put her into the realm of a true mixologist were her invented drinks. A nippy autumn evening inspired Liquid Apple Crisp, a hot drink combining apple schnapps, rum, and a cinnamon stick; one humid summer night she blended what she dubbed a Banana Sangria Slush.

It was 5:30 when I returned from the pool, which meant it was 7:30 back home and Grandma would be mixing up her latest. I had an impulse to call and ask about her newest libation, but my grandmother was old-fashioned and had a slight antipathy/fear of the telephone, especially when long-distance charges were incurred, so instead of bothering the bartender, I changed out of my swimsuit and did what we both promised to do at least weekly: write.

September 1, 1978
7267 Hollywood Blvd., #3
Hollywood, CA 90067

Dear Grandma,

Just to get you situated: Peyton Hall is on the corner and shares a long block with several apartment buildings, one house, and a vacant lot. It's on the residential part of Hollywood Boulevard; the "razzle-dazzle" part starts a couple blocks to the east. I took a stroll down the Walk of Fame yesterday (thinking of you every time I passed the star of one of your favorites—hello, Ray Milland, hello, Tyrone Power!). A woman wearing a stained turban that slid over one eyebrow asked me for a quarter, and when I gave it to her she yelled, "Cheap-

*skate!" and I had to sidestep this tall, blank-eyed guy who motored
by like a purposeful zombie. Twice at street corners I smelled "eau de
piddle"—not my idea of a Hollywood Boulevard perfume!*

*But Charlotte's apartment is really cool. There are embossed
palm trees on the dining room walls (painted over by some lout, but
the shapes are still visible) and a rattan wallpaper covers the ceiling, making me feel like I've taken shelter in a Tiki hut. There're all
sorts of 8x10 pictures of Charlotte on the wall, and enough mirrors
to make you think you're in some low-budget psychological thriller.
Plus all the clothes she didn't take with her she left on the floor.
(And no, I'm not tattling; just reporting . . .)*

My intention to write a nice chatty two-or-three-pager was stopped
by the increasingly loud and snarly growls of my empty stomach. On my
way to the kitchen, I remembered that the eggs I'd fried for breakfast had
emptied my cousin's refrigerator of anything that might be made into
dinner, unless I could whip up something tasty with an almost empty
box of raisins, a murky jar of pickles, and a couple packets of soy sauce.

ALONG WITH SEVERAL INSTRUCTIONS about her car and a bill-paying
reminder, Charlotte had left a roughly drawn map indicating necessary
businesses like "bank" and "cheap manicures." Under a big X she had
written "Ralphs Supermarket."

It was to that Roman numeral I headed, and after stocking up on
essentials, I bought from the store's deli case something I had never
before tasted—a ham and cheese croissant—and ate it sitting on the low
concrete wall that faced Sunset Boulevard.

Sunset Boulevard! Having discovered that the famous boulevards—
Hollywood and Sunset—were just blocks apart and that they ran parallel
to one another, I felt the little flare of confidence that comes when you
start getting your bearings in a new place.

"Whew!" said a woman whose shiny clothing might be considered
skimpy if there'd been a little more of it. Her hoops-within-hoops earrings jangled as she half-sat against the wall near me. "You wouldn't have
a soda in there, would you?"

Looking down at the grocery bag at my feet, I shook my head.

"Coke, Pepsi, I don't care."

"Sorry, I don't—"

"—starving, too," she said, staring at the cars driving by. "Maybe I should run across the street and get a piece of pizza. Or some of that Pioneer Chicken. Nah, pizza's easier to eat. I remember when pizza was sort of—how do you call it?" She snapped her gum; it sounded like a popgun. "Erotic."

She was talking more to herself than me, but I couldn't help correcting her.

"You mean 'exotic'?"

The woman chortled. "Yeah, yeah. Exotic. Course nowadays you can go just about anywhere and find pizza."

I nodded and agreed that, yes, you could go just about anywhere and find pizza, and when a navy blue Volkswagen swerved to the side of the curb, the woman next to me sighed and pushed herself off the wall.

"Been real," she said, offering a little flutter of her fingers as she sauntered to the car. She leaned into the open passenger-side window, exposing a view only the shortest of shorts can offer. After a moment, she stood up and ambled toward me, her hips moving with a definite attitude.

"He's asking for you."

I pointed to my chest. "Me?"

The woman snapped her gum. "That's what I said."

With a flick of her long black curls, she strutted east and I, grabbing my grocery bag, loped toward the car.

"Hey!" I said, seeing the driver was my neighbor.

"You want a ride home?" said Ed. "Or are you too busy working?"

It seems naïve that I didn't know what trade the sociable woman in the shiny red hot pants and metallic silver tube top was plying, but as I told my neighbor, "I never met a prostitute before." (I didn't add, of course, that there were some people—most especially my Aunt Lorraine—who at one time thought otherwise.)

Ed nodded, as if considering my point. "Still, weren't her clothes sort of a giveaway?"

"I just thought she was dressed up. This is Hollywood, after all."

He dropped me off in front of my apartment, and after I threw my perishables in the fridge, we met as planned in the back garage stalls.

"What's that smell?" I asked.

"Night blooming jasmine," said Ed, sniffing deeply. "And eucalyptus."

We passed the pool on our way to his apartment, making plans to crack open a Scrabble board and the bottle of wine he'd intended to present to his date, had his date not stood him up.

"There I was in Silver Lake," he said, "banging on the door until a guy from across the hall sticks his head out the door and says, 'Hey buddy, ain't it obvious she bailed on you?'"

"Ouch," I said.

"Tit for tat!" came a raspy voice.

"Jeez, Maeve!" said Ed as the bodybuilder sprung from the shadows of shrubbery. "Don't jump out at people like that."

"I wasn't jumping out. I was just taking a little air—is that a crime?" She turned toward me, the scorn in her voice matching the scorn on her face. "So, I see it didn't take you long to impress our Mr. Stickley."

"Beg your pardon?" I asked.

Ed sighed. "She thinks we're on a date, Candy."

"Well, you're together and you're holding a bottle of wine," said Maeve. "Isn't that a reasonable assumption?"

There was a little catch in her plaintive voice, and I found myself inviting her to join Ed and me.

"Oh, all right," said Maeve gruffly while Ed proffered me a smile whose vinegar content could have pickled an entire peck of peppers.

6

OUR HOST'S APARTMENT WAS A SURPRISE.

"Goll-eee," said Maeve, imitating the actor who played Gomer Pyle on the old TV sitcom. "These are some fancy digs."

"Thanks," said Ed. "Want a tour?"

We oohed and ahhed over the fact his bedroom not only looked like an adult slept in it—there were no orange crates serving as nightstands, no mattresses on the floor—but that it seemed restful, as if thought had gone into its design and decoration. His bathroom had the same octagonal white tile as the one in my apartment did, but his towels matched and hung from the rod as if folded by a maid. It was his office, though, that most excited me.

"Look at this library!" I said of the floor-to-ceiling bookshelves covering three walls.

"I wish I had a two-bedroom," said Maeve, plopping on a leather chair with wheels. "It'd give me space for a weight room."

"You've sure got a lot of stuff about the Kennedy assassinations," I said, my finger running along the spines of more than a dozen books. "And look at all these CIA titles!"

Maeve swiveled in the office chair and squinted.

"*Who's Really in Charge?*" she read. "*Our Shadow Government in Nicaragua. Secret Presidents—More Powerful Than Our Elected Ones.* What the hell, Ed, are you some kind of conspiracy nut?"

"If you consider wanting to know the truth nutty, then I guess I am."

"*Mrs. Dalloway, A Bell for Adano, Leaves of Grass*," I read aloud, moving on to his expansive fiction and poetry section. "Well, at least you're not completely nuts."

"No, not completely," said Ed. "Now let's go open up that wine—unless you'd like to psychoanalyze the reasons I may or may not have *The Joy of Sex* on hand."

"Do you?" asked Maeve brightly. "Have it, I mean? Because if you do, I'd love to borrow it."

In Ed's living room, Maeve plunked her big sculpted self down on a sleek suede couch and crossed her big manicured feet on top of the coffee table.

"I had no idea substitute teaching was so lucrative," she said.

"Hey, you mind?" asked Ed, nodding toward those big feet and when, with a long aggrieved sigh, Maeve removed them, he put in their place a tray holding the bottle of wine and three glasses.

The bodybuilder's spiel on the unhealthy aspects of alcohol was interrupted when Ed said, "Fine. It's just more for Candy and me."

"Oh all right," said Maeve. "But just one glass."

"And substitute teaching is criminally underpaid," said Ed, steering back onto the conversational road. "Everything in this room was paid for with my game show winnings."

Maeve took a big gulp of wine. "Oh yeah, I forgot you're a big television star."

"What's that supposed to mean?"

Ignoring Ed, she turned to me. "And you. Are you Japanese or Chinese or—" she drummed her kneecaps—"Americanese?"

"Geez, Maeve," said Ed.

"Just asking!"

"I'm a quarter-Finnish," I said, with nursery-school-teacher sweetness. "A quarter-Norwegian and half-Korean."

"And I thought I had an identity crisis!"

"Maeve, really," said Ed, "what is your problem?"

"Who said I had a prob—"

The weightlifter was unable to finish her sentence, overcome as she was by a sudden crying jag.

Mood swings are by nature odd and unexpected things to witness, but this one seemed truly bizarre. Ed's expression telegraphed he felt the same way I did; nevertheless, he got out of his suede club chair and the two of us flanked the bereft Amazon, patting her wide, shuddering back and offering inane assurances like "There, there" and "It's okay."

She picked up real quick on the inanity part.

"It's not okay!" she said, sniffing in a gurgle of phlegm. "It's never okay!"

"What do you mean?" asked Ed gently.

"That 'Americanese' thing—I was just trying to be funny! But I'm just a doofus and nothing—not even a little joke!—ever works out for me!"

This confession inspired another bout of tears (for such a big woman she had a delicate, kittenish way of crying), and when she was all done and Ed refilled her wine glass, she explained how she and her trainer had been confident of her taking home the Miss Dynamo Lady trophy and how she had just that evening heard from said trainer that they'd failed to get her entry in on time and she'd been disqualified.

"And the cash prize is five hundred dollars! The women hardly ever get cash prizes, and we have to fight to get even an ounce of the ton of respect male bodybuilders get, even though we have to work harder because of our testosterone deficit!"

Maeve's face, by virtue of her nearly nonexistent eyebrows, looked naked, and when it crumpled, Ed and I braced for more of her kitten cries, but the big cat drew in a deep breath and lifting her broad jaw to the ceiling sniffed deeply.

"I guess I'll just have to train extra hard for the Valley Vixen event. The cash prizes aren't that hot, but rumor has it the winner'll get free membership at this great gym in Toluca Lake and a year's supply of protein powder and vitamin supplements."

"Speaking of which," said Ed, "anyone hungry?" He retreated to the kitchen and returned with a tray of nuts, cheese, and crackers, none of which he served in their original packaging, further impressing me as to the man's hosting abilities.

Muscly Maeve was curled up on one side of the couch, I sat on the other, and Ed was back in the club chair, and it was in these positions that we did what people will when they don't know each other; we told our stories. That is, Maeve told hers, and we listened.

Watching as Ed topped off her glass for the third time, she told us if she had to describe herself as a kid, it would be tall, homely, and lonely.

"It's not that my parents didn't love me; it's just that there wasn't a lot of time for me. See, Father is a professor of linguistics—he's at the University of Munich now and Mother—well, Mother of course is Taryn Powell."

I knew I wasn't drunk—a few too many Ripple wine binges in my misspent youth had tainted my taste for the grape, and I had hardly touched the cabernet Ed poured—but the bodybuilder's words made me feel as if I were.

"Wait a second," said Ed. "Did you just say your mother is Taryn Powell? Taryn Powell, the actress?"

"No, Taryn Powell the bearded lady. Who do you think?!"

"Wow," I said.

"No kidding," said Ed.

"I don't like to broadcast it," said Maeve, picking cashews from the bowl of mixed nuts. "People are never straight with you when they know your mother's a movie star. Well, was. Now she can only find work on TV."

My grandmother never missed an episode of *Summit Hill,* the nighttime soap opera starring Taryn Powell as Serena Summit, the regal, long-suffering matriarch of a wildly rich and fabulously flawed family.

"I can't wait to tell my grandma that I live above Taryn Powell's daughter!"

Maeve finished chomping nuts and swallowed hard, her red-rimmed eyes threatening to irrigate her face again.

"See, that's exactly what I mean! Now all of a sudden I'm someone *interesting,* when just minutes before you thought I was some freaky bodybuilder."

"I didn't think you were—"

Maeve waved away my weak denial.

"Listen, it's Father—Mother's first husband—I most take after, and proudly so. I followed his footsteps into academia."

"You did?" asked Ed.

"Yes," said Maeve coolly. "I have a master's in physiology."

"Are you a physiologist?" I asked, not exactly sure what that was.

"Right now I'm working as a medical transcriber. It's not my life's goal, but it pays well and I can set my own hours."

"I had no idea," said Ed, balancing a wedge of cheese on a cracker.

"Well, you haven't exactly been eager to get to know me."

Maeve wrinkled her nose, as if Ed's unreciprocated attention had an actual odor to it. Seeking cleaner air, she turned to me. "But it was that study that sparked my interest in bodybuilding. To be the master of my own physical destiny! To fine-tune and mold my musculature! To transform the gangly girl into a powerhouse of womanhood!"

Stirred by her own words, Maeve Mullman stood up, posing with her glass held high. Her T-shirt and baggy warm-up pants couldn't disguise her well-defined body; her muscles were convex and shapely, and I raised my own glass to salute her and her efforts.

"To powerhouses of womanhood!" I said.

"To mastering physical destiny!" added Ed.

"Hey," said Maeve, the celebratory moment fleeting. "Are you making fun of me?"

Both Ed and I averred that we were not.

"Because that's what I can't stand. People making fun of me. I don't mind honest questions—'Why do you lift weights?' 'Why do you like to bulk up like that?'—but I hate people making fun of me."

She banged her empty glass down on the coffee table and bolted toward the door, her long strides making tracks in the thick gray carpet.

"I wasn't making fun of you!" said Ed, and I echoed him, but Maeve exited, slamming the door against our assurances.

"I think," said Ed after a long moment, "a nerve may have been touched."

Shortly after Maeve's departure, I made a less dramatic one.

"Since it looks like she's eaten all the cashews," I said, pilfering through the crystal nut bowl, "I guess I should be going, too."

"Hey, we never got to our Scrabble game," said Ed.

"I would have creamed you."

"In your dreams. And don't go just yet—I've got something for you."

After dashing into the kitchen Ed returned with a six-pack.

"Isn't that the chocolate milk stuff you were drinking down at the pool?" I asked.

"YaZoo. It's chocolate soda. It's one of my game show 'parting gifts,' which I now realize means 'hard to part with,' since no one wants any."

"Well, gee . . . thanks."

Laughing as I reluctantly accepted the six-pack, Ed took out from his back pocket a folded piece of newspaper.

"Here's your real present."

"Want ads?"

"For game show contestants. See here," he said, pointing to red-inked circles, "this one's for *Word Wise,* and here's one for *Use It or Lose It*— although they only have prizes, not cash—and this one's for *The Money Tree.* That's the show I was just on. Call them up and see what happens."

ED OFFERED TO SEE ME HOME, and while I thanked him for his chivalry I reminded him I lived in the same complex and thought I could safely navigate the short distance between his four-plex and mine.

I breathed in the jasmine and eucalyptus-tinged air. After the harsh smoggy daylight, there was something tender and wistful about this Hollywood night that smelled of sachets tucked inside the lace and satins of a widow's lingerie drawer. It was almost dreamy, that soft-scented air, and

I could have walked for miles in it, but instead I turned toward the back of the complex and the pool.

Light shone from behind a shaded window in Billy Gray Green's apartment, but I presumed he was out bartending and like most people didn't want to come home to a dark house. Just in case he was home, I stripped to my underwear in the shadows and slipped into the water, slicing through it in long quiet strokes, thinking of the evening, thinking of the melodrama of Maeve's story, of my own.

7

HERE'S SOME GOOD ADVICE: don't read your old diaries when you're depressed. Earlier that summer I had holed up in my bedroom doing that, and believe me, you can't win: the bright and cheery entries will make you wonder why you don't feel like that anymore, and the sad and whiny ones will make you think nothing changes.

5/12/68

Dear Cal,

Dad gave Grandma a box of chocolate-covered cherries and we drove out to Aunt Pauline's for lunch. I didn't want to go because I had a stomachache.

I hate Mother's Day.

2/24/69

Dear Cal,

One word for the Nokomis Jr. High Talent Show: Huge Success! (Okay, two words.) Miss Lindblom asked me to emcee and it was so much fun! When Dale Ferguson walked off the stage after forgetting the words to "Sittin' on the Dock of the Bay," I said, "I guess he fell in." The audience cracked up. And when Carla Dierks and Paula Peterson came out to dance in their little leotards, a bunch of boys started to whistle and I pretended to crack a whip and said, "Settle down, animals." And not only did I get to emcee, I got to close the show! Paul Dahlquist and I sang "If I Had a Stammer." With Paul's good guitar playing and my okay Bob-Dylan-as-a-stutterer imper-sonation, we got a standing ovation!

6/4/70

Dear Cal,

Finally, FINALLY, at the ripe old age of fourteen, I got my period! Grandma had given me a box of pads when I was eleven years old and it was starting to seem like I'd never need them, and besides, my friend LeAnn Jerdy and I used most of them up making houses (mostly igloos) for our Troll dolls and sleeping bags for Ken and Barbie.

I stayed up late, surprising Dad when he came home by giving him a big hug. He was so surprised he hugged me back, but it didn't take him long to let go and say, "What's this all about?"

"Oh, I just wanted you to know I'm not a hermaphrodite like Charlotte said I was and today I turned into a woman!" That's what I wanted to say—it was sort of momentous news after all—but in the end, all I could say was, "Nothing. Good night."

10/1/71

Dear Cal,

We had a Laugh-Off Assembly at school for April Fool's Day, and the sophomores RULED. Tom Schmitz dressed up in a gray wig and a baggy dress and sang "Folsum Prison" in an old lady voice. Matt Triggs dressed up in a blonde wig and shorts and a tank top and did a cheerleading routine. I dressed up in a man's suit and tucked my hair up into a hat and gave a speech called, "What I Expect from You Brats." The first big laugh came right after I introduced myself as Mr. Welby (our school principal). Afterwards, Mr. Welby came up to me and said he didn't know whether to be flattered or suspend me!

7/29/72

Dear Cal,

Debbie Hutchinson said I wasn't supporting the team. Peggy Brendan said I made the rest of them look dumb. "No," I thought, "you did that all by yourselves."

The thing is, I'd already done it last year; the stupid fundraiser in which we took turns washing cars, or standing on the corner of 46th & Hiawatha, waving signs and hollering "Support Roosevelt's Swim Team! Support the Teddies!" I didn't mind doing any of that; what I did mind was the "uniform" we'd been told to wear—cutoffs ("the shorter the better!") and bikini tops. I didn't like all the guys honking their horns and whistling and how we were all giggly, spraying each other with hoses or how Bonnie Anderson would lean over a car and practically smash her boobs against the windshield while the guy inside sat with his tongue (I hope that's all) hanging out.

So I dressed in my dad's old uniform, the kind he wore before he got promoted to foreman; a one-piece jumpsuit that zips up the front. And I tied a scarf around my hair, like Rosie the Riveter.

And I did what I was supposed to do—shout loud, wave signs, and wash cars—without that icky feeling of giving away something I didn't want to.

Coach came by in the afternoon, and when she saw me she shook her head and muttered, "Typical," but she wasn't able to hide her smile.

2/14/73

Dear Cal,

Another Cry Day. On a scale of 1–10, about an 8.

After English class, I ditched school and took a bus to the Electric Fetus, figuring I might as well buy myself a Valentine. When I was up at the cashier, paying for Exile on Main Street, *I hear this voice saying, "Excellent choice, Candy Bar."*

It was Jim Clark, my childhood crush. I spent a lot of time admiring him from afar (i.e., my bedroom window), watching him jump in and out of cars filled with yelling, joking high school boys and girls, and, once, watching him pose on his front step with his prom date, wishing I was that girl in the pink dress and blonde pageboy who held his hand and laughed when Mrs. Clark pointed her camera and said, "Cheese!" Anyway, from what Mrs. Clark told Grandma, he's had a hard time since he got back from Vietnam, and I admit, I hardly recognized him with his Fu Manchu mustache and scraggly beard.

"Jim Clark, I haven't seen you in forever!"

"Seems that way. You're all growed up!" Then he said that surely I wasn't old enough to be out of school yet, and I said, "No, I'm a junior," and then he said, "A truant junior," and asked if I wanted to go for a ride and I said sure.

He fired up a joint and we drove toward the River Road, listening to "Ride, Captain Ride" and "Smiling Faces Sometimes" and when

"In the Summertime" came on, he said, "Do you know who sings this?
Mungo Jerry. Do you know where the name Mungo Jerry came from?"

"At the Stupid Names for a Band store?"

Jim laughed. "From a T. S. Eliot poem."

Our fun and mellow drive changed when he blurted out how
sorry he was he didn't go to my dad's service because funerals are
hard for him.

"Good old Mr. Pekkala," he said and sighed. "Every now and
then I'd wander over to your garage late at night when your dad was
in there working on his car, or just sitting there smoking. So we'd talk."

"You would?" I said, my throat clogging up. "About what?"

Jim scratched his nametag sewn on the front of his camouflage
jacket. "Everything, really. Cars. Sports. Politics. He was really mad
that Johnson didn't run for a second term."

"He was?"

"Yeah, he hated the war, and he thought Johnson was finally
wising up and would have gotten us out a lot earlier." Jim took a
deep, final toke of the joint. "When I got drafted, he gave me his
lucky Indian head penny. The one he carried all through Korea."

I felt like we were talking about someone I'd never met and
when I told him it was the three-month anniversary of my dad
dying, he said we had to go to Fort Snelling, stat, and pay our
respects. So we drove out by the airport to the cemetery, which is
HUGE and filled with row after row of white headstones that seem
to go on forever. First we stopped at the grave of one of Jim's friends,
and he knelt down, his hands running over the engraving like he
was reading Braille. The date made me feel like my lungs weren't
working: 1949–1968.

A plane roared overheard and I wondered if from way up high,
all those tombstones in all those lines looked like dominoes, and if
you flicked them with a finger they'd all fall down.

My dad's grave didn't have its permanent marble headstone
yet—more unfinished business—and Jim put his arm around me
as we squatted in front of it and I bawled like a baby.

"Life's a bitch, Candy," he said, and then he was crying.

I feel like I don't know anything.

11/19/73

Dear Cal,

Mrs. Freeburg cornered me in the hallway today and said audi-
tions were being held for Hello Dolly *and I'd be perfect for the lead*
role. I said I'd think about it just so she'd leave me alone, and she
said, "Candy, you're one of the most talented students I've ever
worked with. I want you back onstage. It'll be good for you."

Instead of going to Chemistry, I sat in a bathroom stall for all
of second period, but not to play over and over those words about
me being so talented. The reason I locked myself in the can is that
I drank so much this weekend I still felt a little sick. Sick enough to
barf twice.

3/5/74

Dear Cal,

Big college tour today . . . and thanks to the WORST tour guide
ever, I hate my life even more.

6/15/74

Dear Cal,

Shit! This is the second time I've asked the question: am I still
a virgin? All I know is that I woke up in Bryan Emery's basement
with some of my clothes on and some not and a vague memory
of rolling around with a guy who smelled like pot and Slim Jims.
Karen was the only one still there—where'd everyone else go?—and
she had less clothes on than me.

"Man, were you wasted," she said.

"Like you weren't," I said, pulling a squished chunk of Slim Jim
out of my hair.

"Eww," said Karen as we gathered up our stuff. "Is that what I
think it is?"

We both stood looking at the used rubber.

"I hope it's from the guy I was with," I said.

"Same here," said Karen.

They went on and on to an embarrassing degree, the entries recount-
ing my dissolute ways, and I felt sorry and angry at the girl who wrote
them. I stopped reading before I got to my college calendaeiums, knowing they were mostly a robotic rundown of grades and assignments with

the occasional review of a theater department show I should have tried out for, but didn't.

Shoving back under the bed the box of notebooks that proved I was eligible for citizenship in Loserville, I trudged upstairs.

"Listless" would have been an overenthusiastic description of my mood, and after making the huge physical effort of turning on the television, I collapsed onto that on which I was collapsing a lot lately—the couch.

Ignoring the sweet June day outside, I watched a soap opera in which two well-groomed lovers frolicked on picnic grounds while the spurned, well-groomed former boyfriend lurked in the bushes, flashing his well-groomed senator grandfather's pistol. I watched another soap opera in which a well-groomed wedding couple took their vows, while the spurned, well-groomed girlfriend stole away in the backseat of the bridal couple's festively decorated car.

"Now that's what I call a honeymoon surprise," I muttered.

Interrupting the stories of these philandering, violent, but always well-groomed characters were the deodorant, toilet paper, and floor wax commercials, and I was watching Mr. Whipple squeeze the Charmin when something fluttered onto my lap. It was a ticket.

"It's for Heidi Wheaton," said my grandmother, standing behind the couch. "We're seeing her tonight."

My postcollege social life had whittled away to nothing, and I could tell from her expression that she was waiting for me to resist her invitation.

Not having the energy, I said, "Fine."

"Because if you say, 'No,'" she began, ". . . oh, okay. Good."

We took the bus to the State Theater to see the woman whose publicity trumpeted her as "the funniest woman on the planet!"

Heidi Wheaton had been the breakaway star on *Yuk It Up!*, a comedy sketch show, and her ability to play anything from an addled rocket scientist to a larcenous babysitter had won her two Emmys and a wide fan base.

In our velveteen seats, my grandmother and I sat back in the dark theater and for two hours I forgot how bad I felt about my life. We laughed and nudged one another as Heidi reprised her *Yuk It Up!* characters and introduced us to several new ones.

Cool Old MacDonald was a jazz singer whose skat singing involved oinks, moos, and meows. Dottie Dunn was an Avon Lady who needed a little bump—or two—of Johnny Walker Red to give her sales pitch confidence.

Guptula was an East Indian yogi who claimed to have the secret of life.

After arranging herself in a cross-legged seated position, Heidi put her hands on her knees, palms up and with her eyes closed, took several deep and exaggerated breaths.

"You must carefully choose a power mantra," she said in a singsong voice. She opened her eyes, now slightly crossed. "The magic words that will be your guide and compass, your life saber—and no, all you *Star Wars* fans, I did not say 'light saber' but 'life saber' because it is exactly that, something used to slash away that which prevents you from getting your deepest desires. My life saber is—"

Here she quickly said a word that sounded like maykmyneahdubbahl. She said it again, then repeated it so we understood it was *Make mine a double*.

Big yuks from the audience.

"Of course, your power mantra must be a secret," Guptula counseled. "I can tell you mine only because I am more enlightened than you poor Midwestern yahoos could ever hope to be."

I laughed more than I had in a long time, but this wasn't enough for my grandmother.

"Come on," she said, as the theater emptied of its happy, sated audience. "We're going backstage."

Grandma was a polite and unassuming person, and that she steered me toward an usher standing by the stage and said, "We'd like to say hello to Miss Wheaton," did nothing less than boggle my mind.

"Uh, does she know you?" asked the usher, a pimply young man who wore a macramé headband around his forehead to contain a cascade of blond curls.

"Of course she does," said my grandmother, pulling me up the stairs. "And by the way, I absolutely love your hair."

The compliment softened whatever barricades the usher might have put up, and in no time my grandmother and I were behind the curtain.

"Miss Wheaton!" barked my grandmother, as if she were the producer of the show, and the stagehand could do nothing but point.

We followed his finger down a hallway and stood in line with a dozen people. When Heidi Wheaton and another woman emerged from her dressing room and saw us, the comedian whose features were naturally doleful looked even more miserable, promptly turning the other way. The woman with her laughed and taking the comic by the shoulders spun her around to face us.

"I had fifty people waiting for me backstage in Portland," the actress whined, "and this is all you can scrounge up?"

She didn't seem thrilled to go down the reception line, but she did, offering a tired smile as people thanked her for a magical evening, telling her they didn't know when they'd laughed so hard, etc. After she had signed an autograph for a radio deejay, she shook hands with my grandmother, who said, "Miss Wheaton! My granddaughter here is just as funny as you are! Any advice you can give her?"

"Yeah," she said in a monotone. "Life's a shit sandwich. So only eat the bread."

MY GRANDMOTHER FUMED as we walked to the bus stop.

"What kind of advice was that? Honestly, I didn't expect her to be so crude. Yes sir, Miss Heidi Wheaton has lost a little luster in my book! Would it have killed her to tell you something a little more sensible?"

"I still can't believe you said that to her! That I was just as funny as she was!" Feeling almost tipsy from all the laughing I'd done, I laughed again.

"Well, you are—when you want to be!" She tucked her hand in the crook of my arm. "Oh, Candy, remember all those nights we'd watch Johnny Carson and you'd put on your own little show for me, all those times when you told me that when you grew up, you wanted to make people laugh?"

"Grandma," I said, my spirits taking a dive. "I . . . I was just a kid then."

After extending his Happy Hour into Sloppy Hour, a man in a rumpled suit and skewed tie stumbled past us, and my grandmother shook her head at the spectacle.

"And all those school plays and talent shows, oh kid, when you'd steal every scene you were in! And Candy, did I tell you—I just read about this tavern in St. Paul that started hosting comedy nights, and I think you should go down there and—"

"Oh, Grandma, I—"

"—I don't have to tell you how proud I am of all the hard work you put in at the U—good heavens, graduating early!—but now that you've got a degree, well, maybe it's time to finally indulge your old dreams a bit."

Torn between telling her to shut up and bursting into tears, I pressed my lips tight so I couldn't do either, and as we waited for the bus I seethed with anger and resentment that my grandma dare bring up my old dreams—dreams I didn't dare bring up myself.

THE THING IS, Heidi Wheaton's advice had a profound influence on me. Not right away, and not the stuff about the shit sandwich, which, as far as pithy sayings go, didn't strike me as all that pithy. But weeks later, on a stormy summer's night that brought me to a crossroads of terror and absurdity, it seemed only fitting that Guptula, her yogi character, appeared in my head along with the words that would be my own secret power mantra, my life saber. And when Charlotte's apartment offer came just days later—well, like I said, it's all about timing. Time, as my cousin had said, to get a life.

WHILE HOLLYWOOD THROBBED with Friday night energy, I cocooned myself in that pool, in competition with nothing but my own pleasure, swimming back and forth, back and forth, each somersault turn launching me, in an explosion of bubbles, toward the other side. Dolphins understand the mood-brightening effects of a playful swim—you can't fake smiles like that—but my buoyancy was more than physical.

I had gone from a life so stuck that sorting my sock drawer qualified as excitement *and* accomplishment to moving into a Hollywood Boulevard apartment and mock sword fighting with its handsome building manager. I'd turned into such a hermit that the surprise was I hadn't grown a full beard and a preference for flannel shirts, yet in one afternoon I had met more than a dozen people, at least one who already felt like a friend.

Not wanting to snort water up my nose, I had to force myself not to laugh as I did another flip turn. I knew of course that I was in a confined space, a tiled rectangle, but it was the craziest thing—I felt as if a tether had been cut, and I was swimming without boundaries.

8

In an office building on Highland Avenue, I asked the temp agent if she were named after Zelda Fitzgerald.

"Nope. Zelda Kleinman, my mother's best friend. Although I do have an uncle who worked on the Paramount lot the same time as F. Scott Fitzgerald did. He said they went out for drinks a couple times."

"Your uncle went out for drinks with F. Scott Fitzgerald? I love F. Scott Fitzgerald! He could make a whole poem out of one sentence."

Zelda shrugged. "I prefer less poetry and a little more connection to the characters."

I knew a good debate didn't have room for personal attacks so I restrained myself from asking aloud, *Are you crazy?* and we proceeded to have a nice conversation about books before the temp agent was reminded by her secretary that her 3:20 was waiting.

"I like to send smart people to my clients," said Zelda, clicking her pen like a detonator. "Ergo, I think you'll do just fine by us." She looked at the calendar that was spread across her desk like a giant place mat. "I don't have anything at the moment, but when I do you'll hear from me."

Chip, my next interviewer, declared me "impressive." The contestant coordinator of *Word Wise,* he offset his boyish freckled face by dressing like the tenor in a barbershop quartet, in a bow tie and suspenders, his red hair slicked back and shiny.

"You got a perfect score on the general knowledge test," Chip said, peering at me through his horn-rimmed glasses. "That's something of a rarity, even with our caliber of contestants."

I smiled modestly, not about to explain that I had the opposite of test anxiety, and that anytime anyone gave me a pencil and a time limit, I was in heaven.

"*Word Wise* prides itself on its erudition," he continued. "Anyone can play *Password* or *Pyramid* or *Wheel of Fortune*—he practically spat out these last three words—"but it takes erudition to play *Word Wise.*"

I smiled, sucking in my cheeks and lowering one eyebrow in an attempt to look erudite.

"Now, we certainly don't frown on 'bubbly,'" he said. "After all, we don't want the viewing audience to fall asleep. But we don't insist our contestants jump up and down like maniacs, either. Just show genuine enthusiasm."

"I can be genuinely enthusiastic."

"I believe you can," said Chip, marking a little check on the paper in front of him. "And your Orien—your Asian angle's a good one. We don't get a lot of Asians."

LATE THAT AFTERNOON, Zelda phoned to tell me she had placed me at Beat Street Records for an "open-ended assignment" beginning the following week and Chip called to tell me I had made the *Word Wise* cut and was to report for taping on Saturday morning. There was no one at the pool to share my good news with except Robert X. Roberts and June, both of whom had surrendered to the arms of Morpheus; the *Variety* over Mr. Roberts's face fluttering as he snored and Binky the brown-teared dog guarding June from his perch in a hot pink tote bag. I celebrated by swimming forty laps.

The buildings of Peyton Hall—mostly stuccoed and green-shuttered four-plexes—formed a rectangular perimeter, open at the front on the Hollywood Boulevard side. Walking back from the pool, I usually took the sidewalk flanking the east buildings and then turned down the front walk to my four-plex, but being that I was now a person who sought out adventure, I occasionally walked past the big pillared brick building in the center back and made a loop around the buildings on the west side. Taking this route now, I passed a dense rectangle of shrubbery and promptly ran into an old lady.

"Oof!" she said as we collided.

"Oh, I'm so sorry!" I said as she staggered back into the shrubbery, dropping her woven string bag.

Dressed like the matriarch of some Eastern European gypsy caravan, the woman peered at me from her perch in the greenery.

"Here, let me help you," I said, reaching for her.

"Bah," she said, waving me off, and when she was fully vertical she brushed off the sleeves exposed under her cape.

"I didn't see you!" I said. "It seemed like you just popped out on the sidewalk and—"

The woman nodded her head toward the string grocery bag.

"You will carry that for me," she said in an accent thick as borscht. "Yes?"

"Of course," I said, and after picking it up I turned to follow the woman who was already motoring down the path, her skirt swishing it like a broom.

I had figured the old gypsy I had collided with had to be Madame Pepper even before we passed the gargoyle planter and crossed her threshold with the Welcome? mat, and when she took the string bag from me, I stood awkwardly on the small woven rag rug that served as her foyer, wondering if I'd been invited in or dismissed.

It was jarring to step out of the light of a summer evening and into the gloomy glamour of what looked like an Old World apartment with accents provided by an addled Hollywood set designer. The furniture reflected no decorating trends popular within the past century, and even in the worst of circumstances Scarlett O'Hara would never have deigned to make a dress out of the heavy velvet curtains that hung over the parlor windows, brown and nappy as the backside of a flea-bitten bison. Dozens of autographed 8 x 10s of old film stars crowded the walls so that only glimpses of the tropical wallpaper were visible underneath; a palm frond unfurled like a magic carpet underneath a picture of Joan Crawford sitting on Franchot Tone's lap; pineapple leaves formed a spiky tiara from the top of Norma Shearer's head.

"Why don't you go home?" came the old woman's voice from the kitchen. Having been given my answer—I was being dismissed—I turned toward the door.

"Get some clothes on, and when you come back I will have tea made."

"Okay!" I said brightly, adjusting the towel I wore like a shift. I wasn't being banished after all.

"I HOPE YOU LIKE BLACK BREAD," said the old woman, setting a silver coffee service on the table in front of the horsehair sofa. "Black bread and tea with honey—is good for what ails you."

Glenn Miller was playing on the console record player but at a volume so low that "String of Pearls" seemed less a jaunty dance tune than a tease. In a narrow gold vase on top of the upright piano, a stick of incense unfurled a scent that managed to smell both musty and sweet.

"Zo," said the woman, touching the knot of her beaded shawl. "I am of course Madame Pepper and you are the girl who was wanting to borrow a cup of sugar, yes?"

"How did you know that?"

"I am fortune-teller," she said, fingering a tress of the long gray hair that trailed out from under the scarf she wore like a pirate. "Also, Melvin Slyke told me."

She poured a cup of tea and handed it to me. "He is your neighbor, yes? He is hoping you someday make that cake, and that when you do, he will get a piece. I too would accept same. It's not so common that a young person makes cake."

"I love to bake," I said. "My grandmother taught me . . . well, not so much taught me—she was no cook—as allowed me. So yes. Absolutely. When I bake my next cake, you will definitely get a piece."

I knew I was nattering, but how was I supposed to have a normal conversation with someone who announced, "I am fortune-teller"?

Madame Pepper cut a thick slab of bread and slathered it with a half-inch of butter. I followed her example; the bread was good and yeasty with a chewy crust, and as the two of us sat eating and drinking to the companionable clink of silverware and china, I began to relax. That is until the seer looked at me from under the awning of her eyebrows and said, "I could read your fortune but it might frighten you."

"Really?" I said, coughing a bit.

"Yes. Some people don't like to know what lies ahead. Mr. Gable, for instance—"

"—the King of Hollywood," I said, hoping to impress her with my grasp of Hollywood history. "I couldn't believe when the apartment manager told me Clark Gable used to live here!"

"Now and then, when he needed to stay in Hollywood," said Madame Pepper. She stirred milk into her tea and fussed with the pot of honey, signals I took to mean, *You interrupt me, I make you wait.* Silence hung heavy as the drapes before she spoke again.

"His home-home was a big ranch in Encino. Now, as I was saying, Mr. Gable, he always tell me, 'Magda,'—not many I give permission to use my given name!—'Magda, even if you see a bus hitting me tomorrow, don't tell me of it. I only want to hear the good stuff.'"

"Who else did you see?" I asked, a cub reporter wanting the full scoop.

"See? I saw many." She spiraled a hand in the air. "Anybody who was anybody came to see Madame Pepper. Still do. Most wanting of course to know not their fates so much as their fates in Hollywood." Her hooded eyes squinted at me. "You are wanting to be an actress? Because I am seeing cameras."

Even though I thought she was as much a clairvoyant as I was a go-go dancer, my scalp tingled.

"Well, I . . . I am going to be on a game show this weekend."

She slapped the carved wooden arm of the sofa.

"Bingo. Although I am seeing for you more than one dinky little game show. Which is odd because I am not needing to look to the future to see you have none as Hollywood actress."

"Gee, thanks," I said, a flush warming my face.

"You don't have looks for Hollywood actress," she added, in case I wasn't insulted enough.

"Okay, then." I patted my mouth with a yellowed linen napkin. "Thank you very much for the—"

"Sit, sit," she said, only she pronounced it "Zit, zit," and I, who'd been preparing to make a run for it, zat.

As she smiled, remnants of dimples flashed in her sunken cheeks.

"There are reasons to be touchy, but truth should not be one of them."

I didn't disguise rolling my eyes; if she were going to continue to cut me down, I wasn't going to censor my reactions.

"And what if I don't believe that what you're saying is the truth?"

"In general, or as a predictor of the future?"

"Take your pick," I said.

A low guttural laugh crawled up her throat.

"I like you, I am seeing that," she said, nodding. "But it is of no concern to me whether or not you think I am fraud."

"I didn't say you were a fraud."

"In so many words, yes. And I was saying nothing against you, only against Hollywood. You are pretty in your own way, and you could have the acting talent of Sarah Bernhardt, but if you are not pretty in their way, forget about it."

"I've seen actresses who look like me in the movies," I said, defensively.

"Yes, tending to markets or laundromats. Or on that *M*A*S*H* show." She shook her head. "Not for you. You are too big a star."

I came very close to doing a spit take. As it was, I coughed and sputtered and felt tea warm my sinuses.

"Sorry. I just thought I heard you say I was 'too big a star.'"

The old woman smiled, understanding that I was not confused but only wanted to hear her repeat what she'd just said.

"You heard correctly. And now you are thinking, 'Oh, maybe I judged Madame's abilities a little harshly,' yes?"

"No," I said, causing her to snort again. "But, well . . . what do you mean?"

Madame Pepper's bracelets jangled as she arranged them on her wrist.

"Maybe you should hire grammar teacher." She wiggled her awning of eyebrows. "To spell it out for you."

ANY KID WHO LOOKS A LITTLE DIFFERENT gets called names—when I was in the first grade, a big red-faced sixth grader raced over to me on the playground and with chubby hands on his hips asked, "Hey, what are you—a gook or something?"

Occasionally subject to names like Chink, Jap, or Slant Eye, I'd usually ignore them—at least outwardly—but didn't when a boy sitting next to me in seventh grade science asked me if I was related to Charlie Chan.

"Yes, I Charlie Chan," I said in an over-the-top Asian accent, "and you Number One Stupid Shit Head."

The boy gaped at me, and it was obvious from his wounded expression that my response to his slight joke was way out of line.

"Geez, I just—"

"Stupid *Stupid* Shit Head," I hissed, before sleepy Mr. Sonneborg looked up from his desk, swiveling his head trying to detect the noisemakers.

Now the word *star* had been used by a Hollywood fortune-teller in regards to me, and as I alternately skipped and ran back to my apartment, a maniacal giggle burbled in my chest. Madame Pepper was right in thinking I thought her a charlatan, but still, even a charlatan can't be wrong all the time.

9

"Look at my gooseflesh!" said the woman next to me, offering for view her textured forearm.

"Yes, it is cool in here," said Chip, the freckled game show coordinator. "Research shows it keeps the energy up."

"If we freeze to death," said a man behind me, "won't that bring the energy down?"

"All right, people," said Chip, "let's try to forget about the temperature. You've got more important things to worry about."

He led the small group of contestants into a room furnished like a den with vending machines.

"This is the greenroom. This is where you'll take your breaks and have lunch. If you need to use the ladies' or men's rooms, Abby here will escort you."

A young woman with an earnest overbite said, "You really can't do anything outside this room without me tagging along!"

The man who'd complained about freezing to death nodded. "It's because of that big scandal back in the '50s. When they fed that one guy all the answers ahead of time."

"Yes," said Chip quickly. "We are scrupulous about avoiding scandal. Now, everyone, please find your name tags on the table and prepare yourself to be *Word Wise!*"

With that cheerful exhortation, he left the room, leaving Abby alone to stave off scandal.

After we contestants helped ourselves to beverages, we sat at a big oval table and exchanged mini-biographies. Dorothy from Iowa, the woman who'd earlier shown me her goose bumps, was an avid sweepstakes player and was listing the prizes she had won (a boat, a set of real leather luggage, a year's supply of BlockOChoco bars) when Chip reemerged, outfitted with a headset and a clipboard.

"All right, people, it's show time. Up on the docket are Jerry and Carrie." His strictly business contestant-coordinator persona was offset by a surprised smile. "Hey, rhyming contestants. Anyway, Jerry and Carrie, follow me. Abby will take care of the rest of you."

Herded together into a tight group, my (stifled) impulse was to moo as we followed Abby through the studio and into the front row of the bleachers, where a small audience was assembled. We had been advised not to acknowledge any friends or relatives—"We can't risk any passing of signals"—and every contestant took meticulous care not to look up and wave, jeopardizing their eligibility.

"Isn't this thrilling?" whispered Dorothy, sitting to my left. I nodded, and Tina, the fifth grade teacher who was at my right, leaned forward, her hands clutched under her chin.

"The set looks so glamorous!"

It was shiny, that's for sure. On a silver lamé curtained backdrop, metallic letters spelled out *Word Wise!* The host's podium was also silver, and flanked by silver cubes at which the contestants were sitting; Jerry looking relaxed and Carrie looking terrified.

"I hope she doesn't lose her lunch," said Leon, a pharmaceutical salesman from Santa Ana.

As cameramen and people with clipboards and headsets positioned themselves, a man with a lopsided afro raced toward us, clapping his hands.

"Hey, everybody, I'm Jimmy Jay, the show announcer as well as the guy who's going to warm you up!"

His half-dozen so-so jokes about the Flying Wallendas, the Susan B. Anthony dollar, and Love Canal failed to bring up my temperature, but when he asked, "Are you warm yet?" the crowd responded with a hale "Yeah!"

"Good," he said as a camera rolled into position. "Because now it's time to introduce today's celebrity game players. Ladies and gentlemen, put your hands together for Filo Nuala!"

A dark-skinned man who could nudge aside an ox with his shoulders emerged from behind the silver curtain.

"Filo Nuala!" whispered Bob, a blinds and drapery installer. "Holy shit!"

Filo Nuala was a quarterback for the Los Angeles Rams. I knew this not as a fan but as a person with intact senses. You couldn't watch TV, read the newspaper, or listen to the radio without witnessing the American Samoan exhibiting his exploits on the gridiron, hosting a big charity event, or pitching this shaving cream or that breakfast cereal.

Pressing a big hand against his tie, the man sat down at his cube, dwarfing it.

"And joining last year's MVP is this year's Emmy-award winning actress Precia Doyle!"

Now I was getting excited. Precia Doyle was an actress who'd made a career of playing British aristocrats on lots of high-brow miniseries, several of which I had watched through the years with my grandmother.

"She's so tiny!" whispered Dorothy.

After Precia offered a funny little curtsy to Filo Nuala, Jimmy Jay said, "And now, the man who makes *Word Wise* the preferred game show of Mensa members, our host, Yancey Rogan!"

The show's jazzy theme music came on, and a tall, gangly guy in a checkered sport coat loped onto the set, his puffy shag as unmoving as plastic.

"Thanks, Jimmy Jay," he said and looking into a camera that had glided to a stop in front of him, he pointed his finger and said, "Now let's play *Word Wise!*"

It was a tease; first Yancey Rogan had to honor the game show law of engaging in banter before the game playing began, which meant chatting about football with Filo and plugging Precia's upcoming miniseries about all the sexual and political intrigue in Queen Victoria's court.

Next the contestants were introduced, and after Jerry told about his police work—"I've got a pretty quiet beat; seems I chase down more truants than bank robbers"—Carrie, still looking like she needed Dramamine, explained that she was a veterinarian's assistant.

"So I imagine you get on-the-job training as to how to keep the wolves away," said Yancey.

Carrie's head bobbed in several directions so that you couldn't tell if she was agreeing or disagreeing.

"All right, then," said Yancey, smiling into the camera. "You've met our fabulous celebrities and our fabulous contestants—now let's play *Word Wise!*"

I had spent the week watching the show; there wasn't much to it, really; it was sort of like word volleyball, except they kept throwing in a new ball.

The game begins and one team is given a letter, say, *A*. A beep sounds, a light goes on and Yancey gives the celebrity a category of speech, say, *noun*. So the celebrity might answer, "Apple." The play then goes to her partner, and after another beep and light, Yancey gives the contestant another category of speech, say, *adjective*. He might respond with "Anxious." Throughout the round, Yancey can change the category at any time and the players' answers have to reflect that.

If a team misses an answer, if for instance the celebrity says, "annoyed," and her category was still *noun,* the letter A and the remaining seconds go to the other team. When that time runs out, that team is given a new letter and a minute to play their full round. Whichever side racks up the most words at the final bell goes to the Big Dictionary. Occasionally a whistle blows, which means a speed round will be played and the winner of that wins a bonus prize—usually a trip.

"Filo and Jerry," said Yancey, "your letter is E and Filo, your category is *adjective.*"

A beep sounded and a light on Filo's cube went on.

"Empathetic."

Another beep and Jerry's cube lit up.

Yancey said, "*Verb.*"

"Enter," said Jerry.

When Filo's light blinked on, he said, "Egregious."

Whoa, I thought. Here was a football player whose helmet actually protected something.

"Entertain," said Jerry.

"Erroneous," said Filo.

"Jerry," said Yancey after the beep. "*Adjective.*"

"Erratic."

Another beep.

"Filo," said Yancey. "*Noun.*"

"Elephant."

"Elk," said Jerry.

A buzzer sounded.

"I'm sorry Jerry, your category was still *adjective.*" He turned to the women. "Precia, the letter is E, category is *adjective,* and there are still twenty seconds remaining on the clock. Go."

Precia said, "Enormous."

"Carrie," said Yancey after the beep. "*Verb.*"

Carrie looked stunned, as if the light that flicked on her cube was a headlight and she was the proverbial deer, but just when I thought she was going to lurch out and crash into the windshield, she blurted, "Elapse!"

Precia nodded approvingly at her partner and when her light flashed on, she said, "Eminent."

"Exit," answered Carrie.

Beep.

"Precia, *noun.*"

"Existence."

A lower buzzer blatted.

"Congratulations, ladies, you won the rest of your opponents' round; now we'll start your own. Carrie, the letter is J and your category is *verb.*"

The game continued until the final round, and Yancey told Filo his letter was N and his category *noun.*

The light and Filo's word arrived at the same time. "Nimbus."

Beep.

"Jerry," said Yancey. "*Adjective.*"

"Noisy."

We were all sitting forward in our seats, taking everything in. In my mind, I shouted my own answers, *Nadir! Nullify! Nymph!* and imagined my fellow contestants were doing the same thing.

Filo Nuala, who played football in stadiums filled with raucous, beer-drinking fans, didn't seem adversely affected by the respectful quiet of this tiny audience; he was focused and sharp, and it didn't surprise me when he and Jerry won the game.

"Carrie, I'm afraid we're going to have to say good-bye to you," said Yancey. "But let's let Jimmy Jay tell us what you'll be taking home."

"Yancey," said Jimmy, standing in front of a display. "Today's parting gifts include beautiful and unbreakable Melnor dishes—a place setting for six—along with a guarantee that when company comes over, the only thing you will break is bread! Also, Yancey, our lucky contestants will be taking home this beautiful Zirconian pendant and matching earrings by Gerral Jewelers, a case of delicious Rice Doodles, and this very timely clock radio, courtesy of K&H Electronics!"

BY LATE AFTERNOON, there were only three contestants left in the stands and I was resigned to not being called that day when Chip came up to us during a commercial break and said, "Candy, you're up."

Those words had the effect of a blast of desert heat: I felt a deep flush and all saliva in my mouth evaporated.

As I walked toward the set, my legs turned to jelly, their bones to sponges. My heart, which had been running like a steady reliable Ford engine, now revved up like a Ferrari's. My palms sprouted geysers and I wiped them on the sides of my skirt before I shook my partner Precia's hand.

When the red camera light came on, Yancey introduced me to the home audience and then asked, "So what do you do here in Hollywood, Candy?"

I hadn't planned to say anything other than I was new in town and looking for work, but unplanned words tumbled out of my mouth.

"I'm Dooby Carlyle's stunt double."

Filo's laugh was sharp and quick—Dooby Carlyle was his former 6'5" three-hundred-pound teammate who'd parlayed his fame on the field into a new career as a cowboy/detective in the hit action/thrillers *Rodeo Cop* and *Rodeo Cop II*.

I relaxed in the laughter of the audience and the game began. My team, as the contender, got the first turn.

"Precia, your letter is G and your category is *adjective*."

Beep. Her light went on.

"Gigantic."

At my beep/light I said, "Gracious."

"Gleeful."

Beep.

"Candy, *verb*," said Yancey.

My mind made a sharp turn. "Guarantee."

Beep.

Yancey told Precia her new category was *noun*.

"Gutter."

Back to me. "Give."

"Giant."

The low buzzer blatted.

"Precia, I'm sorry, you already used the word 'Gigantic.'"

One of the rules of *Word Wise* was that you couldn't form a verb or adjective out of a noun already used, or vice versa.

Precia bumped the top of the console with her fist and whispered, "Sorry," to me.

Filo and Dorothy were given our remaining time to finish the G round. The football player gave "Gassy" and "Gamine" as adjectives and Dorothy "Galvanize" for a verb, but when her category switched to *noun* and she said, "Greek," the buzzer rang.

"I'm sorry, Dorothy, *Word Wise* does not accept proper nouns."

"Dagblast it," said Dorothy. "I knew that."

The rounds continued, and although Filo and Dorothy made a valiant effort with the letter U ("Umbrage" and "Umlaut" were two of Filo's nouns), at the end of the play Precia and I had three more points, which meant I'd be back the next day as the returning champion.

Returning champion. Imagine that.

10

It was past five when I got home. I changed into my swimsuit and found Ed by the nearly deserted pool.

"Ah, *The Warren Commission Sham*," I said, reading the title of the book resting on his Styrofoam cooler. "More light poolside entertainment."

Ed didn't answer.

"I know you're not sleeping," I said, situating myself on the chaise longue next to his. "And by the way, you're peeling."

"Where've you been all weekend?" he asked, not opening his eyes.

"Oh, here, there," I said casually. "Could be that I was on the ABC lot, taping *Word Wise*."

Ed sprang up in his chair as if a bee had crawled up his swimming trunks.

"You were on *Word Wise*?" When I nodded, he said, "Why didn't you tell me? I would have come down and watched the taping!"

"I was going to, but then I got all superstitious. I didn't want anyone who I knew to watch me if I lost."

"And did you?"

"Eventually. But yesterday I won my first game, and this morning I went back as the returning champion and I won a grand total of four-thousand-seven-hundred dollars and a trip to Tahiti!"

Ed whooped, causing Robert X. Roberts to stir slightly under his *L.A. Times* Sunday magazine.

"Four-thousand-seven-hundred dollars and a trip to Tahiti—Candy, that's great!"

My smile stretched earlobe to earlobe.

"Well," I said, "it's not the kind of money you won."

"On my first game show, I only won three hundred and a microwave oven. So who were your partners?"

"Yesterday I had Precia Doyle—"

"I love Precia Doyle! Not only is she a good actress—she's smart!"

"I'll say. The other celebrity was Filo Nuala and—"

"—Filo Nuala, the football player? He's like Superman, a Rhodes Scholar, all-American, goes to the Super Bowl his second year—"

"—he was pretty good at *Word Wise*, too, but I never got to be his partner. Today when I went back they had different celebrities."

Ed chuckled and lacing his hands behind his head leaned back in his chair. "Okay, Candy, tell me everything."

It was my pleasure.

I told him how my mind had scrambled while playing with Precia Doyle, how fast the lights and beeps and turns were, and how I struggled to remember whether I was supposed to name a noun, an adjective, or a verb. I told him how I had barely slept the night before, so excited I was to go back as returning champ, and that I had won my first game of the day with my new partner, Benjamin Parnell.

"Benjamin Parnell? He's the dean of celebrity contestants—he's been on game shows forever."

THE LATE AFTERNOON SUN was losing its potency, and I blanketed myself with my towel.

"He was nice. I got to go up to the Big Dictionary with him."

This was where the real money was earned. The celebrity sat facing his or her partner, behind whom loomed a big screen that looked like an open book, and on whose pages words lit up. The letter at play would be announced, and the celebrity had to give definitions—for instance, when Benjamin Parnell and I played, Yancey announced, "T—*noun.*"

A little bell rang and after clearing his throat, Benjamin Parnell said, "Call made by lumberjacks when chopping down—"

"Timber!" I said.

We sailed through nouns, verbs, and adjectives, but time ran out before we could get all the way to the last page of the dictionary; twice, Mr. Parnell's definitions had been disqualified for using the root word, and once, I got stuck on his definitions, causing him to skip to the next page. But I had won fifteen hundred dollars, which wasn't bad for two minutes of guessing.

It was when partnered with Sally Breel, star of *Sally in the Morning!* that I won the most money, and the trip to Tahiti in the bonus round.

"Sally Breel!" said Ed. "What was she like?"

"All business. No chitchat at all during the commercial breaks—

she'd sneak a cigarette or get her makeup touched up. And her face was weird—sort of frozen or something."

Ed laughed. "You're really not from here, are you? Sally Breel's the queen of face-lifts."

"But she isn't even that old!"

"She's at least sixty," said Ed. "Which is a hundred-and-two in Hollywood years."

Robert X. Roberts had shuffled off to his apartment and Billy Gray Green had fired up his blow dryer by the time I finished telling Ed all about *Word Wise*.

"Here's to you, kiddo," he said in a fair imitation of Humphrey Bogart. "I'd take you out to celebrate, but I've got a date tonight."

"Anyone I know?"

"Nope." Standing up, Ed shook his towel. "She's a stewardess."

"Ooh la la."

"Well, for just a little regional airline . . . but still." Anchoring his towel with his chin, he folded it into a neat square. "Hey, what about tomorrow night? I'll take you anywhere in the world you want to go—or at least anywhere in the greater L.A. basin."

"Perfect," I said. "I know just the place."

THE COMEDY STORE looked like a black bunker that had been defaced by graffiti artists with good penmanship. Written in white paint were the names of dozens of comics who'd appeared there, and we busied ourselves reading them as we stood in line for the Monday Amateur Night performance.

"This is going to be fun!" said Maeve.

After the night at Ed's apartment, she had left a little cactus plant on my doorstep with a note of apology—"Sorry for being prickly," it had read, "and kind of a jerk, too"—and the hokey but genuine gesture had made me want to put effort into a friendship, and I had invited her to join Ed and me.

"I had a blind date here once," said Ed. "To see Richard Pryor. A friend of mine set me up with his girlfriend's sister and she didn't crack a smile through his whole routine—plus she shushed me when I laughed!"

"I'm guessing that was the last date as well as the first," I said.

"She was one I was glad got away."

We were seated near the back at a small table whose centerpiece was a red glass candleholder wrapped in plastic webbing. After taking our order, our bored waitress returned and, reminding us of the two-drink minimum, plunked down our beverages.

"I don't think there's a danger of overdrinking with these," said Maeve, holding up a glass narrow as a test tube.

The chatter of tourists, college kids, and couples on dates filled the room, and when the emcee bounded onstage, I might have shivered with excitement.

"Welcome, welcome," he said. "Welcome to the Comedy Store's Amateur Night—where comedians have five minutes to live or die!"

The slight man wearing a suit, red tennis shoes, and a five-o'clock shadow introduced himself as Danny Hernandez.

"Yes, my last name's Hernandez, and yes, that's Hispanic. Which means not only am I going to keep things moving on stage, but afterwards I'll get your car if you valet-parked."

"Ba-boom," Ed whispered.

"And now without further ado or further adon't, let's bring up the first act of the evening—ladies and gentlemen, please welcome Ryan Ridges!"

"SOME SAY MY LOVE IS WRONG, some say I'm kinky," sang Mr. Ridges, accompanying himself on a banjo, "but I'll never give up my sweetheart, my little hamster Winkie."

"Get a life, weirdo!" shouted a heckler.

A short sturdy woman—one of only three women to go on—talked about her bad luck with men. "I asked my last boyfriend why he was ditching me for an eighteen-year-old swimsuit model with an IQ of 40, and he said, 'Because I know what's important in a relationship.'"

Like a kid standing in front of a deep-sea aquarium, I was wide-eyed and enthralled, and with the exception of the expensive test tube drinks I loved everything about the Comedy Store. I loved its name, a place where laughter was both merchandise and currency. I loved the convivial darkness we all sat in, softened only by candles, the glowing tips of cigarettes, and a spotlight. I loved watching how each comic approached the stage; one poor guy looked like he was one burp away from vomiting, another strode up like an evangelist, arms held high. I loved listening to their five-minute routines—the bad ones were as instructive as the good ones—

and I even loved the heckling—how the audience cringed when a comic didn't know how to handle it, and how it applauded when he did.

I was in a room filled with laughter, sitting amid an orchestra of high, fluttering, whining, low, chortling, deep, blasting, staccato laughter. It was literally music to my ears, and more than anything I wanted to conduct it.

"Hey, have any of you seen that new Woody Allen movie, *Interiors*?" asked a sleepy-eyed guy in a tie-dyed T-shirt and bowtie. "Man, what happened to Woody? He used to make some funny movies, but if anyone told a joke, I couldn't hear it over all the whining . . ."

Hours—but what seemed like minutes—later, Danny Hernandez took his final bow.

"Thank you all for coming, people, and let's hear it one more time for all the comics who were brave enough to come up onstage!"

Which I vow here and now, I wrote later that night in my calendaeium, *is going to be me.*

11

MY COUSIN CHARLOTTE had left the keys to her 1973 Maverick, along with the instructions: "Use only for emergencies—like if the garage catches fire!" Finger wagging like that most often provoked me to do the opposite, but instead of patching out in the driveway, picking up a group of hairy hitchhikers, and taking pedal-to-the-metal joyrides down to Tijuana for tequila shots, I uncharacteristically obeyed.

I was one of those odd ducks who liked to get around by my good old-fashioned feet or good old-fashioned public transit. At an early age, I had learned to appreciate taking the bus not only for its relative ease and efficiency, but for the world you got to watch on the outside, as well as the one on the inside.

Once a rumpled guy wearing a pungent street cologne staggered on, plopping himself in the seat ahead of my grandmother and me. I remember Grandma tensing and putting a protective hand on my knee as he turned around to face us, but when he opened his mouth, it was not to ask us for spare change but to break out singing "Blue Moon" in a high, soulful voice. After holding the last note, he nodded and turned around in his seat, as if he'd done nothing more unusual than ask us if the bus crossed Nicollet Avenue. Another time, on my way home from the U, I witnessed a wedding proposal, which, unfortunately for the would-be groom, the would-be-bride didn't accept, saying, "Please tell me you're kidding."

It was usually the passengers who provided the entertainment, but on the bus taking me to my first temp job, they took a literal backseat to the driver who sang out each stop on Hollywood Boulevard with his own personal flair.

"Highland. Oh, I wish I was Highhhhh-land."

"Las Palmas—Las Palmass, ass, ass."

When he said, "Bronson! Charlie, Charlie Bronson," I got off.

On the corner of Hollywood and Bronson, Beat Street Records occupied a bright blue two-story building and its interior continued the primary color palate. The reception room was painted a lemon yellow and a red curtain hung behind a small desk. Posters of bands were arranged at odd angles on the wall and underneath a white neon sign reading Beat Street was a blue futon couch.

It seemed fitting that in a room whose decorator could moonlight as a nursery school teacher, a yodeler's trills came over the stereo speakers.

"Oh, hi," said a woman, pushing aside the red curtain. "You must be the temp. If you're not, we don't officially open until ten."

"I am. The temp that is. But I was told to be here at nine."

"That's when the sane people start." She reached out her hand to shake mine. "Solange Paul, one of the sane ones. I'm also the office manager— the one you come to if you have any questions, which you shouldn't, because really, your job's so easy a monkey could do it."

"Hmm," I said. "I'm not sure how to take that."

She offered a sly smile. "Answering phones, typing letters, serving coffee—how hard is that?"

"I don't know that I've ever seen a monkey answer a phone. Not to say he couldn't, but I think he might have a problem taking a message."

"You're right. And a monkey couldn't do the unspoken part of your job and mine, which is to make the men not look as dumb as they are."

Her style of dress did not match her brash, teasing manner; her black hair was processed and cajoled into a pageboy and the skirt of her navy blue suit reached her knees. She wore nylons and pumps with little bows at the toes. She didn't look much older than I, which made me wonder why she dressed like an insurance agent nearing retirement.

A high and plaintive yodel filled the room.

"Elton Britt," she said. "My secret vice. You can't be black and have a thing for cowboy singers."

"Is that a rule?"

Folding her arms, Solange smirked at me. "Yes, it's in the 'Code of Black Behavior' pamphlet we're all given as children. Don't they pass one out to Asians, too?"

"Yeah, but other than the 'No chow mein on Fridays' rule, I can't say I remember any."

We both smirked. Our conversation was like a jousting match, but rather than crying "Ouch" and "No fair" at each other's jabs, we were enjoying it.

"Well, in any case," said Solange, "welcome to one of L.A.'s hippest record companies."

"Is this one of L.A.'s hippest record companies?"

Solange turned off the stereo. "According to our publicity. Now come on, I'll show you around."

A door to the side of the desk opened up into the small break area. Behind the curtain was a big rectangular room and arranged in it were four offices defined by low walls and modular furniture. Unlike the ones in the reception area, the record and band posters hung straight on the white walls. Shelves of albums lined the back wall and to one side of them was a spiral staircase.

"This is where it all happens," said Solange, "contracts, schedules, publicity, A&R—"

"What's A&R?"

"Artists and Repertoire. Tony's our A&R guy—he listens to demos, works with the bands, the songwriters, etc. He also wears leather pants every day, as sort of an homage to Elvis, who he still can't believe is dead.

"That's Ellie Pop's office—she's our publicist. Her real name's Popadopolous—but the nickname fits. Pop, pop, pop—she's all over the place. You get tired watching her." Her hand tipped to the right. "This is where you can find me, and this is Greg Wyatt's office. He's an attorney and keeps—or tries to keep—things legal."

I pointed to the spiral staircase. "What's up there?"

Solange sighed. "Neil Thurman's office. The president of Beat Street Records. His father's Ned Thurman."

She met my blank look with one of surprise.

"Ned Thurman runs RCB—the biggest record company in the world, with the best artists. So of course Neil, his spoiled little son, has a job handed to him at RCB, and when the self-same spoiled little son wants to strike out on his own, Big Daddy springs for it."

"I take it you don't exactly care for the guy."

"Neil? He's nice enough. A little too fond of the"—here she toked an imaginary joint—"but on the whole, okay." With a sudden wince, Solange rubbed her earlobe under her small earring and explained, "Metal allergies."

I reasonably asked why she didn't take her earrings off.

"Because then the allergies win," said Solange, with a final tug to her earlobe. "Now, what we were talking about?"

"Neil the spoiled little son."

Solange cocked her head, studying me.

"I believe I may have been a bit loose-lipped. For all I know, you could be a company spy."

I slipped off my shoe and held it to my ear like a telephone receiver.

"Boss," I stage whispered, "she's on to me."

Stone-faced, Solange regarded me as I put my shoe back on, and just as I thought she might be considering a call to Security, she laughed.

"Girl, you are a strange one. Which in this business is probably a good thing."

9/22/78

Dear Cal,

The highlight of my first two weeks at Beat Street Records: Trevor Dean came in for a meeting and because Neil was running late, he sat down and chatted with me! Of course I had to tell him I listened to his album Soul Station *all through the eighth grade.*

"Do you know what my label wanted to call that LP?" he said. "Trevor Dean: Mod Man. Would have finished off my bloody career before it started!"

Which made me think of my own bloody career, or lack thereof. Am I going to do stand-up or not? If so, how do I actually go about starting it? Guess a little field study is in order, to see what's out there.

"Hey," I said to the curly-haired comic coming out of the Improv. "You were funny."

"Thanks," he said. "That's the goal."

I nodded at the case he held. "Do you always play the trumpet in your act?"

"So far."

"Do you write your own material?"

"Why, do you want to sell me a joke?"

"No . . . I was just wondering."

The comic's smile was easy. "Yeah, I write my own material. I think it'd be weird performing someone else's."

"Well, it was funny."

"Thanks again."

The horn of a car swerving toward the curb asserted itself over the other sounds of traffic on Melrose Avenue.

"That's my ride," said the comic. "Nice talking to you."

My own ride was on the bus, and as it muscled its hefty self through the traffic on La Brea, I leaned my head against the smudged window, reviewing what I'd seen that night. The guy with the trumpet was one of my favorites, and so was a guy who did a mind-scrambling impression of "Johns"—Jonathan Winters doing John Wayne doing Johnny Mathis. The only woman performing in the entire lineup did a riff on the Maidenform bra commercials and how they never featured women doing mundane, everyday things.

"I mean, you never hear them saying, 'I dreamed I shopped for brisket in my Maidenform bra' . . . or 'I dreamed I popped a pimple in my Maidenform bra.'"

I was a comedy vulture, watching and listening to everything, wondering what attitudes and ideas I could scavenge for my own use.

After pulling the buzzer, I was walking up the aisle when the bus driver laid on his horn and braked hard. I lunged forward, grabbing the metal backrest of a seat.

I dreamed I flew through the windshield of a crosstown bus in my Maidenform bra.

12

THE BEAT STREET STAFF huddled around the portable TV in the break room, surprisingly excited to see me on *Word Wise*.

"My boyfriend's watching it at home," said Ellie Pop, racing in. "He loves this show."

As the snappy *Word Wise* music began, Greg Wyatt, the attorney, turned to Neil Thurman and said, "Idea: a novelty album of game show theme songs played by rock-and-roll bands."

"I love it!" said A&R Tony. "Imagine Black Death's bassist playing this—" he strummed an imaginary guitar along with the bright chipper TV music—"or better yet, the *Dating Game* theme song!"

"Shh," said Solange. "It's starting."

Yancey Rogan strode onto the set.

"I've heard that guy's a freak," said Ellie Pop.

"Shh," said Solange.

When Filo Nuala and Precia Doyle were introduced, everyone in the room cheered.

"Shhh!" admonished Solange, again.

No one took offense at her bossy behavior, and I personally was grateful for it, not bold enough to shush anyone myself.

They were disappointed that I didn't get to play with Filo Nuala but cheered when I won my round with Precia.

"Well, I'm impressed, Candy," said Neil at the end of the episode. "How do you know all those words anyway?"

Solange rolled her eyes. "She reads, Neil."

"I tried that once," said my boss affably. "I got a headache."

When my second show aired the next day, the assemblage was reduced by half, Tony, Ellie Pop, and Greg all having previous luncheon engagements.

"I thought you had a date with your dad at Ma Maison," said Solange.

Neil shrugged. "I do. But first I want to watch Candy win millions of dollars."

"I'd like to watch that, too," I said.

They cheered me and booed my opponents, and during the first commercial break Neil informed us that he'd gone to school with Sally Breel's daughter.

"Beverly Hills High," Solange explained. "It's where the elite send their kids to start networking."

Neil laughed.

"No, that starts at the birthday parties. You know Linc Michaels?"

"Of course," said Solange, and to me translated, "big record producer."

"And my best friend," said Neil. "Who I just happened to meet at the sixth birthday party of Nan Norman."

"Yes, Candy," said Solange wearily. "Nan Norman the movie star."

"I remember Mindy Breel because she had one of the first nose jobs of anyone I knew. She was cute, too—before. Afterwards her nose looked permanently pinched—like one of those synchronized swimmers wearing one of those nose-plug thingies." Neil pulled off the band encircling his ponytail. "I wonder what she's doing now."

"Whatever it is, I'm sure she's doing fine. Once you're a member of the Beverly Hills Mafia, you're taken care of for life."

"Beverly Hills Mafia," said Neil with a laugh. "You kill me, Solange." Looking at me, he smoothed back his hair, before gathering it into a ponytail again. "Can I help it if I grew up with rich and powerful people?"

He didn't ask the question with attitude but with sincerity, and there was an awkward moment of silence before we all starting laughing, and then the show came back on, and when Yancey announced that the letter was W and the word was a noun, Sally Breel said, "Wealth!"

This really cracked Neil up.

As the credits rolled, he raced out of the office to keep his lunch date with his father and after Solange turned off the portable television set, she leaned against the counter and folded her arms across her chest.

"Candy, I am truly impressed. You were the best one on that whole show."

I shook my head. "Jerry, the cop? He won sixteen thousand dollars and a trip to the Bahamas."

"I'm not talking about who won the most money. I'm talking about who was the most entertaining. You were so funny! When you had the letter F and you said, 'Fangs' in that vampire voice—that was hilarious! And when—"

The bell on the front door jingled and a voice asked, "Hello?" and I scurried out of the break room to attend to business, which in this case meant signing for flowers—for the third time since I'd been on the job— sent to Ellie Pop.

"How many bouquets do you suppose she gets in a year?" I asked, carrying the heavy arrangement to Ellie's office.

"The smart ones know how valuable publicity is and Ellie's good at her job," said Solange. "When she got the band Hard Rain a front-page spread in the *Herald-Examiner,* they sent her a lemon tree!"

Positioning the vase on Ellie's desk, I inhaled. The smell was deep and sweet, and I was about to ask Solange the weird question that skittered across my mind: what's more beautiful—how a rose looks or how it smells?—but she asked me one first.

"Have you ever thought of doing comedy, Candy? I mean, professionally?"

The rush through my body was like the one I felt when Ricky Pederson and I kissed (well, bumped lips) in our seventh grade cloakroom.

"I uh . . . I uh, yes."

There. I had admitted it. Out loud.

"Is that why you came out here?"

My ears translated her mild question as something hollered by a prosecuting attorney determined to get to the answer that'll crack the case wide open, and I stared at her, my heart pounding so hard I could feel the pulse in my ears.

"Well, I . . . my cousin needed to sublet her place and . . . yes."

13

I WAS SO OUT OF PRACTICE letting people get to know me that when I did, it took on the weight of confession, as if to reveal personal information about myself was a sin. That's how I felt when I shared with Ed and Maeve at the pool what I had with Solange, that I wanted to do stand-up comedy. Their reactions couldn't have been more positive; Maeve surmised I'd probably have my own sitcom by next year, and Ed said he'd head up my fan club.

"So how long have you been thinking of doing this?" Ed asked, after Maeve cannonballed into the water.

"Practically all my life. But it's been a . . . dream deferred for a long time."

Ed smiled. "I've taught that poem. But you've decided not to 'let it dry up like a raisin in the sun'?"

It was the kindness in his voice (and maybe a few renegade premenstrual hormones) that made tears spring up in my eyes. Grateful for the shield of my sunglasses, I shook my head.

"So what was it that made you regenerate this particular dream?"

Maeve swam past us, kicking up fountains.

I watched her for a moment. "Coming out here. Going to the Comedy Store. Taking steps for a change . . . instead of standing still."

"So what's next?"

"More steps, I guess. And getting over being so scared."

"Well, it's a scary thing. Fear of public speaking—let alone stand-up comedy—is ranked right up there with death of a spouse or loss of a job."

"Are you trying to make me feel better . . . or worse?"

Ed's laugh rolled into a shudder as he regarded the bottle of chocolate soda he held perched on his stomach. "Why do I keep drinking this stuff? What grown man in his right mind drinks something called YaZoo?"

AFTER TYPING SOME PRESS RELEASES for Ellie Pop and a letter from Greg informing the manager of the band Firestorm that, no, it was not only impossible but illegal to have a contract rider assuring a blonde and a brunette in the hotel rooms of the lead singer and keyboardist, I sat at my desk, tapping my pencil. My intention had been to work on my act, now that I had decided I was going to have one, but I was tapping far more than writing. Why was it such a struggle to come up with five measly minutes of material? What did I want to say, exactly? Something funny, sure, but what? And how?

Some comics did characters and/or impressions, and while I could do funny voices, I wasn't exactly Rich Little. Should I cultivate a wacky persona like Phyllis Diller or be politically insightful like George Carlin? Or should I take the observational (and popular) "Isn't life weird?" route? The only thing I definitely knew I didn't want to do was talk a lot about myself—(a) who'd be interested in that? and (b) my personal life was too personal.

Bad News Bears Go Up in Smoke! Revenge of the Pretty Baby! High Anxiety Halloween!

Trying to make something funny out of combining titles of recent movies, I realized I hadn't and was crossing out the drivel I'd written when the door opened. I looked up, expecting to see the UPS guy, who this person was definitely not. He wasn't wearing brown shorts, for one thing, and was so skinny that the ratty T-shirt and jeans he had on seemed to weigh him down. He was bald, except for a strip of blue hair that rose in spikes down the crown of his head.

"Hey," he said, surprised.

"Hey," I answered. "It's . . . Francis, right?"

A hint of color bloomed on his pale face. "Uh, actually, it's Frank. *Blank* Frank."

"Oh," I said, not exactly following him. "Well, it's nice to see you . . . Blank."

His blush intensified. "It's not just Blank. It's, uh, Blank Frank. I, um, use the whole name."

"Sorry, Blank . . . Frank."

Solange pushed aside the curtain behind my desk and entered the room.

"Solange," I began, "this is—"

"—I'm sorry," she said, crossing her arms as she regarded the interloper. "I told you before: Beat Street isn't interested in punk rock at this time."

"Yeah, but you'll change your mind if you listen to this," said Blank Frank, digging a cassette tape out of his pocket.

"Look," said Solange, "right now we're just not—"

The musician darted toward my desk and set the cassette on it.

"Take a listen, okay? That's all I'm asking." Backing toward the door, he looked at Solange, palms out. "It won't make your ears bleed or anything."

"It's the 'anything' I'm worried about."

Before pushing through the door, Blank Frank smiled at me. "Just let me know what you think, uh—"

"—Candy. It's Candy."

I'D SEEN BLANK FRANK a few times on the grounds of Peyton Hall, in the company of a man so textbook dapper in his dress that he should have been twirling a walking stick.

"Who's that?" I had asked the first time I saw him. Having accompanied Ed to Limelight Liquors where he'd bought a bottle of wine for another date, we were coming up the Boulevard when I noticed the slim, silver-haired man in a suit and bowtie climbing the steps of the four-plex next to mine.

"Francis Flover," said Ed. "He used to own the Bel Mondo, this nightclub on Sunset that was really famous in the '40s and '50s. He and Robert X. Roberts hate each other."

"Why?"

Ed shrugged. "Some Hollywood slight—who knows? Maybe he didn't like the way Robert X. tipped his hatcheck girls."

"Look at that ascot! He's so—" I searched for an expression I rarely had occasion to use—"natty."

Days later, I ran into Francis—almost literally—as I was coming out of my apartment and he was coming out of my neighbor's.

"Candy, meet one of my oldest pals," Melvin Slyke said, and with great courtliness Francis Flover executed a snappy little bow before taking my hand and telling me he was "enchanted."

Another time, on the way to the pool, I saw him walking with someone whose sartorial tastes lay on the opposite pole from his own; where Mr. Flover wore a bowler hat, this guy wore a blue mohawk, where a fob watch might be tucked into Mr. Flover's vest pocket, thick chains hung in heavy loops from the skinny kid's belt—so much metal he could have outfitted his own private chain gang.

"Candy!" said the older gentleman. He doffed his hat. "Meet my son, Francis Jr."

The younger man ducked his head in greeting, and I saw that he wore a small silver hoop through his eyebrow. It was the first time I'd ever seen a facial piercing and I tried not to stare.

Now at my desk, after reading the label of the tape Blank Frank had given me, I put it into the cassette player and said, "And for all you listeners out there, here's something from a new band called United States of Despair."

I pressed play, and an assault of guitar chords filled the room like the angry voices of a mob.

Solange's reaction was not favorable.

"Turn it down! Better yet, turn it off!"

I half-obliged her by doing the former, and we listened to a voice belonging to a lead screamer shouting over the guitar, bass, and drums. I couldn't make out many of the lyrics, but I did recognize the phrases "death sentence," "shock the septic system," and "annihilation-celebration," which were repeated in a chant.

After we listened to the cassette's three songs, Solange replaced it with one of her own, and the twangy strains of some cowboy band filled the air.

"Ahh," said my coworker, her hand to her chest. "Yodel me back to civility, Otto Gray."

ALTHOUGH I MISSED THE ENTERTAINING DRIVER who announced my stop as Bronson, Charlie Charlie Bronson, I hardly took the bus to work anymore. It was only about a mile and a half from my apartment to Beat Street Records, and I enjoyed getting there on my own two feet—especially after Maeve turned me on to roller skating.

My weightlifter neighbor had turned into my weightlifter friend. Although Maeve had grown up in Beverly Hills, she was fairly new to Hollywood and had decided I was a worthy sidekick in her neighborhood explorations. The first invitation she extended had been to breakfast at Schwab's Drugstore.

"Look," she said, swiveling on her counter stool, "there's that actor who played the bad guy in *The Godfather*."

"Maeve, there were a lot of actors who played bad guys in *The Godfather.*"

We watched as the man in question sauntered to the nearby pay phone.

"Yeah, but that guy was really bad."

The second invitation was to a roller rink on Sunset and La Cienega.

"You've got to try it," she said. "It's great for the quads and the calves—not to mention the glutes—and besides, it's a lot of fun."

Disco was supposedly dying, but not at the roller rink where a blasting throbbing beat accompanied skaters and damaged eardrums. I had skated as a kid on little metal skates that affixed to your shoes and were tightened with a key, and it took me a little while to get used to the heaviness of a boot skate, but once I did, I could skate circles around Maeve. Then again, she could skate circles around me.

"You're smooth!" I shouted over Donna Summers telling me she'd love to love me, baby.

"Why does that surprise you?" asked Maeve, skating backwards.

I shrugged before shouting, "I guess it doesn't!"

"I'm not just some big galoot, you know!"

Maeve presented an imposing-looking figure but it was sheathed in the thinnest skin known to humankind, and I'd learned it was best to ignore her when she went into one of her I'm-so-misunderstood rants. This strategy seemed to work; without attention, the tears threatening to rise out of her hurt feelings would evaporate, and her usual good cheer returned.

A shirtless skater wearing tight vinyl shorts and a black motorcycle cap whizzed by us, twirling around like a music box dervish.

The beginners stayed on the perimeter, tethered to the railing by their sweaty hands. The utilitarians skated beside them, content to move around the rink without falling. The next tier—to which Maeve and I belonged—was composed of fairly good skaters who could easily skate backwards and could do a basic spin turn, whereas the center of the rink was reserved for those who moved like dancers and gymnasts on wheels, executing jetés and arabesques and the occasional flip. As flashy as their athleticism was their dress code, whose basic tenet was that skin should be seen and not covered.

The second time we went to the roller rink I again rented skates, but the day afterwards I bought my own pair and now used them as a means of transportation.

It was a straight shot down Hollywood Boulevard to work, and the polished granite Walk of Fame, from Sycamore to Gower, was a skater's dream surface. During the morning skate the Boulevard was light with traffic, and I'd read the names on the stars I slalomed through: Fred Astaire, Debbie Reynolds, Red Skelton.

Heading west on the way home, my ability to dodge was the more important skill as buskers had set out their guitar and saxophone cases and tourists clogged the streets, armed with maps, sun hats, and cameras.

From La Brea to Fuller, the street inclined, and by the time I got home I had worked up a reasonable sweat and had a perfect excuse to jump into the pool.

Having just skated past the neon Peyton Hall sign, I saw that I might not be getting into the pool as early as I had intended.

"Hey," said Blank Frank, perched on the bottom of the steps that fronted my building. "How's it going?"

"It's going hot," I said, lifting the back of my hair to fan my neck.

"So did you listen to it?"

"Listen to what?" I asked innocently.

"Oh, I don't know—to the traffic. To your conscience. To my tape."

"Oh, yeah," I said, sitting down next to him. "That one." I started unlacing a skate; while I could climb stairs with them on, I'd learned it made better sense not to.

"And . . ."

My mind shouted out two options, *Lie! Tell the truth!* but I decided the latter would ultimately save me time and energy.

"I . . . I liked the energy—wow, it was manic—but I really couldn't understand a lot of the words and the songs all sort of sounded the same."

Chewing his lip, the punk rocker nodded.

"Yeah, we're sorta beginners at song writing," he said agreeably. "And our bass player is just learning how to play. But it's cool that you listened to it. Thanks."

"Not at all," I said, and, surprised by the easy way he took my criticism, I decided to brave the next question. "You mind telling me how you get your hair to stand up like that?"

"Sure. Glue and blow drying. You can touch it if you like."

He bowed his head and I touched a blue spike and then gently bounced my palm against the whole jagged range.

"Thanks," I said, after participating in the weird show-and-tell. "And about your music, even if I had loved it, I'm just a temp. I doubt that anyone would listen to me if I said, 'There's this great band you've got to hear.'"

"You never know. Hey, you should come and hear us live sometime."

"Hey, maybe I will."

"Cool," said Blank Frank, rising. "How about Friday night? Nine o'clock at the Masque." He jumped up and holding his arms out, he zigzagged across the lawn the way a kid pretends to be an airplane, in the direction of his dad's apartment.

14

NOBODY WAS INTERESTED IN JOINING ME at the Masque. Ed had his usual Friday night first date that never seemed to lead to a second; Maeve was going to a movie screening with her mother, and Solange had told me she'd rather lean out her bedroom window and listen to her neighbor's cat, who was in heat and was hellbent on letting both the feline and human worlds know.

"Come on," I said. "It'll be fun."

The look on Solange's face could have recurdled buttermilk. "No, it won't be."

On the way to the pool after work, rehearsing the excuse I'd give to Blank Frank for missing his performance, I saw his father emerge from the laundry room next to the garages, holding a basket.

"Mr. Slyke's," he said, indicating the precisely folded clothing stacked inside. "He's feeling a little peckish, so I offered to act as his manservant—well, at least his launderer. Say, Frank mentioned you might be going to his show this evening. Would I be imposing too much if I asked to join you? I know it's rather late notice and you probably already—"

"—no, no, that'd be great. Let's go together!"

WHEN MR. FLOVER PICKED ME UP, he handed me a cellophane-wrapped bouquet of red and white carnations.

"Thank you," I said. "I'll . . . I'll put them in water."

"And while you do, I'll just say hello to Melvin."

I returned to find my neighbor, dressed in a paisley bathrobe, standing on the landing with Mr. Flover.

"Candy," said Melvin Slyke, wagging his finger. "You keep your eye on this one. Make sure he doesn't do any of that slam-dunk dancing."

"Okay, Melvin," I said as both men laughed.

"And cut him off after two drinks. After three he's a wild man."

"I can see you're getting better," said Mr. Flover. "If only your jokes were."

The two men laughed again and good-byes were said, and minutes later I was cruising down Hollywood Boulevard in a sporty little silver convertible with a dapper gentleman who wore a red carnation in his lapel.

Mr. Flover was telling a funny story about Frank's first guitar lesson when at the stoplight at Highland Avenue, he whispered, "There but for the grace of God . . ."

I followed his gaze to the tall, gaunt figure making his zombie-like trek down the street.

"Do you know that man, Mr. Flover? Because I see him on the Boulevard all the time."

"I can't say I know him, but I know his story. His name is Erwin Paulsen. Although everyone always called him—for obvious reasons—Slim. He was a lawyer—with a firm catering to show business clients."

The light turned, and as the car moved forward I looked back at the man shambling along in rag shoes.

"What . . . what happened to him?"

Mr. Flover's lower lip pushed out as he shook his head. "A house fire. His wife and daughter perished in it. The story was that he was out 'entertaining a client'—a starlet—when it happened."

"Oh, man."

"A number of people—from his old firm, his friends—I know a few, in fact—have tried to help him over the years, but he is . . . unreachable. Unreachable and inconsolable."

A block and a half later, our pensive silence was yanked away when a man darted into traffic. Mr. Flover braked hard.

"Olé!" shouted the jaywalker, who wore a bolero jacket and flannel pajama bottoms. "Olé! Olé!"

"Goodness," said, Mr. Flover, as the man crossed the street, snapping and swirling a ratty red cape. "Be sure to tell me if you see the bull."

THE MASQUE WAS SMALL AND DANK and full of pierced and tattooed people wearing mostly black clothes festooned with holes and/or safety pins.

"I don't suppose there're any chairs," said Mr. Flover.

His supposition was correct, and instead of joining the huddle of people in front of the stage we chose to park ourselves against a grungy, graffiti-decorated wall. Well, next to, both of us making the tacit assumption that to lean against it meant we might stick to it.

"I'd buy you a cocktail," said the ever-courtly Mr. Flover, "but I don't really see a bar, do you?"

I looked around. The only thing that indicated the place was a performance space and not a graffiti artist's old root cellar was a platform stage, loaded with amps, coils of cords, instruments, and microphones.

"I think this is more a BYOB kind of place."

A guy with foot-long purple spikes jutting out of his head bounded onto the stage and screamed at the assemblage, "Are you ready to rock and roll?"

The crowd roared back that it was.

"Then let's bring 'em up! Ladies and gentlemen—if there are any of you out there tonight—give it up for the United States of Despair!"

The dapper Mr. Flover put two fingers to his mouth, adding his whistle to the cacophony.

A motley crew of four jumped onto the stage, and three yanked their guitars off their stands. The drummer plopped down behind his drum kit, and beating his sticks together he shouted, "One, two, three, four!" and within seconds the room thundered with a fast heavy drum and bass beat.

"I pledge my allegiance to the United States of Despair!" shouted/sang Blank Frank, grabbing the microphone. "And to the hypocrisy from which it crumbles!"

The guitars whined like giant mosquitoes as Frank writhed.

"One nation, under Cash, with liberty and justice for no one!"

The crowd was a swarm of violently bobbing heads, their movement as chaotic and random as germs under a microscope slide.

"I don't suppose you'd care to dance?" shouted Mr. Flover and we both laughed, understanding that at the Masque, one jerked or flailed or bobbed, but one did not dance, not even when the band switched from social commentary to songs of romance.

"Hey asshole—you suck, I don't—don't leave me!" bleated Blank Frank. "I rock, you walk—all over me!"

The live music sounded even rawer than it had on their demo tape, and without my having the luxury of turning the sound down, it began to pulse inside my skull.

"Break bones—break hearts—break meeeeeeeeeeeee!"

With that, Frank threw down the microphone and dove into the audience and rode on top of it, like a piece of flotsam on a churning sea of hands.

"Oh dear," shouted Mr. Flover over the noise. "I hope they don't drop him."

The refrain to the song was sung over and over, and when Blank Frank was flung back onto the stage, he grabbed the mike and joined his fellow musicians in continuing the chant, whipping both band and audience into a frenzy. The musicians, their heads bobbing with such ferocity that I feared spinal damage, jabbed their guitars at each other while the crowd in front of the stage lunged and pushed and threw themselves at one another, in a dance that had to hurt. That I didn't see any blood didn't mean none was shed.

They played one hard-driving song after another for an hour and then, with a loud, scary scream from Frank, the band members fled the stage as if a fire alarm had gone off, and even as the crowd shouted for more, they didn't come back.

Finally a dim light blinked on and the audience began to break up, shouting invitations to meet up at the Formosa, the Frolic Room, the Pig N' Whistle. We joined the sweaty stream that emptied out into the alley and stood against the building, waiting for the band.

"Mr. Flover, thanks for coming!" said the spike-headed drummer, enveloping the older man in his muscular arms.

"Yeah, thanks!" said the bassist, leaning in for his hug.

"Mr. F!" said the rhythm guitarist.

It was an odd picture, these tattooed and mohawked punk rockers enthusiastically greeting and hugging Mr. Savile Row.

"Hey, Pop!" said Blank Frank, bumping his guitar case against the doorframe. "Hey, Candy! Guys, this is my friend, Candy!"

The band mates introduced themselves.

"I'm Rock," said the drummer. "Rock Bottom."

"Mayhem," said the rhythm guitarist. "Mayhem Rules."

"Ian Riley," said the bassist, almost apologetically.

"I know you probably have things to do and people to see," said Mr. Flover, "but if any of you would like some fortification before you do those things or see those people, I've got a big pan of spaghetti back at the apartment."

"Sounds great, man," said Rock Bottom, "but I gotta go see my girlfriend at Cedars."

"She's in the hospital?" asked Mr. Flover, concerned.

"She is," said the drummer solemnly, before letting loose a laugh.

"But only because she's a nurse. Pam works the night shift and likes me to join her on her 'lunch' break."

"Pop, we'll just load up the equipment and meet you back at the house," said Blank Frank. "See you there, Candy?"

I answered with words I was saying more and more.

"Why not?"

15

FRANCIS—he insisted all of us dispense with the Mr. Flover and call him by his first name—was the consummate host, piling reheated and tasty spaghetti on our plates and passing around a big wooden salad bowl with the directive, "Mangia! Mangia!"

"My father was in Italy in World War II," said Frank (who'd also given me permission to drop the adjective Blank) as we sat at the heavy oak dining room table. "He orders this from Two Guys on Sunset because he says it tastes closest to the spaghetti of his old Italian girlfriend."

"Maria Donatelli," said Francis, sighing heavily. "What she could do with oregano—well, when you youngsters get older, I'll tell you what she could do with oregano."

"Tell us now!" said Mayhem.

"You're too young," said Francis, with a resigned shake of his head. "You wouldn't know what to do with the information."

"Pop, we're older than you were when you joined the army," said Frank.

"Ah, but we were older back then. God forbid if any of you were in the army now—why, I wouldn't trust any of you boys to load a pea-shooter, let alone a rifle."

As Frank, Mayhem, and Ian defended themselves against this egregious slander, I helped myself to another piece of garlic bread.

This was the side dish to our late-night dinner—good-natured insults and boasts and laughs—and everyone held out their plates for seconds and thirds.

"HEY, CANDY," Mayhem asked, after slurping up a strand of spaghetti. "Do you know you're eating with a Hollywood legend?"

"Please, please," said Frank, "I can hardly be called a legend. Maybe a legend-in-training—"

"—aw, shut yer pie hole. I'm talking about your old man."

"You ran a night club, isn't that right?" I asked Francis.

"A night club," said Mayhem. "That's like calling Disneyland an amusement park."

Ian rolled his eyes. "Disneyland *is* an amusement park."

"You know what I mean. Tell her, Mr. F."

"Well, it is true," said Flover the Elder. " I was fortunate enough to own the Bel Mondo, from right after the war until 1958."

"That's when Sunset Strip was full of night clubs," said Frank. "You know, the kind that wouldn't let you in if you weren't wearing a tie or a corsage."

"Yes," said Francis, looking with bemusement at his son in his mohawk and torn and pinned black clothes. "All the clubs—Ciro's, the Mocambo, the Clover Club, the Trocadero—had a certain dress code and our patrons were happy to honor it."

"Tell her some of the people you booked, Pop."

"Oh, Buddy Rich, Peggy Lee, Frank Sinatra, Martin & Lewis, Billie Holiday . . . any of these names mean anything to you?"

"Pop, come on, it's not like we were born yesterday."

Mayhem nodded. "I love all those people, man. Especially Sinatra. I'll bet he'd have been into punk if he'd been born later."

Francis smiled. "He was a bit of a scrapper back then, that's for sure. Not at all adverse to using his fists."

"Pop's got this idea that punk's all about picking fights with people," Frank said to me.

"Well, it is, sorta," said Mayhem. "Except we smack people around with our music."

"Precisely my point," said Francis. "In my day we wanted to romance people, woo them, entertain them. Smacking was the furthest thing from our minds."

"For us," explained Ian, "smacking just means waking up. That's all we want to do—wake people up."

There was a whiskery sound as Francis scratched his throat. "But isn't it nicer to be woken up with a caress than a scream?"

When Ian asked me what I was into, my self-censor light flickered amber, but instead of braking I raced through it.

"I want to start doing stand-up comedy."

"Stand-up comedy," said Francis. "Well, I'll be!"

"That's radical!" said Frank.

"Make me laugh!" ordered Mayhem.

Impulsively obeying his order, I lunged out of my chair, and two inches from his face, riffed on the lyrics the band had sung/screamed at the Masque.

"Hey, asshole! You suck, I don't—why should I?"

Standing on the precipice of the brief silence that followed, I wondered if I should apologize, but stepped back when the hush was broken by laughter, Mayhem's the loudest.

AFTER DINNER we were invited to "repair" to the living room, where Frank urged his dad to tell us some stories of old Hollywood.

"Old Hollywood is Cecil B. DeMille directing silent pictures," said Francis. "I was part of a far more recent Hollywood."

"Every Sunday people would come over to our house in Beverly Hills," said Frank. "People who worked in Pop's club, celebrities—"

"—yes, everyone got along wonderfully—in fact, my cigarette girl JoAnne met Roger Wilbert—"

"—he was a movie composer," explained Frank. "Won a couple Oscars. He always used to pull out a quarter from behind my ear."

"That's right, Roger fancied himself a bit of a magician," said Francis, chuckling at the memory. "At any rate, after brunch we'd always play Charades or games of that nature, and that's when they fell in love."

"How do you fall in love playing Charades?" asked Mayhem.

"You're right, it wasn't Charades. This was a game in which you'd be given an emotion—for example, happiness—and you'd have to say the first thing that came into your mind. And I'll never forget this, the word given to Roger Wilbert was *awestruck,* and Roger, looking directly at JoAnne, said, "The first time I saw your face.""

"Aww," said Mayhem.

"Apparently, JoAnne was impressed. They were married three weeks later in my backyard."

"Let's play that game now," said Mayhem. "Give me an emotion!"

"Dipshittedness," muttered Ian, but louder he said, "Okay, Mayhem, what's your answer for awestruck?"

"That's easy!" said the wiry and wired rhythm guitarist, jumping up. "The night I saw the Sex Pistols at Winterland. They were unbelievable, man! Cracked the world wide open for me!"

He played an invisible guitar, his strumming hand moving in a blur, his other hand wildly running up and down the fret board.

"And now," said Francis gently, once it appeared the soundless concert might go on a bit longer than we cared to attend, "now, Mayhem, you choose a person and an emotion."

"All right," said Mayhem, making a final grand circle with his hand. "Here's one for you, Candy—fear."

"When I used the bathroom at the Masque."

"Wow," said Mayhem. "You're braver than I am."

Thinking myself clever to bring in the band's name, I looked at Frank and said, "Despair."

Frank's expectant expression sagged, like someone had let the air out of his face. He looked down at his hands and stared at them for a long time before saying, "Living with my mother and that fucking Phil."

The mood in the room darkened as if a light switch had been turned off, and I berated myself (*Good suggestion, Candy!*) as we sat in the dark for a long, uncomfortable moment.

"I was depressed then, too," said Francis softly.

"Uh, aren't we playing a game here?" asked Mayhem. "Come on, Frank, save the sob story for later. Throw someone another emotion!"

The muscles at Frank's jaw bunched and unbunched and I held my breath, thinking he might be just as motivated to throw a punch, but instead he gave a half-smile and looking at Ian said, "Sickened."

"The day Mayhem auditioned for the band," said Ian lightly.

"Oh man," said Mayhem, pulling an imaginary dagger out of his heart. "That was cruel."

"Honesty often is," said Ian, and to Francis, he said, "Jubilant."

"Easy," said the elder Flover looking at the younger. "The day I got my boy back." The father and son exchanged looks, and then Francis added, "And, the first time I did a buffalo scuffle."

"A buffalo scuffle?'" said Mayhem. "Sounds like something they warn cowboys about."

"Excuse me for just a second," said Francis.

He disappeared into his bedroom, and when he returned he was wearing tap shoes that clicked against the wood floor.

"This, Mayhem, is a buffalo scuffle."

His feet were suddenly in motion and, for a man his age, at a pretty good rate of speed.

"Different from a buffalo pull back," he said, demonstrating. "Which of course is not the same as a double pull back."

We watched entranced, as he dug, shuffled, brushed, balled, and changed. He didn't char the floor with a burning energy, but what he lacked in youthful vigor he made up for with a smooth and innate grace that if bottled would have been sold among luxury goods. In between calling out the names of the steps he demonstrated, he hummed "Tea for Two," and when he was finished, he dipped his knees in a little bow.

"Wow, Pop, that was great!" said Frank, and the only one not in agreement was the tenant below us, who was either very tall or used a broomstick to pound on the ceiling a volley of protesting thumps.

AFTER THE PARTY—and it had turned into a party—I sat on my cousin's plaid couch in the darkened living room, looking out at Hollywood Boulevard through the opened window. It was late enough that the only traffic was an occasional passing car, and most of the lights in the apartment building across the street were off. The odd quiet of a metropolis tucked in and put to bed lay heavy in the air, and I hugged my knees to my chest, holding on to a strange amalgam of feelings, of happiness, gratitude, wonder. Wow, how had I gotten to the point that I could feel that combo?

A flash of movement caught my eye and I leaned forward to watch an animal sauntering down the middle of the street. I assumed it was a dog, but as it drew closer I saw from its full bushy tail and fox-like body that it was a coyote—a coyote loping down Hollywood Boulevard. I leaned farther, watching it make its way west, maybe toward its den in Beverly Hills or its girlfriend's lair in Malibu, until it faded into a shadow.

16

10/13/1978

Dear Grandma,

My friend Maeve and I were at the Comedy Store tonight, watching a lineup of "regulars"—comics who've moved past Amateur Night and have their own slot. On the way home, Maeve said she felt bad that the female comics weren't her favorites.

"Well, there were only two," I said.

"That's exactly my point. We've got to stick up for the few that there are."

I reminded her that there were ten men and asked if she liked all of their acts, which she didn't. And neither did I; in fact, there were only three who I thought were really good.

So it's a question of numbers—if there were more women on stage, there'd be more to like! Still, you do root extra-hard for the home team . . .

My game show parting gifts were delivered today and while I'm figuring out who I can give the Rice Doodles to (might be the worst snack food ever), I LOVE my Melnor dishes. They're supposed to be unbreakable, so I threw a couple against the wall and they passed the test! Oh yeah, and Burt Reynolds was in the audience tonight! Not bad for Friday the 13th, huh?

Sending more granddaughter love than you know what to do with,
Candy

WIN BAKER, the guy who marinated in suntan oil, had gotten a part on a soap opera and had brought all necessary equipment and ingredients to whip up celebratory daiquiris poolside. The blender whined as it chopped and pulverized ice cubes and pineapples and rum, and Win filled plastic cups with what looked like slushy urine samples. While doling out drinks was a nice enough gesture, it was basically a bribe: accept my liquor, I get to hold court. Ten minutes of listening to Win Baker expound on Win Baker was an exercise in monk-like patience; twenty minutes, and the monks were reconsidering their vows of forbearance.

"I've got a six-month contract, but my agent says it could easily get extended if my character catches on."

"Catches on what?" I said. "Fire?"

"Now that I'd watch," said Ed.

I was on a chaise longue between Maeve and Ed.

"Over a hundred guys auditioned for this part," said Oily Man, who stood posing with his drink like a product model. "And that was just in L.A.! My agent said more than three hundred read for it in New York."

"What's the name of the show again?" asked Maeve, "*As the Stomach Turns*?"

"No," said Ed. "*The Guiding Blight.*"

Win smiled like a babysitter who hates children in general and his charges in particular.

I smiled back and said, "*The Edge of Trite.*"

"*All My Bastards,*" said Ed.

"*Ryan's Hopeless.*"

"Yeah, those would all be big hits," said Win and, having tired of our adolescent wordplay, turned his back to us.

"Actually, it's *The Break of Dawn,*" he informed Joanie, whose breasts spilled like overripe cantaloupes out of her too-tight bikini bra. "It's been on the air for over twenty years."

"Oh, yeah!" said Sherri Durban, whose own string bikini was missing a few knots. "That's the show with the Nat and Nikki storyline!"

"Exactamundo," said Win. "More people tuned into their wedding than watched the Apollo moon landing."

Ed sighed. "And the decline of Western civilization continues."

It was smoggy, but the all-powerful California sun burned through the hazy skies, and after Ed leaned back in his chair, I followed his cue, basking in the autumnal heat.

On the verge of dozing off under that Big Top of smeary sunshine, I opened my eyes, feeling the energy change around the pool. Someone had arrived who made even Robert X. Roberts take the newspaper tent off his face and sit up and take notice.

"Ma!" said Maeve, standing up and waving her big-muscled arm. "Ma, over here!"

As the actress strolled around the pool toward her daughter, a flurry of whispers filled the air like a cicada's hum. "That's Taryn Powell!" "That's the star of *Summit Hill*!" "That's Taryn Powell!"

"Ma, what are you doing here?" asked Maeve, stooping to accept her mother's kiss (or facsimile thereof; her lips didn't touch Maeve's cheek).

"My friend Sharla," said the actress, and here all ears pricked up, understanding she was talking about her costar, and former Miss America runner-up, Sharla West, "wanted to show me her new kitchen renovation—my God, it's like a fucking mausoleum—marble, marble everywhere, and anyhoo, I thought as long as I was vaguely in the neighborhood, I'd swing by and say hello."

It was as if a new Ice Age had blown into southern California and everyone, including myself, was frozen in place, staring at the woman whose television show was always in the top-ten weekly ratings. Maeve had told me her mother was fifty-seven ("But it's a state secret—you'll be killed if you tell anyone else!"), but Taryn Powell's body underneath its pink nylon running suit looked as lean and supple as someone half—or a third—her age. She wore white-framed sunglasses, a silk floral scarf around her black hair, and around her fingers, wrists, and neck, jewelry with a high number of karats.

"Ma," said Maeve, extending an arm toward Ed and me, "these are my friends—"

"—Hello!" said Win, bounding toward us. "I'm Win Baker, a big fan, and an actor, too. I just got cast in *The Break of Dawn* and—"

"Congratulations," said Miss Powell, giving his extended hand a quick shake before turning her back to him. Win stood for a moment, his mouth slack, and realizing he'd been dismissed, he turned away and said loudly, "Joanie, let me tell you what the casting agent said about my reading!"

The movie star peered at me over the top of her sunglasses.

"You're Candy, aren't you? I saw you on *Word Wise*! You were so good, and it's my absolute favorite game show. So 'erudite,' as they say! I've been on several myself, but I tell my agent, 'Clint, don't you dare book me on *Word Wise* because I'd make a complete fucking fool out of myself!'" She smiled, showing the famous dimple on the left side of her face. "Excuse my fucking French."

"And Ma," said Maeve, "this is Ed."

"Pleased to meet you," said Ed, standing up, and I felt like a bad-mannered lout for staying in my chaise longue, but stupefaction had pinned me to it.

"Likewise," said Taryn Powell, in a flirty tone that suggested that underneath her sunglasses she was batting her eyelashes. "Say, listen, have you kids eaten? If not, why don't you all get dressed and I'll take you out for lunch? Let's all meet at Maeve's in—" she glanced at her diamond-studded watch—"twenty minutes?"

Not needing an answer, she turned and everyone she passed stared at her, emotionally—if not physically—curtsying and bowing.

"Why Robert X.," she said, as the old director stood to greet her. "Still a bathing beauty, I see!"

ALL OCCUPANTS IN OUR BOOTH, except for me, were a little tipsy. My grandma would be furious if my recollection of lunch at the Brown Derby with Miss Taryn Powell was fuzzed up by liquor. She'd want every single detail, from the stars' caricatures hanging on the Great Wall of Fame, to the waiter's regal bearing, to what Taryn ate (she picked at a Cobb salad), to how she looked without her sunglasses (still great, but older), to how she treated the staff (friendly but at no point did you forget who was in charge), to the constant intrusion of fans. So while everyone slugged down Bloody Marys, I demurely sipped iced tea through a straw and pretended I didn't notice everyone staring at us.

Taryn ("Either call me that," she had said, "or 'your highness'") had been regaling us with the story of making her first picture.

"There I was, nineteen years old with only a Miss Ypsilanti credit to my name, and the first day on the set my knees were shaking so hard I thought the sound man was going to ask where the fucking mariachi band was. I only had two lines—'What'll you have, sir?' and 'The cherry pie's good'—and yet when I opened my mouth, could I even get that first line out?" She shook her head. "Not a word. Not a whisper. The only noise on the whole set, other than my shaking knees, were the poor director's sighs. If I hadn't been sleeping with him, I would have been fired for sure."

"Ma, please," said Maeve.

Taryn giggled and elbowed her daughter. "Oh, they know I'm only joking." She leaned conspiratorially toward Ed at the other end of the curved banquette. "Actually, I'm not." She winked, took the plastic skewer out of her drink, and with her shiny white teeth dragged off the olive. With it bulging out of her cheek, she said, "I do remember feeling pretty

demoralized, though. That's when my friend Anne Angelo—God, she
was the greatest actress but could never catch a break—anyway, it was
after that day on set that Annie told me to see Madame Pepper."

"Oh, Miss Powell," said a woman whose frizzy puff of hair was Exhibit
A in the case against home permanents. "Would you be so kind as to pose
for a picture with me? The gals in my bridge club would just go nuts."

"Certainly," said the actress, and as the woman squatted next to the
end of the banquette and leaned into Taryn, a man wearing a lime green
leisure suit instructed them to say, "Cheese" and took the picture, a blue
light fizzling from the flashcube.

"Thank you so much," said the woman. "I've been a fan of yours ever
since you were in that movie about Mt. Kilimanjaro, with William—"

"You're too kind," said Taryn. "And please greet your bridge club for
me."

The woman backed away, bowing, as if she'd just had an audience
with the pope.

To us, Taryn made a face, as if asking, "What are you going to do?"

I was anxious to pick up the conversational thread. "Were you talking
about Madame Pepper who lives at Peyton Hall?"

"But of course. How many Madame Peppers do you suppose there are?"

"Mom's been a client forever," said Maeve.

"I didn't know that," I said.

"Sure, that's how I came to move into Peyton Hall. Mom had asked
Madame Pepper to let her know if she heard about any vacancies when I
was looking for an apartment, and she did."

"You never told me that!"

I, on the other hand had told Ed and Maeve all about my meeting with the Romanian seer, with the exception of her calling me a star,
which I had come to believe had been her idea of a joke.

"Maeve's a little guarded sometimes," said Taryn, reaching out to
stroke her daughter's thin blonde hair. "I think she's suffered having a
mother whose personal life is nothing but fucking fodder for the tabloids."

"Ma!"

"Sorry," she said, patting Maeve's forearm. This might have been
accepted as a conciliatory gesture had she not added, "My God, it's like
feeling up Charles Atlas."

"I've got to go to the bathroom," said Maeve, hoisting herself out of
the booth, and as the three of us watched her stomp off, Taryn said, "I'd
have thought she might consider that a compliment."

Ed was next to excuse himself, and he veered toward the men's room. Seeing an entry point, a man with a sweaty, bald pate and wearing a red poppy lapel pin got up from his table and race-walked to ours.

"Excuse me, I hate to bother you—"

"Oh, no you don't," said Taryn, a tease in her voice.

"I'm such a fan of yours, I'm wondering, would you sign this matchbook?"

At Taryn's nod, he handed her the matchbook and watched as the actress signed it.

"Taryn Powell's signature on a Brown Derby matchbook," said the man. "This is going to be worth some big money someday."

"Don't forget to send me my cut," said Taryn.

She winked and as the fan pocketed the matchbook she was able, with a slight turn, to convey to him that their social exchange was over.

"Isn't Maeve looking well?" she said, draping one arm on top of the banquette. "I am so glad she's growing out her eyebrows. Maybe Marlene Dietrich could get away with seven hairs per eyebrow, but not my Maeve!" She jabbed at the ice cubes in her drink with her skewer. "You know, Candy, she really values your friendship."

"She does?"

Sighing, Taryn shook her head. "Poor kid's been lost for so long."

"I . . . I don't think she seems lost now."

"You don't think a twenty-nine-year old woman who spends hours a day lifting weights is lost? I mean, to what end? Where's the career in that? Or the point?"

Uncomfortable now, and feeling disloyal to Maeve, I was trying to figure out how to change the subject when a tiny flash of light exploded.

"Fucking moron," whispered Taryn, as the maître d' raced over to scold the tourist brandishing a camera across the room. "Let me tell you what I'd like to do—I'd like to follow that sow into the john and snap a photo just as she's settling her big ass onto the crapper."

I had to laugh. Serena Summit, the character Taryn Powell played on *Summit Hill*, was so refined she'd rather choke than use words like "crapper," let alone "ass," or, heaven forbid, "fucking moron."

Taryn laughed too and then tapped my wrist with the long nail of her pointer finger. "Now how's about we talk about you. I was very intrigued when Maeve said you'd seen Madame Pepper. She hasn't taken any new clients for years."

"I'm not a client. I only saw her once."

The star of big and little screens waggled her olive skewer at me.

"Comme ci, comme ça. The fact that she invited you into her apartment is an honor few people realize. She won't even see Maeve—she's got a rule that she won't read family members. She says the 'cross wibrations geet too hay-vay.'"

I smiled at the actress's pretty good imitation.

"So Maeve tells me you're doing stand-up comedy."

I flushed. "Well, I hope to, but I haven't—"

"Where're you performing?"

"Uh, nowhere yet, I'm still writing my act."

"Well, I can't say you've picked an easy field," said Taryn, her words steamrolling over mine, "but really, if showbiz were easy, everyone would be in it, n'est-ce pas?" She drummed her nails on my wrist. "Just don't make yourself a stranger to our dear Madame. She doesn't give her time freely to just anyone. My God, her client waiting list is about three miles long."

Mere weeks ago, the idea of sitting in a Hollywood landmark listening to a Hollywood celebrity advise me to visit a Hollywood fortune-teller would have been filed away in the realm of not just the impossible but the delusional.

Trying to think of something to say amid all this discombobulation, I asked, "How often do you see her?"

"Oh, not that often. Just when I need a good kick in the pants. She's about the only one who's not afraid to give me one."

17

Dear Cal,

If there were a newspaper for comedians, here's what today's headlines would read: "Guts, Prepare to Get Busted: Candy Finishes Writing Her Killer Five-Minute Act!"

To celebrate this momentous accomplishment, I decided to bake a cake. It had been ages since I had solicited my neighbors for sugar, and I had long ago stocked up on ingredients but hadn't had the time or inclination to make use of them. Now I did.

My kitchen skills were inspired by my grandmother, not because she herself was a good cook (elbow macaroni and orange processed cheese had steady and recurring roles in her culinary repertoire) but because she had such high regard for my mother's talent.

"Jo was always so happy in the kitchen, singing and laughing, with you perched on the counter helping her. Oh kid, her Korean barbecue, and this pickled cabbage—kimchee, it was called, and it was spicy but so tasty, and this cold spinach dish, I can't remember the name but . . . well, eating at her table was an event."

When my dad realized he didn't have a place in his pal Kermit's family business, he had moved his little family to Minneapolis and into the upper level of my grandmother's duplex. It was on her kitchen counter I perched after my mom died, but cooking was not something Grandma found joy in, muttering under her breath as she squinted at the recipe book directions.

Gradually, I took over more and more of the cooking, and when I was nine years old I made my first dinner for the two of us.

After her first bite of meatloaf, which I'd glazed with a decorative squiggle of ketchup, Grandma groaned with pleasure and putting down her fork, said, "Are you sure I'm not at the Ritz?"

I became House Chef, always leaving an aluminum-tented plate for my dad when he got home from work. I loved the title, loved the cooking, but after my dad died and I spiraled into that black sad wildness, the only thing I did in the kitchen was scavenge through the cupboards and refrigerator, usually when I was high.

I was twenty when I finally put an apron back on, and it was an occasion that caused my grandmother to weep. Well, her eyes got a little teary.

"Umm," she said, watching me stir the beef stew simmering on the stovetop. "Real food again."

"And there're popovers in the oven."

"Oh, happy days," said my grandmother, pressing her palms together and looking upward.

Like my mother, I was happy to be in the kitchen and I accompanied my cooking and baking with lots of singing—mostly to songs I learned as a sixth grader. Music was an important part of Mr. Meyers's curriculum, and every afternoon from one-thirty to two-ten, he seated himself at the piano and hosted a sing-a-long. His repertoire was heavy on sea shanties, which he encouraged us to sing like pirates, throwing in "Arrgh" and "Aye, matey" at our discretion.

It was these tunes—"Blow, Boys, Blow," "Highland Laddie," "The Drunken Sailor"—that I sang now, the sweetness of those grade-school memories an extra, secret ingredient.

AFTER FROSTING THE THREE-LAYER CHOCOLATE CAKE, I stepped back to admire it. It perched majestically on the plate, like Queen Elizabeth I, worthy of devotion, and I almost whispered an apology before sending the knife through it.

Melvin Slyke, across the hall, was its first beneficiary.

"My cake!" he said, taking the paper plate from my hands. "You finally made my cake!"

"Well, it's just a piece," I said apologetically. "I hope you like it—it's chocolate with caramel frosting."

Melvin's eyes widened behind the smudged lenses of his glasses.

"May I eat it now?"

"Be my guest. Enjoy."

Back in my apartment, I carefully arranged slices onto paper plates and after tenting them with cellophane loaded them into a picnic basket

I'd found in Charlotte's linen closet. Ready to make my deliveries, I skipped down the tiled staircase.

I was glad that Maeve didn't answer her doorbell; I felt obliged to at least offer her a piece, even as I didn't want to hear her rant against the evils of sugar/fat/cocoa.

Francis looked almost tearful, telling me he hadn't had a piece of homemade cake since Eisenhower was in office.

I crossed the lawn, parallel to Hollywood Boulevard, to the last apartment building on the east side.

"Mon Dieu," said Bastien Laurent, as he opened his door to reveal a living room cluttered with photography equipment. "I thought you were Chatelaine."

It didn't take much guessing to figure out Chatelaine was another of the French photographer's aggrieved model/girlfriends.

"Nope, just Candy. Voulez-vous a piece of cake?"

"Candeee," he said in his not-unattractive accent. "Zees is so *mignon. . .* so cute of you."

I shrugged. "I'm a good baker. I thought you might like it."

Bastien accepted the plate and kissed my hand. "Eef I like ze taste of ze cake, I might 'ave to sample ze baker."

"Bon appétit!"

Jaz, the building manager, didn't answer, but turning to leave I heard the slow creak of a door opening.

"There are no apartments available," said the woman standing in the shadows, with an accent that made me feel I'd stumbled onto the doorstep of a cottage in Galway.

"Oh, I'm not looking to rent, I already live here. I—"

"Do you have some problem then? Just put your complaint in writing and we'll have Werner take a look."

Werner was Peyton Hall's Swiss handyman.

"No, no, everything's fine. It's just that . . . well, I made a cake and I thought Jaz—and you—it's big enough for two, might like a piece."

"Oh, did you now?"

Surprised by the accusatory tone of her voice, I said, "Yes. I can't eat a whole cake by myself so I'm sharing it with my neighbors."

The door opened a little wider, and I saw half a lovely face.

"I'm Aislin. Mrs. Jasper Delwyn—Jaz's wife. I'm not trying to be rude, but, well . . . thank you."

I handed her the paper plate with the triangle of cake swathed under cellophane.

"My name's Candy. I'm subletting my cousin, Charlotte—Charlotte Fields's—apartment. I can't believe we haven't met yet, that I haven't seen you at least at the pool."

She had shifted her position, and I now saw the other half of her face, from which bloomed a yellowing bruise.

"Oh my gosh, are you all right?"

"Of course I'm all right!" said the woman, closing the door several inches. "And thank you for the cake. I'm sure Jaz'll enjoy it."

"Like I said, it's a big enough piece—" but the door was shut before I finished.

Ed wasn't home—on another date, I supposed—and I left his piece on his doorstep.

It was nearly seven and the air was like a cool, relieved sigh after the choked heat of the day. Cutting across the path, I headed west and waved to Robert X. Roberts, jaunty in a seersucker suit as he walked toward the parking garage.

I stood on Madame Pepper's questioning welcome mat, not exactly afraid to be there but afraid of disturbing her. I took several deep inhales of the fragrant jasmine-tinged air.

"By not knocking," said Madame Pepper, opening the door, "you are testing my psychic abilities?"

I must have gasped, because she laughed.

"All my senses are sharp, including my hearing. You are not the most stealthy coming up stairs." She looked at the basket I held. "And what have you in there, Little Red Riding Hood?"

"I brought you some cake."

"I must have felt it—the teakettle is already on. Come in, come in."

Her apartment was redolent with a spicy cologne.

"A client," she said, waving her hand. "Television producer. He wonders why he cannot re-create past success. Step one, I tell him, is go easy on the aftershave!"

She indicated I should sit on the sofa while she answered the kettle's whistle.

Setting the heavy tea service on the coffee table and herself next to me, she said, "I am splitting this." She bisected the wide frosted wedge of cake with a knife. "If you do not want to eat your half, I'll save it for later."

"It's all yours. I've got more at home."

As she chewed several bites, she stared at an autographed photo of Jean Harlow on the wall.

"That cake." She paused to take a sip of tea. "That cake is of exceptional quality."

I exhaled, realizing that I had been holding my breath.

"Thank you. I'm glad you like it."

The half piece was quickly eaten and then, with a shrug, she began eating what she had "saved" for later.

"Have you ever had the famous Sachertorte in Vienna?"

I shook my head.

"I have, every time I visit my brother Gavril. And this I like better."

A heat lamp of pleasure switched on and I basked under it.

When she was done, she dragged her middle finger across a smear of frosting on the plate and sucked on it.

"Forgive my manners. So delicious. Perhaps this is where your destiny lies."

"In cake baking?" I hoped this wasn't a prediction; I liked to bake but didn't want it to be my destiny.

She flicked aside a long gray tress of her hair. "Well, then perhaps in making something else people will enjoy."

"I hope so . . ."

"Yes? What is it that you hope?"

"Why don't you tell me?"

Madame Pepper's sigh was tired.

"Candy, I don't need to be fortune-teller to sense it is you who needs to tell me something."

I flinched with surprise. "I do? About what? Doing stand-up?"

She pushed up a jangle of bracelets on her wrist, folded her hands on her lap, and furrowing her luxurious eyebrows, looked at me. The look turned into a stare and a sudden surge of emotion made my heart pound, and I felt a sting of tears in my eyes and then clots of dirt began to fall, some stones, a rock, another, then a boulder, and I was powerless to stop the landslide that I had tried so hard to hold back.

18

IT WAS EARLY SPRING of my senior year of high school, my dad had been gone for over a year and I was living the fractured life of a party girl/pot smoker/academic standout. It was as the latter incarnation that I was visiting a small private college in St. Paul that had offered me a big fat scholarship. I had been paired off with an earnest young woman whose name tag read, "Hi! I'm Ellen!" and whose baggy corduroy pants had been worn free of wale at the knees and seat. As we walked through the tree-filled campus, she recited the history of its architecture and its alumnae, in a way that made neither subject interesting.

Directing me to sit on a wrought-iron bench under the still-bare branches of a cottonwood tree, she asked, "So do you have any more questions?"

Looking at her Earth shoes, I wanted to ask, *Yeah—is whatever comfort you get really worth wearing footwear that looks like turds?* but only shook my head.

"Well, I do!"

This was said with an enthusiasm that had not animated her earlier conversation.

"Gee, Ellen, what's that?"

"Well," she said, pushing a clump of her thick blonde hair behind her ear. "I bet you didn't know I'm minoring in Asian Studies."

"You're right, I didn't." Cranking my voice up to match the brightness in hers, I asked, "Did you know I'm Asian?"

She looked startled, as if I'd pinched her.

"I . . . yes, I assumed so, judging from your . . . well, your facial features. What is your ancestry, if you don't mind me asking?"

"What if I did mind you asking?"

Ellen's fair skin mottled, and even as I enjoyed her discomfort, I recognized that I was being a wee bit of a jerk.

"I'm half-Korean. On my mother's side. She and my father met while he was in the service in Korea."

"I knew it! I knew it because that's the focus of my paper! Korean war brides!"

"Well, isn't that ducky."

She asked me where my parents had met.

"In Seoul," I mumbled, not wanting to share the few details I had.

"Not in a camp town?"

"Camp town?"

"Camp town," she repeated, like I was hard of hearing. "There were a bunch of them—in Bupyong and Pusan, Songtan—all over—and they'd rise up to serve the needs of the soldiers, with clubs, brothels, and whatnot."

Her words had the effect of extreme high altitude, and I felt lightheaded. Breathing didn't seem a natural reflex as much as an effort.

"Brothels and whatnot," I said finally. "Are you . . . are you asking me if my mother was a prostitute?"

"Well, you see, conditions for women were hardly easy at that time and—"

I inhaled a gallon of air. "I seriously cannot believe you just asked me that!"

"It was a cruel reality that the options for these women—"

"Shut up!" I screamed, leaping off the bench, but before I plunged over the small hill that sloped to the parking lot, I told the academic imbecile to leave me and my mother out of her stupid paper.

"Which you'll probably get an F on anyway!" I said, really knowing how to hurt a grad student.

"PEOPLE CAN BE SUCH IDIOTS," said Madame Pepper, holding one side of her face as if she had a toothache.

"It was weird—I was so scared, so angry! Like suddenly I didn't know a thing about my own mother!"

WHEN I HAD GOTTEN HOME, I sat at the kitchen table, my head cradled in my arms, sobbing the afternoon away as my grandmother's hand, steady as a pendulum, stroked my back. When I could finally speak, I asked her what she knew, if she'd ever heard of these terrible things, these camp towns.

Color drained from my grandmother's face, and she blinked several times before taking off her glasses. Faint purple tear-shaped indentations lay on each side of her nose from the weight of the frames, and she massaged them with her thumb and middle finger.

"Yes, I've heard of camp towns." She folded and unfolded the stems of her glasses twice before she put them back on. "And the first time I'm ashamed to say was from my own daughter."

I drew in air so fast it sounded like a hiccup.

"You can't remember this, but shortly after Lorraine moved back from Wyoming, she and your dad had a big blowout. She asked him point-blank if he'd met JoJo in a brothel, because, according to a friend of hers who had a friend who served in Korea, that's how most GIs over there met their wives.

"Candy, I was shocked at what your aunt said but scared for her too, because it looked like your dad was going to throttle her. Instead, in the coldest voice I'd ever heard, he said, 'I have no words for what you are, Lorraine.'

"For the longest time, Arne refused to speak to his own sister. Not like he was ever Mr. HaHa MerryMaker, but Lorraine was aware of his punishment, and so was I, and so was your mom. JoJo felt terrible for this rift between brother and sister—double, I think, because she didn't have any family of her own."

I RAISED MY HEAD to look at Madame Pepper. "Both my mom's parents were killed in the war."

The old woman's face sagged with sadness.

"She never talked about them, except once. On my fifth birthday. My last birthday with her." I drew in a deep ragged sigh. "She had a little party for me and made this beautiful ballerina cake, and after everyone went home I taught her how to use the jump rope Janie Larson had given me. Every time she stumbled or stepped on the rope, she'd say, just like a kid, 'Wait, wait,' and we were laughing so hard. Which is why I was so surprised when a minute later she was crying, just as hard.

"I practically knocked her over with my hug. I wanted to comfort her but wanted more to be comforted by her, because her crying scared me so much. She held me for a long time.

"'I just sad,'" I said, imitating her accent. "'Thinking of my mother. Her birthday, three days from now. She not to be even forty!'"

"Oh, Candy," said Madame Pepper. "The same terrible burdens, for your mother and for you."

I wiped my eyes with the yellowed cloth napkin she handed me.

"Yeah, early orphanhood. What a great legacy to pass on to your kids."

"Excuse me, Candy, but during these years were you talking to someone?"

It took me a moment to understand what she was saying.

"You mean like a psychiatrist?"

"Yes. Psychiatrist. Psychologist. Some sort of professional."

"No."

"Your grandmother, she didn't make you?"

"No. It probably never occurred to her. It didn't occur to me. Really, my family's idea of therapy is 'bucking up.'"

Madame Pepper's frown was deep. "Your friends, then, they helped you through this?"

Shaking my head, I felt a tear piddle down my cheek.

"After my dad died, I sort of closed myself off to my old friends . . . I was only interested in people who could help me get high. Karen Schaeffer was a pretty good friend and my dope dealer, but then she found God—ugh, her church was in this former dry cleaners that reeked of cleaning solvents—and between her trying to convert me and me trying to convince her to restart her dealing career, well, our friendship sort of fell apart.

"But not socializing gave me more time in the library where I'd pore over anything I could find about the Korean War. I never did find much on the subject of camp towns." I swallowed, the memory of speed reading chapters of various battles—Osan, the Pusan Perimeter, Inchon—as sour tasting as bile. "I'd look through the phone book and randomly call people with last names like Kim or Lee or Park and ask them, 'Are you Korean?' Most people hung up, although some asked, 'What is this?' or 'Who the hell is calling?' but no one ever answered 'Yes.' If they had, what would I have asked them? *Hey, Mr. Kim, what can you tell me about camp towns? Hey, Miss Lee, do you know any prostitutes? Do you think my mom was one?*"

MY VOICE MADE A SOUND that I couldn't tell was a laugh or cry, and I slurped my tea for a while, composing myself before I went on and Madame Pepper slurped her tea, waiting.

TWO DAYS BEFORE I WAS TO BEGIN my freshman year at the U (there was no way I was going to a college that enrolled that Earthshoe–Asian Studies dipshit) I woke up on the north side of noon, my head pounding, my mouth tasting of the dry heaves that spasmed up my throat.

I had spent the night at a party whose host was a brother of a friend of an acquaintance, helping myself to their warm beer and cloudy bong. On my way to the bathroom, stepping over a pair of blanketed humps I assumed were bodies, I belched, tasting again the evening's debaucheries. In the bathroom, after splashing cold water on my face, I reached for a towel on the rack, only to find it was my T-shirt.

I walked the mile or two home and was not exactly pleased to see that I couldn't sneak in the house, as my grandmother was in the front yard, watering her hydrangeas.

The look on her face upon seeing the bedraggled, hungover vision that was her granddaughter was not one of anger, or disgust, but of delight.

"Candy! You're home!" she said dropping the hose.

"Sorry I didn't call, but—"

She waved away my apology and dipped her hand into the pocket of her gardening apron, pulling out a letter.

"Look!" she said, waving it like it was on fire. "Look!"

"What is it?" I said, even though it was pretty clear it was an envelope.

"It's from Kermit Carlson," said Grandma, her voice quaking with excitement. "The postman just delivered it!"

It took only seconds for me to rifle through my mental Rolodex: Kermit Carlson was my dad's army buddy and short-lived business partner.

"How . . . ?" I whispered. "Why?"

"I wrote him," said my grandmother, and taking my arm she led me to the front steps where we both sat down. "Right after that college girl said those awful things . . . my goodness, I'd given up that I'd ever hear back . . ."

We both stared at the letter she held.

"How . . . how did you find him?"

"I used the address from a letter your dad had written me. The hardware store. Now come on, open it up!"

"It's addressed to you. You read it."

"Out loud?"

When I nodded she said, "I'm so nervous," and I agreed that that was exactly the way I felt.

Madame Pepper stirred honey into her tea, the spoon clinking against the china.

"Zo. What did the letter say?"

"Oh, all sorts of things . . ." Tears pooled in my eyes. "I memorized the whole thing—I tend to memorize important letters—would you like to hear some of it?"

Madame Pepper nodded and I closed my eyes, scrolling through the paragraphs imprinted on my brain until I found the ones I wanted.

"*Here's what I know about JoJo*," I recited.

"*I was with Arne when he knocked her down on our bicycles (we were both pretty hammered). She was on her way home from work, wearing a gray uniform—not, I can tell you, the getup of a lady of the evening! I'll admit that both Arne and I paid for the services of a few women over there, but JoJo was never one of them.*"

I paused, remembering how my grandmother's shoulder had sagged into mine when she read that.

"*Arne was a pretty private guy and kept his courtship quiet, although once in a while he would say something like, 'Man, that JoJo's something,' or 'She makes me want to dance!' For a reserved guy like Arne, I can tell you, that was a high compliment!*

"*When they were in New Jersey, she was busy with her new baby but sometimes she'd have me over for dinner, and although she was shy about her English, she'd manage to make little jokes. She was so funny! She did an impression of Arne that even had Arne doubled over!*

"*What I remember most, though, was how kind she was to my mother, who was sick with emphysema. JoJo would take the baby and visit her, knowing a baby can cheer anyone up. I remember my mother telling me how JoJo said more than anything she wished her old family could have met her new family.*

"*I'd just like Arne's daughter to know that JoJo was truly a lovely person.*"

19

My grandmother had given me such a gift with that letter that I decided to give her one back, and by the time the residue of my hangover headache subsided, I resolved to give the boot to my profligate ways.

It wasn't exactly cold turkey, but a rearrangement of priorities. Less imbibing of pot and alcohol and more of books. Classes began and I stopped going to parties and started studying. Hard. The more credits I took, the more books I had to read and the more papers I had to write and the busier I was, the better.

That I graduated early with honors was no big surprise, but no big thrill either.

I took on more hours at the pie shop/diner I'd been working at since my sophomore year, thinking it was the taking-a-breather-until-I-figure-things-out tonic I needed, but apparently I wasn't qualified to act as my own pharmacist.

In my polyester uniform that zipped up the front and crepe-soled shoes that squeaked, I served hamburger platters, poured endless cups of coffee, and scooped ice cream for à la mode orders. I liked the pace and flurry, and the atmosphere was collegial, owing to the fact that most of my coworkers were still in college. On break, we shared laughs, slices of banana cream pie, and plans.

Monica was excited about spending her senior year in Spain ("I am going to get *muy* bilingual, you guys!"), Lynn had accepted a summer internship at a paper in Washington, D.C. ("If I don't win a Pulitzer in ten years, I'll buy everyone lunch!"), and Merilou, studying veterinary science, told tales of puppies vaccinated and cows laboring ("You guys, I had to put my whole arm up her 'til I felt the calf's head!").

I lent my laughs, congratulations, or ewww's to these conversations, but they began to work on me like a corrosive, eating away at the false front of confidence I had constructed around me.

Having graduated college, I had met the only goal I had set for myself. Now I was bereft of plans for the future, because, I realized, I didn't believe in the future. Not in a doomsday end-of-the-world future, just my own, which was even scarier. My hopelessness was like a snag in my restaurant-wear pantyhose; it started off small and kept inching upwards, irreparable. Sadness, certainly no stranger, came back as a constant presence, settled in, refused to budge.

I had survived losing my mom and my dad but didn't know how to survive losing myself.

Coming home from work on a stormy summer night, I stopped at a drugstore and bought a bottle of aspirin and two bottles of cough syrup.

My grandmother was in the living room, sitting on the couch and making a face as she sipped a pink-colored drink.

"Oh kid, I won't be making one of these again. It's a Red Russian, because I added cherry juice."

With a little shudder, she set the glass down on the end table.

"Say, *Barnaby Jones* is coming on. You want to watch it with me?"

I declined, claiming I was beat and needed to get some sleep. A timpani of thunder rumbled, and clomping down the basement steps I heard the rush of a sudden rain.

In my bedroom, I took my poisons out of my purse and sat on my bed, thinking over and over, *I am so empty.* I couldn't hear the storm anymore, my ears filled with those words, the sounds of my breathing and the thud, thud, thud of my heart. Dumping the aspirin bottle into my open palm, I crammed the pills in my mouth like popcorn and then I uncapped the cough syrup and took a long swig. I was startled by the flavor; my jaw tingled at the sweetness, and turning over the bottle I saw from the label that I was trying to do myself in with children's cough syrup. Children's "super-grapey!" cough syrup. I sat for a moment, my mouth filled with aspirin melting under a grape oil slick, and the absurdity of what I was trying to do and with what I was trying to do it hit me hard. It was as if some giant force walloped me on the back—not just walloped me but hollered the words of my secret power mantra, my *life saber,* into my head, and with a great exhale, aspirins and grape liquid spewed out of my mouth, spraying the bedside rag rug and the hem of a canopy curtain panel with a purple snow shower. I was mortified and strangely elated.

A CONE OF LIGHT shone from under a yellow-shaded lamp; I had talked through the dusk and into the evening.

Madame Pepper palmed the back of her neck and turned her head, as if working out a kink.

"What do you mean, your secret power mantra?"

"It's from this character Heidi Wheaton did in a show my grandmother and I saw. She plays this Indian yogi who advises the audience to get their own secret power mantra 'to obtain your life's desires.'"

"And what is yours?"

"If I told you," I said, wagging my finger, "it wouldn't be a secret."

"Did you tell your grandmother?"

"No. Like I said, it's a *secret* power mantra."

"Bah," said Madame Pepper waving her hand, "I meant, did you tell her about what you did? About the pills and cough syrup?"

"Oh, no, I'd never tell her that. She'd kill me."

Seeing that Madame didn't appreciate my joke, I added, "She'd be worrying about me for the rest of her life."

"And should she be?"

"No!" A burble of laughter rose up my chest. "That's the thing! It just struck me as so pathetically funny—attempted suicide by children's cough syrup—well, it made me realize how instead of dying, instead of going to sleep for good, I was finally ready to wake up! I had a transcendental moment, like when people get born again!" I let loose a crazy-woman cackle.

"When those words, my life saber, came into my head, something shifted. My real life, and what I really wanted, came out of hiding! And not just out of hiding; it seemed possible! Maybe I could be the real me and do the things I'd always wanted to do; maybe I could get on a stage and make people laugh."

"Ah-ha," said Madame Pepper, as if an image had appeared in her mental crystal ball.

"And then my cousin calls needing a subletter for her Hollywood apartment and boom . . . here I am."

The wrinkles around Madame Pepper's mouth softened as she smiled.

"Boom. Here you are."

"And just today, I'm happy to announce, I finished writing my act!"

Lifting the teapot, I aimed the spout at my cup.

"I think that is sign," said Madame Pepper, watching the trickle of tea dribble out. "Time for you to get going."

"Oh," I said, flushing. I'd forgotten how easy the seer found it to send me packing. "Oh, okay."

"Candy." Grabbing my wrist as I stood up to go, my host snorted a laugh. "Yes, it is late; you probably should go home. But what I really mean is yes, yes! It is time you *get going!*"

20

THE NATURAL FUDGE was a vegetarian restaurant on Fountain Avenue that offered comics a small stage on which to perform while waitresses wearing long madras skirts and not enough deodorant served tofu omelets and vegetable burgers that looked like patties of gravel.

Owing to the general laissez-faire atmosphere, there was not a strict time limit, although if an act was truly dying, the emcee might wander onstage and kindly pull the plug.

The audience had been "entertained" by a guy who fashioned out of balloons lumpy shapes he claimed were aardvarks or bears; a wan guitarist who sang a song about a guy who "left me the way you leave the garbage, out on the street, alone and putrid," and a bearded, wild-eyed comic who seemed less intent on making people laugh than convincing them that the IRS stood for Infernal Republic Stealing and how the US government was full of "imbeciles and idiots that make morons look smart!"

"O-kay," said the emcee, as the comic stalked off the stage, railing about taxation without representation. "I guess this is both a stage and a soapbox. Let's hope the next comic considers it the former. Ladies and gentlemen, Candy Pekkala!"

Did every other citizen on Planet Earth feel the same strange blip at that moment when time stood still? Were birds frozen in flight, ocean waves unable to break, all winds snuffed out?

But then my heart thudded, reminding me of my existence, and I swallowed—hard to do when all moisture had evaporated from my throat—as I moved my legs in a fairly accurate semblance of walking, toward the stage. It occurred to me that I was experiencing similar sensations to those I had when I'd been called down as a contestant on *Word Wise,* and I reminded myself that I'd done all right there.

"Hey," I said, stepping toward the mike. "How's everyone doing?"

A few audience members responded that they were fine.

"It's a pleasure to be here at the Natural Fudge. Although I've been trying to figure out exactly what a 'natural fudge' is. Is it similar to an 'unadulterated donut' or a 'pure peanut brittle'?"

There was a mild—very mild—smattering of laughter at this unscripted reflection, and I scurried back to my written material.

"Anyway, I'm happy to be here. I just moved here from Minneapolis, Minnesota, home of Paul Bunyan, the Pillsbury Doughboy, and the Jolly Green Giant. All three of them, in fact, I dated. Paul seemed like he had an ax to grind, the Pillsbury Doughboy was a real softie, and the Jolly Green Giant was not all that jolly, and bigot that I am, I really couldn't get past his color."

I smiled, remembering to wait for the laughter. It didn't come.

"They say women in Minnesota are as cold as the temperatures there," I said, my heart beating as if I were doing jumping jacks. "Just the other day, I met Brian Wilson of the Beach Boys who told me, 'I wish they all could be California girls . . . except Minnesotans, who are so frigid they think that first base is home plate and that waving is an intimate act.'"

There might have been one laugh, or it may have been a guy clearing phlegm from his throat; either way, it was the lone sound in a vacuum of quiet. I felt as if my body temperature had jumped ten or twenty dangerous degrees, and flitting through my brain was the panicky thought that I just might spontaneously combust on stage.

"Hey, did you read production companies are combining the casts of a couple movies from last year, you know, to make things more cost effective? For example, Benji the dog will be starring with a weirdo with goofy hair in a buddy movie they're calling *For the Love of Eraserhead*."

The silence was so vast that a pin dropping would have sounded like a sledgehammer smashing through glass.

"And who saw *Freaky Friday*?" I didn't wait for anyone to answer; I had no idea if anyone was still awake. "They're going to make a psychological thriller combining that movie with the one where Al Pacino plays the race car driver. They're calling it *Freaky Bobby Deerfield*. He'll only race if he's got his partner—a blowup doll—riding shotgun."

I raced through the rest of my act in front of what seemed less an audience than a collection of grim reapers, wearing black cloaks and holding up scythes, and I either blurted or forgot to say my last few lines, so desperate to flee from an onstage death.

"Hey, nice job."

Barreling out the front door, I turned around to see a nice-looking guy with curly brown hair, sitting on the ledge of the Natural Fudge's front window. A half-second after the memory neurons fired, I recognized him as the trumpet-playing comedian I'd seen at the Improv.

"Surely you jest."

Shrugging at my inability to take a compliment, he stood up. "How long have you been performing?"

"This was my first time," I said, hating how my voice sounded, how I was so close to crying.

"Your first time? Congratulations! You did great!"

"I did not! I bombed!"

"You didn't bomb."

He laughed at my smirk.

"Okay, so you did—but on a scale of bombs—and trust me, I know bombs—yours was harmless. A mere stink bomb." He stuck out his hand. "Mike Trowbridge, by the way."

"Candy Pekkala," I said, shaking his hand. "So where's your trumpet case?"

"It's not like a purse. I don't bring it with me unless I'm going to be onstage."

"You were't going on tonight?"

"No, a friend of mine was supposed to perform, but I guess he chickened out."

"I wish I had chickened out," I said as we began walking. "I can't believe . . . I can't believe how bad I did."

"You didn't do bad," said Mike. "You had a lot of good lines. *Freaky Bobby Deerfield*. I'd see that movie."

"Maybe I went on before I was really ready. Maybe I just need to watch more comics for a while."

"I don't know. It's been my experience that you learn the most from being onstage, not in the audience. By the way, can I walk you to your car?"

"I took the bus."

"I'll walk you to the bus stop then.'"

We wound up walking blocks and blocks down Fountain and when I remarked that we had long passed my bus stop, he suggested we walk back to his car parked near the Natural Fudge.

"So we can talk more. Then I'll give you a ride home."

To me it sounded like a great idea.

"Are you from here?" I asked.

"Nope. Nebraska. I grew up on a farm."

"Wow. A real farm?"

Mike chuckled. "A real farm with real cows and real crops. Mostly corn. Some soybeans."

"How long did you know you wanted to do comedy?"

"I actually came out here with a band. A bunch of guys I'd met in school. We weren't bad, but when two of the guys moved back home, the band broke up. And I realized that as much as I love music, I like making people laugh more. And if I can combine the two, great."

I found myself nodding—a lot. It was the first real conversation I had had with a comic, someone who was doing what I wanted (and had failed) to do, and it was as if I'd been reunited with a long-lost relative.

"How long have you been doing your standup?"

"Almost a year. So I know the Natural Fudge, and every little dive within a fifty-mile radius that has an open-mike night."

A man walking a basset hound passed us, his face as forlorn as his dog's. Fountain was more residential and quieter than the big boulevards it ran between—Santa Monica to the south and Sunset to the north— and the pedestrian traffic was lighter and more neighborly.

"Where'd you go to school?" I asked.

"University of Nebraska, in Lincoln."

"Did you study agriculture?"

"Nope. I was a music major."

"Wow."

"Wow, yourself," said Mike, nudging me with his shoulder. "Now what about you: how'd you come to choose comedy over high fashion modeling?"

It was my turn to nudge him. "Yeah, the magazines are filled with 5'4" Asian Scandinavians."

"If they're not, they should be."

I didn't care that he was joking, and I resisted the urge to skip.

"And you really didn't bomb," he said, once we'd gotten back to his car.

"So what do you call it when no one laughs?"

"People laughed. I laughed."

"But why," I said with all sincerity, "why didn't more people?"

"Should I tell you the truth?"

"Only if it's deeply flattering." When he didn't answer, I gave a quick sigh. "Okay, tell me the truth."

"It's just that . . . I didn't believe you. Whatever you say, you have to make the audience believe that you mean it."

"You didn't believe I went out with the Jolly Green Giant?"

"I would have, if you sold me on the idea."

"How do I do that?"

"Like a poker player who wins the pot even with a lousy hand. Like you believe it yourself."

I pondered this as we drove past a trio of barely dressed women plying their trade on the corner of Sunset and Gower.

"Candy, in a contest between a comic with killer material and no confidence in it and a comic with mediocre material who thinks it's the funniest shit ever, guess whose gonna get more laughs?"

"Comic number two."

"And we have a winner!"

He told me the story of his first time on stage, how a guy yelled at him to "shove that horn up your ass!" and how the drunk lady he thought he was cracking up was actually crying.

When he pulled up in front of Peyton Hall, I wanted to reward him for cheering me up and asked if he'd like to come in.

"I just made some banana bread."

"Banana bread," said Mike, tapping the steering wheel with his fingers. "I love banana bread. But I've got to get home. My girlfriend's probably wondering where I am."

"Oh." I was embarrassed at how deflated I sounded.

"Yeah, Kirsten. We met in college. She works for Alliance/Crocker—the frozen food company? One of us has got to have a real job."

"Oh," I said again. "Well, thanks for everything, Mike. Really nice meeting you." I pushed opened the car door. "Thanks for your advice, too."

"Yeah, I—" he began, but I had already shut the door and was racing up the steps to my apartment.

21

Dear Cal,

Grandma and I went to the movies today—she said she wanted to take her funny girl to see Funny Girl*! It was really good, although that song about a girl not being pretty was dumb—who wouldn't pick being funny over being pretty?*

I USUALLY WENT TO THE POOL after work, and more often than not Maeve and Ed had the same bright idea. We were sprawled out on chaise longues, but instead of regaling each other with what had happened during our workday, I was painfully replaying my night at the Natural Fudge. My feelings were raw; Mike Trowbridge's reassurances had been a temporary cushion I fell against after the bad dream of my performance, but that pillow had quickly been yanked away. And my friends weren't exactly slathering me with the balm of sympathy.

"I don't understand why you didn't ask us to go," said Ed.

"Yeah, way to freeze us out," said Maeve.

"I didn't freeze you out. I just wanted to see how an unbiased audience would react."

"Bullhooey," said Maeve. "You just didn't want to share the experience."

"And now I'm glad I didn't. Because I bombed."

"Which is why you should have had friends with you," said Ed, examining a patch of peeling skin on his shoulder.

"Yeah, who'd want to go through something like that alone? Ed, ick—don't pick at that," said Maeve, leaning over to swat his fingers. She waved her hand then, as if considering swatting me, too. "So here's how it's done, Candy: you tell your friends what's going on in your life, so they can share it. Which is why—whether I bomb or not—you two better be cheering me on Saturday night."

IT WAS A TONIC FOR ME to be an audience member and watch a performance that had nothing—intentionally—to do with comedy.

A banner draped across the stage of the Toluca Lake Junior High School read, Welcome, Valley Vixens! and Ed and I were among a group of about fifty spectators on the folding chairs set up on the polished wood gym floor.

The man seated next to me broke a peanut shell with a quick twist of his fingers.

"You lift weights?" he asked, giving me the once-over.

"No."

"Maybe you should think about it," he said, popping the peanuts into his mouth.

Next to me, Ed snickered.

"Okay, I thought about it," I said to my goober-loving neighbor as he thumbed open another shell.

"And?"

"And I think I'd rather stick to my black belt karate."

"Whoa. No kidding?"

I chopped the air with my hands.

"These babies are insured for a hundred thousand each."

The peanut eater whistled, or tried to.

In the audience, there were a couple of people who looked like they knew their way around a weight room, but the majority had muscles that looked unchallenged by sit-ups, curls, rows, and extensions.

The atmosphere was definitely more sports arena than opera house. Some, like the man next to me, had brought snacks. One woman nursed a baby hidden under a bunny-printed blanket. The older couple next to Ed explained that their daughter had been lifting weights since she saw Raquel Welch in the movie *One Million Years B.C.*

"We tried to tell her—Kath, weights aren't going to help you get what she's got," said the man, holding his cupped hands in front of his chest.

"But Kathy's always been strong willed," said the woman. "And Sy and I realized it's a lot easier to say, 'Okay, honey,' and just go along for the ride."

A thin guitarist, whose droopy mustache matched the slope of his shoulders, plugged an electric blue Telecaster into a pig nose amp and without acknowledging the audience ripped into "Thank Heaven for Little Girls," heavy on the tremolo.

"Maurice Chevalier as played by Jimi Hendrix," Ed whispered.

Judges—a bodybuilder and two normal-sized ones—set themselves and their clipboards at a table across from the guitarist. The royal blue curtain parted and a deeply tanned man with a gray brush cut strode out on the stage.

"Welcome, people, welcome!" he said, clapping his hands. "This is so outta sight! The Valley Vixen Women's Bodybuilders Competition! Who wouldn't want to be a Valley Vixen, man?"

The audience responded with hoots and hollers.

"My name's Ricardo Jones, yeah, that Ricardo Jones"—here he pushed up the sleeve of his Hawaiian shirt and flexed an arm to display a softball-sized bicep—"1968 Mr. Greater Orange County, and it is my beyond-groovatational honor to be hosting tonight's competition because, really, man, isn't it time for the ladies to show off what they've got?"

Cheers rose from the audience; even the peanut eater had reclaimed enough saliva to offer a wolf whistle.

"So let's not waste time—let's bring out the parade, man! Hit it, Kevin!"

The guitarist shrugged his droopy shoulders and as he launched into the Miss America theme song (heavy on the wah-wah pedal), the procession of bodybuilders began.

"Oh my God," whispered Ed, which was my sentiment exactly.

The woman leading the procession had short red hair and a scowl on her face, not an expression commonly worn by a pageant contestant. She had on a bikini that matched her hair color, and before striking her first pose she adjusted, with a determined yank, the triangles of fabric covering her small breasts.

"Ladies and gentlemen, say hello to Susie the Strong from Reseda! Susie enjoys sunrises—especially Tequila ones, right, Suze?—James Bond movies, and riding Harleys with her husband, Lyle! Vroom, vroom, baby!"

"That's my neighbor," said the peanut eater. "Sweetest gal you'd ever want to meet, although she's not the sharpest tack on the bulletin board."

"Next," said the emcee, "from Van Nuys, let's meet Bonnie the Buff."

"More like Bob the Bulky," I whispered to Ed of the masculine-looking contestant. "Or Biff the Brawny."

"Bonnie likes Chinese food," the emcee was saying of the woman whose oiled muscles were the biggest I'd ever seen on a person sharing my gender, "board games like Risk and Stratego—but only if she wins—and the novels of Jacqueline Susann."

"Check out her mustache," Ed said.

"That's from the steroids."

Tears had welled up in Maeve's eyes when I had confessed to her that when I first met her, I thought her build was due to drugs.

"This is all blood, sweat, and tears," she had told me. "I fight fair and I body-build fair."

That particular code of ethics didn't seem embraced by Bonnie the Buff or several other entrants whose musculature was as threatening as their facial hair.

When Ricardo Jones introduced the fifth contestant as Mustang Maeve, Ed and I whistled like we were calling a pack of dogs scattered over three states. She was wearing a lime green bikini and enough oil to toss a banquet of salads.

"Maeve enjoys speaking German—hey, ve got a schmartie here!— the music of Tom and Jack Jones—sounds like she's got a jones for Joneses!—and reading poetry. Roses are red, Maeve!"

While the crowd enjoyed the wit and wisdom of the emcee, Mustang Maeve seemed oblivious to it. She didn't try to tamp down her stage fright with a sneer, like Susie the Strong, but instead wore a smile frozen at half-mast, and she walked as if she were afraid her very footsteps might cause damage to the stage floor.

After the dozen contestants were introduced in the pectoral parade, they posed as a group and then in individual routines. It was obvious that some had been lifting weights much longer than others; Kath the Convex from Ventura had stick straight legs and only a slight rise to her biceps. North Hollywood's Winona the Wild was muscular, but she was also fat, which hid a lot of definition.

During the judges' deliberation, Kevin played "You Must Have Been a Beautiful Baby," and when Ricardo Jones was given the results envelope, the guitarist played the low E note up and down the fret board and gave full play to his whammy bar and wah-wah pedal.

"Ladies and gentleman, third place honors go to . . . Mustang Maeve from Hollywood! And second place goes to . . . Reseda's Susie the Strong!"

It was exciting to watch people who didn't win first prize act like they did. Both Maeve and Susie bounced up and down, clutching one another's arms and when the anticlimatic announcement came, "Which means this year's Valley Vixen is Bonnie the Buff from Van Nuys!" they didn't just embrace the victor but hoisted her into the air.

"You don't see that too often in a beauty pageant," I said to Ed, and repeated the sentiment when we were all in Maeve's car, on the way to her mother's house in the Hollywood Hills.

"How many times do I have to tell you?" said Maeve. "It isn't a beauty pageant. If it's anything, it's an art exhibit, celebrating the bodybuilder as an artist, a sculptor."

"Sorry," I said.

"And she is right," said Ed from the backseat. "I mean, you don't consider a male bodybuilder contest a beauty pageant, do you?"

Maeve brightened. "Yeah! You don't consider a male bodybuilder contest a beauty pageant, do you, Candy?"

I decided not to let on that I considered any bodybuilder contest as sort of weird. Still, I didn't want to let Maeve off the hook completely.

"But didn't you think it was strange that the emcee guy only introduced you by those dumb titles? I mean, what was that about?"

"They have us come up with names like that to make it harder for the creeps—Bonnie said she had a fan who called her over fifty times a day—to track us down. But yeah, I did feel kind of stupid coming up with mine."

"That was your idea?"

"Did you name it after your car?" asked Ed.

"Oh, I get it," I said, tracing the little mustang logo on the glove compartment.

"I couldn't think of anything else that began with an M!" said Maeve. She turned left and into a short driveway.

"Well, here we are," she said, jamming the gearshift into park. "Now remember, I'm not responsible for anything my mother may or may not do."

22

Taryn Powell's famous voice rose from the hot tub as we passed through the high wooden gate and entered the candlelit patio.

"Hail the conquering heroine, everyone," she said, "the new Valley Vixen!"

"I didn't exactly win the title, Ma," said Maeve, "but I did come in third!"

"Well, come on in and celebrate! The water's fine."

"We don't have suits, Ma."

"Well, neither do we," said the TV star sweetly.

"Taryn, you're terrible!" said a man whose silver goatee and mustache were the only hair on his head. He looked at Maeve. "We've all got suits on, hon. At least we did when we got in."

Taryn lifted her hand out of the bubbling water and twirled a bikini top.

"That was then, Derek. This is now!"

"Yeah!" said an auburn-haired woman, tossing a tiny swimsuit bottom over the edge of the hot tub. "It's about time we got this party started!"

Ed's elbow dug into my side, a gesture I knew asked the question, *Do you see who that is?* My nudge back assured him that I did; the person joining Taryn in the underwater striptease was Sharla West, the actress who played her diabolical daughter-in-law on *Summit Hill.*

"Yee-haw!" said a man with a golden mane of shoulder-length waves, getting into the act and throwing his swim trunks out of the tub.

"Oh, great, so you're throwing an orgy," said Maeve.

Taryn reached for her champagne flute in one of the slight recesses that had been built specifically to hold drinks in the hot tub's ledge.

"It's not an orgy," she said and took a sip. "Yet."

The quartet in the pool snickered.

"We'll be inside," said Maeve, turning away.

As Taryn urged us to join them—"The water's fine!"—Ed and I offered feeble waves and followed Maeve into the house.

"Dang," whispered Ed, "I could have sat in a hot tub with Sharla West."

"A nude Sharla West," I said, sprinkling salt into the wound.

After we'd entered her mother's huge white living room, Maeve turned around, hands on hips.

"Hey, you guys are welcome to join the free-for-all. Don't let me hold you back."

Her lips were pinched and she wore her injured-party look.

"No, no, I'm fine," I said.

"Me, too," said Ed, but I could tell if he had his druthers, his would place him in that vat of churning bubbles, squarely between Taryn and Sharla.

"It's just so humiliating!" said Maeve, as tears, the usual accompaniment to her breakdowns, glittered in her eyes.

Ed and I sat down on an immense U-shaped white leather couch in the sunken conversation pit as Maeve began pacing in front of the fireplace.

"She loves acting like she's the racy daughter and I'm the uptight mother! Ewww! How would you guys like to jump in a hot tub with your naked mother and her friends?"

From the look on Ed's face, I could tell her question conjured a picture he didn't want to visualize. As for me, I would have jumped into anything with my mother, naked or not. Still, I understood her point.

"Should we go then?" asked Ed gently.

"No, stay," said Taryn, knotting the tie of her terrycloth robe after she rolled open the sliding glass door and came into the living room. "Maeve, hon, I didn't mean to upset you."

Standing by the fireplace, Maeve considered her fingernails. "Maybe not, but I don't think you tried very hard not to upset me."

The actress opened a silver box on the marble coffee table and took out a cigarette.

Scrambling, Ed reached for the round crystal lighter.

"Do you think I'm a terrible mother?" asked Taryn, after she'd exhaled out her nose, like a dragon.

"Mom!" said Maeve, drawing out the word in two syllables.

"Well, we're not blood-related," said Sharla, entering the living room, "but I will say you absolutely stink as a mother-in-law."

"Sharla," said Maeve evenly. "We were discussing my real mother, not your fake TV husband's one."

"By the way, Taryn," said Sharla, ignoring Maeve. "Derek and Jon are leaving."

"Why? It's still early! Why is everyone leaving?"

"Because some of us have a six a.m. call," said Derek, a towel wrapped around his waist. He was followed by the wavy-haired guy, also half-dressed in terrycloth.

"Sharla and I have tomorrow off," explained Taryn. "But Derek's got to shoot some action scenes out in Simi Valley and Jon'll be jumping out of a burning barn."

"I'm a stuntman," said the wavy-haired guy helpfully.

After their departure, Taryn called for her maid to open another bottle of champagne and suggested it was time to get back into the hot tub.

"Maeve, get suits for everyone, and I promise Sharla and I will keep ours on."

Ed and I looked at each other.

"Uh, I've got to work tomorrow," I said.

"And I've got to teach," he said.

"I'll write you both notes," said the actress. "Now, Mother of God, please, prove to me that youth isn't wasted on the young."

CLIMBING INTO THE HOT TUB, I could see the embarrassment on Ed's face. He was tall and lanky but slightly flabby, and he crossed his arms, trying to cover the soft roll above his waistline. When he sank neck-deep into the water, relief calmed his features.

"So, Ted," said Sharla, "you're a teacher?"

"Uh, it's Ed. And yes, yes I am."

"No kidding," said Sharla, leaning toward him and I saw Ed's Adam's apple bulge as he swallowed. "What do you teach?"

"All kinds of things, but mostly history. Geography sometimes. Occasionally English. Once, art. I don't like to remember that class." He looked at me panicked, silently pleading to help him.

I smiled gamely at Sharla. "He's a substitute."

"And a fine one, I'm sure," said Taryn. "But we simply must talk about you now, Maeve. You say you came in fourth place?"

"Third," said Maeve.

"And she was robbed," I said. "If the whole thing wasn't rigged, she would have won Valley Vixen."

Maeve's big jaw pulled down as she tried to hide her smile.

"She sure had the best-looking legs of all of them," said Ed, and pleasure washed over Maeve's face.

"Gee, I wonder who she gets those from?" said Taryn in a baby voice, lifting a leg out of the water and toward the sky.

"I don't know, Maeve," said Sharla in the same cutesy voice. "I think I could give you some competition, too."

She offered one of her legs up for view, and the two stars of *Summit Hill* spent a long moment pointing their toes and rotating their ankles this way and that.

"Anyway, Mother," said Maeve, "it wasn't first prize, but I didn't expect to be in the top three at all, so it was quite an honor."

Both women drew their legs back into the hot, churning water.

"I'm sure it was, sweetie. You know I would have been there if I could have." Taryn arranged her features into a look of concern and said, "I just didn't want to cause a stir. All eyes should have been on you tonight."

"Or Bonnie the Buff," I added, making Maeve laugh.

"Do you like girls like Maeve?" Sharla asked Ed. "Or do you prefer your women a little . . . softer?"

The heat and steam were making all of our faces red, but Ed's took the color to a whole new level.

"I . . . uh—"

"—Ed," said Taryn, coming to his rescue. "Would you be a good boy and pour me some more champagne?"

"Me, too!" said Sharla, as Ed reached for the bottle chilling in the bucket.

Leaning back, I averted my eyes from the stars in the hot tub and looked up at the stars in the sky, or where they would have been if not obscured by haze and the lights of the city. Turning my head to the left, I saw a kidney-shaped pool illuminated by lamps that were nestled in the gardens and lining the stone paths. Turning my head right, I saw fat lemons hanging from a tree just feet away and limes from another, and the smell of citrus mingled with eucalyptus and what had become my favorite smell—night blooming jasmine. If Minneapolis's unofficial expression was brrr, Los Angeles's had to be ahhh (with a little smog-induced cough at the end).

"So Candy," said Taryn, butting into my reverie, "how's the comedy career going?"

I tried not to flinch, not prepared to tell anyone outside my inner circle about my inauspicious debut.

"I am dying to do a romantic comedy," said Sharla saving me. "*Summit Hill*'s great, but it's so serious. I want to do something a little frothy." She did a little shimmy, in Ed's direction.

"My second movie was a comedy," said Taryn. "*FiFi's Collar*—any of you see it?"

She pushed her lower lip out in a child's pout when only Maeve nodded.

"It was actually quite good. I played Lizette, the French neighbor of a couple who had this crazy poodle named FiFi; my costars were Jean-Paul—"

"—that's my goal," Sharla said, "to do a comedy during hiatus." She leaned into Ed again, this time more aggressively, smooshing one breast against his arm. "Don't you think I'd be good in a comedy, Eddie?"

I surveyed my friend, on whose pink and sweating face was an odd mix of glee, lust, and horror.

"I, uh—"

"—and my fourth movie; yeah, I think it was my fourth," said Taryn, counting on her fingers, "my fourth movie was a comedy called *Herr Professor and Christine*. I was nominated for a Golden Globe award by the way, playing Christine's best friend, Cookie. We shot it in Munich of all places—that's where I met Maeve's father—at the Hofbräuhaus! He had just come from Yale and was working on his doctorate and—"

"—my agent says there's no reason I couldn't be the next Lucille Ball," said Sharla. "I mean we both have red hair, well, mine's auburn, and—"

"—I met Desi Arnaz once," said Taryn. "This was when he was still married to Lucille, and oh my God, the charm that oozed out of that man—"

"—do you like *I Love Lucy*?" Sharla asked Ed. "My mother and I did, but my dad said it was stupid—he much preferred shows like *Car 54* and—"

"—is anyone hungry?" asked Taryn. "Because I can have Verna make some sandwiches and—"

"—I've got to go home," said Sharla, slowly rising out of the steaming water. "Eduardo, can I give you a lift?"

Ed's eyes bulged at the invitation.

"But I came with—"

Sharla posed, water dripping off the camera-ready curves of her body.

"I'll be waiting in the driveway," she said. "In the baby blue T-Bird convertible."

"So you think lil' Miss Arizona and Ed will get it on tonight?" asked Maeve, tossing our swimsuits into the dryer of the fanciest laundry room I'd ever been in.

"Is that what she was? Miss Arizona?"

Maeve shrugged. "Some state that begins with an A."

"Asslandia," I offered. "And no, I think Ed only went home with her because he was too much of gentleman to say no."

We laughed. It had been Taryn and not Maeve who had been in a bad mood after the actress and substitute teacher left, announcing she had a sudden headache and was going to bed.

She didn't even bother seeing us out, which, according to her daughter, wasn't atypical.

"I love her," Maeve said. A soft whirr sounded as she turned on the dryer. "But she can be a little temperamental—especially when she doesn't get what she wants."

"What do you suppose she wanted?"

"Oh, more attention, probably. Or someone to assure her that she's just as attractive as Sharla West—even though she's old enough to be her mother. Sheesh. Did you notice how they had to outdo one another—how our presence was sort of immaterial to them?"

"Ed's wasn't to Sharla."

Now in the car, making our way down the windy road, I asked my friend, "Come on, didn't it bother you when he left with her?"

Chuckling, Maeve expertly negotiated a hairpin turn.

"What, do you think I'm jealous?"

"Well, you like him, don't you?"

"I'd go out with him, sure. But Ed's convinced me that's not going to happen, so I guess I'll have to settle for having him as a friend. From watching my mother, believe me: I've learned the danger of hanging on when it's time to let go."

Gasping, Maeve braked hard, holding her arm out to protect me from making contact with the windshield, even as I was wearing my seat belt.

Her headlights shone on a yellow lab racing across the narrow road, pursued by a terrier, and we watched them disappear into a yard, yapping and barking.

"Lot of bitches out tonight," mused Maeve.

Her joke surprised both of us, and we laughed all the way down the hill.

23

Dear Cal,

While my "bombing" wasn't exactly lethal, a week and a half's gone by and I still feel like I'm picking shrapnel out of my heart. That dead air after my laugh lines, that sense of scrambled panic—uh, I'll have the root canal instead, please. The roar of confidence that had gotten me onstage is now a feeble little meow, and I seriously wonder when and if I'll have the guts to get on stage again.

"Candy, you're kidding me, right?" said Solange when I confessed as much to her. "You don't strike me as that big a baby."

"I'm not a baby, Solange, it's—"

"—you are if you don't get back on stage. Everybody bombs, Candy. That's the nature of show business. That's the nature of everything." Sitting on the blue futon, she leaned forward and picked a copy of *Radio & Records* off the reception area coffee table. "Look at that," she said, flinging the magazine at me. "Brass Jar, a Beat Street band, on the cover."

"I know they're on the cover, Solange." The particular issue had been greeted with much fanfare in the office.

"But what you don't know is I saw them last year at the Whiskey. Where people were booing them. Where a few bottles were thrown. Where they bombed." Her smile was of the told-you-so variety. "And now they've got a hit album and they're on the cover of *Radio & Records.*"

"Well, that's great, but—"

Solange snapped open a copy of *Billboard.*

"And you should read this story about Timber Line. It took them ten years and two lead singers before they got a record deal." I ducked as she hurled the magazine at me. "So I'm not really interested in excuses."

THE PROBLEM, I thought as I skated east on Hollywood Boulevard, was that once I finally got on a stage, I was certain I could do nothing but succeed. That sounds vain, dumb, and ill advised, but to go from my old life to my new one had demanded that I take a huge leap of faith. Which I had done . . . without considering the consequences of a crash.

Stop it, I scolded myself. Solange was right: *Everybody bombs once in a while—it's the nature of show biz.*

Hot winds rattled the halyard of the pole in front of the bank, and the fabric of the flag shook and snapped as if it were in the hands of an angry laundress.

"They're the Santa Anas," June had informed me when I helped chase down her bratty dog. "That's what Binky's trying to run from, the spookiest winds in the world! They're blamed for everything from sparking fires to inspiring serial killers."

Hot and sweaty when I got to the bank, I switched my skates with the shoes I had in my backpack and got into the short line at Lincoln Savings, idly wondering how long I could go without tapping my game show savings.

An angry voice intruded on my reverie.

"Well, that's bullshit! Something's got to be off on your end!"

There was a whispered request asking that the aggrieved customer keep his voice down.

"Why should I when you can't perform simple math? Now let me speak to the bank manager!"

At the end of the counter, behind the far window, I could see the chagrined face of the young teller facing the irate customer, who, by voice and dapper suit, I recognized was Francis Flover.

"Don't just sit there like a peon—get me the goddamned manager!"

I was shocked; this was not the vocabulary or manner of the kindly, gracious man I knew.

"Sounds like someone's not so happy with his interest rate," said the guy ahead of me in line.

The woman ahead of him chortled.

"Or maybe he didn't get his free toaster when he opened up a savings account."

As the two customers yukked it up, I turned around and left.

There were several big concrete planters on the small plaza the bank shared with the Toy Tiger, and I sat on the edge of one, still needing to cash my paycheck but wanting to avoid the embarrassment of Francis seeing me. It was the second strange incident I'd witnessed relating to him, the first taking place the previous weekend.

I had just gotten my mail and was climbing the stairs to my apartment when Melvin Slyke's door opened.

"Dad, it's not just using your car—that man's going to run you out of house and home!"

"Don't be ridiculous!" said my neighbor. "It's just pocket change, Nancy. Pocket change!"

"But he's got a really big pocket!"

"Nancy, sweetheart, I appreciate you coming over, but please, it's not your place to tell me how to spend my money."

"But it's my business to protect you from a shark like Flover!"

Melvin Slyke's daughter stepped onto the small landing just as I slipped unobtrusively—or tried to—into my apartment.

"Thanks for coming over, honey," I heard Melvin say and seconds after I heard his daughter galumph down the steps, there was a knock at my door.

"Sorry you had to hear that," said Melvin.

I shrugged, not knowing exactly what to say.

"Nancy had no right to say those things and I wish you hadn't heard them. Here's the thing. Francis has seen better days—who hasn't?—and if I can pay him for the odd little job that doesn't hurt his pride, what's the harm in that?"

"No harm."

"Exactly. And if I want to take him out for dinner now and again or lend him my car, what's the problem?"

"That little silver sports car is yours?"

Melvin wiggled his bushy eyebrows.

"You probably pegged me as a sedan type, right?"

Now FRANCIS FLOVER PUSHED OPEN the bank door as if he had a personal enmity toward it. While he wasn't quite stomping, he was a long way from skipping, and when the hot wind picked up the vent of his suit jacket, he swatted it down.

There was a tour bus in the intersection and as Francis crossed the street, I wanted to shout, "Hey, there's a piece of Hollywood history right in front of you!" but of course I didn't, there being enough nuts shouting things on the Boulevard as it was.

What had set him off like that? I realized everyone had their bad days, but Francis was a consummate gentleman, one who called a teller "Miss" and not "peon."

Seeing this side of him, I felt bad—bad for him and bad for me. I didn't like being disappointed by someone I wanted to look up to.

5/1/72

Dear Cal,

    My sixteenth birthday! . . . And I spent part of it bawling my head off!

    "Who knows what makes people tick?" Grandma asked me after Dad stormed out of the house. "If a mother can't even figure out her own son, how can she figure out anybody?"

    I think she was trying to comfort me, but sorry Grandma—I'M NOT COMFORTED! I haven't even been sixteen for a whole day, and I feel like I'm about thirty-five—old and worn out and so sad!

The night had started off with such promise. Dad had taken the night off—imagine that!—and Grandma was giddy as she served the birthday dinner she insisted on making. As the three of us shook salt and pepper on our limp unseasoned green beans and sawed away at our well-done steaks, we laughed and joked, acting uncharacteristically like a loving family.

My grandmother had allowed me to make and frost my own cake, but she'd insisted on decorating it, writing in a pink-gel icing, "Happy Sweet 16th!" When it was presented to me, ablaze with candles, I thought, *It is, it is!* and when my dad slid a little box across the table, my heart thrummed.

I untied the ribbon slowly, prolonging the sweet moment, even as I wanted to rip at it like a dog smelling a bone wrapped inside butcher paper.

Opening the box, I'm fairly certain that the thrumming—and my heart—stopped.

"Oh, Dad," I said, picking up the silver locket nestled in the cotton batting. Its thin chain ran between my fingers like a long silver tear. "It's beautiful."

"Open it up," said my dad, his voice rusty.

With my thumbnail, I pushed open the locket's clasp and seeing the lovely smiling face of my mother, I burst into tears.

"Oh, for Christ's sake!" he said.

His words were a slap and I howled my hurt.

"Arne," said Grandma softly, "Arne, it's just that—" but my dad wasn't interested in my grandmother's explanation, and he barreled into the living room. A moment later we heard the front door slam.

I found myself at a strange junction, a place where humiliation, sorrow, and anger met, and my tears dried in that hot, choked place. I didn't understand my own wild reaction at seeing my mother's picture, and I sure didn't understand the reaction of my father.

"What a jerk!" I said, practically spitting. "What's the matter with him?"

"Candy," said my grandmother softly, "he's just—"

"—a total jerk! He barely ever mentions mom's name to me, and then he gives me this locket with her picture in it, and I'm not supposed to be a little floored?"

"You're right, he did overreact." My grandmother's head was not so much shaking as vibrating. "And I honestly don't know what's the matter with him." She picked up the necklace's chain, sprawled on the table like a silver spill, and rubbed her thumb against the locket. "But I think he was scared . . . scared by your reaction."

"I don't care! He should have at least tried to make me feel better!"

"If it would do any good, I'd bust him in the snoot," said my grandmother and her words, her prescription for dealing with my father was so inane, so futile, that we couldn't help it, we laughed.

It was the last birthday present I was to ever get from him, and even though we never spoke of it, I knew it gave my dad pleasure seeing me wear the locket every day. I'd still be wearing it, but to my everlasting shame and regret, one night after a keg party, I woke up to find it gone.

I HAD PLANNED on spending the rest of my lunch hour at the Beef Bowl or browsing the aisles of JJ Newberry's, but I was bummed out after seeing Francis and thinking of my Dad, and having lost the taste for Chinese food or dime store junk, I skated back toward Beat Street Records, the hot wind blasting me in the face as I slalomed around the inlaid stars and upright tourists.

24

"WHAT ABOUT THAT PLACE?" asked Maeve, pointing.

"Looks good to me," said Solange. "Okay with you, Candy?"

I nodded; my senses flooded.

We were walking along Olympic Boulevard, a street whose shop signs were written in Korean characters and underneath them, what I could read, their English translations.

"Korean Bar-B-Q!"

"Nam's Liquor Bar!"

"Jung's Pharmacy!"

While there were white, black, and Hispanic people on the street in Korea Town, they were a minority amid the people who looked like my mother, who looked like me.

"You all right, Candy?" asked Solange.

"It's just so weird. I have never, ever been around so many—" I trailed off, not having the words.

Solange laughed. "Of your people? Imagine how I felt when I first went out to Compton after having grown up in Fresno."

"Or me," said Maeve. "I went to dance school for years, but it was only when I went into a gym with barbells that I felt like I was home."

Noticing the look Solange and I exchanged, Maeve laughed.

"Okay, but it was kinda like what you're talking about."

Flanked by my friends, I was steered into Kee's Bar & Food, and after the hostess told us there'd be a slight wait, we headed toward the bar.

"WHAT DO YOU RECOMMEND?" Solange asked the bartender as we straddled the red leather barstools.

"What's the occasion?" asked the young Korean, in unaccented English.

"We went to this club on Western for open-mike night," said Solange. She tipped her palm toward me. "See, my friend here is a comedian and we were going to watch her perform."

"Really?" said the bartender.

"Only the sign on the door said, 'Closed for remodeling,'" said Maeve.

"But we still want to celebrate," said Solange. "And because Candy's mother was from Korea, we thought this might be a good place to bring her."

I sat hunched like a cretin, hands tucked under my thighs, embarrassed and yet stifling an urge to guffaw.

"My mother's from Korea, too," said the bartender with a smile. "So's my father. Where was your mom from?"

"Seoul," I said. "But I . . . I don't know a lot about her. She died when I was little."

He nodded in sympathy before asking, "Ever heard of Soju?"

In a choreographed move, Solange's, Maeve's, and my head moved from side to side. It was all the answer the bartender needed.

"Now, because you're at a bar and I'm serving you," he said, placing three shot glasses in front of us, "this is a moot point. But if you were at a table, with friends or relatives, you wouldn't fill your own glass. It's against tradition.

"Take your glass," he instructed next, "and hold it in both of your hands. That's a sign of respect."

We did as he advised, and holding a green bottle with Korean characters on the label, the bartender filled our shot glasses.

"What's your name?" asked Solange.

"Bill. Now, usually people drink this in one shot. In fact, you can even call out, 'One shot!'—it's sort of like, 'Bottoms up.' If you don't think you can drink this all in one shot, you can call out, "Pan shot!" which means 'half-shot.' So what do you think?"

"One shot!" I hollered and guzzled down the drink.

"One shot!" echoed Solange and Maeve, both of them mimicking my shudder when they swallowed their drinks.

Bill looked at us approvingly and held up the bottle again in invitation. The three of us shook our heads, with a certain amount of force.

"If we drink any more of that, we'll need to hire a rickshaw to get us home," said Maeve. Her eyes widened as she swiveled on her stool to face me and then Bill. "Oh geez, was that a stupid thing to say? Because I didn't mean anything, I just thought because we were in Korea Town—"

"Ladies," said the hostess, approaching us, "your table's ready."

"Perfect timing," said Solange.

AFTER SCANNING OUR LAMINATED MENUS, crowded with photographs, the lines and dashes of Korean characters and their English translations, we ordered several dishes and as we waited for them, I told them how I was reminded of my grandmother.

"She used to take me to this Chinese restaurant in downtown Minneapolis—it was about the only place she knew I could see some Asians."

The Nankin had big tasseled menus, rice paper wall hangings, and hostesses in traditional Chinese dress, and we considered ourselves very cosmopolitan as we made clumsy stabs at Subgum Chow Mein or Beef Broccoli with our chopsticks.

"Didn't they have any Korean restaurants there?" asked Maeve.

"None that we knew of," I said.

"What surprises me," said Solange, taking a sip of the tea that had been delivered, "is that this is your first time down here. Like I said, when I got to L.A., it was such a relief; I mean, there were whole neighborhoods, cities where black people were in the actual majority. Didn't you want to rush down here to be with your own people?"

"If I wanted to be with my own people, I'd probably rush down to Little Scandinavia, if there were such a place."

"Really?" said Maeve. "That's who you relate to more?"

"That's what I grew up with. That's what I know."

"So you don't feel Korean?"

"Feel Korean?" I shook my head. "No, I look a lot more Korean than I feel Korean." I doodled on the tablecloth with my fingernail. "But the way I look doesn't really match."

"Match what?" asked Maeve.

"The me inside."

"Candy," said Solange, "it's the rare person whose outside matches up with who they are inside."

"I'll bet yours does," said Maeve.

Solange's laugh was big and true. "Oh, right. On the inside, I feel like I'm the finest—I'm talking Lena Horne in her youth; the smartest—Barbara Jordan testifying before Congress; and the wildest—Angela Davis rallying the troops—woman to walk this earth. Does that match up with how I seem on the outside?"

"No comment," I said, regarding my friend with her carefully processed hair, who wore a prim, round-collared blouse, anchored with a tied grosgrain ribbon.

"I get what you're saying," said Maeve. "The me underneath this

doesn't match this." She flexed her biceps. "The me inside is a blobby little baby, with no muscle mass at all."

"We're all blobby little babies inside," said Solange. She took a sip of
tea, studying me over her cup.

"What?" I said.

Tilting her head, Solange's eyes narrowed in suspicion. "Did you
know the club was going to be closed tonight?"

"No! I was excited! Excited that you were going to see me perform."

"Since you neglected on purpose to tell us about the first time," said
Maeve.

"Are you ever—"

"Here we are," said the waitress, and I silently thanked her intrusion
as she set on the table steaming bowls and plates filled with bright vegetables, swirls of noodles, piles of meat, and we happily, and audibly, ate
for several minutes.

"Oh my God," said Maeve in between bites of dak galbi. "I love this
stuff. Did your mom cook like this, Candy?"

"That's what my grandma tells me, but I don't really have any memory of it." I spooned onto my plate some of the spicy chicken and noodle
dish Maeve was lapping up and waited for the usual wash of sadness to
come over me. I sat back in the booth, surprised.

"Wow. I don't know what it is about this place, or you guys, but usually when I talk about my mom, I feel like crying, but right now I don't."

"That's good," said Maeve, passing me a plate of barbecue spareribs.
"I used to not be able to talk about my mom without feeling like I wanted
to punch someone in the face. Now I only want to pinch them."

Her words hung in the air for a moment, like a scent we were trying
to identify.

"My therapist says that's progress," said Maeve.

"My mother and I get along great," said Solange, once we had settled
into a post-laugh relaxation. "Except that she's constantly bugging me to
get married."

"I'm sure that'll happen," said Maeve, "when the right guy comes
along."

Solange shrugged. "The right guy could come along and I'd be totally
uninterested. It's the right girl I'm waiting for."

In the silence that followed, I wondered how to respond, and I know
Maeve was doing the same.

"*Girl*?" I said finally. "Don't you mean *woman*?"

The unflappable Solange seemed, for a change, flapped.

"Then it's okay with you?" she said, her voice small. "Do you still like me?"

"'Like you' in what way?" asked Maeve, planting her big chin on her curled fist.

"Yeah, are you coming on to us?" I said. "Because if you are, I have to tell you—and I think I speak for Maeve, too—I could never date someone who wears grosgrain ribbons as an accessory."

Maeve shook her head. "Why would I want to date my second grade teacher?"

Solange stared at her plate for a long moment, tugging at one of her inflamed ear lobes.

"Thanks," she said finally. "I'm glad you know. My mother still doesn't, and it kills me." She let go of her ear and slumped back in the booth. "Whew."

"Whew's right," I said. "And I thought I was the one who had a hard time letting people in."

"We do what we do to protect ourselves," said Maeve. "But lately I've been thinking secrets do less to protect us than . . . to stifle us."

Solange and I looked at her as if she had just sung "Edelweiss" in a voice purer than Julie Andrews.

"I know, I know," said Maeve, laughing. "I'm smarter than I look."

25

"Look at what my cousin sent me."

"Greetings from Ravenna!!" Solange read aloud. "(See pic of it on other side!)"

"Is she serious? She really thinks you don't understand the concept of a postcard?"

I shook my head. "Read the rest."

In a breathy voice, Solange brought to life Charlotte's childish handwriting:

"Got a couple hours in port so I thought I'd write to tell you I'VE FALLEN IN LOVE!!! *Cray's his name, and he'll be coming home with me, helping me to turn the apartment into a* LOVE SHACK!!! *We'll be getting in on the 30th and you have my permission to use my car to pick us up! Call you when we land!!! XX, Charlotte."*

"You know what that means, don't you?" I asked.

"That your apartment's going to turn into a love shack?"

"Exactly," I said, leaning back in my office chair. "And how much do you want to bet that I won't be welcome in it?"

IN SYMPATHY WITH MY LOUSY MOOD—and because everyone else was out of the office—Solange told me I might as well leave early.

"I'll hold the fort down while you go pout," she said. "Which I thoroughly endorse, by the way."

With my roller skates crammed into my backpack, I dawdled my way down Hollywood Boulevard. At the Broadway Department store, I held out my wrist at the fragrance counter, accepting a spritz of a new perfume called Star Power!

"If I smell like it, does it mean I have it?" I asked the spritzer, a woman who in her white coat looked like a glamorous doctor. Her response was a pitying smile.

I bought a roll of Necco Wafers at JJ Newberry's and while looking in the window at Samuel French, the bookstore that catered to Hollywood historians and those determined to make Hollywood history, I saw out of the corner of my eye a gaunt figure shambling by.

"Here," I said, impulsively handing Slim the candy, and while he accepted it as easily as a runner taking a relay baton, he made no eye contact, said nothing.

At the cosmopolitan newsstand on Las Palmas, I passed a guy in a Tyrolean hat who was reading *Der Spiegel* and was standing in front of the newspaper section, when I was tapped on the shoulder. I assumed it was by the beefy cashier who permitted browsing, but on a limited basis, subject to his stopwatch.

"Hey Mayhem!"

"Hey to you," said the scrawny guy with the purple mohawk. "What's got you so hypnotized?"

"Oh, I'm trying to figure out what paper has the best rental listings. I think I'm going to have to leave Peyton Hall."

"Bummer. I'd say you could move in with me, but right now I'm crashing in my sister's den, which doesn't thrill my brother-in-law—a total douche, by the way—I mean, the guy's favorite band is White Snake!"

"Help you with anything?" asked the cashier, folding his big hairy arms across his chest.

Mayhem's voice was as sweet as the cashier's was not. "No thanks, but I appreciate the offer."

He angled his arm and I took the crook of it, and under the squinty-eyed observation of the cashier we walked like dignitaries along the length of the newsstand.

"Can you believe that a-hole thought I was a shoplifter?" asked Mayhem after we'd turned the corner back onto the Boulevard.

"I don't know that he thought that."

"Well, he should have!" With a gleeful cackle, he pulled the latest issue of *Crawdaddy* from under his loose coat.

"Geez, Mayhem."

"What? There's an article I really need to read."

"You're lucky you weren't caught because—" I didn't expand on what punishment the cashier might have meted out, distracted as I was by the sound and fury of a battling couple charging up the street.

Following my gaze, Mayhem asked, "Who's that?"

"My landlord. And his wife."

I couldn't quite decipher what the pair was saying to one another, but it was obvious from their flailing arms and dark faces that they weren't discussing where to go for tea. Jaz grabbed his wife's arm, and it was when she shook it away that their conversation became audible.

"Bastard!" said Aislin. "Get your fucking hands off me!"

"You don't tell me when to take my fucking hands off you!"

"Let's cross the street," I suggested, too late.

"Hey!" said Jaz, stumbling toward us. "Hey, look who's here, our little subletter! En garde!" He lurched forward in a clumsy thrust, like Robin Hood after one too many flagons of mead.

"En garde," I said with a weak wave of my hand. "Hi, Aislin."

"I say," said Jaz, lifting his sunglasses off his face to give Mayhem an exaggerated once-over. "Is this little piece of shit bothering you?"

"Jaz!" said Aislin. "For Christ's sake!"

"No, I'm not bothering her," said Mayhem, and mimicking Jaz, he lifted invisible sunglasses off his face. "But, I say, I'd be happy to bother *you*."

"I'll bet you would, you little punk," said Jaz, but as he staggered toward Mayhem, Aislin grabbed his arm, forcing him to take two clumsy steps backward.

"Oh, never mind." Realizing he was in no condition to strike a blow, let alone land one, Jaz clasped his hands to his chest. "I apologize. I apologize for my boorish behavior. That better, Aislin?"

His lovely Irish wife, who reeked as much of alcohol as Jaz did, said nothing with her mouth, but her eyes were telegraphing all sorts of profanity.

"So let me make it up to you," said Jaz, with a deep nod of his head. "Be our guests this evening. Come and join us."

"Jaz," said Aislin, "let's go."

"Yes, let's go," said Jaz. "Let's all go."

"Go where?" asked Mayhem amicably.

Seeking better balance, Jaz replanted his feet in a wider stance.

"I am inviting the two of you to join us at an exclusive club, a club at whose doors many clamor—"

"For Christ's sake, Jaz!" said Aislin, pulling at his arm.

"Please tell me you're not Scientologists," said Mayhem.

There were often recruiters in front of the Scientology building on the Boulevard, asking passersby if they'd like to take a free personality test. Not especially thinking my personality needed testing (or grading), I'd always ignored them.

Jaz laughed. "Hardly. Plato's is much more exclusive and a lot more fun."

"Are you talking about Plato's Retreat?" asked Mayhem.

"Right-o, bright boy."

"Jasper, come on!" said Aislin. She yanked his arm with a socket-separating force and hauled him away like an irate schoolmarm. Half-turning as he stumbled alongside her, Jaz gave a jerky wave, and Mayhem and I watched as they reeled down the Boulevard.

"Holy shit, Plato's Retreat!"

"What's Plato's Retreat?" I asked.

"Are you kidding me? It's a sex club! A place for swingers."

I stared at him, and the expression on my face must have matched the shock I felt because Mayhem tipped back his serrated-hair head and laughed.

"Look at me," I said quietly. "Consorting with shoplifters and swingers."

"Well, Candy," said Mayhem, taking my arm. "You're not in Milwaukee anymore."

"Uh . . . Minneapolis."

I SPENT THE MORNING of Charlotte's arrival doing housework, and after making the bed I folded my clothes into a pile and set them on top of the bed. I had taken all my stuff out of the closet and the dresser and now had no idea where to put it. Would Charlotte let me stay on her couch—at least for the night? But then what? Another night? And after that?

My anxiousness was aided and abetted by the coffee I glugged down, and when the phone jangled, I practically yelped.

"Ciao, Candy!" came my cousin's voice.

"Hi, Charlotte," I said, without the exclamation points. "You know, it would have been nice if you told me in advance when you were coming in because now it's going to take me awhile to get there—what airline are you on, by the way? My friend Ed says it takes about forty-five—"

Charlotte's laugh interrupted my scold.

"Candy, I'm not in L.A., I'm in New York!"

"Huh?"

She laughed again.

"It's so wild! We were all set to come back, but then on our last day of work, Cray got a ship-to-shore phone call from his agent! Telling him he had a big audition for *Bellwether*—you know that show about the crime-solving English butler? Anyway, they've written in a part for the new Scottish constable and Cray auditioned for it two days ago. And guess what, Candy? He got it!"

"Well, that's great—"

"—and I met his agent and he's agreed to represent me, too! He says I'm perfect for commercials! Isn't that fantastic?"

"Wow. Yeah. Congratulations." I took a deep inhale; it seemed I'd been holding my breath. "Does that mean you won't be moving back here?"

Charlotte laughed again; honestly, it was as if the girl were being tickled.

"Not for a while. Who knows—maybe not ever, if things work out. I mean, I might as well give Broadway a shot while I'm here, so if you don't mind keeping up the sublet for a while–"

"—no, no, I don't mind, but what about your—"

"—great! And we'll figure out what to do with the car—anyway, ciao!"

I kissed this bearer of most excellent news before setting the receiver in its cradle and racing through each room—my rooms!—in a happy hoppy dance.

Charlotte wasn't coming back! She was going to stay in New York where her boyfriend with the weird name got hired on one of the crappier TV shows dumbing up the airwaves! I was staying at Peyton Hall!

26

Dear Cal,

Progress has been made! My second time on stage (at Pickles, a deli in Glendale with an open mike) and I didn't bomb! I didn't kill either—but still: I DIDN'T BOMB. Only Ed was able to come, and he proved an astute audience member, telling me I raced through my lines (good to know; I'll slow down) and that sometimes I sounded apologetic rather than really believing in what I said. (Same thing that Mike guy said.) So I'll take the criticism and use it to get more of what I got tonight: laughs!

WHILE THE FIRST FRIEND I had made in Hollywood was always generous with his advice and counsel, he had offered surprisingly little about his personal life of late. When he told me about Sharla West calling to invite him to a screening the night after they met in Taryn's hot tub, his voice had been tinged with the awe one might expect from a novitiate meeting the pope or a tourist describing his first visit to the Grand Canyon—at sunset—but further updates lacked the details I was dying to hear.

"Has Ed told you anything about his weekend in Catalina?" hollered Maeve.

"Only that he and Sharla were going there," I hollered back.

"You should hear what she told Mother."

Thwack.

"Do tell."

Splat.

"According to Sharla, they barely left their hotel room."

Thwack.

"No," I said.

Splat.

"She's definitely the pursuer here," said Maeve. "I mean, she's the one who first asked him out."

Thwack.

"I know. Ed was giddy over that."

Whoosh.

"That's it," Maeve said as I failed to return the ball. "I win."

It was late afternoon and we had tromped up to the Hills, a piece of wilderness one block north of our complex. Once an estate, the house had burned down to its foundation and on its vast and overgrown grounds was a cracked and weedy court on which Maeve and I were playing tennis. Maeve was a graceful and powerful player who smacked balls with such force my impulse was to dodge them rather than attempt returning them. She was out of my league skills-wise, but I was just as competitive and made a rallying effort to give her at least a semblance of a game. The balls I hit had half the velocity of those she sent over the net, but let the record show I almost won a set. We had played in steely, concentrated quiet, but by the end of the game, when Maeve's victory was more than assured, we had relaxed enough to gossip.

After gathering up the balls, she pulled up her T-shirt to mop her face. I was impressed by the volume of her perspiration and told her so.

"Thanks for noticing. But don't think it's because you pushed me too hard. I'm just a sweater, that's all." Sighing, she shook the back of her damp dyed-blonde hair with her fingers.

"Not only do I get to be tall and awkward with a face that favors my professor father more than my movie star mother, but I get to sweat more than other people!"

"Maeve," I said, hearing that familiar warble in her voice, "don't even start. We'd just gotten to the good stuff—Ed and Sharla—remember?"

Her sniff was guttural, but she nodded.

"So what else did your mom say?"

"Well," said Maeve. "She says Sharla can't stop talking about Ed—in the dressing room, on the set, at the commissary—it's all Ed, all the time!"

"And it's our Ed she's talking about?"

"Our one and only."

Maeve put the lid on a can of balls and picked up her racket, and we began walking down a path narrowed by tall grass and weeds.

"I tell you, it gives me encouragement," she said, whacking at a weed with her racket. "I mean, Ed wasn't having much luck dating—and yes, he made a big mistake in not dating me—but now, now he's getting it on with the star of *Summit Hill*!"

"'Getting it on with,'" I said, laughing at the expression.

"And get this," said Maeve, targeting another weed with her racket. "Sharla told my mother Ed's the most sensitive lover she's ever had!"

"No!"

"Those were her words!"

We giggled like two junior high girls whose health teacher has just announced today's class will focus on human reproduction.

"Now, Mother made me take a vow to not tell anyone, so you've got to do the same."

I held up my racket. "On my honor."

We followed the path down the hill and toward Fuller Street, whacking at the snarled weeds like landscape architects on speed.

It wasn't unusual to hear shouts and exclamations coming from the Beat Street offices.

"'Genie Girl' is #2 with a bullet!"

"We've got the Brass Jar on *Midnight Special!*"

"*Rolling Stone* wants Summer Stephenson for a cover feature!"

If I were to shout out announcements pertaining to my particular office milieu—"The copier's working again!" or "I updated the Rolodex!"— I doubt it would be received with the same sense of excitement.

More than once, Ellie Pop, who loved the record industry, asked me if I knew how lucky I was to have the opportunity thousands of people would have killed to have.

"Really?" I had asked the tenth or so time she said this. I was wrestling with packing tape as I boxed up promotional albums to send to a radio station. "Thousands of people would kill to get yelled at when they put someone on hold? Thousands of people would kill to make and then cancel lunch reservations or sign the UPS delivery forms?"

Crossing her arms in front of her suede-vested chest, Ellie Pop smirked. "You know what I mean. To work in the record industry."

"Which for me," I said slowly, as if speaking to someone who didn't share my native tongue, "means listening to people yell at me when I put them on hold, making and canceling lunch reservations, and signing UPS delivery forms."

Still, for a temp job, it had its perks, and as the hours of my last day at Beat Street ticked away, I felt a little sad.

"So what should we see?" said Solange. We had decided to honor the occasion of my upcoming unemployment by seeing a movie, and she was sitting on the futon with the newspaper spread before her, looking through the listings. "*California Suite* or *Superman*?"

"Ahh," I said, "to laugh or to lust, that's the question."

"Isn't it always. Or we could go foreign and see—"

The front door swung open and the small reception area was filled with a flurry of people—Neil, Ellie Pop, two worried-looking men in suits, and in leather and stacked-heeled boots the small and shaggy-haired Danny Day, whose debut album *Daybreak* had just been released.

"I told you," he was saying in a nasally Cockney accent, "I ain't gonna do no interview wif no fuckin' Albert Ray!"

"But he's got the biggest radio program in southern California!" said Ellie Pop. "More people listen to—"

"—I don't care! And what the—" Danny Day made a face as if he had just stepped in dog poop, barefoot—"what the bloody 'ell is that?"

Everyone froze and the twangy cowboy music we'd been listening to seemed to increase in volume.

"Uh, that's Spade Cooley," said Solange, rushing to turn off the stereo.

"Is that what kind of record company I'm wif?" said Danny Day. "A fuckin' record company what's playing fuckin' hillbilly music instead of my record?"

Thrusting a pointer finger at Solange, he said, "Get me somefink to drink!"

Neil's laugh was tinged with discomfort. "Danny, you've met our office manager, Solange, and this of course is Candy—"

"—did I ask for a bloody introduction? All I want is a fuckin' drink! Somefink with whiskey in it!"

The curtain swished open as the tiny tyrant and his followers pushed past my desk and Ellie Pop, sotto voce said, "Never mind, Neil'll take care of him."

I was often called on to dispense coffee and sodas to visitors on the main floor, but Neil worked the bar that was upstairs in his office lair.

The thing was, we'd been playing *Daybreak* a lot in the office; it was a great record that featured hard-driving rock and roll and soulful ballads, several of which I'd find myself randomly humming.

"How can a jerk like that make an album like *Daybreak*?" I said as Solange tucked her cowboy cassette into its case.

"I'd like to give him the benefit of the doubt. You know, he's an insecure artist; he's surrounding himself with the wrong people, etc., etc., but the simple fact may be that he's a jerk."

"Yeah, but really: I get tears in my eyes every time I hear the title track. And 'Next to Me'—that's going to be a classic."

Shaking her head, Solange pulled at one of her perpetually inflamed earlobes.

"Why do you keep wearing those?" I asked, as she winced.

"Because of jerks like Danny Day."

"Huh?"

"Take a look up close," she said, leaning close to me.

I stared for a moment at the round little earrings I had always assumed were studs.

Squinting, I saw that the globes weren't entirely round but had tiny lines and ridges in them. "Why, they're—"

"—black power fists," said Solange. "I don't generally point that out to people—they'd think I was some sort of radical, looking to start a riot."

"That pretty much describes your personality," I said.

She smiled.

"But they do help me," said Solange. "It's like wearing armor that no one can see. They protect me and make me feel stronger—even if they do make my ears itch like crazy."

27

December 20, 1978

Dear Candy,

Our first Christmas apart! I sure miss you, girl—and all the good smells that would be coming out of the kitchen if you were here. Mrs. Clark brought over a fruitcake, but it's not the same thing.

Candy, thank you so much for the Summit Hill photo with all the actors' autographs! I get such a kick telling my friends that you're a friend of Taryn Powers and Sharla West! (Oh kid, did you see last week's episode where Serena Summit announced she wanted to adopt the quadruplets the family maid is carrying, not knowing the father is her own son?! Where do they come up with this stuff?)

Say, Pug Amundsen down the block got a snowblower and he's so tickled with it that he's offered to do my whole walk and driveway after every snowfall! So don't feel guilty about not being here to shovel me out!

All for now,

Merry Christmas from your loving
Grandma

P.S. Don't spend your Christmas check all in one place!

I HAD BEEN INVITED by Solange and Maeve to join them in Fresno and Beverly Hills, respectively, and while I would have happily sat at the large dining room table of Solange's extended family, sampling her grandmother's famous deep-fried turkey and her Aunt Onie's cornbread stuffing, or enjoying Taryn's catered dinner before retiring to the media room to watch her guest appearance on a holiday special, I nevertheless had to decline, having already RSVP'd "oui" to the Flovers.

"We don't have a real plan or anything," said Frank. "I mean, we've never been really good at Christmas, but we'd like to spend it with you. I mean, if you're available. If you're not, that's cool. Because I don't—"

"I'd love to," I said, cutting off what sounded like the beginnings of an apology.

It gave me pleasure to share my baked goods with my Peyton Hall friends (my select group had gotten a windfall of four kinds of Christmas cookies, prompting Melvin to propose marriage to me), and occasionally I popped over to Francis's with home-cooked dinners; it gave me an excuse to get in the kitchen and fool around with a few more ingredients than the sacred five (sugar, flour, eggs, butter, and vanilla). He and Frank were grateful almost to the point of embarrassment.

"Hey, guys, it's just meatloaf," I'd say in response to their oohs and ahhs.

Once I brought over a pot roast dinner and popovers, inspiring Francis to say, "This would have been featured on the Chef's Best menu at the Bel Mondo."

It wasn't satisfaction borne out of self-righteousness I felt when making these meal deliveries; I enjoyed the cooking as much as they enjoyed the eating. And I liked being around a father who so easily loved his kid, and vice versa. It was all so new to me.

"I've got my cousin's Maverick," I said, while throwing around ideas as to how to spend the holiday. "We could go somewhere."

"Good idea," said Frank. "Let's drive up to Seattle. I've always wanted to see Seattle."

"Frank, Seattle's nearly a thousand miles away," said Francis.

I nodded. "I was thinking more of a day trip."

"How about the beach?" Francis asked. "Let's pack a picnic basket and sing Christmas carols on the beach!"

Frank shrugged at me. "Pop forgets he's Jewish."

"So's Irving Berlin!" said Francis. "So's Sammy Cahn and Mel Tormé! So we'll sing from their canon—'White Christmas' and 'Silver Bells' and 'The Christmas Song!'"

THE BULLYING WIND BLOWING at Will Rogers State Park yanked at our blanket and we laughed wrestling with it, jubilant when we finally pinned the blanket to the sand, winning the match.

"How come everything else is blowing around but your mohawk?" I asked Frank, and it was true, his blue spikes remained upright and unbending in the gusty air.

"Extra glue," he said.

The picnic basket was stocked with roasted potatoes and chicken, a cranberry-orange relish, garlic green beans, and something that flummoxed my fellow picnickers.

"What is it?" asked Francis, as I held out a container piled with pale speckled cylinders.

"Lefse," I said. "Sort of like a Norwegian tortilla, except it's made from riced potatoes. They're rolled up with butter and brown sugar inside."

Sampling one, Francis judged the pliant wrap to be, "Tasty. Odd . . . but tasty."

"My Aunt Pauline sent me a batch. She makes it every year."

Frank was enjoying a second helping when he said, "Hey, look."

We followed his nod to see a woman in a long skirt standing at the water's edge.

"Isn't that what's-her-name?" he asked, his cheek bulging.

Having no idea who what's-her-name might be, I directed my squinted gaze at the figure who kicked her feet slowly through the froth of ebbing waves.

"Yes, it's Aislin," I said. "Jaz's wife."

A sharp shrill whistle cut through the wind like a knife, and I looked to see the elder Flover with two fingers in his mouth.

The figure on the beach turned and, holding one hand above her eyes, looked in our direction and when it appeared she recognized us, waved.

Francis scooped air with his hand in a "Come here!" gesture, and, nodding, Aislan jogged toward us.

She looked lovely, blooms of color spreading across her cheeks, her blue eyes bright.

"A Christmas picnic on the beach!" she said, collapsing easily on the blanket, tucking her legs under her skirt. "How lovely!"

Her tone validated what we were doing; yes, a Christmas picnic on the beach was lovely.

"Eat," I said, filling a plate and handing it to her.

And she did, with a rapaciousness that rendered the Flovers and me semi-mute, speaking only to offer, "Have more cranberries," or "Would you like more lefse?'"

She signaled that she was done by swiping the paper napkin roughly over her mouth and using it to squelch a burp.

"A thousand apologies," she said, flushing. "But it was so good!"

"I'm glad you could join us," I said. "I'm just . . . surprised to see you here. Is everything . . . okay?"

The last time I'd seen Aislin was on the Boulevard with Jaz, when she'd been obviously drunk and obviously unhappy.

"Everything's fine. I, uh . . . well, the thing of it is, Jaz is in Vancouver—he got a guest spot on *Wiley's Way*—it's this Canadian adventure series and I . . . I just didn't feel like tagging along. And I really couldn't afford airfare to Ireland, so I thought I'd come here . . . because it reminds me of home."

"What part of Ireland are you from, lass?" said Francis and while I would have rolled my eyes at anyone else saying this, out of Francis's mouth it sounded natural, respectful, fatherly.

"Ennis. Do you know it?"

Francis shook his head. "No, but I was hoping against hope you'd say Tipperary just so I could sing that you were a long way from there."

"Well, sir, I'm not going to keep you from singing it, if that's your pleasure."

Francis did not have to be cajoled and he rose to his feet.

"It's a long way to Tipperary," he sang, "it's a long way to go, it's a long way to Tipperary, to the sweetest girl I know."

He captivated his audience of three, who sat on the beach blanket, not wanting to miss a word of the voice the wind thinned. When he sang the last refrain and held his arms out in an Al Jolson How'd-you-like-that? pose, Aislin said, "Do you know the wartime version?"

"Yes. Do you?"

"My da would sing it to my mother as they danced around the kitchen."

Francis offered Aislin his hand and after she took it they began dancing in the sand as they sang,

That's the wrong way to tickle Mary,
That's the wrong way to kiss.
Don't you know that over here, lad,

They like it best like this!
Hooray pour le Français,
Farewell, Angleterre,
We didn't know the way to tickle Mary
But we learned how, over there!

Like kids watching Saturday morning cartoons, Frank and I sat slack-jawed, but breaking out of his trance Frank took my hand, and we joined Francis and Aislin in a clunky sort of two-step in the sand. We all sang the revised refrain several more times, and using the wide beach as our dance floor, stepped and dipped and twirled until we were at the shoreline.

The wind flapped at the legs of Frank's and my shorts, at Francis's pant legs and Aislin's skirt, and as we stood there in a line, the cold water tumbling over our feet, I realized we were all holding hands like kids, looking out at a horizon edged in the glitter of sunlight.

"Perfect time to bring Mr. Cahn into the picture," said Francis and he led us in singing "Silver Bells," and if I had to pick what registered highest on the Thrill-O-Meter that day, it would be hearing the punk rocker Frank, whose onstage voice was mostly snarls and screams but who now sang a tentative but sweet harmony to our Christmas song.

It was dark but not that late when I pulled Charlotte's Maverick into its garage stall, and while I would have been happy to continue the festivities, the Flovers decided to call it a night, Frank citing his father's need to get some rest.

"It is true," said Francis with a wan smile. "In the old days I could dance on the beach and then on a few nightclub tabletops, but the old days are just that."

As I climbed the steps to my building, they stood sentry on the sidewalk, offering their thanks again and wishes for both a good night and a Merry Christmas.

I had shaken the sand out of my clothes, showered, and in the big maroon Minnesota Gophers jersey that served as my pajamas/lounge wear, I squatted in front of the TV, spinning the dial, hoping I hadn't missed Taryn Powell's guest appearance on the *Dill Williams Holiday Special*. Pay dirt. There she was, standing on a corner and outfitted as a sexy, miniskirted reindeer.

"Hey, Big Boy," she said to the wizened comic dressed as Santa, "got anything in that big sack for me?" Her red nose lit up and Dill Williams wiggled his fake white eyebrows, and the two of them launched into a hokey song that offered lyrics like "bag of tricks," and "Santa's gotta get his kicks."

When the doorbell rang, I thought it less an intrusion than a relief.

The peephole did not lend itself to subterfuge; it was a 3"x2" brass door that opened, making it easy to see whoever was standing on the doorstep as well as allowing that person to see inside.

"Hey, Candy," said Melvin Slyke. "Can I come in?"

ON THE TV, to the cop who had appeared on the scene, Santa was singing that he didn't realize he was in a red-light district, blaming his reindeer Rudolph for guiding his sleigh there.

"Oh, Dill Williams," said Melvin, sitting down on the plaid couch. "Good God, is that old geezer still alive? He's older than I am! Here's the ultimate broadcasting riddle: what came first, Dill Williams's holiday specials or the invention of television?"

I laughed and Melvin's gray dentures clicked as he smiled his appreciation.

"That's Maeve's mother," I said, nodding at the miniskirted reindeer being cuffed by the cop.

"Ah yes, the inestimable Taryn Powell. She did a voice-over for a commercial I worked on back in the '60s. 'Queen Crisp,' remember her?"

"Of course I remember Queen Crisp, but I didn't know Taryn did her voice!" In an approximation of the animated sovereign, I cackled, "I order you knaves to eat these most delicious potato chips!"

"Not bad," said Melvin. He looked again at the television, and together we watched as all the guest stars gathered around Dill to wish the viewing audience the "happiest of happiest."

I turned off the television as the credits rolled.

"Can I get you anything, Melvin? I've still got some Christmas cookies left."

"Nah, my daughter fed me well. Not necessarily deliciously, but well." He patted his belly with a spotted hand. "No, what I came here for was, well, Francis had told me he was spending the day with you, and I just wanted to know if everything went all right?"

"Everything went great. He was a little tired when we got home, but I think he had, we all had—" I remembered Aislin's words—"a lovely time."

"Good," said Melvin. "I would have taken him to my daughter's house, but that wouldn't have pleased either Francis or Nancy, so thanks for taking care of him."

"I really didn't take care of him. I enjoy his company and vice versa, I hope."

"Oh, vice versa for sure." Melvin's hands made a raspy noise as he ran them over the knees of his pilly polyester pants. "He thinks you're just about the cat's meow. He told me the last home-cooked meals he had before yours were back in the '50s, when he was still married to Rayna."

"Rayna. Is that Frank's mother?"

Melvin nodded, his face like a doctor's affirming a bad diagnosis.

"It's weird, I've never heard Francis or Frank talk about her."

"That's because she was a big reason, no, *the* reason for all of Francis's troubles. The tax stuff—piffle—compared to what she did!"

He stared at the blank television screen for so long I began to worry that he was having a ministroke or something.

"Melvin?"

"Francis was very forward-thinking," he said, his gaze still on the TV. "When he opened the club in the late '40s, he brought in a woman as his business partner! Gladys had handled his studio when he was a dance instructor back in New York." Finally he turned to me. "I'll bet you didn't know Francis was quite a hoofer, did you?"

I nodded. "He tap-danced for me once."

Melvin had already begun to talk over me.

"The two of them made a great business team, plus they enjoyed each other's company. Gladys and her husband, Phil, got along swell with Francis and Rayna. They were so close they even named each other godparents for their kids.

"Anyway, I'll make this short—"

This had to be a first.

"—because if I talk too much about it, my blood starts to boil." Melvin's mouth scrunched up and he stretched his fingers before balling his hands up in a fist. This he did several times, as if it were a calming exercise.

"The thing of it is, one evening Frank's looking for Rayna—she came to the club all the time for dinner or to see a show—and he finds her shtupping Phil in Gladys's office!"

"Francis caught his wife shtupping the husband of his business partner?"

"*Finally* caught them. It came out that Rayna and Phil had been carrying on for over a year. Both couples divorced and then Rayna the bitch—excuse me—and Phil the bastard got married, but not before Francis attacked Phil and sent him to the hospital for nearly a week. Beat him up pretty bad."

"Oh . . . my," I said, borrowing my grandmother's response to monumental news.

"My wife—God rest her soul—and I used to go to the Bel Mondo all the time. That's where Francis and I met, and to watch that man go through all he did . . . well, it was just terrible. The scandal, the shame. It was only because he had a hell of a lawyer that he avoided a jail sentence. Then Rayna takes little Frank with her when she and Phil the bum move back east, and poor Gladys wants nothing more to do with the club—the scene of all the love crimes, you see—so Francis buys her out, losing first his family, then his partner. A couple years later, Vegas is taking away so much business and on top of that Francis isn't paying his taxes—really, I think he just didn't care anymore—and he loses the club. He went from a man who was king of a real Hollywood kingdom to . . . to what Queen Crisp called everyone—a knave."

Melvin fondled his whiskery chin with a liver-spotted hand. "Everybody wanted to be Francis Flover's friend when he ran the Bel Mondo, and nobody wanted to acknowledge his existence after all the trouble. Robert X. Roberts, for example." Acrimony darkened his voice. "When his own career wasn't exactly going gangbusters, he was a regular at the Bel Mondo, and never said no to a free drink or a ringside table, but afterwards, he wouldn't give Francis the time of day. Francis won't even go to the pool because he's afraid of running into that bastard!" Melvin shook his head. "Sure, some people with consciences have thrown him work over the years—mostly script reading, although Janus Weinberg—hell of a guy—had him on his studio's payroll for years; had him coaching the dancers on *The Jackie Kenner Show*. He just barely hangs on, though, and well, you can see why I worry about him."

I felt as if I had been slugged with information. "I'm glad he has you to worry about him."

"Ha! Tell that to Nancy! She thinks her poor old dad's being taken advantage of by a devious schemer!" Melvin's cheeks rounded before he expelled a long sigh. "Pardon the soliloquy, Candy. I just wanted you to know." Clamping his hands on the knees of his houndstooth pants, he braced himself to stand up.

"I'm glad you had a good time. I'm glad you helped Francis have a good time."

As I opened the door for him, Melvin proffered a scratchy little kiss on my cheek.

"Hope that doesn't get you all riled up," he said with a wiggle of his eyebrows, and he shuffled across the short landing to his apartment.

28

"CHARLOTTE!" I said, opening the door to the tall blonde. "What are you doing here?"

"Just making sure you haven't pawned all my stuff," she said, strolling into the apartment.

"The pawn store wouldn't take it," I said, slipping as easily as she had into our push-pull relationship. "But, really, what are you doing here?" My voice was light, even as I seemed to have broken out in a sweat.

She twirled once before flopping on the plaid couch. "I forgot how sunny this room gets. Do you have anything to drink? Pop, iced tea? Anything cold?"

Like a compliant servant, I ran hunched and splay-footed to the kitchen, and to Charlotte's credit she did laugh, but when I returned to the living room and threw a plate against the wall she yelped.

"Candy, what the hell?"

Handing her the glass of lemonade I held in my other hand, I apologized. "I just wanted to show you the dishes I won on *Word Wise*. They're unbreakable." I picked up the plate and handed it to her. "Here, you try."

Looking at me like I was crazy, she nevertheless took the plate and Frisbeed it against the wall. It clunked to the floor, all in one piece.

"How much money did you win on that game show, anyway?" asked Charlotte and when I told her, she nodded. "I made twice that on the cruise ship."

Taking a long sip that emptied the glass of half its lemonade, she wiped her mouth and said, "Ahh. Okay, so here's the story, Glory: Cray and I are here on business for a couple days."

"Are you going to stay here?"

When she said no, I could have done a cartwheel. And a back flip.

"They put us up at the Beverly-Wilshire! We've been here since Thursday and we're leaving tomorrow. We're driving my car back, too—that is, if you haven't totaled it."

"Car's untotaled."

"Cray's meeting with some big shots from the network, so I had him drop me off on his way to the studio. I thought it'd be fun if we got a head start on New Year's Eve. Ever been to the Toy Tiger?"

"CHARLOTTE FIELDS," said Billy Gray Green, leaning over the bar. "You just made the end of the year better and the prospects for the new one dy-no-mite."

"Oh, Mr. Gray Green, how you do go on," drawled my cousin, batting her eyes. "Now what's the recommended drink to get this party started?"

"Ever had Sex on the Beach?"

"Every time I'm in Malibu," said Charlotte.

Not being the focus of anyone's attention, my eyeballs took a tour around their sockets.

"So how's New York treating you?" asked Billy, setting before us drinks that were not sand colored, as the name would imply, but a gaudy orange.

"New York's treating me fabulously," said Charlotte. "I've got a theatrical and a commercial agent. I've already been on tons of auditions; in fact, I've got a reading for a soap the day after I get back. For the part of Suzanna Jade, Eden Valley's newest temptress."

Charlotte tossed her hair and struck a pose.

"You're hired!" said Billy Gray Green.

"Hey, bartender!" A man in a party hat waved his empty glass and bleated a paper horn.

While Billy Gray Green attended to the guy who was probably not going to see in the New Year in any state of consciousness, Charlotte suddenly shot up, as if a joy buzzer had been activated on her bar stool.

"Cray!" she said, waving her arm wildly. "Cray, over here!"

The man approaching the bar looked as if he were out of another time and place—at least his face did, much of it obscured as it was by big muttonchops and a handlebar mustache.

"Ciao, bella!" he said, opening his arms to catch Charlotte as she tumbled into them.

"Ciao innamorato!" answered my cousin.

Gee, I thought, *I wonder if anyone's been to Italy lately.*

Their kiss was long and sloppy, and I swiveled on the barstool until Charlotte finally came up for air and shoved her make-out partner toward me. "This is Cray, Candy! Isn't his mustache cute? He's growing it for *Bellwether*. He films his first episode next week! Do your Scottish accent, Cray!"

"Ach, the infamous Candy." Taking my hand, he laid his whiskery lips on it. "The one who wrecked Charlotte's first dance recital."

"Oh brother," I said to my cousin. "You're still telling that old story?"

As five-year-olds, we had both been enrolled in Miss Mila's Tippy Toes dance class and that I had been the inadvertent star of the recital by milking my mistakes was an unforgivable offense to Charlotte.

"It might be an old story," said my cousin, flicking aside a hank of her long blonde hair, "but it doesn't mean it's not important."

As the bar's population swelled along with the sound decibel, we thanked Billy Gray Green for our on-the-house drinks and waded through the crowd, pushing through the doors into the cool night air.

"Where should we go first?" asked Charlotte as they discussed their party options, of which there were many.

"And we've got to go to Blake's," said Cray. "There'll be a ton of industry people there."

"Blake created the show *Dustin Drake, DDS*," said Charlotte. "Ever seen it? It's a riot."

"Yes, but—"

"—to Blake's then!" said Cray, bending his knees and motioning for Charlotte to get on his back.

"Hi Ho Silver!" said Charlotte, climbing on.

I followed the piggy-backers as they crossed the plaza and toward a town car parked curbside like a big black cat.

"Compliments of the *Bellwether* people," said Cray in his serviceable brogue as a chauffeur opened the passenger door.

The couple groped each other as they got into the car while the chauffeur stood at attention, a Mona Lisa smile on his face.

"Candy," said Charlotte, leaning over Cray to talk to me through the open door. "Are you coming or not?"

It took me less than a second to say, "Not." I gave a little wave. "Thanks, anyway. Happy New Year!"

I watched their car merge into traffic, relieved that I wasn't in it.

During a lull in their bar groping, Charlotte had taken enough interest in me to turn away from Cray and say, "Grandma tells me you're temping at some record store."

"Record company. But the job ended." I felt no need to fill her in on what else I was up to because the interest wasn't there, and more so, I had learned to protect what was precious from the sharp claws of my cousin.

It might have been a smart career move to go with them and mingle elbow-to-elbow with people instrumental in making sitcoms about dissolute dentists, but I didn't feel ready to introduce myself as a comic and didn't want to explain what I did for a living—"I'm a temp!" (a guaranteed conversation stopper at a Hollywood party). And there'd be all those smiles I'd have to fake as Charlotte introduced me to some assistant director or screenwriter who'd look back and forth at the two of us before saying, "You're cousins? Really?"

I thought about going into Limelight Liquors to say hello to the depressive Ukrainian chess pro who worked the cash register, but there was a line of revelers inside and so I crossed the street, heading toward my apartment. I had nearly passed the first rectangular blocks of shrubbery that flanked the staircases leading to each Peyton Hall four-plex when someone said, "Happy New Year, Sandy."

The voice was suave and accented, and I looked up to see Jaz, the building manager, sitting on a chair next to the potted plant on his small landing.

"Candy."

"Sandy, Mandy, Candy . . . what's in a name? That which we call a rose / By any other name would smell as sweet."

I nodded. "Well, Happy New Year to you, too . . . Spaz."

The building manager held up a bottle of champagne. "Touché. And for that, you must share a quick glass of bubbly with me." With his other hand, he crisscrossed and jabbed the air, unable to greet me, it seemed, without some imaginary swordplay. "Or perhaps you'd like to go a few rounds first?"

His pronunciation was extra crisp, as if he were trying very hard not to slur his words, and although I would have rather kept walking, I climbed the steps, feeling charitable because of the holiday.

"I'll pass on the duel, but I'll take the champagne." I nodded toward a row of stacked plastic glasses next to his chair. "You're expecting company?"

"On New Year's Eve, one should be prepared," he said, twisting the top glass off the stack and filling it with champagne. "Here you go."

"So where's Aislin?" I asked, taking a sip.

To my great surprise, he did not offer a casual, "In the loo," or "Watching Guy Lombardo." Instead, he set down his glass and, stretching his mouth as if trying to stifle a yawn, he slumped forward in his chair, buried his face in his hands, and began to cry.

As he sniffled and snortled, I stood frozen even as I wanted to flee.

After a long awkward moment, he lifted his head, and drying his tears with a drag of his fingers, he said, "She's gone, you know."

"What do you mean? I just saw her on Christmas."

He nodded. "She told me on the telephone all about your little beachside picnic. She sounded so happy, but when I got back from Vancouver on Thursday, she was . . . gone."

"Gone?" I was suddenly scared for Aislin. "Are you sure she's not just taking a trip or something?"

Jaz swiped at his nose with the back of his hand. "She left me a note. Well, actually a Christmas card. Left it propped on the kitchen table, against the little cactus plant we got in Joshua Tree. It read"—he looked up like a child about to recite his lessons—"'This will be a Merry Christmas for me as I've finally decided to give myself the gift of leaving you. Don't bother looking for me because even if you find me, I'm never coming back.'"

His Technicolor blue eyes widened as if registering what he'd just reported.

"Where," I asked, taking a step forward then rocking back, "where do you suppose she went?"

Jaz shook his head and exhaled a sigh that was close to a moan.

"Most of her family's still in Ireland, but she's got a sister in Boston. Maybe there." He finished the remaining champagne in his glass and looked at me for a long moment. "Why are you standing like that?"

"Like what?"

"Crouched over. Like you're about to run a race."

"Maybe I am."

Jaz's smile was weary. "Don't worry, the invitation to Plato's has been revoked."

"Please. Don't make me gag."

A question that had nagged at me popped out of my mouth before I could consider the wisdom in asking it. "Did you ever hit Aislin? Is that why she left?"

Color faded on Jaz's face.

"Because the first time I ever met her, she had a big bruise on the side of her face. She tried to hide it behind the door."

We stared at one another. I was breathing fast, as if I'd just sprinted up and down the stairs instead of merely spoken a few sentences.

Breaking the stare, Jaz looked at his glass.

"I never hit her," he said, his voice low. "But I did throw a cream pitcher at her. After she threw a sugar bowl at me. I know that's no excuse—I could throw a lot harder than she could—" His words were choked by a sob, and he leaned forward, as if he were trying to expel it. His plastic champagne glass fell to the cement with a little bounce. "God, I never meant to do that!"

His fingers made a cage over his face and he cried behind them. "I never, ever meant to do that!"

I stood there, to use an expression of my grandmother's, like a dumb cluck. Several New Years seemed to pass before I laid my hand on his shuddering shoulder and patted it.

Finally he lifted his tear-streaked face, laughing a little by way of apology.

"My movie is supposed to start production in March. Did I tell you I'll be playing Errol Flynn?"

"Only every time I drop off the rent."

"Aislin was so excited when I got that part."

Five minutes with the guy and my emotions vacillated from amusement, pity, disgust, and now pity again, but a softer kind.

"She said something nice about you at that picnic," I said.

"She did?" He swiped a finger under his right eye. "What was that?"

"Well, we were sharing little Christmas memories, and she said that the two of you had spent your first Christmas together in Madrid."

"Yes, yes, I was in a touring company of *Guys and Dolls*." Jaz smiled at the memory, and I saw how truly handsome he was when he wasn't trying so hard to make sure I noticed.

"She said you played Sky Masterson and that when you sang, 'Luck Be a Lady Tonight,' all the young señoritas swooned."

"She said that?"

I nodded.

"That was nice of you to tell me that. Thank you." His mouth bunched up and he stared at his hands for a moment. "And who knows, if she said that . . . maybe she will come back."

"Maybe she will. Happy New Year, Jaz."

The building manager picked his glass off the stoop and after refilling it held it up in a toast. "Happy New Year, Candy."

THE SONG "YOU LIGHT UP MY LIFE" streamed from the radio of a passing convertible, and from the stereo of an apartment across the street Mick Jagger sang that Lord, he missed me, and as I walked to my apartment, I repeated my secret power mantra like a chorus. I considered how its message applied to the events of the day, the year about to close, and no doubt would apply to the year about to begin. Maybe that would be my resolution: to be a devoted yogi with a serious practice of brandishing my life saber.

Another resolution: I would ring in the New Year by baking a cake. When I got back to my apartment, I started humming as I got out the flour and eggs. A yellow cake with my famous fudge frosting.

29

IT HAD BEEN MY INTENTION to start out 1979 by greeting the dawn with an early-morning swim, but on the way to the pool I came across Madame Pepper taking out her garbage.

Startled, we both gasped, and after we caught our breaths she whispered, "What are you doing up so early?" just as I asked, "What are you doing?"

I gave my explanation and she held up a plastic garbage bag.

"I always empty the trash on January first. It's good for the soul—and for the apartment."

"But you didn't feel a need," I said, gesturing at her copper-colored beaded gown, "to take off your party dress from last night?"

"This I just put on," said Madame Pepper, holding out her shawl like batwings to better expose her dress. "For the second part of ritual."

"Which is?" I asked, following her to the garbage bins.

After she'd tossed in the knotted plastic bag, she brushed off her hands and smiled, like someone about to reveal a secret and wanting to enjoy it by herself for just a moment more.

"Why don't you join me?"

"Join you for what?"

Impatience scuttled across her heavy features. "For second part of ritual."

"Okay," I said, intrigued. "I'll just get some clothes on and I'll meet—"

"—I am thinking it's perfect the way you are."

I was barefoot and wearing an old terry robe over my swimsuit, but the old woman's expression taunted, *I dare you,* and never good at turning down dares, I said, "All right. Let's go."

We stole quietly through the grounds of Peyton Hall and to the sidewalk and didn't speak until we were nearly at the La Brea intersection.

"Wow," I said, looking down the expanse of Hollywood Boulevard. "There's nobody here."

"Precisely," said Madame Pepper. "It is the first day of New Year and we have one of the most famous streets in the world all to ourselves."

She took my arm. "Since 1942, Candy, every January first, I have walked down to Vine and back as the sun comes up. And always in fancy clothes, as the ritual demands."

"And you do this because—"

"—because I am able! Because it reminds me, that worldwide symbol of mystery and allure and dreams—is right here!" She flung her free arm east. "And here it is that I make my resolution to accept mystery and allure and dreams for another year!"

"Why, you old Hollywood romantic," I said, giving her a little nudge with my hip.

"When there's nothing else to believe in, why not choose romance?"

This was not the blithe response I was expecting.

"What's that supposed to mean?"

The old woman's fingers tightened around my bicep.

"Candy, how do you think I got here?"

"Here to Hollywood?" I asked, and when she nodded I said, "By plane? No, wait; they hadn't been invented yet."

"Ha, so funny. But, you are right, I did not take plane. A boat. In 1933. I was twenty-two years old."

I did some quick calculations.

"You're younger than my grandma."

"You sound surprised."

"I never thought I'd defend my grandma's leisure suits or the dye jobs she gives herself . . . but they are a little more youthful than shawls and long skirts and head scarves."

Madame Pepper snorted a laugh.

"You remind me so much of my sister, Sophie. She also was smart aleck."

"Is she in America, too?"

"Sophie? Oh, my Sophie's long gone. She died in the war. Not in your mother and father's war. The one before it."

I shivered in the cool morning air, wishing I were wearing more than a swimsuit and robe.

"I'm sorry."

"Me, too," said Madame Pepper. "Ah, Greta Garbo."

We stopped for a moment, looking down at the star of the Swedish actress.

"My friend Polly said she had the prettiest shoulders. They were broad, like yours."

"Tell me more," I said, and covering the hand she had tucked in the crook of my elbow with my own, we walked slowly, the hem of Madame Pepper's long dress dusting the smooth granite of the Walk of Fame.

We walked far enough in silence to convince me she didn't want to honor my request, but then she began speaking, in a dreamy voice so soft that I had to lean in toward her.

"Friedrich Pfeffer was cinematographer, an artist! Most of his work is in silent pictures, but also he filmed *A Star to Hold* and *Gentle Lies,* which can be seen on the late show. But most importantly—to me—he was my husband."

"Pfeffer," I said, "so Pfeffer is—"

"—yes, I anglicized it. You have to make things easy for Americans."

I smiled at the insult.

"We met in summer of 1931. He was older than I by a dozen years and already established in the European cinema. He was part of a German crew filming a movie in my hometown, Bucharest. I was exiting Dancescu's Bakery with my marmalade rolls as he was entering for his tea biscuits, and it was either love at first sight, or lust; either way, it didn't take long before we were sharing a bed." She frowned at me. "This shocks you?"

"Why would it?"

"The young sometimes think that premarital sex is their discovery."

I let my jaw drop. "Is that what you meant, that you were having sex? Because I thought you were just sharing a bed, you know, for sleep!"

The fortune-teller snorted.

"Just like Sophie."

Her quick laugh was replaced by the long sad whisper of a sigh.

"A year after we marry an offer from Hollywood arrived and of course Friedrich takes it. I would have loved Sophie to come with us, but she now had married also, to Josef, a doctor."

She turned again toward me and to a casual observer it might look as if the old woman were looking directly at me, but the storytelling veil had dropped over her eyes, and I knew that in her gaze she wasn't seeing me but the people of whom she spoke.

"With Friedrich's help, I got work in costume department—it's true, in Hollywood, it often is who you know. That is where I first met my friend Polly, although she left MGM for Paramount and Edith Head. I loved the work, loved not just the artistry but being the ear to so many stories. You fit someone, you dress them, you hear their stories!

"My letters to Sophie were like confections, filled with descriptions of this strange world I found myself in, where oranges, grapefruits, and lemons hung like jewels from backyard trees, and where air was perfumed with this jewelry fruit, and also flowers which I had never seen. And how she loved for me to tell her the gossip! I would write of a dinner party where the person across the table, asking to 'Please pass the butter' might be Carole Lombard or William Powell. 'Tell me more!' she would write, and for two years my letters were filled with this glamorous piffle. Then Friedrich died."

I drew in a quick breath of surprise.

"Of stupid accident on the set! They were shooting in sound stage and he falls off the crane! The crane he had been on hundreds of times before!"

"I'm so sorry."

Madame Pepper's nod was slow. "There was much to be sorry about at that time. I was of course devastated and angry, too—how could he fall off crane and make me a widow at twenty-four?—but I am thinking at least this is worst my life will know.

"Time passes; that is its cure and curse. Sophie's letters, usually so bright and filled with news of their baby Anica, or Josef's patients—once a butcher paid his bill with spoiled sausage making Josef joke, 'Was my care that bad?'—grew darker with news of Hitler, and I beg them to come to America. Begged."

Madame Pepper's lush eyebrows lowered as she squinted her eyes, as if the memory was a bad headache.

"Josef's family on his mother's side was Polish, and he and Sophie and little Anica were visiting these relatives in September of '39." We walked at least ten steps before she said, "In Wielun, Poland.

"It was a surprise bombing on the city. By the Germans. The beginnings of the war, and my sister and her family perished in it."

"Spare change?" asked a ragged woman, stepping out from behind a ticket kiosk by Grauman's.

Madame Pepper shook her head, and I stated the obvious, "We didn't bring our purses."

"The Supreme Court justices are all aliens," said the panhandler. "Except for Thurgood Marshall. He's from Baltimore."

"I would have gladly paid for that information," I said and two seconds later I apologized. "When things get too heavy, my reflex is . . . never mind. Please. Go on."

"Yes. That is all I could do: go on." She stared ahead, nodding her head. "All during the war, I was frantic to get my mother, my father, my brother Gavril here, but they wouldn't leave—even in wartime! Bucharest was bombed and they survived, but for my parents it was a survival that finally wore them out. Both died several years later, not able to believe what had become of their world."

We stepped on one, two, a dozen stars, and when she didn't speak again, I said, "I'm so sorry. So sorry for what you had to go through."

"Yes," said Madame Pepper. "But I am not alone in having sadness. You, too, know it."

"I do. We're in the same sad club."

"The Club of Sorrows."

"The club that no one wants to be a member of."

"The club where people get turned away for not having enough pain."

"That's right," I said. "We're exclusive. You've got to know death and devastation to join our club."

Our laughter was of the resigned, Whaddya gonna do? variety.

"Look here," said Madame Pepper, stopping to examine a star. "Vivien Leigh. If I could have a different face—hers I would have. Or Hedy Lamarr's—who could have been her sister."

As we began walking again, Madame Pepper took my hand, and we swung them, like kids.

"So tell me more about your ritual," I said. "What made you want to ring in the New Year by walking the Boulevard? By walking the Boulevard in an evening gown?"

"It is the end of 1941," she said after a moment. "I had been dropped off from a party in Beverly Hills—the fanciest, most festive New Year's Eve party I had ever known. Pearl Harbor had been struck only weeks before and now the war, already such a terrible reality for me with the death of Sophie and her family, was real for Americans. But that party! Everyone—the stars, the producers, the directors, all of Hollywood royalty—danced and ate and drank, and at midnight we clung to each other singing 'Auld Lang Syne,' and, Candy, there were no dry eyes.

"No one, it seemed, wanted that party to end, but finally I was chauffeured home—I had just moved into Peyton Hall—by a director who'd worked with my husband Friedrich. It was nearly dawn when I climbed out of that car, a little *betrunken* from the flow of champagne, but instead of going to my apartment, I decided to take walk down Hollywood Boulevard. Being tipsy did not save me from how I felt—so sad and hopeless, wondering, Who knows? Maybe the bombs come here and this street will be no more. Maybe next year, I, like my husband, like my sister, my niece, my brother-in-law will be no more. So, Candy, the first time I walk it; well, it was more a stagger, and I was not so much the romantic."

"I wish you'd have let me change."

"Why? You are cold?"

"No." My robe was belted tight and the rising sun was doing its job to warm me. "No, I would have liked to dress for the . . . specialness of the occasion."

Madame's smile was sly. "I am thinking walking down Hollywood Boulevard in swimsuit is special enough."

"All right, then." Letting go of her hand, I took off my robe and draped it over my arm, so that I was indeed walking down Hollywood Boulevard in my special-enough swimsuit.

With my shoulders back and head held high, I strutted down the Walk of Fame as if it were my personal runway. Madame Pepper began to issue forth her peculiar little snorts, and the more she laughed the more I turned up the performance, tossing my robe to her so that I could leap and dance around the stars unencumbered. To be jumping around and shimmying on Hollywood Boulevard in my faded old swim-team suit made me feel wildly liberated and wildly addled; I was like a newly defected ballerina from the Bolshoi who'd gotten kicked in the head during a pas de deux.

Across the street, near the closed-up newsstand, a stooped man pushing a shopping cart paused in his collection of cans and bottles to offer a loud, shrill wolf whistle.

Inspired by my newfound fan, I wished Buster Keaton a Happy New Year and did a cartwheel right over his pink, black, and gold star.

Madame Pepper cackled as I greeted the various stars I danced by.

"Happy New Year, Nat King Cole! Happy New Year, John Barrymore! Happy New Year, Licia Albanese, whoever you are!"

We crossed the street and standing on a star, I struck a glamorous, you-may-photograph-me-now pose.

"Happy New Year, Betty Grable!"

"I danced with her at the USO Club," shouted the shopping cart man. "Her and Evelyn Keyes!"

"Happy New Year, Evelyn Keyes!"

A woman folding up the cardboard that had served as her mattress looked up from the recessed corner of a storefront.

"And Virginia Mayo!" she said, her smile revealing only three teeth whose tenancy along her gum line didn't look to be long lasting. "I was her stand-in back in the day. We were the exact same size."

"Happy New Year, Virginia Mayo!"

I could have continued offering up best wishes to all the stars lining the street, but when a police car turned on to the Boulevard from Cahuenga, Madame Pepper handed me my robe.

"Who knows what is considered creating a public nuisance these days," she said.

By eight o'clock that morning, I was in cool, chlorinated water, amusing myself in the pool I had all to myself. I turned backward somersaults, raced against (and always beat) imaginary opponents and walked on my hands in the shallow end. When I pulled myself out of the water, I collapsed onto a chaise longue and, offering myself up to the pale morning sun, dozed off. Seconds, minutes, or hours later, I heard a voice ask, "Why are you smiling?"

"Ed!" I said, opening my eyes. "An nou fericit!"

"On new what?"

"It's Happy New Year in Romanian. Madame Pepper taught it to me."

"Well, Happy New Year in Romanian to you, too." The aluminum legs of the chaise longue scraped as he pulled it close to mine.

I had seen him briefly when I was making Christmas cookie deliveries, but he was no longer a poolside regular, trying to unload his bottles of YaZoo to unsuspecting tenants and reading one of his conspiracy books.

Giving him the once-over, I asked, "Have you lost weight?"

He patted his firmer belly. "I've been doing sit-ups."

"You *are* in love."

"Last night Sharla made me dinner," said Ed, stretching out on the chaise. "She said she'd been invited to a dozen parties—she counted—but she didn't want to share me with anyone on New Year's Eve."

"Wow," I said, and watched Ed's pink skin get pinker.

"I know what you're thinking: will wonders never cease? And the answer is: I sure hope not."

In her funny, tiptoe walk, June entered the pool area, a cigarette clamped in her mouth, her little white dog with its brown tears peeking out of its tote bag.

"Ed, don't take offense at this—"

"—whenever people say that, I know that's exactly what I'm going to take."

"It's just that the two of you seem so different."

"Tell me about it," said Ed, shrugging. "But different can be really good."

"You're right . . . but do you feel—"

"—out of my league? Hell, yes, how could I not? I've been stood up by everyone from a keypunch operator, to a claims adjuster, to a woman I know for a fact had a shoplifting record—and now I'm going out with a real-live Hollywood actress?" He rolled up his towel in a cylinder and propped it behind his neck. "That a guy like me is with someone like Sharla . . . well, go figure."

"She's the lucky one."

"Uh-huh," said Ed unconvincingly.

We both settled back in our chairs, faces lifted to the sun like flowers.

Minutes passed and then Ed said, "So why'd you have such a blissed-out smile on your face, Candy?"

I considered his question for a long moment.

"I'm just really glad to be here."

"I'm glad you're here, too."

"I stayed up late last night baking a cake. I'm going to have a big piece of it for lunch.

"Not your famous yellow cake with fudge frosting?"

"None other."

"I'm not doing anything for lunch," said Ed.

"You are now."

PART II

30

MAEVE PICKED AN ODD PLACE to lecture me on the need to get tough and go on a "comedy regime."

"Like when you were swimming for your high school team, you'd practice every day, right? Do a certain amount of laps, some sprints, try to better your times, apply yourself daily to the goal of doing your best at the next meet."

I could only giggle.

"Really, Candy," said Maeve, examining the padded cups of a red lace bra, "if I called myself a weightlifter but only lifted weights now and then, what kind of weightlifter do you think I'd be?"

Again I giggled.

"The thing is, Candy, if you're going to do something—do it."

The saleswoman smiled at us from across the room, risking a crack in her plastered orange makeup. She had to be at least in her fifties and yet "low" would have been a modest description of the neckline of the skintight sweater that plunged past her sternum, exposing as much of her pushed-up orangey breasts that could be exposed in a public place that wasn't a strip joint.

Another giggle thrummed up my throat; I'd been practically vibrating with them since we'd stepped out of the hurly-burly of Hollywood Boulevard and inside Fredrick's of Hollywood, as quiet and lushly appointed as an off-hours New Orleans bordello.

"You really buy your underwear here?" I'd whispered.

"Not all of it, but some."

"But it's so . . ." I looked around at Barbie doll-shaped mannequins wearing black corsets, push-up bras, satin girdles, and lacy garter belts. "Weird."

"It is not," said Maeve. "It's sexy. And I like to wear sexy, pretty things next to my skin—what's wrong with that?"

"I don't know . . . I guess I never saw the need."

"So you're a white bra and cotton panties girl?"

"Eww, Maeve, don't say *panties*. I hate that word."

A contingent of Japanese tourists pressed through the door, oohing, ahhing, and—yes—giggling as they gaped and pointed at the feathered peignoirs, the negligees with peek-a-boo cut-outs.

It was when Maeve was narrowing down her bra selection that the pep talk began.

"It's like this, Candy: I work out two hours a day. I've got several very specific routines that work different parts of my body. I keep track of my reps. I eat foods that'll help me burn fat and add muscle. I do things on a daily basis that help me achieve the goals I've set. What do you do?"

"You know I've been—"

"Mother's told me that when she was starting out, she'd visit at least one casting and talent agency a day—sometimes the same ones she'd been to the day before—and every night she and her girlfriend Anne would get all dolled up and go to nightclubs to see and be seen by the Hollywood big shots." In the direction of the saleswoman, she waved a hand clutching the red lace bra and a sheer beige one. "I'd like to try these on, please." She turned to me. "And while I do, I want you to seriously think, step by step, what you're going to do to best reach your goals."

I held up a black G-string with ruffles.

"Wear this onstage?"

1/9/79

Dear Cal,

Maeve's right, of course; Madame Pepper's right. I've dipped my toes in the comedy waters, have even plunged in a few times, but haven't stayed in, plugging away, lap after lap after lap. I have failed to be serious about being funny. So here's my schedule that I swear on a stack of comedy albums I'm going to stick to:

Get Up—Swim

Work on act, i.e., Write! Write! Write!

Perform at least three times a week, without fail, and then refine by writing about each performance; what worked, what didn't, what the crowd was like, etc.

And finally: Stop being a baby!

Zelda had a three-week position for me at a record company in Century City, but that I had already worked at Beat Street made it easy to turn down.

"I'm on a month-long sabbatical," I said impulsively. "To concentrate on my comedy career."

"Well, let me know if and when you want to supplement the joke telling with some actual cash," said the temp agent.

I kept to my write-perform-and-refine goals, getting on stage at least twice, and usually three times a week at the Natural Fudge, Pickles, and a North Hollywood bar called Wally's. The audiences were never big (one night at Pickles, I stood before seven people and two of them were Maeve and Solange), but constancy had sprouted my confidence and it grew with each performance.

As valuable and needed as the open mikes at these places were to beginning comedians, they were like small towns, burgs, compared to the dazzling capitol cities that were the Comedy Store and the Improv, and every comic's goal was to impress the cities' mayors, Mitzi Shore and Budd Friedman. The action was at these two clubs, where casting agents and managers went trolling for clients, where there were whispers as reverent as prayer: "The Carson people are here!" Even Amateur Night at the Comedy Store felt special; most of the comedians wore jeans, and yet it seemed we were all dressed up.

Yes, *we*. After a grand total of eleven performances on the B side, I had signed up and was waiting to play the A side, the Comedy Store, and standing in the back of the room, watching one five-minute act after another, I reminded myself that I had just as much right to be there as than anyone. (Judging from the caliber of this particular evening's talent, a definite right.)

When the emcee finally said, "And now let's give a hand to Candy Ohi" (!), I allowed myself three seconds of frozen terror before barreling through the audience like a locomotive, my secret power mantra providing a chuga-chug-chug forward momentum.

Onstage, the emcee gave me a pat on the back before exiting and there I was, standing with a black curtain behind me and the Comedy Store audience in front of me, although onstage I couldn't see anyone past the front row.

"Hey, everyone, how're you doing?" I said this nervously, and wrung my hands, as if I had a confession to make. I looked to the left and to the right, and to the left and right again, making them wait. Finally I spoke. "Okay, why don't we just get this out in the open. I know you're all aware that there's something different about me." (Here I took a long beat, nodding slowly.) "Yes, I am double-jointed." I held my fingers up, bending them at the top knuckle and heard a couple of laughs.

"It's been rough—it's hard when there are so few people like you; when you're always in the minority—when you're only valued for a simple party trick."

There were a few more laughs but a loud voice trampled through them.

"Confucius say, 'You're not funny!'"

A hush filled the room and I felt a pinch of panic, but determined not to let it spread I forced myself to smile and turned to focus my attention on the source of the voice, a guy who all evening had been heckling comics.

"Really? Because your girlfriend says you are. Funny, that is. Or to quote her, 'hilarious.' At least in the bedroom."

There were some Oooohs, a few laughs, and a shouted, "You tell him, girl!"

I smiled at the heckler, as if he were a welcomed guest.

"I take it, sir, you're making an observation about the way I look?"

"Damn straight," he said. "I've never seen a Chink chick do comedy before."

"And I've never seen a Neanderthal sit up straight and drink out of a straw . . . but life's strange that way."

There were one or two laughs and then, like popcorn heating, two, three, four more.

"You're . . . you—" sputtered the heckler.

"How did you get here, anyway?" I asked. "Did you turn left on Sunset when the rest of the hunters and gatherers in your pack made a right toward the grasslands of Griffith Park?"

Ladies and gents, the ripple of laughter grew into a wave and I floated on top of it.

Knowing my grandmother wouldn't appreciate the gory details of my lying bruised and bloodied onstage after a comic bomb, my letters home describing my performances had been on the censored and rose-colored side. But now, now that I had experienced my first big success in front of a full house, I called her the next morning, even before I made my coffee.

"Candy?" she said, and after I assured her there was no emergency, I explained how I'd killed at the Comedy Store.

"Oh, kid! Killed is good, right?"

"Killed is great. Especially considering the heckler I had."

"Why would anyone want to heckle you?"

"Because that's what they do. They drink too much, or they want to be onstage themselves but aren't, so they try to get laughs sitting in the audience."

"Well, I don't go for that at all!"

I could picture my grandmother, grabbing the collar of some drunken wise guy and warning him, "One more peep and I'll give you a knuckle sandwich!"

"And guess what else, Grandma? You know how Charlotte uses Fields as a stage name? I decided to use one, too."

"So you're . . . Candy Fields?"

"No, Ohi. Candy Ohi."

"Kandiyohi like the county?"

I laughed, knowing she'd understand the reference. "And for mom."

"I like it," she said softly.

Reliving the entire evening for her, I told her the nice things the emcee and some other comics had said, and how an audience member had tugged at my sleeve and asked me when I'd be appearing next.

The silence that followed was long enough that I had to ask my grandmother if she was all right.

"I'm just so proud, Candy. Candy Ohi."

"Thanks, Grandma. My friends think—"

"—oh, honey, I'm sorry, I've got to go."

"What's the matter?"

"It's just that I'm sitting by the window and I see my company's here."

I asked if Mrs. Clark, her next-door neighbor was coming over for coffee.

"No," said my grandmother with a little giggle. "Alice's brother Sven."

After my father died, and I had permanently moved in with my grandmother, she'd rented the upper apartment to a woman named Alice O'Rourke.

"Sven O'Rourke?"

"O'Rourke was Alice's married name. Sven's last name is Hanson."

"Grandma! Details, please."

"Well, after you left, Alice started inviting me up for a couple of her Friday night pinochle games, and, well—" another giggle adorned her words—"Sven and I sort of hit it off."

"You and Sven sort of hit it off?!"

"Yes, and I invited him over for coffee this morning, and he's coming up the walk with—well, they're all wrapped up, but I can tell they're flowers! Gotta run—love you!"

After hearing the hang-up click, I admit to the clichéd gesture of holding the receiver out and puzzling over it like a cave man who'd stumbled upon it while out stalking Mastodons.

Did my grandmother have a boyfriend?

Wow. I didn't know whose news trumped whose.

1/24/79

Dear Cal,

The creep who went on before me must hate women because his act was just one ugly, gross line after another (and no, none was funny, at least to all sentient beings in the audience). When I got onstage I said, "I believe in evolution, but it's not true that all of us descended from apes. Some obviously are the spawn of jackasses . . ." (Big Laugh.)

2/4/79

Dear Cal,

Okay, spent the morning writing nothing but political material. Here's an example: "There's trouble at Camp David—things were going fine until Anwar Sadat pushed Menachem Begin out of the canoe and Menachem retaliated by short-sheeting Anwar's bunk. Jimmy the counselor is threatening to ban them from the Friday night belly dance and gefilte fish fry."

2/8/79

Dear Cal,

Solange brought Neil to Pickles to watch my act. He left right after I was on to go see a band, but before he did, he said if Beat Street ever did comedy albums he'd sign me! The likelihood of that is pretty nil, but still!

2/18/79

Dear Cal,

First time at the Improv—and had a good, bomb-free five minutes! Besides me, the only other woman was PJ Rand, who I saw the first time I went to the Comedy Store. She's really funny and we sort of formed a mutual-admiration society.

She told me her real name was Priscilla, but her agent (!) said she'd have a better chance getting her sitcom scripts read if her name wasn't so "feminine." (Shades of S. E. Hinton, I guess.) She said there wasn't anyone who handled hecklers better than me (!), and I returned the compliment by telling her she got the biggest laugh of the night. She'd been talking about the differences between men and women and how her boyfriend had told her one night that if she lost about fifteen pounds, wore some makeup, and grew out her hair, she might kind of resemble Farrah Fawcett.

"'You know what,' I answered, "If you capped your snaggle teeth, quit your job as a line cook at Taco Bell, and got a Ph.D. in astrophysics, you might kind of resemble Carl Sagan.'"

While my calendaieum entries proved I had my nose to the comedy grindstone, rent, utilities, baking ingredients, etc. still had to be paid for, and while I had made great use of my sabbatical, I called Zelda and told her I was available.

"So you're willing to type more than punch lines?" she asked, and laughed at her own joke.

I was sent on a weeklong assignment at Paramount Studios, and although it was typical office drudgery—typing, filing, answering phones—within the drudgery there was enough Hollywood mystique to make the job interesting. First, I got to go through the big white Paramount gate (it was like passing through a glamorous Check Point Charlie, but instead of Communist East Berlin, you got to enter Fantasy Land) and on my way to the animated television production office that employed me, I'd pass airplane hanger–sized sound stages, bungalows with signs reading Writers or Casting, and the occasional actor dressed like an astronaut or a lion tamer.

The first morning I typed checks for the voice-over actors of the Saturday cartoon *Mildred's Mummy*, the actress voicing the sixteen-year-old Mildred earning a sweet $15,000 per episode, and the actor playing the centuries-old Mummy pulling in five thousand more. Age before beauty, I guess.

I filed headshots and résumés, although I didn't quite understand why voice-over actors needed headshots. I took messages from actors, agents, and managers: had there been a casting decision on the new series *Clancy's Clubhouse*? What sort of accent should the character Milo the Marmet have? And when would the residuals from the summer reruns of *Farm Yard Follies* be released?

I eavesdropped on arguments between the two brothers who led

Joe-Jack Productions—arguments that ranged from the quality of a
script to last week's ratings to who called their mother more often. From
what I could tell, it was the short, stout Joe who instigated, and the short,
stout Jack who yelled louder.

Next I was sent for a three-day assignment to Eminence, a literary
agency in Beverly Hills. Their clients included novelists and nonfiction
writers, but their big money came from screenwriters.

"Do you know we represent Robertson Foley?" asked Lawrence, an
agent who liked to loiter in the reception area, tying and retying the
sleeves of the cardigan sweater he wore draped around his shoulders.

"He wrote eight novels—he was up for a National Book Award
twice—but sales?" Lawrence made a puhhh sound and looked skyward.
"He was lucky his wife had gainful employment as a college professor.
Then he writes the screenplay for his novel *I Smell a Rat*—it's a box office
hit, plus it's nominated for a Guild award, and suddenly the guy's in the
money! He writes another adaptation—this one from his novel *Journey
Back,* and not only is he in the money, he's submerged in the money!
So he ditches the professor wife and marries the actress who played an
amnesiac in the second movie, and now he's writing an original screenplay for a cool two million dollars!"

"I saw *I Smell a Rat,*" I told the agent. "Now I'm going to read the
book."

"Don't bother," whispered Lawrence conspiratorially, one hand held
to the side of his mouth. "The book's got a lot of boring stuff that was
cut out for the movie."

The literary agency was a block away from Rodeo Drive, in whose
ultra-swanky shops and boutiques the rich and celebrated wrote checks
for designer gowns in the same amount normal people wrote for a down
payment on a house, for jewelry that equaled their yearly salary times ten.

The windows of JJ Newberry's were crammed with dime-store clut-
ter, and in those of Frederick's of Hollywood mannequins posed in black
garter belts and leopard-spotted negligées, but what was being sold inside
these Beverly Hills stores was harder to discern by mere window shopping. One featured an arrangement of black suede cubes with a sprinkle
of single diamonds; in another, glass pyramids rose up from a ripple of
blue silk scarves.

Wandering under the white and yellow striped awning of Giorgio's,
I was relieved to see a clothing boutique with actual clothing displayed

in the window, and remembering Robb, a fellow tenant and pool-hound, worked there, I decided to say hello.

I stood in the entrance, breathing in air that even smelled expensive. A woman approached me—if she was a security guard, she was awfully well dressed—and with her head slightly cocked, she offered a warm smile and said, "Welcome to Giorgio's! My name's Cynthia. May I help you find something?"

"Uh, yes. Actually, I was hoping to find Robb—"

"—oh, Robb's not working today," she said as if it pained her to give me the news. "But I'd be happy—"

"—excuse me," I said, practically pushing the gracious salesperson aside to better gape at the apparition approaching me.

"Candy!" it said, "I didn't know you had such expensive taste."

"Madame Pepper! What are you doing here?"

Taking my arm, she waved at the salesperson, who rushed to open the door for us and wished us both a wonderful afternoon.

"You look as though you've seen a ghost," she said, once we were outside and standing under the awning.

"Well, I . . . I just . . . look at you!"

Madame Pepper patted her hair, done up in a scarfless, demure bun. Her layers of gypsy clothes had been replaced by an olive green dress and a matching olive jacket.

"When in Rome," she said. Looking over my shoulder she raised her index finger, and I turned to see who she was signaling to wait.

A chauffeur standing next to a Rolls Royce thumbed the brim of his hat.

"I meet a client here every month," she explained. "She likes to top off a morning's shopping with a little chat with me. We have a mimosa in the bar." She nodded toward the store. "Did you know they've got a bar in there?"

"Figures."

"The car belongs to same client. She doesn't want me bothering with taxis or whatnot."

"Wow. People really do believe in you, don't they?"

"Because I give them reason to," she said with a weary patience. "Now I've got to get back to Hollywood. Can we give you a lift?"

"I'm temping—the office is just two blocks away. But Madame Pepper," I said, anxious to update the seer, "I've been at the Comedy Store twice already and the Improv once, and I'm not bombing! And I've got a stage name—Candy Ohi!"

"Candy Ohi," she repeated, raising her head like a dog smelling something on the wind. "I like it. Is name for a successful comedian."

"Thanks."

I accompanied her on the short walk across the sidewalk.

"I'm glad things are going well," she said as the chauffeur opened the car door for her. "I—oh!" She stopped, half inside the luxurious leather cavern of the backseat and half out. "I just had wonderful idea. We need to celebrate! Go back in Giorgio's and find a dress. A fancy dress you can wear to an awards show."

"What?"

"Or at least to a fancy party. Many of which you'll be invited to, now that you're successful comedienne, Miss Candy Ohi."

"I just had . . . just a couple of good nights," I said, flummoxed. "And there's no way I could—"

"Don't worry about the cost, just tell Cynthia that Madame Pepper will take care of it." She settled in the backseat and winked at me. "Which means my client will. I am on her charge account and her feelings get hurt if I don't use it."

"But I can't—"

"Yes, you can. I mean it. And after you get the dress, bring it over to show me. And cake, too, if you feel so obliged."

ON MY LAST DAY at the literary agency, after Lawrence had told me that he'd just sold a screenplay about a telepathic farm boy—"It's like *Carrie* with tractors and combines"—I answered the telephone to hear Zelda's voice.

"So how're things going at Eminence?"

"Eminently."

My temp agent's laugh was nasal.

"Listen, Candy. I've got your next assignment. I'm sending you to the Rogue Mansion."

When I regained my ability to speak I said, "The Rogue Mansion? Ha! I don't think so."

I was not about to degrade myself in this Citadel of Sin (as its religious detractors called it), this Bastion of Bull*#@! (a term coined by a feminist magazine), and there was no way I was going to put on the little kitten ears and tails Rascalettes wore as accessories to their satin, swimsuit-like costumes. This last part I said aloud.

"They only wear those at the Rogue Clubs. This is the Rogue Mansion."

"That's even worse. That's where they have all those orgies in the grottoes, right?"

Zelda sighed.

"All I can tell you, Candy, is that it's a clerical job. You'd be working for Rogue Industries, wearing normal clothes. 'Attending orgies in the grotto' is not in the job description."

"What is the job description?"

"I've got the work order right here," said Zelda. I heard a shuffle of paper. "Typing and filing. A proficient knowledge of the English language/motion pictures a plus."

"A proficient knowledge of the English language/motion pictures a plus?" I repeated. "What's that supposed to mean?"

Zelda sighed again. "They didn't go into detail, Candy. Now do you want the job or not?"

I wanted a job, not necessarily that job, but beggars and temps can't be choosy.

31

"I can't believe you're going inside the Rogue Mansion," Ed said, grinding the gears of his Volkswagen as we climbed a hilly section of Bel Air. "It's every boy's dream to spend a day—make that a night—at the Rogue Mansion."

He was between teaching assignments and beyond happy to drive me to my temp job.

"I'm surprised you haven't been here with Sharla. Doesn't *tout* Hollywood come to Donald Doffel's parties?"

"If she's been invited, she hasn't brought me along."

"Maybe she doesn't want to subject you to all that temptation."

Ed smiled. "Maybe."

After driving alongside a stone fence, the kind built to guard castles rather than ordinary domiciles, we pulled up to an elaborate iron gate with statuary of nubile young women flanking it. The grounds were visible through the slats, and Ed craned his neck to get a look.

"Don't strain anything," I said, opening the car door.

There was a large rock into which a speaker had been outfitted and it was into this rock, Zelda had informed me, that I was to announce my presence.

"Uh, hello," I said, leaning toward it, "I'm uh . . . I'm Candy Pekkala and I've been sent here by Hollywood Temps?"

Waiting for a moment, I looked at Ed who returned my worried expression with a thumbs-up sign.

I tried again but before I'd gotten the last syllable of my name out, the gate opened.

This was worth two thumbs up from Ed, and a wiggle of his eyebrows.

With a wave, I thanked him for the ride and plunged into the emerald grounds that surrounded the Citadel of Sin and the Bastion of Bull*#@!

Deirdre, a gangly, middle-aged woman who stooped to compensate for her height, met me at the front doors, which were tall and wide enough to admit a pair of elephants.

She explained that she was Doff's secretary and that I was to follow her. And so I did, up three staircases whose walls were lined with Rascalette and celebrity photos, and to the "attic," which housed the video offices and library.

"These fine people—Denny and Trudy—will tell you everything you need to know," said Deidre, and she ducked under the door's threshold, leaving me in a room my high school audiovisual club would have salivated over.

"This is your desk," said Trudy, sniffing her pink-tipped nose every couple of seconds. "What you'll be doing here is typing up descriptive labels—production credits, cast lists, synopses for Doff's videos. He watches *a lot* of TV, and he likes to be an informed viewer."

"Of all sorts of things," said Denny, with a wink I chose to ignore.

AT NOON I was in the kitchen, filling my plate in a luncheon buffet line.

"Have you ever had a free lunch like this?" said a woman who was exactly the same height as me. Her hair, too, was black but cut short and spiky.

"No," I said, spearing a big prawn, "I brought a bag lunch but then I was told lunch is on the house."

"It's from the party Doff throws every night," she said, lowering her voice to a whisper. "Pretty swank for leftovers, huh?" She ladled seafood salad onto her plate. "It's my theory that they give you all these niceties to make you feel like it's okay to be working in a place like this. I'm Terry, by the way. Where do you work?"

"Up in the video room. I'm a temp."

She directed me outside, where we dined at a wrought-iron table under a eucalyptus tree.

"I started as a temp, too," Terry said, spearing a scallop with her fork. "I took the job thinking I was sorta like Margaret Mead, exploring a secret culture, you know? I was only going to work long enough to save money for a trip around the world, and then they ask me to stay on permanently and offer me a raise and all sorts of benefits, which I really needed—and whoosh—I'm sucked into that which I despise."

"It's such a strange place—on the way to the bathroom I passed a girl wearing a sarong who asked me if I knew the way to San Jose."

Terry chuckled. "That'd be Barbie Tenucci, April's Rascalette. She's trying to be a singer so she quotes Burt Bacharach lyrics a lot. Plus if she's not stoned, she's asleep."

Terry explained that she worked in Doff's office, which was like working in NASA's Command Central.

"Everything goes in and out through our office. The Rascalettes' breast implant appointments, Doff's oral surgeon bills—he's getting all new teeth—letters and phone calls from old movie stars begging to be invited to the Halloween party . . . even fried chicken samples from the kitchen that Doff rates. I really have no idea what that's about." She sighed. "It's like working in a Fun House, only it's more weird than fun. How's it up in the video room?"

"Well, I've only been up there a couple hours, but so far all Denny and Trudy have done is watch TV, while I type up labels like, 'Doff crowns winner at annual Bikini Ping Pong tournament,' or 'Doff crowns winner at annual Bikini Volleyball tournament.'"

"Lucky you. I was on the phone for three hours, trying to track down the kind of sheets they use in this Caribbean hotel that Gina Mills insists Doff gets for the Mansion."

"And Gina Mills is . . . ?"

Terry tsked in mock indignation. "Only Rascalette of the Year! Only Donald Doffel's new girlfriend! Geez, Candy, where've you been?"

"Out of the loop, I guess. Thank God."

TERRY LIVED UP IN THE HOLLYWOOD HILLS and generously offered to pick me up every day, pulling up in her little Saab promptly at eight fifteen. She wouldn't accept gas money from me either.

"Listen, I am just so happy to have a normal person to share this bizarre experience with me! My friends think I'm a sellout, my sister would love nothing more than to be a Rascalette, and everyone I work with thinks Doff's the Second Coming."

I nodded. "I told my grandma where I was working and she said, 'Oh, Candy, just make sure you wash your hands when you get home.'"

Terry barked a laugh.

"My dad asked me if I could get an autograph of the 1963 November Rascalette! Although he'd freak if he knew my sister would pose for the magazine in a minute."

The thing was, it was a good temp job. When we got to work, Terry and I ambled into the kitchen, helping ourselves to pastries or fruit or cereal and coffee from the big kitchen urn, and while she went to her second floor office, I continued upstairs, occasionally seeing in the hallways a sheepish-looking television actor or movie star who'd spent the night being rogue-ish with one of the Rascalettes.

One morning I might thumb the encyclopedic books about movies that constituted my research library so I could type up things like "*Born Yesterday* (1950) starring Judy Holliday as a tutor assigned by her tycoon lover (Broderick Crawford) to teach him proper etiquette" and "In *Splendor in the Grass (1961)*, Elia Kazan directs Warren Beatty and Natalie Wood in a story of sexual repression, social hypocrisy, and mental illness." Later I might watch a movie to write a critique, or view several videotapes so that I could provide information like "1977 October Rascalette, Jann Diomedes, shows how to make grape leaves on *Dinah & Friends*" or "Aubrey Dale, 1975 June Rascalette, brings her pet ferret to *The Merv Griffin Show*."

Regarding the porn movies, all I had to do was type the movie title on a special label marked with a big X and thus was saved the monotonous task of writing the same synopsis, "People having sex."

At noon, the entire Rogue Mansion staff repaired to the sumptuous buffet table to load up their plates, and at three o'clock a butler delivered coffee, tea, and cookies from an ornate silver service. Employees were made to feel not just valuable but coddled.

"It's all a plot," said Terry. "The oppressor makes oppression so nice that nobody wants to rise up anymore."

"Somehow I can't see Gina Mills wanting to rise up," I said.

"But who really knows? Maybe she started out as a temp—maybe she'd grown up reading Betty Freidan and Simone de Beauvoir, and suddenly, the free lunches, the afternoon tea, the double-overtime pay—maybe it all got to her and made her want to take her clothes off and pose for *Rogue* magazine."

"And why not?" I said in a robotic voice, as I started to unbutton my shirt. "Donald Doffel is my lord and master."

32

By day I typed movie synopses and cast lists, passing Rascalettes in the hallways, pressing myself against the wall so as to not bump into their mammoth fake breasts (I hadn't even known things like fake breasts existed, but Terry told me Rascalettes had silicone implants as casually as the rest of us had our teeth cleaned). And once I passed Donald Doffel, who, befitting his legend, always wore a silk robe over silk pajamas, a bottle of Dad's Root Beer clamped in his hand.

By night—at least Sunday, Monday, and Thursday nights—I appeared at my favorite open mikes at the Improv, the Comedy Store, the Natural Fudge. I had abandoned Pickles; the deli/comedy club never attracted much business, plus I always left there reeking of, yes, pickles, and Wally's in North Hollywood switched its format to strictly country-western singers.

"I can't believe how much I love being onstage," I said to Francis Flover, whom I had run into at Ralphs Supermarket on a Saturday morning. He'd been staring at the rows of cereal boxes with the concentration of an art gallery patron.

"Frank says you're a natural," said Francis, after he'd made his selection and we headed down the aisle. "I'm very sorry I haven't been able to get to one of your performances myself, but—"

"Oh, don't apologize," I said, suddenly alarmed at the slow and halting pace with which he pushed his cart. "Of course, I'd love to have you see me, knowing show business like you do, but I know you're a busy man."

Francis looked at me with a pained expression.

"Please, Candy. I am many things, but at this stage in my life, busy is not one of them."

His groceries only filled half a paper bag, but I offered to carry them and was glad I did, because he could barely make it up the two slightly inclined blocks to our apartment complex.

"I'll bring you over dinner tonight," I said as I put away Grape Nuts, a can of coffee, eggs, a pint of cottage cheese, and three oranges. "And next time, I'll do your shopping for you. At least until Frank gets back."

Frank and his band had been delighted and astounded to have booked a two-week tour that took them to small clubs throughout California.

"You're as sweet as your name, Candy," said Francis as he walked stiffly toward his dining room bar. "And as much as I'd love to offer you something tantalizing to drink, the liquor cabinet seems bereft of everything but soda water."

"Soda water would be great."

"Excellent choice."

The front windows of his apartment were open and a car horn blared on the boulevard and someone shouted, "Move over, ass-wipe!"

From the bar, Francis sighed.

"This used to be an address of some civility," he said, pouring two glasses, and as he handed them to me I couldn't help but notice the tremble in his hands. "Now the lunatics run the asylum."

As he walked toward the couch, his gait was spongy, as if he didn't trust the floor's surface, and when we sat down, it took him a moment to catch his breath.

After several sips of water, he sat taller, seemingly rejuvenated after taking his old-man vacation.

"Now, Candy, I want you to tell me all about this new career of yours. What's your strategy?"

"My strategy?"

"Peggy Lee, for example. Her strategy was to lock you in her bedroom when she sang."

"It was?"

Francis arched a silver eyebrow.

"And Eartha Kitt. Her strategy was to bring you to a little dive that the cops were ready to bust, and then force you to spring for a diamond necklace at Tiffany's."

"Oh."

"Now, Martin and Lewis, of course their strategy was to bring you into their private clubhouse, where tuxedos and clown suits were both acceptable apparel."

I nodded as if of course I knew that.

"So you see, my dear. All great performers have a strategy. And I'm curious as to what yours might be."

"I . . . I'm flattered that you think I have one, but the only strategy I have is that I want to make people laugh."

Considering this, Francis nodded.

"Get that album under there," he said, pointing. "If you please."

I hefted a leather-bound book from underneath the coffee table and handed it to him.

Setting it on his lap, Francis blew off a puff of dust and smoothed his hand over its tooled cover.

"This is about all I have left of the Bel Mondo. Dust and photographs."

I leaned into him.

"That's Ward Bond," he said, opening the album on the table our thighs made. "Recognize him?"

I studied the man's face. "Wasn't he in—"

"*Sergeant York. It's a Wonderful Life. The Maltese Falcon.* On and on."

"Oh yeah."

"He could play a tough guy, a tough guy with a heart, and a funny tough guy."

"And that's Ethel Barrymore." His drew his fingers across the photograph, as if he were petting it.

"She wasn't as good looking as her brother John or as accomplished as her brother Lionel, but I tell you, no one could liven up a party like Ethel."

He turned the pages slowly, taking me on a tour through a bygone era.

There were pictures of Joanne Woodward and Paul Newman, Stewart Granger, Ava Gardner, Lana Turner.

"Look at you next to Humphrey Bogart," I said. Francis often posed with many of the stars whose short biographies he narrated, and in all the photos his hair was combed back and shiny with brilliantine, his smile dashing under a mustache. "You look like a movie star yourself!"

"Tuxedos are a great equalizer. But I daresay, even a street bum from back then was better groomed than some of today's stars." Francis shuddered. "My own son wouldn't have been able to get past the coat room of the Bel Mondo." Pointing to photographs of Doris Day and Jean Simmons, he asked, "Can you imagine Frank and Mayhem Rules on the dance floor with her or her?"

"No," I said and we shared a laugh.

I pointed to a lovely woman in a white dress. "Who's this?"

Francis leaned closer to the album.

"Ahh. Leonora de la Graza. She was from Brazil, and if I had a list of the ten most beautiful women, her name would be number one. Considering the company I kept, that's high praise indeed."

"Was she in the movies?"

"She should have been, but she made the mistake of publicly criticizing someone who had the power to hire her, Louis Melchor. He was a studio head, notorious at the time for naming names in front of the House Un-American Activities Committee. You ever hear about all that communist infiltration nonsense?"

I nodded.

"When Leonora showed up at the club—this photograph is from that night, when she first got there—the audience begged her to get onstage and perform her big hit, 'Little Canary.'

"She obliges us, but after she sings the song and is taking a bow, she sees Mr. Melchor in the crowd and says, 'Hola, Senor Melchor—have you sung like a birdie today?'"

Francis shook his head. "I remember it as if it were yesterday. There was absolute silence, and then some lugs started booing her, and although I'd wager there were more people who'd have liked to cheer her on, nobody did. One could criticize Louis Melchor in private, but he was far too powerful to criticize in public. Hedda and Louella, Hollywood's most influential—too influential—gossip columnists, got a hold of it and it was all over the papers, and Leonora's movie career was over before it began. All for having the guts to say what everybody else was thinking."

He stared at the photograph, one finger under his nose as if stopping a sneeze.

"What happened to her?" I asked.

He shrugged. "She left town. I think she went back to Brazil, where I hope she led a rich and satisfying life. Which is what I hope you will have."

"Well, thanks," I said, a little taken aback at the benediction.

"Just remember, Candy, show business is cruel, but then again, so is life. It's up to you whether or not to get undone by it."

It was getting harder to hear him; his voice only a degree above a whisper.

"Are you all right, Francis?"

He cleared his throat and spoke with a little more strength.

"Look at this one, Candy," he said, pointing to a photograph on the album's last page. "It was taken just down the street."

I leaned in closer.

"Oh, at the Roosevelt Hotel!"

"We were at a party there after a movie premiere, I forget which one. See how some of us have champagne glasses? It was so crowded we spilled out of the hotel and into the street." He chuckled. "That's me," he said, pointing to a man wearing a top hat and lighting a woman's cigarette. And that's Rita Hayworth—well, her elbow—right there. Too bad you can't see the rest of her in the picture, because she was something else."

"Everyone . . . everything looks so glamorous."

"It was a different world." He carefully unmoored the picture from its triangular corner tabs. "Here. I'd like you to have this."

"Thanks." The word didn't feel quite big enough.

We sat on the couch, our knees a quarter-inch from each other's. Several measures of mariachi music rose up from a passing car's stereo and then June's voice, scolding her yapping dog. We listened until both voice and bark faded down the boulevard, and Francis's deep sigh didn't speak of regret; it shouted it.

"Melvin told me he told you about my troubles," he said. "I would have preferred he didn't. I'd like you to think of me as I used to be rather than—"

"Francis, I think you're—"

He lifted a trembling hand in protest.

"—I *was* something, but one ill-chosen act made me something else. Of course, that's no excuse; even a murderer was something else before he pulled the trigger."

"Francis, let's—"

"—the thing is, anyone can rehabilitate. I just didn't know how. At least to the level I should have." He stopped then, seeing my face. "Pay me no mind, Candy. Those photographs just put me in a melancholic mood. Even old men can get the blues." He snapped his fingers and wagged his head, as if the last sentence were lyrics to a song.

Several minutes later, he apologized for needing to keep an early date with his mattress, and when I left his apartment I felt uneasy, as if I weren't going to see him again.

33

3/30/79

Dear Cal,

Comedians are striking against the Comedy Store! The strike was so short, I only got a chance to join the picket line once. The comics prevailed, though, and even though their victory won't affect those of us performing on Amateur Night, my goal of course is to get a regular slot there, which will now be a regular PAID slot!

EMERGENCY VEHICLES LIGHTS PULSED and my heart pounded as I stood off to the side, watching the paramedics shove the stretcher into the back of the ambulance.

"What happened?" I whispered.

"I don't know. He seemed fine and then all of a sudden he passed out cold."

"I want to go with him! I've got to go with him!"

Terry and I watched as the twenty-three-year-old bikinied Gina Mills, on roller skates, chased after the ambulance carrying her fifty-nine-year-old boyfriend.

"Doff! Doff!"

Deirdre, secretary to Mr. Doffel, trotted over to the sobbing Rascalette, who'd been practicing her figure-eights on the tennis court when she heard the commotion and skated over hill, dale, and flagstone driveway to get to the downed Doff.

"All right, everybody back to work," said Deirdre, and as a group of cooks, office workers, and gardeners dispersed, she led Gina toward the mansion, clumsily trying to match her on-foot stride with Gina's on-skates one.

"Ow!" she said as Gina ran over her toe. "Watch it, will you?"

Gina wailed harder.

Deirdre rolled her eyes at Terry and me before asking what we were doing standing around when there was work to be done.

Doff was back hours later after his physician gave him a diagnosis of simple overexertion.

"The good doctor seems to think it might have something to do with the especially energetic calisthenics I engaged in with three willing young ladies last night. Seems I should have had some breakfast to restore all those calories I burned off."

He had delivered this news to his office staff, and Terry related it to me on our drive home.

"Ewww," I said, sticking my head out the window.

"Tell me about it," said Terry. "I just about barfed. As if I want to hear any details about that old lech's sex life."

"Everyone else wants to," I said, reminding her of the recent *L.A. Times* article Deirdre had copied and posted on every department's bulletin board. It had gushed that *Rogue* was experiencing its biggest subscription year ever among men of an age desirable to advertisers, and that a survey of these same young consumers indicated their favorite part of the magazine was the Rascalette fold-out pictorial, with Donald Doffel's "This Rogue's Corner" column in second place.

"You know what you should do, Candy?" asked Terry as she pulled up in front of my apartment building. "You should work the Rogue Mansion into your act."

"I'd probably get sued," I said. "For invasion of ickiness."

THE THING WAS, it didn't matter what material I wrote for my act; I was having trouble sticking to any of it.

There were comics who wrote their own acts, even writing the word *beat* in parentheses to remind themselves to pause; comics who hired out writers; and there were comics who liked to wing it, talking about whatever came to mind. It was scary enough trying to make people laugh on stage and scarier still to attempt it without material, and so the comics who worked this way were in a distinct minority, a minority in which I was finding myself more and more.

"First and foremost, you've got to have an act," advised Danny Hernandez, who emceed Amateur Night at the Comedy Store. "Sure, you can improvise a little, but no one's going to book you if you don't have a rock-solid act."

It was my intention each time I got onstage to do at least one of the five-minute acts I'd written, but a minute or two into it I'd get distracted.

On stage at the Improv, I noticed a couple sitting off to the side. The woman's hair was sprayed into a blonde helmet and the man wore a black shirt with a white satin tie.

"Hey, look," I said, "It's Pat Nixon out on the town with Vito Corleone."

The woman laughed along with the audience, but to describe the guy as "stone-faced" would be attributing more animation to his face than was there.

"Don't worry, Mr. Corleone," I said, with an acquiescent little bow. "I won't tell Dick."

I didn't intend this lasciviously but it sounded that way, and the crowd erupted in laughter and applause.

"Wow, who'd have thought, Pat Nixon out on the town with a big Mafia don? Then again, I guess she's always had a thing for criminals."

The more I got into it, the looser Vito got, until his scowl was replaced with a big grin, and when my five minutes ran out, he cupped his mouth with his hands and shouted, "More!"

This was a really fun discovery; people tended to like getting insulted from the stage (at least the ones who weren't totally plastered). If your insults were funny enough. Or stupid enough.

"I see you love New York," I said to a woman whose T-shirt said as much. "You're lucky—I just broke up with Philadelphia."

There was a huge groan, but sometimes the fun came in not just refusing to give up a bad joke but elaborating on it.

"Okay," I said, "it wasn't me who ended the relationship. You know Philadelphia's all about freedom."

When I saw a guy wearing a cowboy hat, I said, "And what do you do, Curly?"

"I like to ride the range!" he said, and pleased with himself, he nudged his wife.

"So are all your appliances covered in spur marks?"

After letting the laugh settle, I said to his wife, "Does he try to rope the refrigerator, too? Corral the mixing bowls? Hog-tie the step stool?"

I was having so much fun.

"Candy Ohi, huh? I like it. And I can't believe how much you've improved from the last time I saw you."

"I should hope so," I said, and shuddered at the memory.

Mike Trowbridge swiveled on the barstool. "What was that, three, four months ago? Man, you're a totally different performer."

"Thanks," I said and sucked on the straw of my margarita. We had run into each other in the back hallway of the Comedy Store, and hearing that I'd be going onstage, he'd watched my act. Afterwards, we went next door to the Hyatt House for a drink.

"Really, Candy, you had them right where you want 'em: in the palm of your hand."

I batted my eyelashes. "Tell me more."

He considered me for a moment.

"Okay, you've got a very pretty smile."

This I was not expecting and I ducked my head, discovering how interesting my drink coaster was.

"So," I said, taking a deep breath. "How's Kristin?"

"Kirsten. And she's fine." He laughed. "You know, I'm not betraying her by saying you have a pretty smile."

A fire flamed on my face. "Of course you're not. Anyway. So . . . what were you doing at the Comedy Store on Amateur Night? You're a regular."

"I was in the Main Room, doing improv." He took a swig of beer. "Have you tried that?"

"No. I'm not exactly sure what it is."

"Sketch comedy, except you make it up on the spot."

"Yikes."

"It's not much different from ad-libbing during your monologue, only you get to play different characters. It's fun."

So is sitting here talking with you.

"What else has been going on?" asked Mike. "Are you still at the record company?"

"No, I'm at the Rogue Mansion now."

Mike stuck his finger in his ear and wiggled it.

"Sorry, I thought you said you were at the Rogue Mansion."

"I did. I'm temping there."

"They have temp Rascalettes?"

"I'm not a Rascalette, although if you think about it, they are sort of temporary. I mean, they get a new one every month."

"Doesn't matter, they live forever. Take the July 1969 Rascalette—she will always have that title."

I cocked my head. "Sounds like you have a passing familiarity with *Rogue* magazine."

"Are you kidding? Jim Dooley's older brother had a stash of them under his bed, and the day we found them was the day I understood the existence of God."

We wound up talking for another hour, and although most of the conversation was focused on comedy, I did manage to learn that his favorite old band was the Kinks and his favorite new band the Clash, that we both much preferred *The Andy Griffith Show* to *Mayberry RFD* and that he liked *The Munsters* over *The Addams Family.*

"Whoa," I said. "And I was beginning to respect your taste."

"You've got to admit Herman Munster was a lot funnier than Gomez Addams."

"But the music," I said and when I began to hum the theme song, Mike joined me, both of us snapping our fingers at the appropriate cues.

Even though I only had to cross Sunset Boulevard to catch the bus that dropped me off right in front of my house, I accepted Mike's offer to give me a ride home, but this time I didn't make the mistake of inviting him up for homemade baked goods, which just happened to be chocolate chip cookies.

"I'll try to see your act again soon," he said. "You're doing all the open-mikes, right?"

"Pretty much. The Comedy Store, the Improv, and the Natural Fudge. I was doing Pickles but I didn't like the—"

"Smell," said Mike. "I know, I used to perform there, too. Anyway, I think your days of open-mike nights might be coming to a close. You're ready to move up."

"From your lips to the Comedy gods' ears."

34

"Zo, how is showbiz treating you?"

"You tell me. You're the soothsayer."

"That is true," said Madame Pepper with an acidic smile. "And that is why I am foretelling that you will be picking up the check."

We were sitting in one of the dark booths at C.C. Brown's, treating ourselves after having seen the movie *The China Syndrome.*

"For all we know, planet might explode tomorrow," Madame Pepper had said glumly as we left the theater. "Might as well eat ice cream."

When our aproned waitress served our hot fudge sundaes, we dug our spoons into them, pushing aside thoughts of melting nuclear reactors and annihilation.

Even though the movie's subject matter was disturbing, we had enjoyed the drama and craftsmanship of the actors and happily discussed whether the movie's stars, Jane Fonda and Michael Douglas, were worthy successors to their fathers, and we both agreed they were.

"It's much easier for children of movie stars to get into the business," Madame Pepper had said as we walked down Hollywood Boulevard toward the ice cream shop. "But for those children, I think the shadow of doubt is always there: 'Could I have done this on my own?'"

Now as she wiped a trail of hot fudge off her chin, Madame Pepper said, "And as to your comedy career I will tell you: yes, you will be successful as you want to be."

I rolled my eyes.

"You do not have much faith in my clairvoyance, do you, Candy?"

I folded the napkin on my lap and folded it again.

"I . . . if I had faith in anyone's clairvoyance, it would be yours, Madame Pepper."

She snorted a laugh.

"You know, very important people pay me a lot of money to help them."

"I know! And they send Rolls Royces to pick you up and take you to fancy Beverly Hills boutiques! But when you say 'helping'—isn't that sometimes just another word for 'making stuff up'?"

Holding her spoon, Madame Pepper's hand stilled in midair.

"I don't make stuff up."

"Oh, come on. How does a person go from dressing movie actors in costumes to reading their fortunes, anyway?"

My voice was playful, but I wanted—had wanted for a long time—to hear her answer.

"It was an evolution," she said, stressing every word, "from recognizing I had the gift to realizing I could help people with it."

"The gift? Then tell me this, why don't people with the gift ever help people who really need it? Like, say, did you know something was going to happen at Three Mile Island? And if you did, why didn't you do anything about it; and if you didn't, why not? Does the gift have an on-off switch?"

The heavy valance of her eyebrows lowered, and I braced myself for a not-very-pleasant response.

"That is reasonable question," she said, surprising me. "Why can't those of us with the gift predict major events, disasters, catastrophes? Well, of course, some try to show off, and that is why we are so often discredited. Most of us can only work in a smaller framework; we need to be in the presence of those we are helping—"

"—to 'sense their vibrations.'"

"Yes," said Madame Pepper simply. "There are those of us whose gifts are large enough, big enough to see outside the framework, but fear keeps the general public from recognizing their sight."

I shrugged and helped myself to more ice cream. She mimicked my shrug and attacked a puff of whipped cream clinging to the parfait glass.

"Zo," she said after a time, "you have worn your dress yet?"

"No. For some reason, I haven't been invited to any of those fancy parties or award shows you foretold."

She smiled. "You will."

I had modeled the black sleeveless dress for her as soon as I got home the day I'd met her in Giorgio's, and she had sat on her horsehair sofa, applauding.

"It fits you perfectly," she said. "And those little sprinkles of sequins—not too much and not too little—beautiful."

"Thank you. Cynthia helped me find it." I felt the rise of tears in my eyes. "I still can't believe you bought it for me."

"Bah," said Madame Pepper, waving her hand. "Like I told you, it's my client who pays. And she is richer than a king, so why not make use of her benevolence?"

Now as the waitress lay the check on the table, Madame Pepper was quick to pick it up, and quicker to hand it to me.

"Time for you to pay bill, so we can ditch this place."

"How is it," I said, with a laugh, "that you say slang words like *ditch* and still drop your articles every now and then?"

Madame Pepper looked more offended than when I had questioned her psychic abilities.

"Articles? I have dropped articles?" She made a big production of looking to her left, to her right, on the floor.

I sat back in the dark wooden booth and smirked. "Articles, like *a* or *the.*

"Oh . . . articles like *a* or *the.* Tell me Candy, do you speak another language beside English?"

The internal embarrassment vents suddenly turned on, blowing hot air onto my cheeks.

"Well, I took three years of French in high school, but—"

"I speak four languages, Candy. Romanian, German, Russian, and English. And all well enough to have a conversation on any topic with a Romanian, a German, a Russian, and Englishman—or an American. In Romanian, of course, I speak like a poet. In the others, I am slightly more pedestrian and will drop occasional articles."

I stared at my fudge-smeared dish, the vents turned up to high.

"Sorry. I'm an idiot."

"That I would not dispute," said Madame Pepper.

I GOT HOME TO FIND AN ELECTRIC BILL, the latest issue of *Cosmopolitan* (Charlotte subscribed to it and I was happy to read it), and my grand-mother's weekly letter in my mail box. The headlines on the magazine's cover—Lose Weight While Pleasing Your Man! or Don't Ticket Him in Your Erogenous Zones!—were tame compared to the words my grandma wrote. I placed a long-distance call and when she picked up, I said, "I just got your letter."

My grandmother giggled for a good ten seconds, and I had the odd sensation that I was on the phone with a thirteen-year-old.

"Pretty exciting, huh?" she said.

"I'll say. I would like a few more details, though."

"Well," she said, drawing two musical syllables out of a plain one-syllable word. "We were on our way to the Pannekoeken Huis after church—"

"After church? You don't go to church."

"Maybe not regularly," she said, a little huff to her voice. "But certainly on holidays. Anyhow, Sven sings in his church choir, so I've started attending services. He's got the loveliest voice, Candy—a bass!—which I can pick out even when the whole choir's singing!" There was more of her girlish laugh. "In any case, we were on the way to the restaurant, when he just blurted out, 'Let's get married' as easily as he might have said, 'I'm in the mood for some French toast!' And I said, 'Okay!'"

I couldn't help but be delighted by the delight in her voice.

"So when's the big day?"

"Sometime this summer, we hope. And Candy, I want you to come home and be my maid of honor."

"Maid of honor?"

"I plan to ask Charlotte and Patti as well. I want all my granddaughters to be my maids of honor." Her voice lowered to a whisper, as if we had eavesdroppers on the line. "But between us, know that you're my number one."

Sweet inspiration rose on a rush of love.

"Then I'm giving you an early present. You and Sven are going to Tahiti."

"What?"

Before she could continue her protest, I explained that the game show rule only specified that any trip won had to be taken within a year, and that I could transfer the prize to someone else, and didn't she remember that I had offered to take her as my guest anyway, and she had said, oh no, Tahiti is for lovers and didn't that describe an engaged couple . . . ?

And then I said, "Come on, Grandma, I really want to do this . . ."

I breathed in a huge column of air and after a moment of silence, my grandmother unleashed a low string of giggles.

"Tahiti," she said finally. "Oh, kid."

35

OCCASIONALLY, I had to make a certain delivery that millions of American men would have paid cash—and lots of it—to make for me. Unfortunately, I had no idea how to tap that market, and so it was I alone who had to enter Donald Doffel's bedroom.

Never lingering, I always felt slightly creepy and mildly panicked as I race-walked across the expanse of thick carpet, trying not to look up at the mirrored ceiling. Flanking his round bed draped with its fur throw were two nightstands, and it was on the nearest nightstand I was instructed to place my delivery of a half-dozen VHS tapes. Deirdre always called to tell me when to make these deliveries, apparently knowledgeable of the room's vacancy.

But even the most efficient secretary makes mistakes.

"May I ask what your intention is?" came a voice, the unmistakable, gravelly voice of the Titan of Titillation, the Sultan of Salaciousness, the Master Rogue himself, Donald Doffel.

Had I not already put down the stack of cassettes, I know I would have dropped them; as it was I nearly jumped, and losing my balance I stumbled sideways, right onto the fur pelt on the round bed.

"Mr. Doffel!" I said, scrambling off the bed, "I'm sorry to have disturbed you." Mortification propelled me toward the door and escape. "But Deirdre told me—"

"—well, Watson, methinks if she knows Deirdre, she's not some reprobate off the street who's come into the inner sanctum uninvited."

"Oh no, sir. I work here—up in the video room—and I was just delivering your tapes."

I was near the door, so close to making my getaway, when with a rustle of his robe, he put his arm out. Obeying the silk-draped semaphore, I stopped dead in my tracks.

"I'm sorry, but if you could see your face." Mr. Doffel shook his head and chuckled. "I haven't seen anyone look so scared in here since Shirley Oxendale's first visit."

He allowed himself a little sigh of laughter before nodding toward the French windows.

"Come, sit on the balcony with me, Candy."

Another shock. "You know my name?"

"I know all my employees' names, even the temps. Especially the temps who do such good work. And speaking of names, please call me Doff. Only my tax attorney calls me 'Mr. Doffel,' and I don't like to be reminded of him."

I felt as if I'd entered an alternative reality even more mind-bending than the alternative reality that the Rogue Mansion inherently was.

On the balcony that overlooked a garden in which the topiary was shaped like female forms, he gestured for me to sit on a wrought-iron chair and he sat at another, a small table between us.

"Shirley Oxendale was October Rascalette 1969," he said. "That's another thing I remember, every single Rascalette who has appeared in the magazine, and the order of their appearances. In any case, Shirley was an Indiana farm girl who knew all about crop rotation and conservation tillage, but she didn't know a thing about the little world I'd created here at the Rogue Mansion. Consequently, her first look at my boudoir was one that made an impression."

I tried to smile but there was no moisture in my mouth and my upper lip snagged on my teeth.

"You look as if you'd rather be anywhere else than here," Doff said, not unkindly.

"No, it's just that . . ." I didn't know how to finish the sentence because I would, in fact, rather be anywhere else.

"I've got a refrigerator full of sodas," he said, with a nod, "or I can call and have something hot sent up—some tea or coffee?"

"Uh, no thanks." Not wanting to appear ungrateful, I added, "But thanks anyway!"

Shifting in his chair, Doff sat back and folded his hands on his chest.

"Then I won't keep you long, Candy. I just wanted to say I appreciate the work you've done on the video covers. Your synopses are very well written, and occasionally quite humorous."

I felt the burn of a blush. There were times, when describing a Rascalette at some function or on a television show, I'd let loose a double entendre or a bit of sarcasm.

"I'm sorry if—"

"—sorry? I just complimented you. 'Raelynn Otis, March Rascalette 1972, on *Dinah's Place!* demonstrates how she keeps in shape jumping rope. Ratings, among other things, bounce.'"

My blush deepened.

"A tad juvenile," said Doff, "but juvenility certainly has its place, especially here. And your movie synopses! I loved what you wrote about *The Sin of Harold Diddlebock.*"

"Thanks. Mostly I just embellish stuff from the movie guides, but when there's time, I like to watch the movie myself and throw in the occasional critique."

"It's the occasional critique that I enjoy. 'In his cast, Preston Sturges has created a magic kingdom, from Harold Lloyd, the movie's king, to its duke, Jimmy Conlin, and its earl, Franklin Pangborn.'"

"Wow. You do have a good memory."

"It's photographic." He lifted his entwined hands off his chest and, placing them behind his neck, leaned back into them. "And I agree completely with what you wrote about Preston Sturges and Harold Lloyd. Geniuses, both of them."

"I'm glad I got to watch the movie. I'd never heard of it, or them."

"A sad commentary. Sometimes the world doesn't embrace what it so obviously should."

"Can I . . . can I ask you where you get these movies?"

"I don't know, can you?"

So the man was a grammarian, too.

"May I, Mr. Doffel," I drawled, "may I inquire as to the methods by which you obtain these motion pictures?"

The Regent of Raunch smiled.

"You may. From the personal libraries of my friends in the movie industry. Not only can I get a copy of just about any old movie, I screen yet-to-be-released movies here nearly every night. Me! A kid from Wichita Falls who'd skip school to sneak into twenty-five-cent movies he couldn't afford!"

His smile was wide and true, and I glimpsed the wonderstruck teenager in the tanned and wrinkled face.

"Now tell me, Candy, a girl of your abilities surely has bigger desires than office temping. What are—"

A phone on a stand behind him rang and Doff turned to pick it up. After a short conversation consisting of two yeses, a no, and one "Tell him we don't endorse that sort of behavior," he hung up, brushed the lap of his robe as if he had spilled on it, and rose, offering me his hand.

Feeling a little silly, I took it, standing up myself.

"Candy, I thoroughly enjoyed our conversation. You were about to tell me where your interests lie?"

We passed through the French doors and into the bedroom.

"I'm doing stand-up comedy."

"Stand-up comedy? Seriously?"

"*Seriously* meaning 'Am I concentrating my efforts on it?' or *Seriously* meaning 'Surely you jest'?"

"The former. Seriously."

We both smiled at our word play.

"You've chosen somewhat an atypical field for a young woman."

Well, not everyone can be a Rascalette, I thought.

"Nevertheless, good for you," said Doff. "According to Mark Twain, 'The human race has only one really effective weapon and that is laughter.'"

"Hmm," I said, considering this. "Weapon against what?"

He looked at me, surprised. "Against life, of course."

We were both silent as he escorted me across his bedroom and through the door into the hallway.

"Good luck, Candy, and remember: be bold. As Goethe says, 'Boldness has genius, power, and magic in it.'"

With that final piece of advice, the Master Rogue turned left, toward the grand stairway that led down to the great hall, and I turned right, to the narrow staircase that led up to the video room, passing Gina Mills in several scraps of white fabric I think was supposed to be a tennis dress. She was leaning against the wall, arms folded, and the look she gave me was both suspicious and confused, and—I couldn't help it—I looked to the ceiling and fanning my face said, "Yeow!" just for the fun of it.

36

4/18/79

Dear Cal,

Solange invited me to Beat Street for Summer Stephenson's record launch and after Summer had lip-synched what the record company hopes will be her big hit, I asked Neil why Summer's manager was wearing a tiny spoon on a chain around his neck.

"Is he on a baby foot diet or something?"

"Uh, Candy . . . that's a coke spoon."

"Why doesn't he just drink it out of the bottle like the rest of us?"

A look of pity flashed on his face before he realized I was kidding.

"Oh, ha ha," he said, nudging my shoulder with his own. "I'd say save it for the stage, but then again, you want laughs so maybe not."

Everyone's a comedian . . .

5/1/79

Dear Cal,

I'm 23 years old today! Happy Birthday to me! Maeve and Solange took me out for Thai food, and now I've got a brand-new love.

6/3/79

Dear Cal,

M. Pepper and I saw Alien—*we had planned on going to Hamburger Hamlet afterwards, but the movie took away our appetites.*

8/17/79

Dear Cal,

Great Night at the Natural Fudge!

I had introduced myself to the audience as being Korwegianish.

"Half-Korean, a quarter-Norwegian, and a quarter-Finn. Yes, I'm descended from those considered the funniest people on earth, those laugh-riots—the Asianavians. Who hasn't rolled in the aisles listening to comics like Thor Kim or Yoo Suk Peterson? We've even got our own Three Stooges—Ole, Lars, and Dong."

"Kiss my ass!" shouted a man from the back of the room.

"My mistake," I said. "Ladies and gentlemen, it appears we have a fourth Stooge."

It was rare, in the mild-mannered herbal-tea-drinking atmosphere that was the Natural Fudge, to have belligerent hecklers, but beer and wine were also served, apparently too much of it to this guy, as again, he yelled, "Kiss my ass!"

"Sir," I said slowly, "Do you really think the more you shout that, the more willing I'll be to do it?" Tapping my chin with my fingers, I looked upward, as if seriously pondering his words and in a dreamy voice, mused, "Hmm . . . maybe he's not really being crude and obnoxious. Maybe he's making me an offer I shouldn't refuse—maybe his butt's got magical powers like the Blarney Stone." I looked back at the heckler. "Does your butt have magical powers?"

"I'm here to see Freddie, not you!"

I had no idea who Freddie was but nodded.

"Oh, well that explains things." To the rest of the audience, I explained, "Freddie's an improvisational contortionist. He bends his body into weird positions based on audience suggestion." I cast a pitying look at the heckler. "But when Freddie comes out, you should ask him to kiss his own ass, because that would be the real act of contortionism, not kissing yours. Unless you and he have made previous arrangements?"

"All right!" he said, both agreeably and nonsensically, and he was silent for the rest of my act, which included a bit on my tenuous dating life ("I've had to lower my standards a bit . . . 'my type' no longer means 'handsome and witty' but 'conscious and speaks English at least as a third language'"), a couple of impressions (my Beverly Hills panhandler getting the biggest laughs), and an exchange with Mindy, a waitress who wore a tank top accessorized by tufts of underarm hair and who, I had discovered, was always up for some good-natured ribbing. She provided me an opening when she dropped a plate.

"Oops, another customer review of the Eggplant and Okra Surprise," I said.

"I wish we served an Eggplant and Okra Surprise," Mindy said. "It sounds yummy."

"She's high," I said to the audience.

"High on life. And maybe a little Maui Wowie."

I looked at the audience. "This is a good time to remind you to tip your waitresses. Especially Mindy. She's saving up to buy a razor."

AFTERWARD, I joined Terry, Francis, Frank, and Mayhem at a table.

"Candy!" said Mayhem. "That was radical!"

"Bravo!" said Terry.

"Way to deal with that 'kiss my ass' asshole," said Frank.

"'Krugerrands,'" said Mayhem, reciting a line my Beverly Hills panhandler used, 'Spare Kruggerands?'"

"If I still had my club," said Francis, "I'd book you. For the weekend."

As far as compliments go, I could ride on that one for a while.

"Excuse me, Candy?" A woman with a corona of springy brown curls and a face dotted with moles approached the table, hand out.

As I shook it, she said, "Claire Hellman—yes, just like the playwright and the mayonnaise. But I'm not related to either. Listen, I just wanted to tell you, I thought you were wonderful."

After I asked her to repeat herself, I thanked her and introduced her to my tablemates. Her warm smile froze when I got to the man seated next to me.

"Oh, my God," she said, "you're Francis Flover?"

Looking slightly perplexed, Francis said, "Yes . . . unless you're delivering a summons."

Grinning, Claire Hellman squatted next to the table and took Francis's hand.

"My mother told me all about the Bel Mondo—she said she practically lived there."

Sitting up a little straighter, Francis asked, "And who was your mother?"

"Winifred Hellman. Well, back then she was Winifred Jarret."

"No. Winnie Jarret is your mother?"

The woman's curls trembled as she nodded.

Francis turned to illuminate the rest of us.

"Winnie Jarret worked in publicity for one of the studios, which meant she was often at my club, babysitting movie stars who found it hard to monitor their excesses."

Claire laughed. "She loved it. She said where but Hollywood would they pay you to dress up, see great entertainment, and share a table with people like Peter Lawford and Mitzi Gaynor?"

"And how is your lovely mother?" asked Francis.

"Oh, fine. Living in the Valley with my dad. She quit working when she got married and had me and my brother, but she passed on her love of showbiz to both of us. Eric's an agent, and I'm a filmmaker."

"Isn't that wonderful!" said Francis.

"Well, here's the wonderful—or maybe synergistic—part," said Claire, and seeing a chair at the next table, she got up from her squat and pulled it over.

"You guys don't mind, do you?"

We all shook our heads, everyone wanting to hear the wonderful and synergistic part.

"Okay, obviously, I didn't know you were sitting here, Mr. Flover—"

"—please, call me Francis."

Nodding, Claire continued. "I just wanted to congratulate Candy here on a great act." She gave me a little salute, which I returned. "But meeting you, I'm reminded of all the stories my mother told me about the Bel Mondo, and by the way, I'm sorry for your later troubles, Mr. . . . uh, Francis, but what I'm thinking is—wow! I'd love to interview you and get your own reminiscences on film! It'd make a great documentary—a real look back at the old, glamorous Hollywood, and I could intersperse interviews with stars and use archival photographs, but you'd really be the centerpiece, because my mother always said, 'Francis Flover wasn't a studio head, but he ran Hollywood after hours.'" Claire brushed back a handful of curls. "Whew! Sorry, when these ideas come to me, I tend to get a little excited."

"I can see why," said Frank. "A documentary about my father is a great idea."

"This is so wild," said Terry. "When my date picked me up for prom, well, we were both sort of hippies and I guess our clothes reflected that, because my dad looks at my mom and says, 'Can you imagine those two at the Bel Mondo?'"

At that moment, Mindy the waitress stopped at our table.

"Can I get you guys anything?" she said and looking at me, she smirked. "Or do you prefer to be served by someone with a little less body hair?"

"Oh," I said, swiveling my head as I looked around the restaurant. "Is Bigfoot working tonight?"

8/30/79

Dear Cal,
    My One-Year Anniversary in Hollywood! I bake a pineapple-upside-down cake and share it with the usual suspects.

9/15/79

Dear Cal,
    I get a slot at the Improv!

"I hope you know how many people spend years getting to where you got in a couple months," Gary Arnstein said one evening in the Improv green room. "Especially when you don't even really have an act."

"I have an act," I said. "It's just fluid."

"Fluid's not gonna get you on Carson," said a comic named Jim Clausen.

I had heard this from comics and club owners: "You've got to hone your act—do it over and over and over." That was my intention every time I stepped onstage, but it seemed I could never stick to the script.

"Take me, for instance," said Gary. "I was doing Amateur Nights for three years before I moved up."

"Shoulda done them for a couple years more," said another comic.

"Should still be doing them," said Jim. "Although with you, Arnstein, practice doesn't necessarily make perfect."

"You should talk, Clausen. I saw your act last Saturday." Gary shook his head and in a deep news-anchor voice said, "Bomb rocks L.A. comedy club."

Jim twirled his middle finger.

It was typical, I had learned, that anytime comedians got together there was a constant jockeying for position, a top-this mentality. Everyone was constantly "on," which was exhilarating until it became tiring. There was as much testosterone-fueled swagger as on a battlefield, and as testosterone wasn't my dominant hormone, I tended to stay in the demilitarized Zone of Estrogenia, throwing an occasional grenade mainly for my own amusement. Comics were wary of the women—and there weren't many of us—who invaded their turf, and for me it wasn't important to compete with them offstage. If we'd all been onstage together, it would be an entirely different matter.

A CALENDAEIUM ENTRY in October read, "Last day at Rogue Mansion—how will they survive without me?" Underneath that I had scrawled, "small party—nice," and it had been, with the Rogue Meister himself accepting a piece of cake and thanking me for my good work.

"A piece of you shall be forever entombed in my video library," he said, to which I replied, in a muffled voice, "Help, let me out!"

Terry fretted on the drive home, wondering aloud who she was going to make fun of the Rascalettes with.

I reminded her that our friendship wasn't over and that we were scheduled to have brunch that Saturday.

"Yeah, but who am I supposed to get on-site relief with? I mean, just today Jackie Vining—she's next month's Rascalette—told me she's changing the spelling of her name to J-a-q-u-e-e because 'it's more classy.'"

"Is that classy spelled 'q-u-l-a-s-s-y?" I said.

"See! That's what I mean." She turned onto Sunset Boulevard and more to herself than me she said, "Geez—what am I doing with my life? I should be tagging endangered species in the rain forest or running with the bulls in Pamplona. How did I wind up at the Rogue Mansion?"

37

I SIGNED WITH THE TALENT AGENCY the Starlight Group, and my agent was Eric Hellman, who had, on the recommendation of his sister, Claire, come to see me perform. During our very first meeting, Eric was surprised when I told him I didn't want to do TV commercials.

"You mind telling me why?"

"I figure if I wanted to be a salesperson, I would have applied at Dayton's."

Now his face (fairly handsome and, like Claire's, fairly mole ridden) registered blankness.

"It's the best department store in America. It's based in Minneapolis."

"Candy, surely you're aware," said Eric, no doubt filing the information I'd just given him in the useless trivia drawer of his brain, "that commercials are a stepping stone? I have a client who was seen in a rug shampoo commercial, and now he's shooting a romantic comedy with Goldie Hawn! And what about sitcoms? Please tell me you don't have anything against sitcoms."

"I just don't want to do anything dumb," I said, not liking how small my voice sounded. "Or that feeds into stupid stereotypes."

Eric nodded. "Duly noted."

He booked me on my first college tour, in which I traveled with four other comics in a minivan as far south as San Diego and as far north as Santa Rosa. This was exciting in itself, but what set the Thrill-O-Meter's needle to sway was that one of those four other comics was Mike Trowbridge.

"Well, look who's here," he said, as we loaded our bags in the back of the van. "Miss Candy Ohi."

"None other," I said casually, giving my suitcase a shove.

EVERYONE ON THE TOUR WAS FUNNY, although Lance Gill's ability to make me laugh diminished the more I got to know him; he had one of those egos that demanded the modifier *insufferable*. In the van or restaurant booths, he liked to lecture us on the art of comedy, offering unsolicited tips as to how we could improve our act.

"You, Boris," he said to the guy who had emigrated from Russia five years earlier. "You've got a good thing going—people feel sophisticated laughing at a guy who's from behind the Iron Curtain—but your jokes need to be updated. That bit about Khrushchev is tired, man."

"What he mean, tired?" asked Boris, slathering his accent on extra thick. "If people are laughing, this means they are sleepy?"

"Yeah, Lance," said Solly Berg, who'd given up a career as a science teacher to go into comedy. "Boris's act kills. There's nothing tired about it."

"I'm only trying to help," said Lance.

"If that's help," said Mike, "I'll wait for the next ambulance."

"Yeah," I added. "If that's help, throw me a rope that's not frayed."

"Da," said Boris, chuckling. "If that's help, I'll take life-preserver not made of cement."

WE DECIDED TO TAKE TURNS EMCEEING, and Mike had the honors during our show at UC–Santa Barbara.

"You're in for a real treat," he said and, before introducing Boris, lifted his trumpet to his lips.

"Those Volga boatmen are real partyers," said Mike, after playing the song's slow "Yo-oh, hee, hoe," refrain. "And so's the next comic, live from Russia—it wouldn't be so good, of course, if he was dead from Russia—ladies and gentlemen, Mr. Boris Yvanovitch!"

When it was time to introduce me, his trumpet accompaniment was "My Funny Valentine."

"Now Candy Ohi's not really my valentine," he said, "but she is funny, and she does have a beautiful heart-shaped . . . ass."

After the show, we gathered in Solly's room, giving each other notes, and if stares were lasers, mine would have cauterized Mike's retinas and blinded him.

"About that 'heart-shaped ass' bit," I said. "It's a wee bit sexist, wouldn't you say? I don't hear you mentioning anyone else's body parts."

"You're right," he said, accepting the joint Solly passed to him. "I just thought it would be funny because everyone thought I was going to say 'face' and then I said 'ass.' But okay, it's the first—and last—time I'll use it."

"I thought you girls liked guys noticing your bodies," said Lance. "I mean, isn't that why you dress the way you do?"

"Lance," I said, holding up my palms. "Take a look. Aren't I wearing the same thing as you?"

"Well, actually, his shirt is gray and yours is black," said Boris. "And you of course are not wearing a tie."

I waved off the joint Mike held out to me.

"What I mean is most girls like guys noticing their bodies," said Lance. Taking the joint, he took a deep inhale. He held his breath but continued talking in a clenched voice. "You can't tell me you dress like a guy when you're not onstage."

"I didn't know wearing a black shirt and black pants constituted 'dressing like a guy,'" I said. "Next time I'll make sure I have your wardrobe approval before I go onstage."

Lance shrugged and let loose a cloud of smoke.

"Why wait?—I'll tell you now: you'd probably do a lot better if you wore a skirt, or something that showed a little skin."

"Jesus, Lance," said Mike.

"Yeah," said Solly, mid-toke, "you're sounding like one of those sexist pigs all the cute little gals are talking about."

Solly winked at me, in case I hadn't caught that he was joking. Lance just smirked.

"All I'm saying is Candy should make it easy for all the people who'd rather be looking at her than listening to her."

"By *people*," I said, keeping my voice neutral, "do you mean *men*?"

"Well, yeah. At least half our audience. Because unfortunately, as hard as you might try, most guys probably aren't going to think you're funny."

"If I weren't so stoned," said Mike, "I'd ask you to step outside."

"Don't do me any favors," I said, and deciding I'd be better entertained watching the late show in my room, I stood up.

"Candy, Candy," said Mike, his hand outstretched. "Don't go. Lance's views are not representational of the views at large."

He rendered this announcement in a I'm-a-serious-newscaster voice.

"Da," said Boris. "Just because Lance has got a problem appreciating funny women does not mean we do also."

"Amen," said Solly. "My girlfriend's hilarious. Especially without her clothes on."

"Ha ha," I said, but smiled, knowing that even while sticking up for me, jokes must be told. I sat down.

"Hey, Solly, don't bogie that," said Lance, holding out his fingers, and he gulped in what was left to be gulped of the joint that had burned down to a glowing ember.

"And my mother," said Mike, "my mom's the person who made me want to get into comedy. Wit's her middle name."

"And my mother!" said Boris. "My mother's middle name meant same!" He spoke a word in Russian that sounded a little bit like "octopus."

As the men in the room laughed, trying to pronounce the Russian word for wit, I got up again, leaving the room foggy with marijuana smoke, repeating silently and with just a touch of weariness my power mantra.

MIKE INTRODUCED ME DIFFERENTLY in Santa Cruz, playing on his trumpet several bars of "Doin' What Comes Naturally" from the musical *Annie Get Your Gun.*

"Ladies and gentlemen, what Candy Ohi does naturally is make people laugh. At least that's some of what she does naturally. The other stuff is frankly none of your business."

Our shows were very well received, although the audience in San Jose seemed to tacitly agree to make it Student Heckler Night, and while Mike and I flourished in these circumstances, it threw off the others, in particular Lance, who was proud that he was the show's closer and was nearly apoplectic when a couple of audience members kept shouting, "I want Candy!"

Having entertained ourselves in the bar afterwards by repeating some of Lance's clunky insults ("You know what a moron looks like? Get a mirror!"), Mike and I giggled our way down a motel hallway that smelled of cigarettes and Fritos, and when we got to my door, he wrapped his arms around me and confessed, "I want Candy, too."

Floored and excited, I answered, "I want Mike," and after I jammed my key in the lock, we pushed the door open and tumbled into the room and onto the stiff, flammable bedspread covering the concave mattress.

We were inhaling one another with kisses, our hands frisking one another like thorough arresting officers, and I would like to report here that some wild, tawdry sex ensued, but ensue it did not.

"Oh, Candy," groaned Mike, pulling himself away from me. "Oh God, Candy, I'm so sorry. I can't do this to Kirsten."

He rolled off the bed.

"Sorry!" he said, lunging for the door as if he'd heard a fire alarm.

It was shocking to go from being in the throes of lust to being so suddenly abandoned, but what was worse was to be abandoned by a nice guy who didn't want to cheat on his girlfriend.

I was thankful that our make-out-and-nothing-more session happened near the end of the tour rather than the beginning; at least the awkwardness wouldn't be prolonged. Nervous when we all met in the motel restaurant for breakfast the next morning, I saw Mike feeding pennies into the Lions Club gumball machine but pretended I didn't.

He was braver than I. "Look, Candy, I was a jerk and I'm sorry. I hope—"

"—at least you have hope," I said dramatically. "Now that you've dashed mine."

Mike looked at me warily and then seeing something in my eyes, smiled.

"So we're friends?" he said, offering me a cherry gumball.

"Since we can't be anything else," I said, holding up my palm.

"Guys," said Boris, slapping a folded copy of the *San Jose Mercury* newspaper against his thigh. "Guys, we got reviewed, and it's good!"

MELVIN HAD COLLECTED MY MAIL while I was on tour, and I took a nice big stack down to the pool, happy to see Ed on a chaise longue. It had been a long time since we'd been together poolside.

"What is it this time?" I asked, noticing the book splayed open on his stomach. "Secret alien landings or a government run amok?"

"Neither," said Ed, and as I settled into the lawn chair next to him, he passed me the book.

"*Love, Trust, and Who Takes Out the Garbage?*"

The long look I gave him asked, "Are you kidding me?" and Ed's flush darkened his already pink skin.

"I know, I know. I can't believe I'm reading it—let alone bringing it to a public place."

"Are you and Sharla having problems?"

"Don't mince words, Candy. And no, we're not. Well, not many. Some." He opened the cooler. "Good news—the YaZoo's officially gone." He handed me a can of Orange Crush. "To tell you the truth, Candy, I don't know whether I'm coming or going with her. She just seems . . . well, she's sure not like you."

"Should I take that as a compliment?"

"Definitely," said Ed, opening his can. "What I mean is—you don't have any of those feminine wiles . . . you're just a regular person. She's like, I don't know, I just can't figure her out. She spends so much time on how she looks; wouldn't you think a person who looks like Sharla would be fairly confident in herself? Once I waited for two hours while she got ready, and she winds up crying because she 'doesn't have anything to wear'! Still, as much as she drives me crazy, I'm crazy about her."

Nodding at the book on his lap, I asked, "So who does take out the garbage?"

"Usually not the person who brings it in, but I didn't have to read a book to figure that out." He shook his head, leaned back in the chaise longue, and shut his eyes.

"Don't think you're off the hook," I said as I rifled through my mail. "You're still going to have to explain that feminine wiles stuff . . . oh!"

Ed opened one eye.

"It's from Terry," I said, waving a postcard. "My friend from the Rogue Mansion?"

Opening his other eye, Ed nodded, having met her at one of my comedy performances.

"She's in Nepal!"

"Nepal, cool."

"I haven't seen her since before my tour, and I was going to call her today!"

"So what does she say?"

I stared at her neat handwriting for a moment before I read the card.

"'It took me a while, but you leaving the R.M. finally inspired me to do the same. What do I need benefits for? I'm young! So here I am looking up at Mt. Everest—I don't have the urge to climb it, but I always wanted to see it!'"

Ed and I laughed the way you will over a good surprise.

"That's great," he said, shutting his eyes again.

Thumbing through bills and bank statements, I came across a tissue-thin blue airmail envelope.

My gasp sounded like a little huuh.

"What now?" said Ed. "Did she fall in love with a sherpa?"

"No," I said, tearing open the envelope. "It's from my grandmother." I unfolded the letter and with greedy eyes scanned the first few lines. "Oh, my God!"

Ed sat up. "Candy, is everything all right?"

"She . . . she, well, oh my God, she got married! At the courthouse, before they left for Tahiti! She says they wanted the trip to be a real honeymoon!"

I turned to Ed, feeling the prickle of tears in my eyes.

"My grandma got married!"

"So it seems."

I read on, each sentence inciting from me a sigh or an exclamation.

"That must be some letter," said Ed.

"It is. Listen to this last paragraph." I cleared my throat and began to read.

Candy, my husband (I love that word!), Sven, is taking a nap now and snoring in a nice, fluttery way, and if I look out one window I see a blue blue ocean, and if I sit by another I see two lovely maids dressed in sarongs (they call them pareus) chatting under a palm tree.

Who'd think that I'd ever be in a tropical paradise with a man I had found love with, after I thought love was just a memory? Thank you so much for this gift of a Tahitian honeymoon (a real Tahitian Treat, ha ha), but so much more, thank you for the gift of being my granddaughter. As Sven (my husband!) likes to say, "Ain't life grand?"

XXX and some Os,
Grandma.

Ed and I sat quietly for a while, and then nodding toward the mail on my lap, he said, "So that's it? Just Nepal and Tahiti? Nothing from Outer Mongolia or Barbados?"

38

Not only did Claire Hellman have lots of ideas, she acted on them. She was her own high-voltage transformer, humming with so much energy that I joked I didn't dare touch her for fear of getting shocked. Within months of thinking of making a documentary about Francis and the Bel Mondo, she had managed to get a public television contract and funding and had already begun interviewing him.

"He is so excited," said Frank. "He met with Claire again yesterday at the Chateau Marmont, and he comes home whistling. He's whistling more than he's talking!"

We were in a guitar shop on Sunset, viewing the instruments on the wall as if they were pieces of art, which, to Frank, I suppose they were.

"Claire told me she's getting some great stuff. She says your dad's a great storyteller."

Frank's nostrils flared and he pursed his mouth, moving it from side to side.

"Sorry," he said, after a moment. "I'm just so happy for him."

I looped my arm through his. "Me, too."

"Hey you," said a greasy-haired sales clerk in a tone that suggested we were riffraff instead of potential customers. "Aren't you in United States of Despair?"

Frank, as surprised as I was, stared at the clerk.

"Yeah," he said warily, as if waiting to hear the clerk's negative review. "Yeah, I am."

"I thought so," said the clerk, wagging his head. "I've seen you guys at the Masque, and the Whiskey. You're radical, man."

"Thanks, man," said Frank gruffly.

The sales clerk gestured to a guitar on the wall. "You want to try out this Stratocaster? I saw you looking at it."

"Sure," said Frank, and despite his tough-guy mien his eyes shone with excitement.

MAEVE'S FATHER WASN'T THE SUBJECT of a documentary, but she was as proud of him as Frank was of Francis.

"Candy, you can't believe how his students adore him," she said, as we sat in dappled shade on the rickety bench facing the Hills's tennis court. Winter was here and while the temperature was in the midseventies, there was a thinness to the late-afternoon light. "Egon said he's the best teacher he's ever had."

"Who's Egon?"

Maeve pressed her lips together, but her smile quickly broke the seal. "This guy I met. At the university."

Maeve had just come home from a trip to Germany, and we had celebrated her return with a game of tennis. It might have been more of a celebration for me, since it was the first time in our history that I had beaten her. She blamed her defeat on jet lag.

"Uh, think you could spare a few more details?"

"*Jawohl!*" Maeve tucked a section of her lank blonde hair behind her ear. "He's tall—taller than me, and I can't tell you how thrilling it is to look *up* to a guy—and his English is flawless. Flawless with the kind of accent you'd expect to hear from someone narrating a fairy tale."

"Oh, brother," I said. "You've got it bad."

"Candy, he's the first guy I've ever felt . . . I don't know, at ease with. Like I don't have to apologize for anything. Anytime we were together—having coffee or taking a walk—I never felt any of that nervous dating ickiness."

We laughed, at both the words *nervous dating ickiness* and the shared understanding of what a lousy state to be in nervous dating ickiness was.

"Egon makes me feel like I only have to be myself with him and oh, Candy, he's so smart. Smart, kind, and he doesn't think it's weird that I'm a bodybuilder. In fact, he thinks my body is *schön.*"

"*Schön's* good, *jah*?"

"*Schön* is *zehr* good."

Deciding to have dinner together, we wandered down the path, and as we debated whether to go to a Thai place or Musso & Frank a sudden cry stopped us cold in our tracks.

"Did you hear that?" whispered Maeve.

My nod was frantic.

There was a romantic ruin to the Hills—it could have been the estate of Gloria Swanson in the movie *Sunset Boulevard,* years after William Holden's body was pulled out of the pool. I liked playing tennis on the dilapidated court (the ghosts of movie moguls arguing whether a lobbed ball was in or out), plus it was nice to escape into its almost jungle-like greenery set in the middle of a city. Still, there was an element of creepiness that made it a place I'd never venture into alone; the guy with the beard and a rucksack most likely was a hiker, but there was a chance he was the Hillside Strangler; the teenaged couple smoking pot by the crumbling chimney was probably skipping school, but they might be a modern-day version of Bonnie and Clyde, trigger fingers itchy.

There was another sob, and a tortured, "God! God damn it!"

Trying to figure out where the noise was coming from, Maeve and I bumped into each other.

"There he is," I whispered, pointing to a figure sitting amid the gnarled, aboveground roots of a fig tree.

We watched as the man put a bottle to his lips.

"He's drunk," said Maeve.

I squinted. "It's Jaz!"

We looked at each other, asking silent questions with nods and shrugs. The man was obviously in distress: should we approach him? But didn't the fact that he'd hiked up here convey a certain wish to keep his distress private? Deciding that his misery might be elevated by discovery, we tacitly agreed to leave but hadn't taken two steps when Jaz's voice stopped us.

"Hey!" he cried out. "Hey you!"

He struggled to stand among the thick fingers of roots but sank back down, his bottle clunking against the wood.

"Shit! Shit! Shit!"

Now more concerned than wary, Maeve and I raced over to him, asking him if he was all right.

"Do I sound like I'm all right?" Examining the bottle he thanked it for not breaking and took a sloppy swig of its remains. Whiskey dribbled down his chin, and when he wiped at it with the back of his hand his bloodshot eyes filled with tears.

I felt a stir of fear; something was really wrong.

"Jaz, is Aislin okay?"

The handsome, inebriated building manager jerked his head.

"Aislin? Have you heard from Aislin?"

"No. I just thought . . . well, from the way you're acting, I thought something might have happened to her."

"I haven't heard a word from that whore, other than the whore wants a divorce."

The look Maeve and I shared said it was time to go, and as we turned, Jaz wailed, "Don't go! Please!"

He sounded so pathetic we had to stop.

"Okay, but if you talk about Aislin like that again, we're leaving."

"Yeah," added Maeve.

"But she left me!" wailed Jaz. "She left me and now I've got nothing! No wife and now I've lost the best job of my life!"

"You got fired from Peyton Hall?" asked Maeve.

He made an odd noise, like a dog whose tail had been stepped on, followed by a bellowing "Ha!" and then he slumped against the tree trunk, pounding his knee as he laughed.

Maeve and I stood like befuddled scientists, watching our test monkey throw an unanticipated fit.

"Hoo, hoo," said Jaz, finally, wiping his blue and red eyes. "That's a good one! Managing Peyton Hall is the best job of my life!" He pulled at his nose as the final vestiges of laughter rumbled out of his chest, sighed, and tried to stand up but was unsuccessful, plopping down, hard. After some dips and weaving, he staggered upward like a boxer who'd been hit too many times.

"But no, Mary," he said, looking dully at Maeve, "my very best job, or should I say job offer, was playing the role of Errol Flynn."

"Jaz," I said, "what happened?"

"They're not going to make the bloody film! They strung me along all this time, but the green light finally turned red. And I'm out."

"Oh, no," I said.

Jaz's head wobbled and with a great sigh, he took a step, nearly falling on the tree roots.

"Here," said Maeve, and rushing forward, she put one arm around him. "Candy, get him on the other side."

FLANKING HIM, we stumbled down the path, through the broken gate, and onto Fuller Avenue, consoling Jaz as he alternately raged and wept.

"What am I supposed to do now?" he asked, his voice high as he overpronounced his syllables. "Go back to Vancouver and play another fucking mountaineer on *Wiley's Way*? Which, as piss-ant as it was, was the best part I'd had in a year! But all those little piddly piss-ant parts didn't matter, because I knew I was going to play Errol Flynn. In the biggest movie of the year, of the decade! People were finally going to know who Jaz Delwyn was!"

Instead of walking all the way to Hollywood Boulevard, we cut between two of the apartment buildings facing Fuller—one was Madame Pepper's—and made our way across the center grounds of Peyton Hall, past the neon sign, and across the lawn to Jaz's apartment.

"Mr. Delwyn!" said Werner, holding a sprinkler. "Are you all right?"

"I've been shot," said Jaz.

"Wass?" said the Swiss handyman, alarmed.

Both Maeve and I sought to reassure him; I shook my head and Maeve said, "No, he hasn't."

Jaz lurched to a stop, and Maeve and I made adjustments to keep him upright while keeping our balance.

"Yes, I most certainly have," he said to Werner. "Shot through the heart by the assassin Hollywood."

39

IN OLD MOVIES, to denote the passage of time, calendar pages shuffle and fly out of frame as if propelled by a good stiff wind. We were in a new decade—had anything ever sounded as modern as 1980?—and it seemed I had barely scribbled notes on a month's first day when I'd scribble notes for its last. The pages of my own datebook flew as if in a tornado, with the usual notations of business—*3/1/80—Weekend gig up in San Francisco at the Holy City Zoo!*—and pleasure—*6/4/80—Lunch at Barney's Beanery with Solange; maybe I should have gotten the Classic Chili instead of the Fireman's* . . .

A notation in my September calendaieum of that year combined business and pleasure, but mostly pleasure: *Screening of* The Man Behind the Bel Mondo*!*

"I TELL YOU, this gives me chills," whispered Melvin Slyke as the limousine pulled up in front of Peyton Hall and the chauffeur hopped out, opening the door for the guest of honor, Francis Flover, and his entourage—Frank, Melvin, and me. "The man is finally getting his due."

Even in his timeworn suits, Francis had always looked dapper, but in a tux he looked ready for his close-up.

"At one point, I think I had five tuxedos in my closet," he confided to me. "This is the only one I held on to. I must say I was proud no seams had to be let out!"

A screening room in the old Gower Studios had been rented and among the throng of people that stood outside of it were Claire and her brother, Eric. She waved us over with the ardor of a traffic cop on NoDoz and introduced us to some of the muckety-mucks at the public television company that had bankrolled the production.

"Isn't this exciting?" said Claire, taking Francis's arm.

"It is," said the old man, and taking her other arm, he dipped her, suave and assured. The crowd clapped.

It was not the last time.

As we watched the film—a mixture of old photos, movie clips, and current interviews—there was often applause: when Evie Carlyle, a popular 1950s singer, held Francis's hand and sang her signature "Old Man/ My Baby"; when Dixie Ribedeaux, the movie star, told how Francis kept a stock of crayfish in his freezer, instructing his chef to make something out of it whenever Dixie, a homesick Louisiana native, came into the club; and when Bryce Huntington, an actor hired whenever Rock Hudson wasn't available, said, "It's easy to be classy in public, but Francis Flover was classy when no one was watching. I couldn't get a job for seven straight months, and every day for two-hundred-fifteen days—I counted!—I ate dinner, my only meal of the day, at the Bel Mondo. On the house. And Francis never made me feel like I was taking charity; he always said, 'What the hell, Bryce! Right now I'm up—you'll be there in no time!'"

At the end of the film, Francis looked into the camera and said, "And that was the Bel Mondo. Real glamour and not-so-real glitz. Onstage talent that brought you to your feet and offstage drama that sometimes brought you to your knees. It was pure Hollywood, and for a while I was lucky enough to be part of it."

As his image faded and a photograph of him welcoming fur- and jewel-draped stars into the Bel Mondo came into focus, the credits rolled and the audience erupted into applause, bravos, and shouts of "Speech! Speech!"

Claire, holding up her long skirt in a bunch at her hip, bounded up the steps to the narrow stage, gesturing frantically for Francis to join her.

"Thank you all so much for coming!" she said. "Thanks to my mother, Winnie—" she waved to a woman in the front row—"Hi, Mom!—for telling me and my brother—Hi Eric!—all those wonderful stories of the Bel Mondo when we were growing up, and thanks to Jack Williams and Tricia Bayer of NBS for agreeing to finance Francis's story. And ladies and gentlemen—" she held out her arm—"Francis Flover!"

Onstage now, the documentary's star gave a curt yet suave bow and the crowd again went crazy.

When we had all quieted down, he looked out into the audience and said, "Tonight has been a dream." His voice broke and he took a moment to collect himself. "When I was at the Bel Mondo, I . . . I saw so many dreams come true, and just as many dreams unravel. I am proud to have been part of a community that doesn't discount dreams but encourages them. Thank you, Claire, thank you, everyone, for encouraging mine one more time."

It was a beautiful moment, and that Melvin Slyke honked when he blew his nose and Frank practically squeezed my hand into pulp only added to it.

IT WAS ONLY FITTING that Francis got a Hollywood ending. Three days after the screening of *The Man Behind the Bel Mondo,* he died in his sleep.

I had just made a turn at the deep end of the pool and was gliding through the water when I became aware of motion, then yelling, and a sudden splash.

"Candy!" cried Frank, flailing his arms in the water as he lunged toward me. "Candy, Pop's gone!"

He grabbed me, and I grabbed him back; fortunately, we could touch bottom at this point and weren't in danger of drowning each other.

He wailed as I led him across the shallow end of the pool, and when we got to the short ladder he seemed stumped as to what to do, and I helped him grab the railing so he could pull himself out.

That effort used up all his energy, and he crumpled on the cement, sobbing.

"Pop's dead," said Frank, lifting his face off the pavement. "Pop's gone!"

The few people who were at the pool—Sherri, Robb, and Bastien— had rushed over and helped me get Frank up and lead him to a chair. Robb wrapped a towel around Frank and stood behind him, keeping his hands on his shoulders. I knelt in front of him, taking his hands. Sherri and Bastien stood on both sides of him, their hands on his arms, all of us understanding that what Frank needed now was touch.

He cried so hard I thought he was going to throw up.

"Pop!" he'd holler between sobs, "Pop!"

When his teeth began to chatter, I told him we were going to get him in some warm clothes, and four people in their swimsuits formed a phalanx around the one in soaking wet jeans and T-shirt and escorted him back to my apartment.

Insisting he take a hot shower, I sat on the toilet the whole time, afraid he'd collapse in the stall. When I heard the water turn off, I said, "There's a towel on the rack and a robe on the door hook. I'll be waiting in the living room."

It was there that Frank told me the whole sad story, how'd he woken up early (strange for him; he usually didn't greet the day until the day was half-spent) and felt an odd quiet in his father's apartment.

"It was more than quiet," he said, clutching to his chest the mug of tea I made for him. "It was like a deep quiet. Like something big had been turned off. I went into his room, even though I didn't want to, and there he was, lying on his bed with a smile on his face."

"He was smiling?"

Frank nodded and offered a jagged smile of his own.

"I always thought it was a bunch of bullshit when people talked about dead people and said, 'Oh, he looked so peaceful,' . . . but he did. He looked peaceful. I'm freakin' out, though—I don't want him looking peaceful—I want him looking alive! And I called the ambulance and Melvin heard the sirens and he came over, and he even went with them when they came to pick up Pop. I couldn't even do that for him!"

"Frank," I said, pushing the words past the huge lump in my throat, "you didn't need to do that for him. You'd done everything you should have. You were a great son."

"He was a great pop," said Frank, and he collapsed to the floor on his knees, burying his head in my lap. His usual upright spikes of hair were draped against his head like a stringy blue scarf, and I petted them over and over and over.

On the day of his father's funeral, Frank was a different man. Greeting mourners (Francis would have been thrilled at the turnout of old Hollywood), he was dignified and stately, a comfort to those who needed comfort.

"To tell you the truth," he told me and Claire at the cake and coffee reception we held poolside, "I was worried about him a long time ago. He was getting so . . . frail. But then you," he lowered his head, looking at Claire, "you came along and it was like he was young again."

"I wish he could have lived to see the television broadcast," said Claire, her voice warbling.

"He didn't need to," said Frank. "The night of the screening, when he got all that applause from the Hollywood community—that's what he called it, 'the Hollywood community'—well, that's all he needed."

"How you doin', man?" asked Mayhem, carrying a plate loaded with pieces of the three different cakes I had baked.

"Fair to middling. I was just telling them how much Pop dug that documentary."

Mayhem nodded. "Dug he did, man. I just wish he could be around to see it win an Oscar."

Claire's laugh was a one-syllable "Hah." "It was made for television, Mayhem. It's not eligible for an Academy Award."

The skinny rocker skimmed off the cake's chocolate frosting with his fork. "Then there needs to be a fucking rule change."

40

"Oh, Candy, that was absolutely wonderful! I knew you were going to be good, but I didn't know you were going to be that good."

"Thanks . . . I think."

"I've never seen her laugh so hard," said Sven. "And that's the God's honest truth."

"Thanks, Sven."

My grandmother and step-grandfather (it had never crossed my mind that I'd ever use that term) were on what they called an extended honeymoon, which included a trip to the West Coast.

Having them in the audience was an odd experience, and after repeating my life saber over and over as I walked up to the stage, I reminded myself not to change anything because of their presence.

Just do what you usually do. Let them judge you on that.

In the course of my fifteen-minute set, I talked about the news of the day, including the upcoming presidential election.

"I don't think I want an actor in the White House," I began.

"Reagan *was* an actor," shouted a burly guy in the second row. "But after that he was a damn good governor."

"Yeah, but when he realized he couldn't hire a stunt double to do the boring stuff, the day-to-day governing stuff, he wanted out of his contract."

There were some laughs, some whistles, and some boos.

"And what about that Nancy Reagan? Have you noticed she can't stand next to her husband without wearing that weird smile? She looks like the Mona Lisa on 'ludes."

"That's disrespectful!" shouted Burly Man. "How come you don't say anything about the Carters?"

"Listen, peanut farmers get enough abuse. I mean, Jimmy Carter could be the most brilliant man who ever lived, but you've got to admit, having the words *peanut farmer* on your résumé takes away some of your gravitas."

My grandmother only had one caveat to her praise.

"I wish you wouldn't make fun of Jimmy Carter," she said softly on the ride home. "I like him."

"Well, heck, I like Ronald Reagan," said Sven. "But that doesn't mean you can't poke fun at him." He leaned forward so that I could see his wink. "All's fair in love and comedy, right, Candy?"

"Exactly, Sven."

As FIRST-TIME VISITORS to southern California, the newlyweds had a checklist of things they wanted to accomplish and seeing me perform was #1. Following that was visiting #2—the ocean; #3—Beverly Hills; #4—Hollywood Boulevard; and #5—Griffth Park Observatory.

They celebrated each item checked off. My grandmother got a particularly big kick navigating the Map of the Stars as I drove their rental car through the swanky flats of Beverly Hills.

"Oh kid, that's Lucille Ball's house! And Jimmy Stewart's! Oh my goodness, Sven, isn't that Sandra Dee?"

Sven peered out the window. "That little blonde gal walking her Chihuahua? Looks like her, but wouldn't she hire people to do that for her?"

The observatory isn't something my grandmother would have had on her list, but she recognized the value of compromise in marriage.

"He's the stargazer in the family," whispered my grandmother as we leaned back in our seats, watching the planetarium's laser show. "This sort of stuff makes me kind of dizzy."

A big thrill, however, was not plotted on their checklist. Having heard from Maeve what a fan my grandmother was of *Summit Hill,* Taryn Powell made the kind gesture of inviting us onto the show's set.

"For crying out loud!" said my grandmother. "What am I supposed to wear to something like that?"

"We'll have to get you an evening gown," I said. "And a tux for Sven."

"Where are we going to find—" began my grandmother, and then seeing my face, she stopped. "Oh, ha ha. She's kidding, Sven."

"Now THIS OF COURSE IS OUR LIVING ROOM," said Taryn, sweeping her arm. "Scene of many of the Summits' biggest dramas."

"Oh my," said my grandmother, pointing to the huge fake stone fireplace. "That's where you shot Judith Partridge."

"She was holding a knife to my son's throat. What was I supposed to do?"

"What this room needs is a recliner," said Sven of the room decorated in expensive antiques, or facsimiles thereof.

Taryn laughed. "Spoken just like Baird Davies."

"Her third husband," explained my grandmother. "He was a real man of the people—a mechanic—and probably Serena's greatest love. But then he died when he took the new Jaguar out for a spin."

"The brakes had been tampered with," said Taryn, and with a laugh she added, "you *are* a fan, aren't you?"

"Like Candy says, I never miss an episode."

"And now she's got me watching it," said Sven.

We got a tour of the kitchen set, where, my grandmother explained, the estate's maid had canoodled with Serena's son—not the son who had the knife held to his throat—but Jed, the handsome but cheating financier.

"That was supposed to be a one-episode fling," said Taryn, "until we got so much mail about it."

"Because she got pregnant with quadruplets!" said Grandma.

As we toured, Taryn greeted an electrician working on a row of lights, chatted with a woman from the wardrobe department who asked if Taryn had approved her yacht race costume, and conferred with someone carrying a script. This glimpse into a working television show was all very heady for my grandmother, but the pinnacle of excitement came when, while touring the patio set lush with fake potted plants, she met Rianna Summit, aka Sharla West.

"Good heavenly days," said my grandmother softly.

"Did you see what they have me wearing for the yacht race?" Sharla asked Taryn. "It's absolutely hideous." She pivoted slightly—all good beauty queens have mastered the pivot—and tossed back her glossy auburn hair. "Hey, Candy. Taryn told me you were bringing by your grandparents."

It was weird having her refer to Sven as my grandparent, but I let it pass and introduced both of them.

"I absolutely hate you," said my grandmother, holding on to the hand Sharla offered. "But I mean that in the very best way. Rianna Summit is the best bad-girl on television."

Sharla made a face at Taryn that asked, "See?" before treating my grandmother to a full-wattage smile. "Thank you so much. It's a real acting job because I'm the exact opposite of Rianna."

"Not quite the exact opposite," said Taryn with a smile rivaling Sharla's in its dazzling insincerity.

SVEN WAS AN EASY TRAVELING COMPANION who not only was up for anything we wanted to do, but insisted that my grandmother and I spend a little "girl time" by ourselves.

"You two go have a cup of coffee," he'd say, opening up his wallet and handing us a ten. "And some dessert while you're at it."

We took him up on his offer and money several times (he insisted), and when we went to Schwab's Drug Store we brought along someone I'd been dying for my grandmother to meet, Madame Pepper.

For the outing, the seer didn't wear her work uniform; both women wore pantsuits and surreptitiously checked out each other's. (There wasn't much stylistic difference in their polyester slacks and buttoned short-sleeved tunics, although my grandmother accessorized her peach one with a scarf and Madame Pepper adorned her scarlet one with a brooch.)

Sitting at the counter, sipping our coffee, my grandmother enthused about how excited she was to be at Schwab's, considering it was where Lana Turner was discovered.

"Actually, that's a myth," said the waitress whose hair spiraled in coronet braids around her head. "She was discovered at another coffee shop—the Top Hat."

"Baloney," said another waitress putting dirty cups into a bus tray under the counter. "How do you know that's not just another myth?"

As we dug into our pieces of pie, Madame Pepper made the casual announcement that Lana Turner had been one of her clients.

"It was right after *The Postman Always Rings Twice*. She was at the peak of her fame and beauty, but all she wanted to know from me was if she ever was going to find true love."

The trajectory of my grandmother's fork from pie plate to mouth halted.

"Lana Turner was one of your clients?"

"Grandma," I said as Madame Pepper offered a shrug and took a bite of her pecan pie. "Madame Pepper is soothsayer to the stars. She's seen everybody."

One of those scruffy-looking actors who often plays the part of the defendant in television movies got up from the end of the counter to answer the ringing pay phone.

"He got the part," said Madame Pepper, just before the man's "Yes!" resounded through the restaurant/drugstore.

"What's it like?" asked my grandmother softly, as she set her fork on her plate. "What is it like to see people's future?"

My eye rolling was only intended for my amusement, but apparently the Madame was privy to it and she laughed.

"Your granddaughter thinks I'm a bit of a fraud."

"Not a bit."

"Candy!" my grandmother scolded.

"No, no, she does not insult me," said Madame Pepper. "It is the nature of our relationship to tease one another. A little game we play." One final sip finished her coffee and she set the cup on its saucer.

"Miss!" said my grandmother. "Could we get some more coffee, please?"

"Sure," said the waitress, bringing the pot over. "But just so you know, we charge for refills."

Having been at Schwab's with Maeve, I was familiar with this policy, but my grandma wasn't, and she gaped at the waitress.

"You charge for refills?"

I knew this practice was an abomination to people who came from the part of the country that invented—and embraced—the bottomless cup of coffee.

"It's because of all the actors," said the waitress. "They'll sit here all day, drinking gallons of coffee, waiting for their agents to call. So the boss says they've got to pay for refills. But I'm from Iowa," she said, filling our cups. "And I don't always enforce it."

My grandmother sipped at her contraband brew and then asked quietly, "So when did you realize you had the gift?"

"The gift?" I said. "Grandma, Madame Pepper is a businesswoman. If she's got the gift of anything, it's the gift of salesmanship."

"I understood from a young age," said Madame, leaning toward the counter to better speak around me and to my grandmother, "that the veil that covers much was not so opaque for me."

I laughed, at both the sentiment and its clunky expression, and my grandmother nudged me, hard.

Offering a patient, slightly sour smile, Madame Pepper continued.

"For years I tired to ignore it, but after my husband died and I had no one to rely on, I decided it was time to make use—and a living—off my talents. And I am happy to tell you that your new marriage will be both long lasting and loving."

I wasn't about to make fun of that pronouncement, but had I the slightest inclination to, seeing my grandmother's smile would have stopped me. After a moment her expression grew serious.

"And what about Candy?"

"Well, Candy, as you know, is a giver."

"Oh, absolutely," agreed my grandmother. "She's always been willing to share what she's got."

I felt as if I were eavesdropping on a conversation about someone I didn't know.

"Yes, I have benefited from what she shares," said Madame Pepper. "From cakes to cookies to jokes to friendship. There aren't too many young girls willing to give these things to an old lady."

"You're not an old lady," said my grandmother, defending a fellow member of her generation. "But I know what you mean. Candy had a lot taken away, but she never stopped giving herself."

"And she will be rewarded for that."

Not prepared to hear this sort of answer—not prepared to hear this sort of conversation—I coughed a bit as I swallowed my coffee.

"So you see big things for Candy?"

"Oh yes. I see big changes coming."

"Oh brother," I said, knowing that if I didn't make a joke, I was going to start crying. "'Big changes coming'—that's right out of Fortune Telling 101."

While my grandmother tsked at my irreverence, Madame Pepper winked.

"Matter of fact, I got an A in that class."

41

THE FIRST BIG CHANGE that Madame Pepper predicted had to do with Peyton Hall.

"Did you see this?" asked Melvin Slyke, after banging on my door. He thrust a piece of paper in my face. "Did you read this goddamned letter?"

I hadn't seen or read anything, including the newspaper, due to the fact it was seven a.m., and I had only gotten home a few hours earlier, having gone to Canter's Deli with several comedians after our sets.

Stepping back—Melvin was shaking the letter in front of my face and I didn't want to get a paper cut—I saw an envelope that had been slipped under my own door. Melvin noticed it, too.

"That's it! That's the letter, Candy!"

Its contents were brief and to the point. Our apartment complex had been sold to a developer who had plans to demolish it and build a high-rise, and we had three months to move out.

"You see that?" said Melvin, pointing one of his narrow artist fingers at the print. "Three months! In three months we have to be gone!"

I stood there mutely, feeling as if someone had punched me in the stomach.

"I'm glad Francis isn't around to see this," said my neighbor, and trouncing back to his apartment he added, "I'm calling my lawyer!"

WHEN CLAIRE PHONED with a last-minute invitation to meet her and Eric at Michael's, I told her sorry, but Solange was on her way to pick me up for dinner.

"Have her come, too. The more the merrier!"

We joined them sitting in a gold vinyl booth, and after our hellos and Hollywood air kisses Claire asked, "So how's Frank Jr., doing? I worry about him."

"You should be," I said. "He just got evicted!"

"What?"

"We all did! They're going to tear down Peyton Hall and build a high-rise!"

"They can't tear that place down," said Claire. "It's a Hollywood landmark."

"If you can get more renters into a high-rise," said Eric with a shrug, "then the landmark'll have to go."

"That's pretty cold, Eric," said Solange.

"Cold, but true. When do we let a little history stand in the way of profit?"

"Well, look at Rome," said Solange. "Look at Athens. Look at Bagdad and—"

"—you tell him," said Claire, nodding in approval.

"I'm talking about Hollywood," said Eric. "And Hollywood's an American city where unfortunately, old is not considered gold."

"My brother the poet," said Claire, bumping Eric's shoulder with her own. I can't say that struck me as a particularly hilarious line, but Eric and Claire felt differently; both burst out laughing.

"Gee, I'm glad they're getting such a charge out of my potential homelessness," I said to Solange.

"Here you are," said the waiter, setting down a silver champagne bucket.

Watching him pour four glasses, I asked, "Am I missing something?"

"Candy, believe me, I'm sick about Peyton Hall," said Claire, "but we'd already planned this celebration."

"Celebration of what?" I asked.

"Of new experiences."

Eric raised his glass. "And starring in them."

"I cannot wait to find out what you're talking about," I said, clinking everyone's glass with my own.

THE MAN BEHIND THE BEL MONDO had given Claire Hellman that much-coveted commodity in Hollywood: attention. People who wouldn't take her calls prior to its air date were now inundating her with theirs. Everyone wants to work with a success, and her documentary had set ratings records, and because of so many requests it already had an encore performance.

"Of course I want to keep making documentaries," Claire said. "Real stories about real people. But I'm not adverse to a few side projects either, especially when one virtually drops into my lap."

"Remember when we brought a couple of people to see you at the Improv a few weeks ago?" said Eric.

"Yeah," I said, clueless but excited.

"Melanie Breyer was one of them." Claire took a sip of champagne. "So Melanie—from the Breyer Candy family, by the way—and I were talking after she saw you onstage, and she was saying she'd love to do a show with you—"

"Something new and fresh," said Eric. "Comedy, but not necessarily stand-up—"

"We were talking about how there are so few women comics compared to men, and then we got to talking about nighttime television talk show hosts, and how they're all men."

"Starting with Steve Allen and Jack Paar," said Eric. "And Johnny Carson, of course, and Joey—"

"—Bishop and Merv Griffin and Dick Cavett and Tom Snyder," said Claire nodding. "And this is the really great thing Melanie said to me, Candy: 'Women stay up late, too—when's there going to be a female host?'"

"Well, there's Joan Rivers," said Solange. "She's great."

"But she's only Johnny's guest host," said Eric.

"So then," said Claire, her smile stretching from one side of her mole-filled face to the other, "we got the great idea of producing a talk show! With you as host!"

The Crystal Room of Michael's Restaurant was full of mirrors and chandeliers; it didn't take much effort to see your own reflection. There's no noun form for *stun* but there should be because mine reflected it. Stunningness. Stunnition. Stundom.

"Oh . . . my . . . God." My skin seemed alive, prickling with excitement. "A late-night television talk show?"

"Oops," said Claire as she and Eric exchanged looks. "I guess we should have been a little more clear. This would be a late-night talk show for the stage. I'd direct it in the theater Melanie owns. The Swan on Melrose."

"Oh," I said, the skin tingling fading.

"I saw Marty Robbins at the Swan Theater," said Solange. "It's a beautiful venue."

Claire shot Solange a look of gratitude.

"It'd be the perfect showcase for you, Candy," said Eric. "We're setting up a meeting this week, okay?"

"Okay," I said with a smile that probably could have been bigger.

42

DURING THE FIRST MEETING I had with Melanie Breyer, I confessed how I thought my childhood dream of hosting a television talk show was coming true, and how disappointed I'd felt upon learning the show was meant for the stage.

"But now that I've thought about it, I'm excited. I think it'll be a blast."

"Great," said Melanie. "That's what we want it to be."

Sitting in her office at the Swan Theater, we batted around ideas.

"Certainly we want an element of improv in the show," said Claire, "but we see it as a scripted show."

"So it would basically be a play about a talk show?" I asked.

"Yes," said Melanie. She templed her fingers in front of her chest. "We obviously haven't exactly thought everything out, but, yes, it's basically a TV talk show . . . onstage."

"What we're thinking," said Claire, "is a really fun, loose production. We'll work from a script, but we'll hire actors who, like you, aren't afraid to improvise."

"Speaking of the script," said Melanie, "I'm assuming you'd like to be a part of writing it?"

I nodded. "Definitely. But I'd need some help."

"Eric represents lots of writers," said Claire.

"And I know some," said Melanie. "We'll solicit material and then arrange a couple meetings so you can see who you click with and who you don't. And if there's a comic you think you might want to work with, bring him or her onboard. Remember, we'd like to open in late March, which gives us over four months. You think that's enough time?"

"I'll make sure it is," I said, rubbing my hands together.

TWO DAYS LATER at the Comedy Store, I ran into the person I wanted to work with.

"Candy Ohi!" said Mike Trowbridge, approaching me as I was leaving out the side door. "Were you on tonight?"

I nodded.

"Did you kill?"

My shrug was modest. "Some maiming might have occurred."

Mike laughed. "I'm on in ten minutes. Wanna watch?"

I did.

"I LOVED THAT BIT ABOUT YOUR GRANDPA showing you how to dress," I said afterward, when we had walked next door to the bar at the Hyatt House. "Tell me that first part again."

Comics are usually not shy about honoring requests.

"Mikey," he said, making his voice warble with age, "Mikey, of course a man puts on his boxers first—you've got to protect your valuables, naturally—but after that, I like to put on my tie. It tells the day you believe it's worth getting dressed up for."

"And he really did that?" I asked, wanting to know how much was fact and how much was comic embellishment.

Mike held up his palm. "Honest to God. He'd be standing there in his underwear and a knotted tie—a loose knotted tie—around his neck."

The waitress served our drinks.

"I liked that song you played for that couple when you found out they were on their honeymoon."

Sipping his beer, Mike nodded.

"Thanks. Can't go wrong playing 'When I Fall in Love,' to newlyweds." He paused to slake his thirst again. "I saw you in La Jolla a couple months ago, and I think I just missed you in San Francisco—"

"—you were at the Holy City Zoo?"

"I was booked there the day after you left." He took a long sip of beer. "So other than that, what have you been up to? What's new?"

And so I told him.

"Are you kidding me?"

There are a lot of ways a fellow comic could deliver a line like that—with disbelief, with jealousy, with anger—but the only thing I heard in Mike Trowbridge's delivery was glee.

He slapped the tabletop and laughed.

"Candy, that's fantastic! An onstage talk show—what a great idea!"

"You mind turning down the volume, pal?" asked half of a hung-over rock and roll couple in the next booth.

Leaning across the table, Mike whispered, "Your own show!" and that was when I asked him if he'd like to write for it.

He sank back in his seat as if I'd pushed him.

"Are you serious?"

"Yes! You know how much I like to improvise, but we still haven't quite figured out the premise and—"

"—of course, I will, Candy. It'll be a blast!"

I beamed. My sentiments exactly.

A PAPER AIRPLANE SLID ALONG the makeshift runway of the conference table.

"Lunch?" was written on one of its wings and on the other I carefully wrote "Sure" and shot it back in the direction from whence it had come.

"Great," said Mike, standing up at the opposite end of the table. "Let's go."

In front of divided piles of material, he and I had spent the morning reading through jokes, essays, monologues, and sketches. Claire and Melanie had given me and Mike carte blanche to select the writers, and it was a laborious task, interrupted occasionally with laughter or groans.

"I'm really not very hungry," I said, studying the diner's menu.

"Me neither," said Mike, "I just thought I should eat something other than those Breyer Bricks."

Heir to a candy fortune, Melanie stocked glass bowls throughout the small offices of the theater with the family product, including Breyer Bricks (gold-wrapped chocolate squares), Breyer Dazzles (fruit chews), and Breyer Moos (milk chocolate caramels).

"I know," I said. "Growing up with all that candy, how can Melanie not be a four-hundred-pound diabetic?"

"And still have her own teeth."

We both ordered chicken noodle soup and after it was served began to talk shop.

"I never knew there were so many bad writers out there," said Mike.

"Ugh! All those mother-in-law jokes! I thought they went out with Henny Youngman."

"Some guy once asked me if I was influenced by Henny Youngman."

"Why? Your jokes aren't that dumb."

Mike smirked. "It was the music angle he was referring to. Although I like to think I play trumpet better than he played violin."

I squeezed a cellophane packet of crackers and dusted my soup with its crumbs.

"So who would you say has influenced you?"

Helping himself to the cracker basket, Mike copied my crushing and dispersal technique.

"As a kid, I loved Red Skelton. And Bob Hope in his movies and TV specials. Now I don't think there's anybody better than George Carlin and Richard Pryor. How about you?"

"I loved Red Skelton, too, and I loved Lucy and Carol Burnett . . . but more than anyone, Johnny Carson."

"And now you're doing your own talk show!"

As I returned Mike's smile, a helium gas of happiness rose in my chest. "I know."

BY THE END OF THE AFTERNOON, we sat back, exhausted from the reams of jokes and anecdotes and stories we had read, discussed, and judged. Agreeing on the list of writers we wanted to interview, we called it a day, and as Mike made some final notes, I fashioned a paper airplane myself and wrote on it "Dinner . . . and?"

My aim was good and the airplane sailed across the room, landing in front of its target. My heart thumped as I watched Mike read its two-word invitation and then thudded when I saw his face. He looked a little seasick, which wasn't promising, considering we weren't on a boat.

"Uh, sorry, Candy," he said, a flush coloring his face. He forced himself to look up at me. "It's just that . . . well, Kirsten and I have something planned tonight."

"No problem," I said, the contagion of his flush spreading to my own face. "Just a suggestion."

We busied ourselves straightening up already-straight piles of paper and gathering up our pens and notebooks, and the good-byes we said were stiff and awkward.

I called Kirsten all sorts of names on the way home but reserved the biggest name calling for myself: *Dumb shit. Why couldn't I just have written "Dinner?" Stupid jerk. Why did I have to write the rest? Loser.*

Lowell Balin was a comic who didn't believe humor, like testosterone, was manufactured mainly in the scrotum, and we hired him along with my friend PJ Rand.

Melanie didn't pay us a huge amount of money to write a script, but for all of us, at this stage in our careers, getting paid at all was a bonus. Meeting around performance and work schedules (PJ waited tables and Lowell worked at a book store) we four writers met in the theater's small conference room, hammering out ideas. We called the show *The Sorta Late Show* (an 8 p.m. curtain time didn't exactly qualify as late) *with Candy Ohi* and decided that while we would have a cast of characters and several set scenes, it would ultimately be a different show every night. I would play the host as well as a few characters, à la Johnny Carson's Carnac and Aunt Blabby.

"But remember, I don't want to do any stereotypical Asian characters—no laundresses or Samurai warriors or stuff like that."

"Belushi's already done that Samurai character, anyway," said Mike. "But how about a Samurai Laundress—"

My look stopped him.

"Kidding," he said, laughing. "Just kidding."

Since I was using my real name (well, my real stage name) for my character, we decided we'd use the real first names of the actors who were hired and then figure out a fake last name.

"Okay, so we've agreed your sidekick is a big dumb macho guy, right?" said PJ, flipping pages of a yellow legal pad. "And the show's director is a member of the Daughters of the American Revolution and the wife of the president of CANS?"

CANS—Columbia/American/National Broadcasting System—was the fictional network of our fictional talk show.

"And then we've got the stoned cameraman and the depressed makeup girl."

"The casting sessions are going to be so much fun," I said.

"Yeah," said Mike. "Especially now that I don't have to go through one myself."

At my suggestion, both Claire and Melanie saw Mike's act and agreed that he should play the show's bandleader. Mike had already enlisted his old band mates to make up *The Sorta Late Show* Band.

"I'm almost done writing the show's theme song," Mike told me. "I can't wait to play it for you."

"I can't wait to hear it."

43

THE FLYER TUCKED UNDER MY DOOR gave the particulars of the first meeting of Tenants United!

About thirty people were assembled on the east side of the pool, under Billy Gray Green's apartment windows, and the talk as I entered through the gate ran more to shouting than conversational.

"This place is a landmark!" said Melvin Slyke. "You don't tear down landmarks!"

"What about the lease I signed?" said Bastien. "I must honor the lease, but you don't have to?"

"This is our home!" said June, holding up her mangy white dog.

"Yeah!" said Vince Perrogio. "I've been here since they built the place! I've written my best books here!"

A slight man in a tailored suit stood in front of the group, his hands clasped behind his back, looking no more ruffled than if he were accepting compliments on his alligator shoes.

"People, look. We're well aware of the attachments people make to their homes. Of course we are. But you, as renters, must also be aware that the owners of a property have a right to do whatever they wish with their property."

"This isn't just a property!" said Vince. "It's Peyton Hall!"

"For the first time," I said, sidling next to Ed, "I'm thinking I might want to read one of his books."

"Read Raymond Chandler instead," whispered Ed. "Perrogio's a poor imitation."

"Mr. Delwyn?" said the alligator shoe guy, and Jaz, looking like he was ready to face the gallows, slunk forward.

For a building manager, Jaz had not been much of a presence around the building he managed. When I ran over with my rent check or some homemade cookies, he'd half-open the door, offering a dim, apologetic smile. Where he once was like one of the showy bird of paradise plants that sprang up around the complex, now he was a withered and colorless houseplant.

"Uhh," he said, standing next to the man in the suit, but not looking 1 percent as comfortable, "well, you heard what Mr. DelaCruz had to say . . . and um, I think we should all thank him for coming here today, which he . . . um, certainly didn't need to do. And with that, uh, thank you, and—"

"Wait a minute," said Ed. "Are you saying this is a done deal? That there's nothing more we tenants can do?"

"That is correct," said Mr. DelaCruz. "The wheels are in motion. The complex will be torn down. A new building will be built."

A chorus of "No's!" was unleashed by the crowd and with a brisk nod serving as a good-bye, Mr. DelaCruz picked up his alligator briefcase and made his way to the gate, Jaz loping after him like a dog hoping he'd earned a treat.

After they exited, Melvin whistled for quiet.

"If we're united, we'll beat this. Now who's with me?"

There was a unanimous show of hands, and by the time the meeting broke up we had elected Melvin president of our tenants' union and Sherri as our secretary. Vince Perrogio asked to serve as sergeant at arms/ bouncer.

"Because, really," he said, rubbing his thick hands together, "I'd like nothing more than to throw the bums out on their ears."

After the meeting disbanded, I decided to take a swim, but not before inviting Ed over to dinner. "Maeve'll be there, too and we're going to decorate my Christmas tree. So if you and Sharla don't have plans—"

"We don't. She's on location in Monterey. What time?"

EVERYONE TOOK TURNS throwing an unbreakable game show dish against the wall (my tried-and-true party trick), and afterwards we sat down to the Yankee pot roast dinner that had been simmering all day in my Crock-Pot.

Ed led off the conversation by telling us of a recent fight he'd had with Sharla.

"She's convinced she's going to get an invitation to Reagan's inaugural ball."

"So's my mother," said Maeve. "She was in a play once with Nancy. Although she voted for that John Anderson guy."

Ed shook his head.

"Well, not only did Sharla vote for Reagan, she also contributed—a lot—to his campaign. An invitation's pretty likely."

"So what was the fight about?" I asked.

"I told her I wouldn't go with her."

Maeve stared at Ed. "You told her you wouldn't go to a presidential inauguration ball? Why not?"

Anger was like a drawstring, pulling tight Ed's features.

"Because I went to school at Berkeley when Governor Reagan said our campus was, and I quote, 'a haven for communist sympathizers, protesters, and sex deviants!' I was there during the People's Park protest, when he sent in the National Guard. Where I got gassed!" Ed's pink face deepened in color. "I'm a public school teacher, Maeve, and Mr. Reagan is not a fan of public education. Tit for tat. I'm not a fan of his!"

We sat for a moment in a silence cloudy with his anger.

"And Sharla doesn't respect how you feel?" I said finally.

Ed sighed before offering a rueful smile. "Sharla respects how I feel when she feels the same way."

THE TREE DECORATION took all of five minutes (it was a three-foot artificial tabletop model I'd gotten at JJ Newberry's), and as we all stood back to admire our masterpiece I tipped a lamp shade, and the concentrated light that shone on the tree also cast Ed's shadow on the wall.

"Ed," I said, seized with artistic inspiration. "Move closer to the wall!"

"Why? What's wrong?"

"Nothing. I'm going to immortalize you, that's all."

"With that?" asked Maeve, looking at the thick black marker I dug out of the end table drawer.

"Yeah. I'm going to trace his silhouette."

"You can't draw on the walls with that! You'll never get your cleaning deposit back."

"Maeve, this place is going to be torn down," said Ed.

"Don't say that!"

"Yeah, Ed," I said, irritated. "You were at the meeting today; we're not going to let it be torn down. Besides," I said, turning to Maeve, "when *I* decide to move out—if I ever do—I can always paint over it."

Ed sidled up next to the wall. "How do you want me to pose?"

"In profile," I said. "Pretend you're walking."

Ed was a compliant model, freezing into position as I dragged the marker alongside his leg, around his butt, up his back and around his arm and hand, over his shoulder, head, and around the features of his face, and back down the other side of the body.

"Okay, now sign your name on the inside," I said when I was finished and handed him the marker.

In clear, teacherly handwriting, he wrote *Ed* inside one leg and *Stickley* inside the other.

We all admired the handiwork, and then Ed traced Maeve who stood flexing her biceps.

"Wow," I said, squinting. "You made her look like Popeye."

"Well, I do look like Popeye," said Maeve, nodding her approval. "Okay, Candy, I'll draw you now."

I stood in profile, trying to pose like an Egyptian hieroglyph.

"Oh, that's good," said Maeve. "But lift your leg up higher."

Maeve was a slow and methodical tracer, and struggling to keep my balance, I told her to hurry up.

"Maeve," said Ed, watching from the plaid couch, "you've got to have the pen closer to her body. It looks like she's got elephantiasis in that leg."

As I began to protest, there was a pounding on the door.

"What the—" I said.

"Hey, don't move," said Maeve. "I'm almost done."

"Candy!" said Frank, bursting through the door Ed opened. "Candy, did you hear?"

My heart pounded as I dropped my pose.

"Hear what?"

"John Lennon's been shot!"

The phone rang. It was Mike.

"Candy, did you hear? John Lennon's been shot!"

A minute after that Solange called, and then Claire, and after that I left the phone off the hook.

It was a strange night. We watched TV for a while but were turned off by the reporters whose reverence for the topic was undone by a breathless sort of excitement reserved for big scoops.

I lit several candles, and I told my friends how as a little girl I'd watched the Beatles on *The Ed Sullivan Show* with my grandma.

"Anytime the camera would pan to the audience, I'd stand up and go nuts, copying those screaming teenagers." I smiled at the memory. "And then my grandma stood up and screamed with me."

Ed said that after getting the excellent news that he'd flunked his physical (flat feet) and wouldn't be drafted to Vietnam, he drove around along the Pacific Coast Highway singing "Revolution" at the top of his lungs.

"When I moved back with Pop after he got custody, he bought me *Rubber Soul*," said Frank. "I think he wanted me to know he was still a hip guy, you know? I remember he said, 'Norwegian Wood' was just about the prettiest song he'd ever heard."

I passed around a box of tissues.

"John was my favorite Beatle!" said Maeve, wiping away tears. "I got in the only fight in my life over him. It was in the eighth grade, and DeAnn Hoffman said he looked like a pointy old lady and that anyone who liked John better than Paul was a moron. So I punched her in the stomach and she punched me back and we wound up rolling around on the gym floor."

She inhaled a deep sniff.

"You know what Miss Unger, the P.E. teacher, said after she'd pulled us apart? She said, 'Don't you know, girls, that all you need is love?'"

After a moment of processing, we laughed, needing the release.

"She didn't tell you to get back?" asked Ed.

Frank snorted. "Or just let it be?"

This started a tribute, all of us trying to remember titles of Beatles' songs to memorialize one of their creators.

"Do You Want to Know a Secret?" I said, to which Ed replied, "I Want to Tell You."

When Frank scolded, "You Can't Do That!" referring to the newly drawn silhouettes on the wall, I apologized, saying, "I'm a Loser."

Then picking up the marker, I asked Frank if he'd like to pose, because it could be a really cool wall, "With a Little Help from My Friends."

He stood facing the wall, one arm crooked and the other held high up at a diagonal, and when I was done tracing him, he took the pen and printed his name down his neck.

We all sat on the plaid couch studying the four silhouettes on the wall.

"You were posing like you were playing the guitar, right, Frank?" said Maeve.

"Yeah."

"It doesn't really translate," said Maeve. "Can anyone draw a guitar? I think someone should draw in a guitar."

"I think it's a great tribute," said Ed.

"What do you mean?" I asked.

"It reminds me of the riderless horse they had at President Kennedy's funeral processional. The horse with Kennedy's boots put in the stirrups backwards? So I'm thinking Frank's holding Lennon's invisible guitar is kind of like that."

"Man," said Frank, "I wish I could say that's what I was thinking."

"Maybe you were," said Maeve. "Just not consciously."

44

"PERFECT," said Madame Pepper, admiring the old pink taffeta gown I'd found in a used clothing store on Vermont Avenue and a cardboard tiara I made out of a cereal box.

The old seer wore the same shawl over her copper-colored beaded dress, and we left the complex with a giddiness reserved for those seizing the New Year while the rest of the world—at least Los Angeles—slept.

It was our third annual stroll down Hollywood Boulevard, and I was happy to usher in a year already full of promise.

But Madame Pepper's mood, I soon surmised, had not risen to the heights of my own.

"Are you all right?" I asked as we crossed La Brea and entered the boulevard's commercial section.

"*All right* is relative term," she said. The hand she had tucked in the crook of my arm was spotted and veiny.

"Why don't you," I said, trying to dismiss the thought that the tough old bird seemed fragile, "define it as it's relative to you?"

"My friend Polly's moving. I have always lived next door to Polly."

"Don't worry—we've got all sorts of plans. Melvin's lawyer friend is helping us and he says he's going to tie up the owners with injunctions, and then we're going to petition the city council to have Peyton Hall declared a historical landmark and—"

"—bah," said Madame Pepper, with a wave of her hand. "Won't happen."

I didn't know if that was a prediction borne of intuition or pessimism; either way, I didn't like how it made me feel.

"Where is she moving to?" I asked.

Madame Pepper's sigh was heavy. "The Motion Picture Home! Polly's going to move in with a bunch of old people!"

"Well, she is old, isn't she?"

"Only four years older than I!" Madame's gruff expression warned me not to say anything, but after a moment her features softened into a smile.

"That is the thing, Candy; despite all evidence to the contrary, I am young. Inside I am nineteen years old and full of life, and yet every time I look in mirror, I wonder, who is this impostor?" She chuckled. "Zo, I don't look in mirrors much."

The skirts of our party dresses swished along the granite.

Dawn had arrived, a rosy loveliness rising from the edges of the eastern sky, and if a bus had deposited an actress from Abilene or a dancer from Dubuque on Hollywood Boulevard at this hopeful pink moment, how could they not think, "Yes, of course; this is where dreams will come true."

"How is your grandmother?" asked Madame Pepper companionably.

"Good," I said. "Sven's got a little cabin in northern Minnesota, and they went up there for Christmas."

"Brrr," said Madame Pepper. "That does not sound so inviting."

"Grandma said it was really cozy. She said they sat in front of the fireplace reading to one another from the stack of *Reader's Digest Condensed Books* Sven's got up there. And they saw the northern lights twice!"

Madame Pepper stopped, clutching my arm. "The northern lights! Oh, Candy, have you ever seen them?"

I shook my head.

"They are . . . a marvel. I saw them when I was a young girl, fifteen years old. We had taken a trip way up to Finland to visit an uncle who'd emigrated there." Madame's hand pressed against her chest. "Candy, the sky was alive with color—greens and violets and pinks! My uncle, a scientist, explained what we were seeing, but my ears closed to his voice, thinking, 'This is beauty and mystery so far beyond your words of science.' I thought just because there are explanations for things does not mean we really understand them."

We swung our held hands.

"And then that night, the wolves cry. Howling into that cold, Finnish night and Sophie was scared and I am a little, too, but I make my voice sound deep and know-it-all like my uncle's and tell my sister not to be afraid, that she should feel lucky, because she gets the privilege of listening to wolves telling jokes."

"Wolves telling jokes?"

"That is just what Sophie said. After each wolf howl I would laugh and say, 'Oh, that's a good one' or 'Oh, I never heard that one before,' and then Sophie gets into act, and as the wolves are crying we laugh ourselves to sleep."

"What a nice way to fall asleep."

Madame Pepper squeezed my hand. "It was."

Seeing the tall man shuffling toward us, his eyes fixed straight ahead, Madame Pepper reached into the cavern of her dress bodice and pulled out a folded bill.

"You're up early, Slim," she said, holding it out to him. He didn't break his stride as his fingers closed around the money.

We didn't get all the way to Vine; we thought Ivar was a good enough turnaround point, and on our way back a few people had come out of their nighttime hiding places to begin their first morning of the New Year.

An agitated, bearded man pushing a shopping cart passed us, muttering something about Beelzebub being alive and well and working as an upholsterer in Boise, Idaho.

"Another reason to love Hollywood Boulevard," said Madame Pepper, as we passed him, giggling. "Where else could you learn of the current career and location of Beelzebub?"

An actress named Gwen Clark who had starred as the second lead in a '60s sitcom about a veterinary clinic was hired to play Gwen McGillicutty, the befuddled, upper-crust director of *The Sorta Late Show,* and Harry Jansen, a big, brawny guy, got the part of my sidekick, Harry Chest. The other regulars included Mac Mork, the stoned cameraman, and Rose Williams, a new comic I had met, who played the depressed makeup girl, Rose Blush.

At the first read-through of the finished script, a constant thrum of excitement coursed through my body, so much so that I would fold my arms across my chest just to keep myself planted in my chair. The laughs were full and frequent, especially when we got to the parts we'd marked improvisational.

"So tell the audience a little bit about yourself, Harry," I said, during one of our improvised couch chats.

Examining his fingernails, Harry said casually, "Well, you know, Candy, I was quite the big man on campus. I was first in my class at Harvard."

"You went to Harvard?"

"Yeah, baby." With his fingers entwined, Harry stretched out his arms and cracked his knuckles. "Harvard Barber College. It's in Pomona."

Gwen was great at playing the addled, out-of-her league director Gwen and was no slouch as an improviser, either.

"Mac," she said to the cameraman, "you can come to work stoned, or you can come to work not stoned, but you can't do both."

"Whatever," said Mac.

After the actors left, we writers conferred with Melanie and Claire.

"So the monologue changes every day," said Claire, reading from her notes.

"Yeah," said Mike. "We'll change things just to keep it topical."

"We'll have set pieces," I said. "For instance, Rose will also play the zoo expert, Mac'll be the playboy actor, and Gwen'll be the tone-deaf torch singer."

"Yeah, and we'll all act in the commercials," said Mike.

"We think it'll be fun for the audience to see us playing different roles," I said. "Plus it's cheaper than hiring a bunch of actors."

"Cheaper," said Melanie. "I like that. This is going to be so fun."

She wasn't going to hear a dissenting voice from any of us.

AFTER THE RUN-THROUGH, I was walking back from the bathroom when a hummingbird collided with the back of my shoulder.

"What the hell?" I muttered, wondering what had torpedoed me, figuring the likelihood of a hummingbird attack in a theater was fairly slim.

Looking behind me, I found an airplane fashioned out of a piece of cardboard, its nose slightly damaged from its impact with my deltoid. It was fine and sharply folded, but it wasn't its sleek construction that got my heart pumping, but the message scrawled on it.

"Dinner . . . and?"

Mike appeared from the corner he had ducked behind after launching the aircraft. He stared at me and I stared at him.

"What about Kristin?" I asked, finally.

Mike shrugged. "*Kirsten* and I broke up."

"You did?"

"I moved out. Into an apartment two blocks from the Formosa."

"I love the Formosa," I said, feeling a little light-headed. "Maybe we could go there for dinner."

"And . . . and like I said, my apartment's two blocks away. We could have dessert there."

45

"Candy!" came the less-than-dulcet tones of my cousin's voice over the telephone. "What's this Grandma says about a 'talk show show'?"

"I'm in a show about a talk show. It's opening in two weeks."

"Where at?" asked Charlotte, the way an investigative detective might question a suspect she'd rather slap.

"At the Swan Theater."

"The Swan Theater? I saw James Taylor there!"

There was a long pause, and in it I imagined her exhaling out of her nostrils smoke that had nothing to do with a cigarette.

"So how've you been?" I said, figuring as long as she called me, we might as well converse.

"I've been just fine," she said, her voice clipped. "I've got a callback tomorrow for a hairspray commercial."

"Congratulations. I hope you get it."

"You do not! You never want me to get anything!"

Other than left field, I had no idea where this sentiment came from and had no response, which was fine, as Charlotte wasn't done talking.

"Why is everything going so good for you? Why do I have to struggle when things just fall into your lap?"

I slumped on the couch as if my spine had suddenly dissolved.

"Things just . . . fall into my lap?"

"Of course they do! You're the one who's always been Grandma's pet! You're the one who she spent so much time with! Who got to live with her—"

"*Because my parents died!*"

Charlotte's words fell over mine. "Who could never do any wrong in her eyes! Even when you were a big druggie, it was always 'Candy this' and 'Candy that,' and now it's 'Candy's got a big show she's putting on!' And you know what really pisses me off? I'm the reason you're in Hollywood! I'm the one who gave you my apartment! Do you think any of this would have happened to you if I hadn't given you my apartment?"

My heart forgot its regular rhythm and was galloping like a spooked horse.

"First of all, I wasn't a big druggie—I just smoked a lot of pot, okay? And secondly, you didn't give me your apartment. I sublet it, remember? As a favor to you!"

"Hah! I can't believe it! I sublet it to you as a favor!"

"Hah!" I said, mimicking her. "You don't do favors unless they benefit you!"

"You just can never thank me, can you? Is it because you've always been jealous of me? Well, guess what: I can't help it that I'm what you've always wanted to be! I can't help the way I look, can't help that I'm blonde and blue-eyed!"

My heart was now Sea Biscuit, straining for the finish line.

"Don't you mean *bland*? Bland and blue-eyed?"

I heard a gasp and then a click, and dropping the receiver in its cradle I promptly burst into tears. When the phone rang again, I snatched it up, ready to hear Charlotte's apology, ready to offer mine.

"Hello?" I said, my voice hopeful, even through its thickness.

"Candy? What's the matter?"

It wasn't Charlotte, unless she was very good at impersonations.

"Oh, Mike!" I said, "I just had a terrible conversation with my cousin!"

"Is your grandmother all right?"

"My grandmother? No, not that kind of terrible—everything's fine with my grandmother. It's just that she—" My last words bobbed on the wave of a sob.

"Candy, I can hardly understand you," said Mike. "I'm coming over, okay? We'll take a walk, okay?"

I sniffed. "Okay."

"EVEN THOUGH WE DON'T EXACTLY GET ALONG," I said, after having recounted the entire phone conversation, "we still love each other. Or so I thought. I mean, we're cousins! We grew up together!"

Mike pulled me closer to him as two young women trotted by us on horseback. We were up in Bronson Canyon, in an area that had been the location of many shot-in-L.A. Westerns, hiking up a path toward stories-high rock outcroppings.

"But I didn't know that she hated me!"

"I don't think she hates you, Candy. Sounds to me like she's jealous of you."

"You haven't seen my cousin."

"I've seen her picture in your apartment."

"And you don't think she's beautiful?"

"Not like you."

"That's a good one." My laugh was bitter. "I'm a lot of things, but beautiful is not one of them."

Dropping my hand, Mike enveloped me in his arms.

"You are beautiful, Candy. You have the most lovely mouth." He kissed it. "And the cutest nose." He kissed it. "And the most beautiful, soulful eyes." He kissed my right eyebrow, then my left, and when he was finished he stepped back, holding me at arm's length, appraising me. "You have the shiniest hair I've ever seen, and the most perfect body ever assembled. In one word, well, two: you're beautiful."

I had to laugh. "No, I'm not. But thank you."

"Yes, you are. And you're welcome."

A man sporting a crew cut, tennis shoes, and stretchy shorts that looked like underpants approached us, his face, pate, and bare chest slick with sweat.

"That's an attractive look," I whispered as he raced by, his breathing laborious chuffs. "One you should think about."

"Good idea. Forget the tuxedo—on opening night I'll wear a Speedo and my old purple Keds."

"Opening night," I said, my voice dreamy. "I can't wait."

We walked farther, my hand in Mike's back pocket, his in mine.

"Charlotte's right about the apartment, though," I said. "If she hadn't come out here, and then needed a subletter, where would I be? Would I ever have done stand-up? Be ready to open a show that has my name in the title? No! I'd still be at the pie shop, asking if you'd like to try today's feature."

"I would, thanks. With whipped cream. But come on, Candy. You kept up the rent on your cousin's apartment and then took over the lease, and for that you're going to give her credit for your whole career? Give me a break! And quit asking yourself those stupid questions. 'What if I would have done this?' 'What if I hadn't done that?' The thing with those what ifs is, you'll never know. Don't waste your time with them."

"Thanks, doc," I said, pinching his butt.

"Hey, I charge extra for that."

I took a big inhale, loving that in the middle of Hollywood the air could smell of nature, of dirt and weeds . . . and of horse manure.

"Yikes," I said, sidestepping the freshly dropped briquettes.

We walked in the cooling air, as shadows spilled over the surfaces of the rocks.

"I wish my mom could see the show," I said softly.

"I know you do, Candy. But maybe she can."

"You believe that?"

Mike shrugged. "I might. Who knows? You forget my grandfather was a Lutheran minister."

"The one who puts on his boxers first and then his tie?"

"No, the Lutheran minister one. He usually wore a clerical collar."

"So you believe in Heaven?"

"Absolutely. But in my heaven, after the angels have put in their time playing harp all day, they get to relax a little. They climb off their clouds and head to the nearby peanut gallery, where they drink beer and get rowdy, waiting for the next good act on Earth to take their shot at entertaining them."

"Oh, great. So now I'm picturing my mom heckling me from on high."

"Not heckling. Laughing. Applauding. Yelling at all the other angels to shut up, 'cause my daughter's on!'"

"No, she wouldn't say it like that." Demonstrating how my mother would tell a group of boisterous angels to put a lid on it, I said, "Prease, prease, no talk! Candy on! My daughter Candy on!"

"What would your dad say?" said Mike.

"Oh. Oh . . . I don't know."

"He'd probably say, 'Yeah! That's my girl!'"

"I don't think so," I said, my throat thickening.

"You don't think so, but you don't know."

Mike bumped my hip with his, but it wasn't until we'd walked for a while that I bumped his hip back. I was surprised at the wave of sadness that had washed over me—not at its strength but its lack thereof. It was like standing under a shower that had always released a torrent of water and now only mustered a trickle.

I hooked my finger through Mike's belt loop and he did the same to mine, and we continued sauntering down the road where Hopalong Cassidy and Gene Autry had in days gone by sauntered.

46

"Did I tell you how fantastic you look?" Mike whispered.

"A couple times," I said. "But don't let that stop you."

Finally, I was attending a special-enough occasion to wear the black dress Madame Pepper had bought for me.

"He's right," said Ed, overhearing. "You look great, Candy."

"Amen," said Taryn. "A dress like that's an investment, and you invested well."

"If everyone can stop talking about Candy's dress long enough to remember it's *my* party—" here Maeve winked at me—"I'd like to make a toast."

Maeve cleared her throat and held out her glass. "To the man I always dreamed of!"

"To the woman far better than my dreams!" said the man next to her.

"To grandchildren—eventually!" said Taryn.

We were at Marconi's, an ornate-bordering-on-kitschy Italian restaurant, to celebrate the news of Maeve and Egon's engagement.

"Maeve's father used to take me here when we were dating," confessed Taryn, the party's host. "And I thought since Maeve's getting married—"

"—Ma," said Maeve as her mother's voice broke.

"It's just that I'm so happy for you!" said Taryn. "Despite my crappy influence, it seems you've found true love!"

"To true love," offered Sharla. "To true, supportive love."

The last part of her toast was directed at Ed, with a smile that veered more southward than north.

"So you've set the date?" I asked Maeve.

"We're not sure." She was nestled—not easy for a big woman like Maeve—under the arm of her betrothed, with a permanent grin plastered across her face. "But we're thinking late fall."

"And she plans to live in Munich!" said Taryn. "What am I supposed to do with my baby so far away?"

"It's just for a couple of months, until Egon finishes his studies," said

Maeve. "You can come and visit anytime you like." She looked at the rest of us. "She'll love the attention: *Summit Hill*—or should I say, *Die Spitze Summit*—is huge in Germany."

"Yes, very popular," said Egon. "My mother—it is her favorite program."

"My future son-in-law comes from a woman of taste!" said Taryn.

"So, Mike," said Sharla, aiming at him a full-wattage smile, "tell us all about your show!"

"It's not my show," said Mike, taking my hand. "It's Candy's—"

"—he's the bandleader," I explained. "He plays trumpet, and he's our top writer."

Mike laughed. "When did I get that promotion?"

"Top in quality. The pay grade remains the same."

"Maeve has said it is about a chat show, ja?" said Egon. "I am finding this very interesting, a theatrical play about a television chat show."

"We hope others'll share your opinion," I said. "But we're pretty excited."

"What are you going to do about guests?" asked Taryn.

"We've got a regular cast who'll play different—"

"—because I'd come on the show. I'd be one of your guests."

"You would?"

"That would be great," said Mike.

"I'd come on, too," said Sharla. "I love the stage. In fact, I just did a staged reading at the Westview Playhouse last month. Ed saw it, didn't you, honey?"

Ed nodded. "She was incredible."

"Not to change the subject," said Taryn, looking at Egon's plate, "but I just realized my future son-in-law ordered exactly the same cheese manicotti dish that Maeve's father always ordered!"

After our plates, smeary with sauce, were taken away, Joanie Welles took the microphone off its stand at the front of the restaurant.

Our fellow Peyton Hall tenant wasn't our waitress but had come to the table earlier to say hello, and Ed had explained to everyone that he had heard her sing at the restaurant several years earlier. He didn't elaborate as to what he had thought about her performance or her desire to be bigger than Streisand.

Joanie took a deep breath, and the tops of her breasts puffed out over her peasant blouse.

"First, might I say it's an honor to sing to a group that includes Taryn

Powell and Sharla West—" here the other forty or so diners in the restaurant, who'd been sneaking looks at our table all evening, applauded, and the *Summit Hill* stars modestly dipped their coiffed heads—"and it's also a pleasure to sing to my friends—one just got engaged! So here goes."

A guy I'd earlier seen carting bus tubs sat down at the piano and played a glissando and a few chords, and as Joanie Welles raised the mike to her mouth, Ed pressed the side of his knee to mine.

"I'll bet you a hundred bucks it'll be a Streisand song," he whispered.

"Pee-pul," sang Joanie, and if Ed and I pressed our legs together any harder, someone's femur was going to snap.

Maeve shot us a knowing look as we steeled ourselves not to laugh, but as Joanie continued the song, it was apparent she could not only carry a tune but caress it.

Her voice was sweet and true, and because she seemed to believe the words she sang, you believed them, too.

The diners gave her a hearty ovation, and when she approached us, hat sheepishly in hand (singing for her supper, indeed), she looked as if she were going to cry.

"I was so nervous singing in front of all you!"

"You shouldn't have been," said Taryn, taking a crisp fifty-dollar bill out of her leopard-skin wallet and dropping it into the hat. "You were wonderful!"

"Joanie," said Ed. "I . . . I don't remember you singing like that."

The waitress made a face. "You saw me when I was just starting out. When I might have taken my Streisand worship a little far."

"I loved your version of 'People,'" said Maeve.

"That was what I had to figure out," said Joanie. "My version. When I tried to sing like Barbra . . . well, I'd just get so intimidated. And when I'm not comfortable singing, I tend to go a little flat."

Sharla opened her zebra-striped wallet, and when Ed took out his, she said, "Don't worry about it," dropping three twenties in the hat, casually glancing at Taryn to make sure her costar noticed whose big tip was bigger.

AN AFTER-DINNER INVITATION to soak in Taryn's hot tub was extended, but its only takers were Maeve, Egon, and Sharla.

"If you don't mind driving yourself," said Ed to Sharla, "I'll just get a ride home from Candy and Mike. I've got to teach tomorrow."

"Mr. Excitement can only take so much," said Sharla.

Ed smiled, the way a beleaguered parent smiles at yet another smart-ass and not-so-funny wisecrack his bratty kid makes.

HE WAS QUIET ON THE SHORT DRIVE HOME, and when Mike pulled up in front of Peyton Hall, Ed thanked us for the ride, practically jumping out of the backseat.

"Do you mind if I don't go with you?" I asked Mike, whose late set at the Comedy Store I'd planned on watching.

"Not at all," said Mike. "Find out what's bugging him. I'll see you tomorrow."

It was dangerous to kiss him good-bye—it was easy to forget everything when my mouth met Mike's—but I forced myself away after a good fifteen seconds and opened the car door.

"I love you," I said, and gasped, hit by the surprise and the truth of my announcement.

"I love you, too," said Mike and we stared at each other, like two spies who've finally exchanged the right code words, and then I tumbled out of the car and ran after Ed.

When I caught up to him by his apartment steps, he seemed agitated, even angry, but when I told him I just thought he could use some company, all the air went out of him in a great sigh, and he said I was right—he could.

"I know you have to get up early tomorrow," I said, "but it's such a nice night out, why don't we go sit by the pool?"

"Good idea. Especially since I don't have to get up early tomorrow."

Following the path, we made our way to the back of the complex.

"Did you hear Billy Gray Green's going out with Siri Kenner?" said Ed quietly, looking up at the bartender's apartment.

"The weather girl?"

Ed nodded as he took off his shoes and rolled up his pants legs. "I guess she comes into the Toy Tiger a lot. The TV station's right down the street." Taking off his sports jacket, he draped it over my shoulders. "It's a little cool. And it'll protect that snazzy dress of yours."

I took off my sandals and we sat on the pool's edge, dangling our legs in the water.

"I wonder how you get to be a weather girl," I said. "Do you have to have a real interest in the weather, or is it mostly about being in front of a television camera?"

"I'd say the latter. But for all I know, Siri Kenner has a Ph.D. in meteorology and has had a lifelong interest in weather patterns since she saw a twister take down the local post office. "'There were letters,'" he said in a falsetto voice, "'and packages flying everywhere!'" He shrugged. "Then again, what do I know?"

The water rippled softly as I swung my legs in a slow circle.

"If you really don't have to work tomorrow," I said, "why did you tell Sharla that you did?"

"Because it's over."

Ed's cheeks puffed up as he expelled a long sigh.

"I knew it was, a long time ago, but I just couldn't give myself permission to believe it."

"Why not?"

"Uh, because she's Sharla West? Because there's no way a woman like Sharla West should have ever gone out with a guy like me in the first place?"

"Sharla West doesn't deserve a guy like you."

"You know what I mean." Ed sighed again. "It was fun, really fun for a while, especially at the beginning. Seriously, I was besotted."

"*Besotted.* Good word."

"To think that a beautiful woman—a Hollywood actress!—wanted to be with me; well, it was easy to ride that wave for a long time."

I nodded and we both stared out at the water. The pool lights were on, making it glow a fluorescent sea green.

"I never really liked how she treated you."

"It took me a long time to notice. Again, blame the besotted factor. I didn't mind being her coat rack—you know, holding her purse while she glad-handed all the important people . . . but what really started to bug me was her lack of curiosity about anything but herself. And when I wouldn't go to that inauguration ball—"

"—I can't believe you turned down a chance to go to the White House."

"Actually, it wasn't at the White House. It was at the Smithsonian."

"Still!"

Ed shrugged. "There'll be plenty more inaugural balls in my lifetime."

"Sure. Invitations to those are a dime a dozen."

Ed's laugh was rueful. "Hey, don't make me regret taking a stand." He leaned back on his hands. "It sure is great about Maeve, isn't it?"

"Yes. I've never seen her so happy."

"You seem pretty happy, too."

"I am," I said, with a little catch in my throat.

"Aw, Candy, I'm so glad. Glad for you and Mike." He clamped his arm around my shoulder, and making his voice sound old and rusty, he said, "Does my heart good to see young couples in love. Gives me hope for the future!"

47

IF I COULD HAVE BOTTLED MY EMOTIONS during the first show, that bottle would have exploded from the sheer force of its effervescence.

It was almost a full house (Melanie was good at publicity) and included in the audience were my favorite people: my grandmother and Sven, Madame Pepper, Ed, Maeve, Solange, Frank, and Melvin. The words of my secret power mantra rang in my head as Mike's bouncy theme music began and his announcer's voice filled the theater.

"Ladies and gentlemen, it's the Contessa of Comedy, the Duchess of Droll, the Empress of Entertainment—put your hands together for Miss Candy Ohi!"

The words of my life saber blasted in my head, as if screamed by three dozen cheerleading squads with bullhorns.

The curtain parted and I strode out briskly, wearing the suit and tie the costumer had found for me in the boys' department of Buffums. I took my mark in the spotlight and struck an I'm-conveying-seriousness pose, bending one arm and holding it against my waistline, the other at my side.

"There is nothing wrong with your television set," I said, stealing the line and intonation used in *The Outer Limits*. "Do not attempt to adjust the picture.

"What you are seeing is real: a woman—a Korean American woman—hosting a nighttime television talk show. Now I know there are some of you out there who don't think it's a woman's place to host a nighttime talk show, so let's meet one of them right now. Ladies and gentleman, the sexist pig I get to call my sidekick—Harry Chest!"

A spotlight shone on Harry sitting on the couch, his legs spread wide. He gestured to me as if his hand was a gun.

"Contessa of Comedy," he said in the broad Brooklyn accent he'd decided to use, "give me a break! You know where you should be right now? You should be at home in bed with your man watching this show, not starring in it."

A few boos rose out of the audience, which brought Harry scrambling off the couch.

"Ah, shut your traps!" he said, hands clenched. "You're nothing but a bunch of henpecked losers!"

The boos increased.

"Sit down, Harry," I said, and then looking out into the fourth wall, which served as my camera, I said, "For those of you at home, we've got a fight brewing here in the studio audience. I'm hoping it'll break out in fisticuffs, with the audience winning."

"Cut!" said the actress playing Gwen McGillicutty, our director. She raced out onstage wearing a tweed skirt, a cardigan sweater, and comfortable shoes. She looked like a British dog trainer and her voice was old-money-lockjaw. "Harry, you're simply going to have to stop harassing Candy. She is the star of the show, after all!"

"Just because she slept with the president of the network!" said Harry.

Gwen looked more confused than usual. "But . . . but my husband's the president of the network!"

The show rolled on. During our first "commercial break," the actors playing Harry and Mac now played kids sitting at a table who didn't want to eat their Death cereal.

"I'm not gonna try it—you try it!"

After pushing around their bowls, Harry said in a cute little voice, "I know, let's get Mikey!"

My Mike, playing the little brother, dug into his bowl and after a moment clutched his throat and keeled over.

"Death Cereal," came the prerecorded announcer's soothing voice, "so tasteless, so healthy, so good for you, you might as well die."

In other parodies of well-known commercials, we pushed products like Alkie Seltzer (we all played lushes trying to stop burping) and Eczema Shaving Cream, where the Swedish bombshell (me in a blonde wig) begged Mike, playing an old pervert in a trench coat, to not take it off!

After I finished my monologue and we got to the interviewing part, I sat at my desk and in hushed tones, said, "Ladies and gentlemen, it's a thrill for me, and I know it will be for you, to bring out our very first guest, the lovely and talented Taryn Powell!"

The audience applauded and a moment later gasped, no doubt expecting Gwen or Rose to play the star of *Summit Hill.* Instead, the real Taryn Powell sashayed onto the stage.

I had called her up the day after Maeve's engagement dinner to ask her if she'd been serious about coming on our show.

"Absolutely. Write me up a little script—make sure it's funny—and I'll be there opening night."

A vision in a white-beaded gown that picked up light like a prism, Taryn threw kisses to the audience on her way to the couch.

"You could have dressed up," I pouted, as she sat down.

She cast a cool eye at me. "I might say the same to you."

The audience laughed.

The writers and I had conferred with Taryn in a fifteen-minute conference call batting around ideas, and when we asked her if she had anything special she wanted to do that she hadn't done before, she practically squealed with delight and admitted to a special skill, which we then wrote into the script.

"So Taryn—"

"—please, *Miss* Powell."

"So, Miss Powell, everyone knows you from the hit television series *Summit Hill*—"

"—I love that show," said Harry. "All the broads on that show have such nice bazonkas."

"Harry, please," I said. "Try not to be such a buffoon."

"He is right, though," said Taryn. "We do have some nice bazonkas."

I let Taryn and Harry share a little moment before I said, "Could you tell us about your new movie?"

"Well, of course; that's why I'm here. You didn't think I'd come on if I didn't have anything to plug, do you?"

She explained how she'd gotten the much-coveted part in the biopic of Katrina Nemorov, the Ukrainian gymnast who'd dazzled the world at the last Summer Olympics.

"But Taryn," I said, "Katrina Nemorov is . . . what, twenty-two?"

Taryn glared at me. "What's your point?"

"Yeah," said Harry, "what's your point?"

"Well," I said, pretending to get flustered, "you're a . . . bit older! Plus, she's a gymnast! How are you going to portray a gymnast who got perfect scores for her floor exercise and uneven parallel bars routine?"

"This is how," said Taryn, and standing up she whipped off the detachable skirt she had specially made. The audience cheered and whistled as she posed like Betty Grable in what looked like a sparkly beaded white maillot and went wild when she did a handstand.

The applause surged as she walked, on her hands, past my desk, turned around, and walked back.

"So," she said, after she had jumped onto her feet and brushed her hands together. "You were saying?"

Also appearing on the show was champion Swiss yodeler Hulda Himmler (played by Rose who could really yodel) who tried to give me a lesson. Mac played the third guest, an up-and-coming soul singer who couldn't get in tune with Mike's band.

When Gwen gave me the cue to wrap it up, I stepped to the front of the stage and thanked the audience for staying up for *The Sorta Late Show.*

"And remember," I said, "laughter's a medicine that can lighten a heavy heart, that can put a cold compress on a worried brow, that can—

"—hey, tootsie," said Harry, pulling an imaginary zipper across his mouth. "Enough. Now how's about we slip into your dressing room? We can go over some post-show notes while you give me a massage."

The lights blacked out.

THE REVIEWS WERE GOOD. The *Herald Examiner* said, "They've assembled a wacky cast over at the Swan Theater, and a wacky premise, 'Let's put a late-night television talk show onstage!' but somehow it all works and everyone has a good time from the beguiling host (Candy Ohi), to her jackass sidekick (Harry Jansen as Harry Chest), to, and especially, the audience."

According to the *Los Angeles Times,* "*The Sorta Late Show with Candy Ohi* is a freewheeling and funny nod to television talk shows. . . . Taryn Powell displayed a delightfully comic (and limber) side that impressed and surprised this reviewer."

"Bandleader and trumpeter Mike Trowbridge," reported *Daily Variety,* "leads a jazzy quintet and amid the song parodies and witty intros is some seriously tuneful music." (That was fun to read aloud to Mike; he in turn read aloud the part that said, "The talk show hostess is funny and charming with enough confidence to let everyone else be funny and charming, too.")

I DIDN'T MONKEY MUCH with the daily monologue that PJ and Lowell wrote because I could count on it to be topical, politically charged, and funny, but it didn't take long for me and the rest of the cast to get loose and make the written scenes even more improvisational. If any actor decided to go off script or invent an entirely new scene, everyone else was more than willing to go along. It gave the show a wild energy that the audience loved and participated in. They booed Harry Chest's outrageous comments, and Mac, the stoned cameraman, couldn't ask his signature line, "Where's my pipe?" without having members of the audience shout things like, "The band's got it! or "The last guest took it!" which might result in a whole new direction for a scene to take.

Everyone was having fun, and we, ladies and germs, had a hit on our hands.

48

THE REPORTER FLUFFED HER HAIR and ran a fingernail between two teeth, but when she was given the signal, she was camera-ready.

"I'm standing here with Melvin Slyke," she said earnestly, "long-term resident of Peyton Hall, the Hollywood Boulevard apartment complex that's slated for demolition."

"Not if we've got any say about it!" said Melvin, leaning into the reporter's microphone.

"Yeah!" chorused the group of tenants standing under the Preserve Hollywood Landmarks! banner we had erected on the front lawn.

"Yeah!" agreed Maeve and I, seated at a table offering the chocolate Preservation Cupcakes! we had spent a whole morning baking.

"Tell me, Mr. Slyke," said the reporter, studied concern settling on her face, "what's so important about this place? Why get in the way of progress?"

"Progress?" said Melvin, waving his arm. "Take a look around you! You think a high-rise, a big tall box could ever match this graciousness, this oasis we've got right here?"

"But Mr. Slyke," said the reporter, "the complex isn't even fifty years old; certainly not historic in—"

"I'll tell you what historic is," said Melvin. "A place of grace and elegance that housed and continues to house a Hollywood community! Not just big stars like Clark Gable or Shelley Winters or Claudette Colbert, but directors, soundmen, costumers, screenwriters. Me, I was an animator for years, and my neighbor, Francis Flover, was the famous night club impresario—"

"But how do you really expect to stop the complex owner from doing what he's rightfully entitled to?"

"We're standing up for what's rightfully right!" said Melvin. "This place deserves to stand! Hollywood residents, call your city councilwoman and tell her Peyton Hall deserves historic landmark designation!"

"Thank you so much, Mr. Slyke," said the reporter, and turning her bright, professional smile on for the camera, she said, "Reporting live from Hollywood, this is Deena Lynde."

AFTER FOLDING UP THE CARD TABLE and taking down the banner, I presented Melvin with a cupcake.

"They all sold. But I saved this one for you."

He kissed the frosting and licked what remained on his lips.

"Nice job, Melvin," said Vince Perrogio. "We're going to get this place saved yet!"

Sherri Durban nodded and shook a cigar box. "And Candy, your cupcakes brought in a hundred and eight dollars!"

"Not just my cupcakes. Maeve helped me."

"Don't tell my trainer," said Maeve. "He doesn't even want me in the same room with sugar."

Carrying Melvin's card table up the stairs for him, I stood at the landing as he fumbled with his door key.

"Melvin, you don't seem so excited about the rally. I thought it went over really well."

"I was hoping for that reporter from the *Times* to come."

"Well, we had that one from *L.A. Weekly.*"

"True, true," said Melvin, and turning the key he pushed open his door.

"Just put the table right there, if you don't mind," he said and after I leaned it against the wall, he added, "Don't mind me. It's just battle fatigue. I'll get a good night's sleep and wake up rejuvenated and ready for action."

"Remember, we've got a three-tiered plan," I said, mimicking the nasal voice of Baines Wallem.

The lawyer who'd taken on the case to save Peyton Hall as a favor to his old friend Melvin had assured us that he was going to (1) tie everything up with injunctions, (2) petition City Hall about historical landmark status, and (3) get as much publicity as possible.

"That's right," said Melvin. He kissed my cheek. "And thanks for the cupcake, honey."

"We will prevail!" I said, using Melvin's favorite saying.

"Darn tootin'."

Shutting the door to my own apartment, I settled myself on the plaid couch, fingers laced behind my head, staring up at the rattan wallpaper plastered to the ceiling. How many actors, comics, writers, directors, dancers, and musicians had lain prone while reciting their lines or jokes aloud, plotting their scripts, framing their shots, choreographing numbers, or humming a few bars while under the Tiki hut? How many Hollywood dreamers had gazed on the embossed palm trees on the dining room walls and the real ones out the window, cooled themselves in the pool, instructed drivers giving them a ride home to "pull up by the green neon sign"? A shiver skittered up my back. I couldn't bear the idea of losing this place. I had not only made the best friends of my life at Peyton Hall, I had made the life I'd always wanted. A life I loved.

A MUSICAL CALLED *WAITING . . . FOR GODOT!*, based on the less-punctuated play, had been on the Swan Theater's schedule, but the first composer quit and the second composer was close to that, complaining to Melanie Breyer that there was no way his music could support, let alone be enhanced by, lyrics like, "Why, oh, why, is that Godot / so very, very interminably slow?"

The *Waiting . . . for Godot!* team's failure to come up with mutually satisfying music and lyrics was our success; we were extended, filling the slot of the show whose desire to combine the existential with entertainment had not been met.

At the loose production-meeting-cum-brunch Claire held at her house every Monday morning (our day off), we discussed many things, including which stars, from the many requests that flooded her office, we'd have on the show.

"You know what Mia Lennox's agent told me?" Claire said, passing me a bowl of fruit salad. "She said, 'Being on the *Sorta Late Show* is like being on *Dean Martin's Celebrity Roast*. It might be a little painful at times, but everyone loves to do it because they get to show people that they have a sense of humor.'"

"I didn't know Mia Lennox had a sense of humor," said Mike, of the notoriously vain actress whose father was the movie producer Curtis Lennox.

"She was terrible in that movie about that talking dog," said PJ, dousing her scrambled eggs with hot sauce.

"Still, that movie did huge business," said Claire. "And I think it's pretty flattering that her agent said that."

"I say no to Mia Lennox. Let her be content to be in her father's next blockbuster." Melanie's tone was harsh, and noticing our response to it she blushed.

"Sorry," she said, "It's just that . . . well, as an heiress myself, I guess I'm kind of sensitive to people succeeding in the family business without actual effort. I've met Miss Lennox a few times and, believe me, she doesn't just expect things handed to her on a silver platter, she expects them to be placed on her lap so she doesn't have to do any heavy lifting."

I admit it gave me a sense of power to know I could veto someone, too. I was pretty open to whatever guest Claire and Melanie wanted to have on, although when Sharla West's name came up, my answer was immediate: nope.

"I don't like her," I said simply, "and I don't want to pretend I do."

We had a guest star on an average of twice a week, and while we had to work hard to rescue Chase Peavy, who might be at home in teen-marketed movies but who froze onstage, generally our guests were good sports and able to easily milk whatever laughs were to be found in the material we wrote for them. We had tried to get Heidi Wheaton (wouldn't that have been a personal coup?), but she was in London with her one-woman show, the same one-woman show my grandma and I had seen. A costar of hers from *Yuk It Up!* was available, however, and said it would be a distinct pleasure to improvise with us.

"Say, Harry," I said to my sidekick, "guess how many Emmys Carol Ernhart's been nominated for?"

Harry shrugged. "Don't really care. Their whole voting system's corrupt."

"Why do you say that?"

"Because I've never been nominated for one."

"Well, Carol's not just been nominated four times, she's won once! So let's bring the Emmy winner out—ladies and gentlemen, Miss Carol Ernhart!"

The large woman, dressed in a caftan embroidered with little reflective discs, raced out onto the set and flung herself into Harry's lap, surprising the applauding audience, as well as Harry and me.

We'd been told by Carol's people to "expect anything," and we were not about to let a little surprise slip us up.

"Baby doll," said Harry, "I've missed you, too!"

With a look of disgust, Carol unpeeled the arms Harry had clamped around her.

"You're just like them!" she said, moving to the other side of the couch, nearest my desk.

"Carol," I said, "who? Harry's just like who?"

A loose rule in improvisation is that rather than ask questions, you provide information, but thinking Carol had a particular direction she wanted to go in, I decided to ask the questions that would help get her there.

"You know," said Carol, "the same people who are after you!"

I waited a beat, for her explanation of who these people were, but when it didn't come, I said, "Oh, those people. The Most Beautiful Women in the World judges."

This got a big laugh from the audience; Carol Ernhart was a large woman, and while she wasn't homely, she had a lot of expressions that made her look as if she were. And I certainly didn't have an attic full of Miss America sashes and tiaras.

"Yes," said Carol nodding frantically. "And they're in cahoots with Those Searching for the Brain Closest to Einstein's.'"

"E equals mc squared," I said.

"Shh!" said Carol. "They're backstage right now! And their aim is to find all of us incredibly beautiful and supremely intelligent women for their own devious purposes!"

"I'll see about that!" said Harry, rushing backstage.

"Should I be worried?" said Gwen, from the other side of the stage.

Mike, in the music pit, stood up and offered a resounding, "No."

Harry rushed back onstage. "Girls, girls, you're safe! Totally safe! They got their directions mixed up—they thought they were on the set of *Let's Make a Deal.*"

The audience laughed at Harry's reference to a game show that did, for a fact, feature beautiful women who posed by curtains, doors, and prizes.

"Of course!" said Carol. "Everyone knows that the women on that show all have Ph.D.'s in either physics or rocket science."

This inspired Rose to come onstage and strike a pose.

"Hi," she said in a cheery voice, "before I show you what's behind Door #2, let me share the exciting news that I've rewritten the Pythagorean theorem."

We had a high old time, and at the end of that particular show we took our bows with Carol Ernhart to resounding applause.

This wasn't uncommon. My grandmother and Sven had seen the first week of shows, and while it was thrilling to hear Grandma's voice inciting everyone to stand up and shout, "Bravo!," after they went back to Minneapolis the audience was still shouting bravos and we were still getting standing ovations. Which was a whole 'nother thrill.

49

I TOOK A LONG SWIM before I gave Madame Pepper a ride to the airport. Typical for the early hour, the pool was empty and the water had the sting of chlorine not carefully measured. I liked that, though—it made it seem more of a cleansing ritual than exercise, although why I thought I needed to be cleansed I had no idea. Maybe I just liked the smell of bleach.

The air was gray and misty, a secret to those who'd wake up later to a bright and sunny Los Angeles that had burned away the moisture, and for several laps I did a languorous backstroke, feeling the heavy water under me and dewdrops on my face.

"YOU TAKE HIM," she said to me, as she closed the door to her Hollywood apartment for the last time. "He is good guard dog."

I looked at the gargoyle planter with its teeming jade hair and promised I'd give it a proper home.

"Nice car," said Madame Pepper as we loaded her luggage in the Ford Cougar I'd gotten several months earlier.

"You say that every time I give you a ride."

"Fine," she said with a sniff. "Although I am not complimenting you, I am complimenting your car."

I drove west on Hollywood Boulevard.

"You are not taking freeway?"

"Nah. La Cienega. It's nicer. And just as fast."

"I don't want to miss my flight."

"You won't."

We drove for a long time in silence, and it wasn't until we had turned onto Stocker Street that Madame Pepper said, "Zo, the show's good?"

"It's been extended. Again."

"You must take it on the road. I'll be the first in line to see it in Vienna."

Madame Pepper had taken her brother Gavril up on his open invitation to come live with him and his family.

"Unfortunately, I haven't heard of any plans for an international tour."

Hearing the whine in my voice, she said, "You're going to do fine without me, Candy."

"Is that a belief, or a prediction?"

A long moment passed and I looked over at her. She was squinting out the window, her arms folded, her heavy eyebrows a ledge over her face.

"Okay, now you *are* scaring me."

"Why? You don't believe in what I do."

"No," I protested, "I believe you're very good at what you do."

I matched the old woman's smile with one of my own.

A pickup truck whose side panel read "Palmdale Dates" sped by in the right lane.

"Someone needs dates stat," said my passenger, and that she knew—and used—the word *stat* made me laugh.

"Zee, I too can be comedian."

"A lot of people can," I agreed.

"Yes, but to be funny onstage is a separate talent from being funny in real life. And vice versa. Will Hoover was my client," she said, of the comic who'd had a very successful sitcom about a hapless jewelry store owner. "And not once, never, did he make me laugh in my home." She shook her head. "But is not good to speak of clients."

"But is fun," I said, in her accent.

By the time I was on Century Boulevard and nearing the terminals, I started blinking back tears. Madame Pepper reached over and patted my arm.

"I feel the same way you do, Candy. Only I am not a crier."

Pulling over near the Pam Am signs, I put on my car flashers and helped the traveler load her old-fashioned leather luggage onto a cart.

"I could park. I could park and come sit at the gate with you."

"No. I don't like the good-byes that go on and on."

"It's just the good-byes I don't like," I said, and a rush of emotion and all that I was losing made me open my arms and grab my friend. "Who am I going to see matinee movies with?"

"Matinee movies are fine to see by yourself," she said, squeezing me tight. "But you will miss me at C.C. Brown's when you don't have my hot fudge sundae to pilfer."

"Will you write to me?"

"If you'll write me back."

Releasing our hug, we held each other's elbows, and I saw a sheen of tears in the old woman's eyes.

"Aha!" I said. "I knew you liked me!"

"Like you? Bah! Like a rash! Like a toothache! Like a shot with a big long needle!"

"I love you, too."

Now there was more than just a sheen of tears in her eyes, but she dispensed of them quickly with her thumb and forefinger.

"Allergies." She unclasped her purse and searched for something inside it. "Zo," she said, taking out her wallet. "How much do I owe you?"

"For what?"

"For ride to airport?"

"Madame Pepper, you insult me. Put that away."

With a smile, the old woman honored my request. A businessman rushed past us and we stepped aside to give more room to a mother dragging a duffel bag and little boy with equal impatience.

"Perhaps then you will accept as payment, oh, an answer to a certain question?"

"A freebie fortune? Great!"

Her lips pursed in a semi-smile. "Ask me anything. Anything at all."

"Okay." Thinking this was not a time to bunt but to swing hard, I asked, "What is the meaning of life?"

The seer put her fingers to her temple and after a moment, nodded her head.

Opening her eyes, she said, "You decide."

"I decide what the meaning of life is? And you had how many clients paying you how much money for gems like that?"

"Well, every now and then I throw in a little abracadabra. I can tell people the plain truth, but everyone always wants the abracadabra, the clairvoyant flash that will cause the goose bumps."

"Goose bumps would be good."

"For that, listen to Maria Callas sing 'Sinfonia.'"

"Fine. Good-bye, you old gypsy."

"Good-bye, you young wisenheimer."

We both held our arms out, and as we met in a final hug, she said, "Just remember, Candy," and then whispered a few words into my ear.

LEAVE IT TO THAT OLD ORACLE to really be tapped into the spirit world, to lift the veil that separates the known from the not-so-known, to take messages from sprites and angels . . . or not. I mean I must have let the words slip at some point during our many conversations, right?

That she had repeated my *secret life saber* had flabbergasted and delighted me, and on the drive home from the airport I laughed like a crazy person, to the point of being a highway menace.

LIKE THE FIRST DOMINO TAPPED, Madame Pepper's departure started a chain reaction I did not like at all.

"You can't go," I said, when Frank told me he was packing up.

"The rent's a lot cheaper where me and Mark are going," he said, and in response to my questioning look, he added, "Mayhem. He's going by his real name now."

"Why?"

"He got a new day job. With an advertising agency. He says nobody wanted to hire anyone named Mayhem."

"What about the band?"

"Oh, we're still playing. We've got a late set at the Frond on Saturday. You and Mike could come by after your show."

"So where are you and May—uh, Mark—going to live?"

"Not far. We got a place on Cherokee. Our landlord's in the band Night Noise, so he's cool about making noise."

"Especially at night, I'll bet."

"Ha. I hope you're funnier than that in your show. Which reminds me, can I get some more comps? I know you're sold out, but you still gotta have some comps, right? I'd really like to see it again Friday night, but this time with my girlfriend."

"Girlfriend?"

He twirled the chains looped on his jeans.

"You don't have to act so surprised."

"Well, shouldn't I be? I haven't heard you say anything about a girl-friend."

"Yeah, Paula. I just met her. At the Roxy. And if she's gonna become my girlfriend, I've got to impress her. So I thought I'd take her to your show."

"Can't beat flattery. There'll be tickets at the will-call."

ONE DAY AFTER DROPPING OFF MY RENT CHECK, I saw a tenant carrying a spotlight down his front steps.

"Bastien!" I said, racing up to him. "You, too?"

The photographer's shrug was languid and, I thought, very French.

"I need my home life to be calm so that my work can be wild. I cannot live with this uncertainty."

"Bastien, Melvin is planning another meeting with our city councilwoman—"

"Candy, you know what I know: it is a lost cause. A beautiful cause . . . but a lost one."

Joanie Welles, whom we invited to sing one night on *The Sorta Late Show* (fun!), found a little cottage up in the Hollywood Hills, and June was moving into an apartment a block away.

"I can't bear to go any farther," she said, looking more disheveled and patched together than usual.

Coming from the pool, I had seen her struggling with a twine-tied cardboard box and offered to carry it. It smelled like BENGAY and whiskey.

"And Binky," she said, walking in her funny tiptoed way toward the garages. "This is the only home Binky's ever known!"

The mangy dog was tucked into its hot pink tote bag and looked at me dolefully, brown tears smeared under its eyes. I would have reached out to pet it if I hadn't known its penchant to nip.

"God," she said, as she opened the trunk of her beat-up old Chevy Nova. "Not only do I feel like it's the end of an era, I feel like it's the end of *my* era."

She sniffed and I offered a consoling pat on her skeletal arm.

"Don't worry," she said, and she was standing so close to me that I could see her thin lips underneath a purple smudge of lipstick. "I'm not going to cry. I haven't cried since Lizabeth Scott got the part I should have had in *I Walk Alone*. Now that one hurt."

MELVIN TOOK EVERY MOVE PERSONALLY.

"Don't they know that the more we stand united, the likelier it is that we win? If a chain is only as strong as its weakest link, well, then we've got a damn flimsy chain."

I had brought him a batch of oatmeal raisin cookies and quickly realized the short-and-sweet delivery I had planned was a pipe dream. He had insisted I come into his apartment to look at his most recent flyer.

"What's this?" I asked, picking up from his worktable a picture of Bugs Bunny with boxing gloves.

"Inspiration," said Melvin. "I drew it during the Looney Tunes Lockout, when we were fighting Warner Brothers for the right to unionize."

"Looney Tunes Lockout? Did you win?"

"We sure did. And you know why? Because we stuck together. Why can't people realize that what seems impossible isn't if you're willing to fight for it as a team?"

"There are still a lot of tenants left."

"You're right." He took a cookie off the plate. "I just get a little disheartened sometimes." Taking a bite, he grunted his pleasure. "You make these for the troops, Candy, and no one'll want to leave." He took another bite, and another, and after he'd eaten two cookies, he handed me a flyer on which he'd drawn Cupid holding a house key. The hand-lettered words said, "Love Peyton Hall? Then Don't Give Up On It! Meet by the pool Sat. morning at 10!"

And then my kindly neighbor, who liked nothing more than to talk, told me it was time to go—didn't I know I had a show to rest up for?

50

LITTLE WOMEN! HAD A FINISHED SCRIPT, a finished libretto, an all-drag cast, and unlike *Waiting . . . for Godot!* was ready for production at the Swan Theater, and although we still had great box office, Melanie had a contract to honor.

There are some closing night parties in which the prevailing emotion is relief (whew, this dud is over!), but ours was filled with a mixture of pride, affection, and of course laughs.

"To the most fun I've ever had as an actor!" said Harry Jansen, raising a glass.

"Although I can't say I'll miss his Harry Chest character," said his wife, Eve. "That's a role I told him he'd better never bring home."

"Shut up, woman," he said, cupping her behind, "and get me a beer!"

After the final curtain, a catering company had set up tables bearing the kind of food that would earn Michelin stars, if caterers were included in Michelin ratings.

"I thought your song with Mike was my favorite thing of the night," said Maeve, "until I bit into this." She held up a half-eaten crab dumpling.

"Try the steak Diane," said Solange, pointing her fork at her plate. "Before they're all gone."

Mac joined our little group, and my grandmother greeted him by asking, "Where's my pipe?"

"Candy told me you had it," he said in his stoner's voice. "So let's fire it up and have a toke!"

"Oh kid, you kill me."

The groups kept shifting; the party was a true mixer in that everyone kept moving, grazing at the tables, telling stories, reminiscing, and laughing.

At one point I joined my agent Eric and Mike's mom by the desserts.

"I was just telling Betty here that I've never been on a farm before, and she invited me to the fall harvest," said Eric.

"Yup, it's about time you get out of your three-piece suit and into some overalls," said Betty. "See how the real world lives."

I had been nervous about meeting Mike's parents, but their kindness—and Betty's irreverent humor—had put me immediately at ease.

"And you," she said, giving me the once-over. "You're awfully good onstage, but I'd like to see what you can do in a cow barn."

Mike's dad, John, was talking to Sven, Ed, and Lowell about UFO sightings.

"Uh oh," I said, sidling up to Ed. "Don't scare them with your Roswell stories."

"My Uncle Leon never set foot in New Mexico," said John. "But he was in France during the first war, and to his dying day he swore he saw a UFO hovering over the Vesle River."

"I don't know," said Sven. "Seems in a war zone you might get confused about a lot of things."

"I'm writing a screenplay about aliens," said Lowell. "Only they don't arrive in UFOs, they infiltrate cereal boxes and multiply in bowls of cornflakes."

Bell-like clinks rang out as Claire and Melanie, standing on our set, tapped spoons against their glasses.

A "Shhhh" traveled across the stage until there was silence.

"For a group that's hard to shut up," said Claire to Melanie, "they did pretty good."

"They probably think we're going to hand out cash bonuses," said Melanie.

"Sounds good!" said Harry.

"Sorry, all we've got for you tonight is our gratitude."

"Doesn't sound quite as good!" said Harry.

There was more back-and-forth and more laughter before Claire said, "Seriously, you guys, this was one of the most fun adventures in my entire show business career, and I want to thank all of you from the bottom of my heart."

Her voice wavered a little, and Melanie, draping her arm around Claire, said, "That goes double for me. It might be closing night, but who knows, with a show like this there might be another opening night."

A frisson of excitement zipped around the room.

Melanie raised her hand. "I'm not making any promises: the Swan's booked up for the next eighteen months, but I'd be surprised if this was the last of *The Sorta Late Show*."

Cheers flew up to the rafters.

"And now," said Claire, "I think we need to bring up the person who every night brought everything together: the best host in sorta late-night entertainment, Candy Ohi!"

As I moved through the crowd, I smiled—hard—hoping the effort would rein in my emotions. Up on the platform, I took a seat behind my desk, gesturing for Claire and Melanie to sit down on the couch. I took a deep breath.

"I want to thank everyone for all the fun we had—the writers"—I nodded at Lowell and PJ and Mike—"the actors, Harry and Gwen and Mac and Rose, the band—" The composure I thought I had captured darted away and my voice cracked. "Whoo!" I said, fanning my face.

"We love you, Candy!" shouted Mac.

"Love you back," I said. "And if you're looking for your pipe, I gave it to the police officer waiting for you in the lobby."

The laughter soothed me, but when I saw my grandmother and Mike standing close to each other, I about lost it all over again. Mike scrunched his face and flexed his muscles in a be-strong gesture.

"Hey," I said, "you guys don't want to hear me talk—you've listened to me talk through this whole run. Everything I feel about this show is in the song Mike and I sang tonight."

That was the only cue Mike and the band members needed; they hustled over to their instruments and after an intro full of fancy trills and runs, Mike set down his trumpet and began singing our rewritten lyrics to the tune of the song Bob Hope and Shirley Ross sang in *The Big Broadcast of 1938*:

Thanks for the Memories,
Every night at eight, it's magic we'd create,
and if it wasn't magic, still the levity was great,
How lovely it was . . . .

When we sang it during the show, I had stayed seated at my desk, but now I got up and went over to Mike, and he and I stood inches apart, singing to one another stanzas about gaffes and laughs, wit that bit, taking chances and knowing glances. When we got to the last refrain, we waited after each line, allowing people to sing it back. Finally, everyone onstage sang the last verse together:

So thanks for the memories,
There's Ibsen and Shakespeare, their dramas have no peer,
But as for laughs we outdid Hedda Gabler and King Lear.
Thank you . . . so much.

As the voices faded, Mike put his arms around me, dipped me backwards, and laid a big juicy kiss on me.

"Okay, people," he said, lifting his head to take a breath, "move along, there's nothing to see here."

"That's right, go about your business," I said, clinging to Mike in a horizontal hold, "so we can get back to ours."

51

AFTER THE CLOSING of *The Sorta Late Show*, I was sorta in a funk. Grandma and Sven went back to Minnesota; Betty and John went back to Nebraska; Lowell went back to work at Book Soup; and PJ picked up more waitressing shifts at the Cock 'n Bull.

"Actually, I don't mind it," she said. "I like the hustle of a restaurant. And I steal stuff from the customers all the time."

"Remind me never to sit in your section."

"You know what I mean. Character traits. Tics. Sometimes whole lines of dialogue."

I missed our writers' meetings, the way we'd crack each other up as we threw out lines. I missed going to the theater in the late afternoon for our preshow rehearsals, missed getting show notes after curtain each night, missed our postshow dinners at Canter's or Denny's or Barney's Beanery.

While Mike had kept up a twice-a-week late-night booking at the Improv during the run of the show, my performance lust was pretty well satiated by what we did at the Swan Theater. But I had booked a spot that Friday night at the Comedy Store, knowing, as one of Solange's cowboy singers counseled, it was time to get back in the saddle.

On the fifth day (I was still counting) after *The Sorta Late Show* closed, I took a long morning swim. Normally, I could expect a few regulars to be lounging around the pool—I mean, it wasn't dawn or anything—but Robb and Bruce had moved to Beverly Hills, Sherri Durban found an apartment in the Valley, and even Robert X. Roberts had packed up his velour robe and was very likely snoring under his newspaper tent beside some other (definitely dinkier) apartment pool. His departure had unsettled Melvin.

"Robert X. Roberts has been here as long as I have! It's like all the officers are abandoning ship!"

By now almost half the tenants had moved out, and resignation was beginning to seep into the complex, although Melvin and I kept busy convincing one another that the cavalry, in some shape or form, was about to swoop in and rescue us.

Back in my apartment after my swim (forty laps), I checked the movie listings, and debating between *The French Lieutenant's Woman* or *Mommie Dearest,* I called Mike.

"You want to join me on the Boulevard for a movie?"

"My audition's at two."

"Oh, yeah, I forgot. For that new sitcom, right? *Pete's White?*"

Mike snickered. "It's *Pete's Wife.*"

"Well, break a leg."

"I've only got three lines. How can I screw that up?"

Knowing there were a million ways, we both laughed.

"Okay," said Mike, "How about if I come by tonight? I'll bring dinner."

"Only if you get the part."

"Even if I do, they won't tell me today."

"Excuses, excuses."

"So what time?"

"How about seven? And don't bring anything—I'll cook. And I'll ask Maeve and Ed. And maybe Solange can come. We'll have a little dinner party."

"Sounds good. Should I bring my pajamas?"

"Do you plan on wearing them?"

Mike's chuckle was lascivious. "No."

BLINKING MY EYES against the bright sun, I left the movie theater, lonesome for Madame Pepper and thinking how much she would have illuminated my viewing experience of *Mommie Dearest.* An autographed picture of Joan Crawford, had, after all, hung on her wall, and the seer had confided, "Joan was only star to write me regular thank you notes for my services!"

Across the street, clots of tourists stooped in front of the hand- and footprints at Grauman's. I walked east with no particular destination in mind, inviting the melancholy of missing Madame Pepper to settle into my already blue state. In her last letter, she had talked about living near the Freyung, one of Vienna's old squares, and while it had many charms, it couldn't compete with the Boulevard.

"You can take the old Romanian out of Hollywood," she had written, "but you can't take Hollywood out of the old Romanian."

"Hey, Slim," I said to the white-haired man shuffling toward me. Slim nodded but as usual didn't make eye contact. As he passed, however, I was struck by something different about him.

"You smell good," I said reflexively.

"British Sterling!" he barked, without turning around.

A laugh blurted out of me. These were the first words Slim had ever spoken to me, and I received them as I would a surprise bouquet of flowers. I ambled down the street and by the time I had positioned myself in front of the Frederick's of Hollywood window, gaping at its latest display of lingerie that played peek-a-boo, my low spirits had climbed out of the basement and were on their way to the second floor.

I've got to hustle, I thought. *I've got people coming over tonight.*

Turning around, I made my way west on Hollywood Boulevard, past a clarinetist squeaking through "My Way," past a wild-haired woman who was babbling about Jesus's imminent return at four-thirty-three that afternoon, past a young couple studying a map of Hollywood and arguing in southern accents about the best route to take to the Farmers' Market on Fairfax. I paused for a moment, ready to offer directions, but they looked resourceful enough, and they might discover something unintended—and extraordinary—by finding their own way. Hollywood was like that.

At Ralphs I bought ingredients for a dinner I had a particular hankering for: a hamburger hot dish (and there would be no skimping on either cheese or sour cream), drop biscuits, and a nice green salad. Dessert would be a yellow cake with my special fudge frosting.

When I got home I saw the red light of my answering machine blinking twice.

"Candy, Candy, is that you?" came my grandmother's voice when I played back the first message. "Are you home? Listen, Candy, I just wanted you to know how much fun Sven and I had out there . . . can you hear me? Kid, I hate these things, I can't tell if—"

The second message came from someone more accustomed to answering machines, and as I listened to it, my hands flew to my mouth. I played it again and my hands repeated the gesture. Listening to it the third time, I hugged myself, my body thrumming. Then I called my grandmother.

The pirate songs that accompanied my cooking were sung with extra verve and volume as I measured and sifted, chopped and browned, boiled and baked, and by the time the doorbell rang, the apartment with the

Tiki hut rattan-wallpapered ceiling and the interior and exterior palm tree views smelled like a quarter of all Minnesota kitchens at suppertime.

I was glad I had thought to include Melvin, who was in a mood similar to mine earlier in the day, depressed by having heard the news that the petition to have Peyton Hall declared a historical landmark was denied.

"I fear there'll come a day when the unique and individual will be trampled by the same and the standard," he said as we entered the dining room.

I picked up a plate and hurled it against the wall. He stood gaping at me.

"Be my guest," I said, handing him one. "They're unbreakable."

THE TOSSING OF THE DISHES went a long way in cheering up Melvin.

"I'm not saying there's no chance for Peyton Hall," he said, when we were all seated at the table. He buttered a biscuit. "It ain't over 'til it's over."

"Candy, this smells so good," said Ed, helping himself to the hamburger hot dish.

"You've got to give me the recipe," said Maeve. "This is the sort of food Egon loves."

"And how is Herr Egon?" asked Ed.

"Wunderbar. Fabulous." She sighed. "Far away."

Solange had had a long and tiring day at Beat Street, having had to console Danny Day, whose latest single had failed to make it to the top of the Hot 100 list the hour it was released.

"He came into the office ranting," she said. "He had a whole list of people he wanted Neil to fire, including Neil."

"Who owns the record company," I explained to the others.

"So is he going to fire himself?" asked Mike.

"Yeah, but then he'll rehire himself at double the salary," I said and laughed at my own joke.

Ed reported that he had had an excellent day in ninth grade civics.

"We've been studying our founding documents, and I've been having the kids write additional amendments to the Constitution, and my third-hour class—oh my god, some of their stuff was priceless."

"Give us an example," said Solange.

"Congress shall make no law respecting school lunches and the serving of vegetables, particularly of the green bean variety," said Ed. "And then there's this boy Sean—he's smart as a whip—for extra credit he takes it upon himself to rewrite the Preamble to the Declaration of Independence, and he begins by writing that 'All men *and* women are created equal' and proceeds to turn it into this completely wild feminist tract."

"Go, Sean," said Maeve.

"It's kids like that who make me want to teach full time," said Ed. "Which I've decided to do next year."

We toasted Ed and the certain jump in IQ scores lucky junior high kids would soon experience.

Mike told us about his audition for a three-line part as a beleaguered library patron.

"First they say, 'Pretend you're really mad, so with my mouth like this—" Mike clenched his teeth—"I say, 'But it was shelved in Nonfiction! It's a novel! What's this world coming to?!'"

"That was a pretty good Kirk Douglas impersonation," said Melvin, nodding.

"That's what I was going for. Then they ask me to do it in a foreign accent."

"So how'd you do that?"

"But eet wus shevlt in noun-feekshone," said Mike, in a broader-than-broad Scandinavian accent. "Eet's uh no-fel! Vhat's da verlt co-ming to?"

"Oh, so you went with Spanish," said Ed.

We ate and drank and joked and left the table with exaggerated groans of satisfaction, and after everyone had settled themselves in the living room, I asked Mike to help me serve the coffee and cake.

"Candy, what's going on?" he asked in the kitchen. "You're so ... giddy."

"Am I?" I said, laughing.

He'd been the last to arrive, and I hadn't had a chance to share my news with him. Now I did.

"Candy, that's sensational!" he said, grabbing me in a hug that lifted me off my feet.

"I didn't want to tell anyone—well, except my grandmother—until I told you," I said but he swallowed up the last few words when he planted his mouth on mine and gave me a loud, lip smacker of a kiss.

"Hey, young lovers," said Solange, leaning against the door frame, her arms crossed. "Any chance of us getting that cake?"

"Coming right up," I said and laughed for the hundredth time.

"THAT'S SOME WALL," said Melvin, as I refilled his coffee cup. He squinted behind his magnified glasses at one of the drawn silhouettes and its signature. "Oh, *Blank Frank*," he said, smiling. "You know he stopped by to see me the other day. He's grown out his mohawk! He looks like Francis!"

"I know," I said. "I asked him to come by, but he had a date."

"HEY, MELVIN," said Maeve. "You should be on the wall. Seeing as what a part of Peyton Hall you are."

"That's a great idea," I said and after completing my coffee-refill duties, I got the black permanent marker. "Melvin, you figure out how you want to pose and one of us will draw you." I waved the pen. "Who's feeling artistic?"

"Well, I *always* am," said Melvin, raising his hand. "But, tell you what: rather than having my silhouette up there, may I draw something freehand?"

"Be my guest." I handed him the marker.

Mike put his arm around me as I sat between him and Solange on the plaid couch; that we shared a secret made me even giddier.

Melvin padded over to the wall, the seat of his herringbone polyester pants so flat and droopy you had to wonder where his butt went. He stood studying the wall for a moment before turning to look at me. Cocking his head from one side to the other, his hand was suddenly on the wall, the pen moving fast. After each glance directed at me, he'd made a few more strokes with his pen until he stepped aside.

"Ta da!" he said.

"Candy," said Ed from the plaid chair. "It's you!"

"My interpretation of our lovely hostess," said Melvin.

"It looks just like you!" Maeve said, and she was right. It was a caricature—all my features were exaggerated—my mouth looked like a bow and my eyes were barely two diagonal slashes—but the owner of those features was beyond doubt.

"Oh, Melvin," I said, laughing. "That's great! Do another one!"

"With pleasure." Melvin fixed his squint on Mike and his pen on the wall, and in what seemed like seconds he was finished. This earned applause; he had drawn Mike so that it appeared he was gazing at me, with puppy dog–like devotion.

"Hey, you've got me looking—"

"—besotted," said Ed, giving me a knowing look.

"We used to do this all the time in the studio," said Melvin, after his rendering of Solange, with a no-nonsense yet sly expression that limned her perfectly. "And we'd time each other, see which one of us could draw the others the best and the fastest."

"Did you usually win?" I asked.

"Well," Melvin bowed his head, smiling, "yes."

We all sat rapt, watching the old animator work his magic. I was tucked under Mike's arm, and every time his hand squeezed my shoulder, I pressed my leg against his.

Melvin almost ran out of space, our heads appearing above or between the already-drawn silhouettes. I heard Maeve gasp when he finished with her portrait; it was funny and exaggerated like the rest of ours, but somehow he had captured the blobby little baby inside the fierce bodybuilder.

Ed's reaction to Melvin's depiction of him, on the other hand, was one of protest.

"I've got more hair than that!" he said, palming the top of his head as if to make sure.

We applauded Melvin as he made his way back to his chair, and his smile was so wide I thought his dentures might fall out. This thought of course made me laugh.

"Honestly, Candy, what is going on?" asked Maeve.

"Yeah, what gives?" said Solange. "You're so . . . bubbly."

"Candy, come clean," said Ed. "Are you on medication?"

Mike nudged me. "Better tell them."

"Okay!" I sprang off the couch.

Standing next to the little table the answering machine was on, I felt my heart racing.

"I'd like to share something with you." I pressed the Play button.

"Candy?" came my grandmother's voice. "Candy, is that you?"

"Wait," I said, pressing Stop and skipping ahead to the next message. "Okay, here we go."

"Hi Candy, this is Eric," came the voice of my agent and I heard Solange shush the group.

"Great news—I just heard from the Carson people! They saw *The Sorta Late Show* and now they're coming to see you Friday night at the Comedy Store. I know you'll knock 'em dead. *The Tonight Show*, Candy! Love you."

The beep ending the message sounded, and feeling a little weak-kneed

I pressed my spine against the wall. My friends stared at me and I stared back, astonishment muzzling us into silence until Maeve's congratulations set off everyone else.

Mike stood up.

"To Candy!" he said, and everyone joined him in raising their coffee cups high, and after the toast Melvin emptied his cup with a long swig before flinging it across the room.

It bounced, as my unbreakable dishes always did, against the wall.

He was like the point man firing the first shot, and a volley of cups followed and a splash of coffee darkened the flexed arm of Maeve's silhouette and a dribble ran down Solange's caricature and a spray of drops decorated the invisible guitar of John Lennon's that Frank's silhouette held.

I was awed, watching this celebratory throwing-of-the-cups-spilling-of-the-coffee, and so moved, I hurled my own cup against the wall.

It exploded, as if it were crystal, bone china, or porcelain and not my unbreakable Melnor—with its guarantee that "When company comes over, the only thing broken will be bread!" And yet, I had *shattered* it.

THE BEDROOM WINDOW facing the Boulevard was open and only occasionally would the deep night quiet be stirred by a passing car. If I shut my eyes, I could imagine myself at the ocean; the in-and-out-going waves the soft and steady sighs of Mike's sleeping breaths. But I couldn't shut my eyes; I was wired as a circuit board.

I had sent my guests home with pieces of cake—my version of a hostess gift—and when Melvin said his good-byes, he kissed my cheek and said, "Kiddo, you really know how to throw a party."

Now the weight of his compliment struck me: Yes! That was all I ever wanted to do, all any comic really wants to do—throw a party. A little laugh bubbled up within me; all night I'd been a fault-line generating little tremors of giggles, snorts, chuckles.

For the fifth or one-hundredth time, my agent's voice came into my head, telling me that the Carson people were coming to see my act!

More laughter stuttered through me and my agent's voice was drowned out by the words of my secret power mantra in the voice of my mother: *Best to laugh.* It came again, in Madame Pepper's whisper at the airport: *Best to laugh.* Both of them together, singing a chorus I always knew: *Best to laugh, best to laugh, best to laugh.*

EPILOGUE

TODAY, there are a lot more women who wield real comedy power, but as of this writing there is still no one of the fairer sex hosting a major late-night talk show. Joan Rivers had a brief run at it, but in terms of not getting any respect she could teach Rodney Dangerfield a thing or two. Cable TV has begun to wise up, but as far as network television goes it's still a petulant boys' club that's in no hurry to expand its membership.

Melanie Breyer was right about *The Sorta Late Show with Candy Ohi*: there was a life beyond the Swan Theater, and we took the show on the road, playing in twenty-one cities. The highlight for me was performing in the same theater in which my grandmother and I had seen Holly Wheaton. The highlight for Mike was having his college town, Lincoln, Nebraska, present him with the key to the city.

"Dang, it doesn't fit," he joked, struggling to put the two-foot-long ceremonial key onto his key ring.

Because of the tour, I didn't get to hunker down with Melvin Slyke and Vince Perrogio, the last holdouts, after a long tough fight, to leave Peyton Hall.

I was, however, back in town to watch a wrecking ball crash into what had been the east side of my apartment. Mike, Ed, and I stood across the street on the other side of Hollywood Boulevard, and every time the chain swung and the ball smashed into the stucco and wood, I felt it in my stomach.

"Oh, my God," I said, watching the tiled wall of my shower collapse.

As Ed's camera clicked, the vise of Mike's grip tightened around my shoulders, and when we watched the last wall tumble—the one decorated with silhouettes and caricatures and splashes of coffee—he held me up when my knees turned to pudding.

CONCENTRATED AS THEY WERE on fame and glory, my girlhood dreams didn't leave much space to envisage a guy like Mike Trowbridge, which goes to show you how limited girlhood dreams can be.

I married him in the black cocktail dress with the smattering of sequins that Madame Pepper had insisted I get for special occasions. I also wore it to the Emmy Awards, when Mike and I were nominated for writing an episode of *Blades!*, a sitcom about a women's hockey team. (My calendaeium entry for that day reads: *Oh, well, it was an honor to be nominated.*) My favorite go-to apparel for swanky events, it was worn to dinner parties in homes with Malibu and Brentwood zip codes and a reception honoring Ed as Los Angeles Public School Teacher of the Year.

Six years after I had entered Giorgio's, shyly whispering to the cool, blonde Cynthia the code words, "Madame Pepper wants you to help me find a party dress," I wore it, for the last time, to my benefactor's funeral.

We had kept up a correspondence after she moved to Vienna, and when my book *Wise Acre* was published, I sent her the second publisher's copy (my grandma getting first dibs).

"I am so proud of you," she wrote in her thank you card. "Very funny, and such deft use of *articles.*"

After her funeral service, Taryn Powell and I rode the train together, heading to Munich and a reunion with Maeve, Egon, and Andreas, my godchild (!).

"Ah, riding the rails," said my seatmate, as we settled into a club car booth, the windows offering a moving postcard of the green Austrian countryside.

"To Madame Pepper, a true Hollywood legend," said Taryn, after the white-gloved waiter delivered our drinks and we clinked glasses. "Responsible for more Hollywood careers than MGM and Warner Bros. put together."

"You really think that?" I said, impressed.

After a moment, Taryn said, "No," and we shared a laugh.

"But you believed in her powers, didn't you?"

The actress raised her eyebrows. At least I think she did: thanks to the pinches and pulls of a recent face-lift, Taryn's lovely visage now wore a permanent expression of mild surprise.

"It's easier for me to believe in clairvoyance than a lot of other things."

"Like what?"

"Oh," she said, twirling the speared olive in her glass. "World peace. Lasting love."

Looking at me, she chuckled. "I know, I know. Both you and Maeve would make strong cases about the lasting love business. And I wish you luck."

"Which we'll probably need," I said, not cynically. Showbiz—and life in general—had taught me that however and whenever luck comes your way, you tackle it and hold on.

A glass of white wine, the slight swaying of the train, and jet lag made me both sleepy and contemplative, and I considered telling Taryn what Madame Pepper had whispered to me when I'd left her at the airport all those years ago. But I hadn't even told Mike the words of my life saber, even as I understood he embraced their philosophy. No, how the Hollywood soothsayer came to know my secret power mantra is a puzzle I'm content to be amused and a little awed by.

THE BLACK COCKTAIL DRESS had felt a little snug at Madame Pepper's funeral and the reason I had suspected was confirmed by my gynecologist.

Loren Barney was born two and a half years before his sister, Lily Bea. There are many reasons children resent their parents, but so far neither of ours thinks giving them middle names inspired by favorite characters on *The Andy Griffith Show* worthy of severing family ties. As to their first names, Loren was a baby book name we both liked; Lily of course was named after my grandmother—with whom, happily, both my kids got to spend lots of time, thanks to Mike agreeing to my suggestion of sorta-bicoastal (one East Coast, one landlocked state) living.

"We can keep our apartment in Manhattan. And buy a little house in Minneapolis. By the creek. Or one of the lakes."

We'd moved to New York when Mike was hired as the head writer for the hit sitcom *You're My What?* We could have been hired as a team (see Emmy nomination), but I declined, choosing to stay at home with our bambinos. That was a big surprise—how much I enjoyed being a mother. Besides, I was working on my second novel (the first finding its permanent, and proper, home in the bottom of a file cabinet). My published book of essays had been an expansion of my calendaieum notations; now I was discovering that the joys (and frustrations) of writing fiction were equal to the joys (and frustrations) of performing stand-up. I still booked comedy gigs, although more and more I was accepting only those within driving range, the allure of touring and telling jokes fading when compared to that of staying home and telling bedtime stories.

Our realtor found us a bungalow by Minnehaha Creek, and one of my first decorating tasks was to hang pictures of Hollywood Boulevard in the bathroom and my cocktail dress on the wall of our bedroom.

If I had a super power, it would have been one that shielded my grandmother from that which we all must face, but after she suffered a stroke, I did what I humanly could, which was to be with her in her last days. Sven, parked on one side of the bed, was mute with grief, so it was up to me and my aunts, Pauline and Lorraine, to hold my grandmother's hand, to caress her wispy dyed hair, and recount the news of the day— the everyday family events that somehow ratchet up to the extraordinary when they're about your loved ones. Once while telling her about Loren's kindergarten girlfriend and Lily getting into the flour bin and creating a blizzard in our kitchen, I like to think she smiled, but it may have been a twitch.

When the nurse told us in her soft earnest voice that it was time to say good-bye, I said, "Oh kid!"

Grandma, always my best audience, would have laughed at that, but as she had more important things to do, I kissed her cheek and told her that I loved her, so grateful that I wasn't telling her anything that she didn't already know.

Even though it's been decades since I lived in Peyton Hall, I still have a recurring dream about it, and the night before last, back in Hollywood, I dreamed it again. It's always the same: most of the four-plexes have been torn down and the pool has been paved over, but tenants are still squatting in the back buildings, which are missing walls or steps or rooftops. They're not nightmares, but there is a sense of disquiet and loss when I wake up.

"What do you suppose they mean?" I've asked Mike. "That I didn't finish what I wanted to in Hollywood?"

"Do you feel that way?"

"No. Except for being on *The Tonight Show* with lousy guest hosts."

The needle on my Thrill-O-Meter couldn't have registered higher when I was booked on the Carson show—twice!—but it fell notches backwards when a guest host—twice!—sat behind Johnny's desk. It's a small bone of good-natured contention (good-natured on his part) that the one time Mike appeared as a comic on the show, Johnny was hosting.

I look at my husband now, his hair still curly but more gray than brown. He's wearing airplane headphones and an eye mask (he's not afraid to fly but prefers not to see what's underneath him—especially when it's an ocean).

Yesterday Ed had asked us how we had gotten so lucky, and both Mike and I, at the same time, said, "*I* got lucky."

Ed laughed. "See, that's what I want. Someone to be in sync with."

"You're not dead yet," said Solange. "Look at Kay and me. I'd just about given up on ever finding love, and then there she was."

"Was she aware of your musical tastes?" I asked, as a nasally voice yodeling about a good-time gal gone bad was piped through the sound system and into their backyard.

"She's got a theory about cowboy music and menopause," said Kay, twirling her finger near her temple.

"Sure, call me crazy," said Solange. "But I'm telling you, minor key music is soothing—it helps minimize the intensity of hot flashes."

I fanned my own sweaty face. "Then crank it up."

It was a mostly fun, three-day trip to Hollywood. The not-so-fun part was visiting Claire, who was battling the Big C, which I wish someone would figure out how to diminish to the little c.

"You know what cheered me up during that crappy chemo time?" she asked, fondling the stubble where her tangled mane once sprung. "Watching footage I shot of you all at the Swan Theater. Why didn't I ever make a movie about that?"

"Guess you were too busy making *Without Papers* and *What's the Matter with Men?*" I said, citing just two of her many award-winning documentaries.

"When I get my strength back, I'm going to make a movie of *The Sorta Late Show*. Who knows? Maybe it'll revive your comedy career—or better yet—maybe somebody'll offer you your own TV talk show."

"Which you'll direct."

Claire's laugh was weak in volume but full in spirit.

"They wouldn't know what hit 'em."

The fun part was staying with Solange and the backyard barbecue she hosted the last night for some old friends.

"He's his mother's son," said Frank, as we watched Loren execute a

pretty swan dive into the pool. We were standing at the picnic table, load-
ing our plates up with seconds.

"And look at the Facebook friends," he said, nodding at my daughter
and his son flirting with one another. "Looks like they get along pretty
well off-line."

"I love that they stay in touch," I said. "Lily says they even write letters
to each other now and then."

"You're kidding," said Frank's wife, Paula. "The kind with stamps? I
had no idea Nate even knew how to write a letter, let alone mail it."

"Well, he is a communications major," said Frank, and our laughs
were echoed by those of Lily and Nate as they struggled to throw one
another into the deep end of the pool.

THE DECEMBER NIGHT HAD FADED GENTLY, as December nights in southern California do, and Ed and I were the lone holdouts, the two who
didn't want the party to end.

"This reminds me of the night we—"

"—sat out at the pool at Peyton Hall," said Ed, nodding. "The night
I broke up with Sharla."

With our hands tucked under our thighs, we dangled our legs in the
tepid water.

"I just saw her in a Lifetime movie," I said. "She was playing the feral
mother of a scorned bride."

Ed laughed. "I'm glad I missed that one." He shoved the water with
his foot. "Hey, speaking of old actors, did you see Jaz in that Masterpiece
Theater series? He played the butler."

"Not just the butler. The *diabolical* butler. He was great. I was so
happy to see him."

"And what about that cousin of yours? If she had a career, I've missed it."

"Ahh, Charlotte. She married some big-shot hedge fund guy and got
a huge settlement when they divorced. I guess he's in jail now, and she's
in Miami, with a boyfriend who wasn't even born yet when we were living at Peyton Hall."

The night-blooming jasmine was our tender and melancholic perfume as we talked about Aislin, Joanie, Bastien, and those who had joined
Francis Flover: June, Robb, Vincent Perrogio, Robert X. Roberts, and my
favorite animator/union organizer, Melvin Slyke.

"And get this," I said, "Frank told me Mayhem—uh, Mark—cashed in the stock options from his advertising agency and now he's sailing around the world!"

We laughed, delighted by life's twists and turns and the surprising way people seize them.

"Maybe he'll run into Terry," I said. "I just got a postcard from her last week. She's teaching kick-boxing in Sao Paulo!"

I then told my old friend of the latest installment of my recurring dream about Peyton Hall.

"Well," said Ed. His sigh was long. "It was a magical place."

"Really, you think that? I mean, I do, but I didn't know you did."

"If magic is possibility . . . or the unexpected . . . no, if magic is an *invitation* to possibility and the unexpected, then sure, Peyton Hall was loaded with it."

LOREN AND LILY are a few rows behind us in the plane, and I resist the temptation that I've already given in to several times—to turn around and wave to them. They are adults, after all . . . and what adults! Loren's getting his master's in music composition at the University of Minnesota and Lily's a sophomore at Columbia, studying economics, of all things. They're smart and kind and fun, and I have no idea how I spawned them.

The flight attendant, who looks like me—or me thirty years ago—gives me a glass of tomato juice and smiles.

"Are you traveling for business or pleasure?" she says in a soft voice, solicitous of my sleeping (snoring) seatmate.

The question throws me, but after a moment, I say, "A little of both."

This trip is Mike's Christmas present to me, inspired by our son's computer research. Loren wasn't able to find any living relatives of my mother but he cyber-managed to track down a woman who worked with Jong Oh at the metal stamping factory in Seoul. We're meeting Hana at a teahouse on Itaewan Street, the same street on which the looped bicycle rider that was my father plowed into the sober pedestrian that was my mother.

The accident that started it all. The accident that my bloodied mother could have stomped away from, hurt and angry, but instead chose to react to with a little joke. The joke that led to a courtship, to marriage, to me.

I open my leather-bound calendaeium and write the words that fill my heart, the phrase I've found that has now superseded *Best to laugh* as my life saber: *Maykmyneahdubbahl.*

Nah, just kidding. Of course, it's *Thank you.*

ACKNOWLEDGMENTS

PEYTON HALL WAS A REAL COMPLEX on Hollywood Boulevard, one that I lived in and, like Candy, still dream about. It was old-school Hollywood, and some tenants had been around Los Angeles since the 1930s and were always happy to talk about the golden days when the very air—so fragrant with orange blossoms—made them nearly tipsy. Most of the characters in this novel are made up or composites, but two are based on real people: Herman Hover, who ran Ciro's for a time, and his son, Ian Hover, who introduced me to punk rock. Thanks to fellow tenants Sharon Orfeli, Eddie Fields, Jeff Slyke, Mike Sobota, Todd Everett, Aben Kandel, Oliver Ferrand, Peter Chaconas, Art Fine, Kari Haugland, Larry Becker, Kathy Bick, and to those I knew only by their first names, Des and Katie, Sherri, June, Judy, Anne, and Michael.

Thanks to Bev Baz, my singing partner during our morning drives to work at the Playboy Mansion.

To all those in the business of comedy: it's a noble profession, and I'm honored to have worked with so many people whose goal it is to make people laugh. Those in San Francisco and Los Angeles include Freaky Ralph Eno, Andy Garcia, Dana Delaney, Rick Overton, Gail Murray, Dan McVicar, Gail Matthias, Rachel Lovey, Jamie McGovern, Danny Mora and Robert Aguirre, Jason Micheal Passorelli, John Bates, Kevin Nealon, Fred Asparagus, Sam Kinison, and Brian Bradley. Big huzzahs to comedy impresario Dudley Riggs, who's given scores of funny people a place to be funny. As part of his Brave New Workshop touring company, I performed in Midwestern towns and cities with Mo Collins, Mark Copenhaver, Melissa Denton, Steve Schaubel, Danny Schmitz, Greg Triggs, and Tom Winner, whom I thank for the kinds of laughs that work out your abs better than sit-ups. Also on the Riggs home stages and others, I have had great fun working with Lee Adams, Laura Adams, Renee Albert, Doug Anderson, Leslie Ball, Mark Bergran, Bill Bliseath, Ken Bradley, John Brady, Andrea Beutner, Michelle Cassioppi, Dennis Curly, Jim Detmar, Rob Elk, Maile Flanagan, Beth Gilleland, Peter Guertin, Marshall

Hambro, Leon Hammer, Robyn Hart, Cheryl Hawker, Judy Heneghan, Kimberly Hofer, Michelle Hutchison, Drew Jansen, Brian Kelly, Wendy Knox, Rich Kronfeld, Tom McCarthy, Kevin McLaughlin, Gene Larche, Priscilla Nelson, Steve O'Toole, Mary Jo Pehl, Melissa Peterman, Stevie Ray, Dan Rooney, Joel Sass, Dean Seal, Kirsten Seal, Barb Shelton, Peter Simmons, Wendy Smith, Peter Staloch, Dane Stauffer, Denise Sumptor, Sandy Thomas, Jeff Towne, Nancy Walls, Mike Warren, Kevin West, Wayne Wilderson, and Phyllis Wright. Apologies and free drinks to those funny people I inadvertently left out.

For giving me a regular slot all these years, I thank Kim Bartmann, Kristin Van Loon, Bryon Gunsch, Barb Otos, and the staff of the fabulous Bryant–Lake Bowl.

Big inestimable thanks to the University of Minnesota Press.

To my family: thanks for the continuous laughs.

Lorna Landvik is the author of ten novels, including the best-selling *Patty Jane's House of Curl, Angry Housewives Eating Bon Bons,* and *Oh My Stars.* She has performed stand-up and improvisational comedy around the country and is a public speaker, playwright, and actor, most recently in her one-woman all-improvised show, *Party in the Rec Room.* She lives in Minneapolis.